SOMETHING OLD

DIANNE CHRISTNER

SOMETHING OLD

THE PLAIN CITY BRIDESMAIDS

BARBOUR
PUBLISHING

ISBN 978-1-61626-231-0

All scripture quotations are taken from the King James Version of the Bible.

For more information about Dianne Christner, please access the author's website at the following Internet address: www.diannechristner.net

Cover design: Mullerhaus Publishing Group

Published by Barbour Publishing, Inc., P.O. Box 719, Uhrichsville, OH 44683, www.barbourbooks.com

Our mission is to publish and distribute inspirational products offering exceptional value and biblical encouragement to the masses.

ecpa Member of the
Evangelical Christian
Publishers Association

Printed in the United States of America.

DEDICATION

To my mom, who has a good word to say about everybody. Even during a season of intense physical pain, she spread the word about my books. To my mother-in-law, who also experienced a rough year. Yet Anna repeatedly asked, "Is your book out yet?" Finally, I can place it in her lap.

Thanks to my agent, Greg Johnson, who believed in my writing and persevered, opening doors of opportunity that led to the Plain City Bridesmaids series. Thanks to Becky and the superb Barbour Publishing team for enhancing my manuscript throughout editing, marketing, and production.

Dad, thanks for your prayers and my Mennonite upbringing. Jim, I appreciate your daily love and devotion. Rachel, you are my encourager. Leo, you are hers. Mike and Heather, you are patient, especially before deadlines. Kathy and Chris, I cherish your supportive e-mails. Timmy, thanks for your website assistance. Gkids, want to see your name in print? Hi Makaila, Elijah, Vanson, Ethan, and Chloe!

Reader, I'm humbled you picked up *Something Old* and ventured into Plain City to spend time with Katy Yoder and her friends. I hope our paths cross and invite you to meet with me on my website: www.diannechristner.net.

Most thanks go to God, my helper and highest inspiration.

Ouch! Stop it!" Ten-year-old Katy Yoder howled, her head pinned to the back of the car seat until she could uncoil Jake Byler's fingers from her ponytail. She glared at the unrepentant boy—though she secretly relished the attention—and flipped her hair to the front of her buttoned blouse. In return, he flashed her a lopsided grin.

With Plain City, Ohio, one hundred miles behind them, the van continued to eat up the asphalt and soon veered off the interstate onto a dusty road that could churn soda pop into butter. The boys whooped, but Katy's stomach did a little somersault. Under normal circumstances, curvy roads turned her green, but she was also fretting over the unknowns of her first camp experience.

The driver shut off the ignition in front of a rectangular, log building. With ambivalence, Katy scrutinized the green-lettered sign identifying Camp Victoria. The side door slid open, startling her as the boys scrambled over her, all elbows and knees, to exit the van. She squealed a protest and piled out after them. Then the children jostled into the parking lot and remained in a cluster like a group of balloons, where they drew attention, not for their festive splash but for their plainness.

Jake, who had pulled Katy's ponytail twice on the road trip, curled his lip and elbowed Chad Penner. Katy turned to see what tickled them. Her cheeks flamed to watch the boys act like first graders over some girls in shorts and brightly colored Ts.

She tossed her black ponytail and nudged Megan Weaver. "Stupid boys. Act like they never saw shorts before."

"Probably not on church girls," Megan replied. "Those girls are looking this way. Should we go talk to them?"

Lillian Mae Landis, the third friend in their tight trio, frowned at her navy culottes. "I wish my mom would let me wear shorts."

For Katy, her homemade culottes afforded more freedom than her normal below-the-calf skirts, and she would die before she showed her legs. She smoothed the cotton folds that clung to her legs and studied the other girls. "I hope they're nice." She gently bit her lip, wondering if they knew how to play Red Rover. Or would they take greater pleasure in calling her ugly names like "Plain Jane"?

One of the shorts-clad girls waved.

"Let's go," Lil urged.

To Katy's relief, it turned out that a girl in green shorts had a cousin who lived in Plain City. The common acquaintance gapped the bridge between the Mennonite girls in shorts and the more conservative ones wearing culottes, which was fortunate since their sleeping bags and duffels all landed in the same cabin.

After participating in a long morning of organized activities, the Plain City girls took advantage of a few minutes of relaxation. Katy squinted up through glistening leaves, trying to locate an angry, chattering squirrel.

Lil propped an elbow on a bare, chubby knee. "Let's name ourselves after something that comes in threes." Their counselor had just divided their cabin in teams of three and given them fifteen minutes to name their group.

Katy gave up on the squirrel and tried to ignore the tight-fitting shorts Lil had already borrowed from a cabin mate. *Things that come in threes.* She twirled her long, black ponytail and thought about the picture books she'd read to entertain her younger siblings while her mother shelled peas. "There's the three bears, three Billy goats, three little pigs—"

"Nah." Lil tilted her leg this way and that. "Everybody'll think of those."

"How about the Trinity?"

"Yeah, I like it," Megan's face glowed. Katy wasn't sure if Megan was excited about her suggestion, or if she sported a sunburn. She was the only person Katy knew whose skin was as pale as white chinaware with hair as light as yellow thread. Lil was light-complected, too, but her freckles camouflaged it.

With a scowl, Lil said, "No way. Too holy."

"She's right." Megan reconsidered, nibbling at the tip of one of her blond braids.

Lil's blue eyes lit with cunning, and Katy inwardly cringed. "Three Bean Salad! Nobody else will pick that name."

"Huh?" The other two scowled. *Leave it to Lil to think of food*, Katy thought.

"Don't you see? It's perfect. Megan is the green bean since her parents are always talking about stewardship and recycling. I'm the garbanzo." Lil shimmied her shoulders and singsonged, "Gar–ban–zo." She pointed at Katy. "And you can be the kidney bean."

"What? I hate it. Do you even know what a kidney does?"

"You're just a kid with a knee. Get it?"

Katy watched Lil pat her bare knee again. "That's stupid. My knees never show." She hoped Lil got the point that at least *she* was a modest person.

"Sometimes they do in your culottes," Megan remarked.

Katy's ears turned pink. "What?"

"I only saw them once in the morning relay." Megan sighed. "Never mind. Would you rather be the green bean?"

"Red's *her* favorite color," Katy tossed her head toward Lil and pulled her culottes down below the middle of her shins. "If Lil's so set on it, let her be the kidney bean."

Megan turned up her palms. "Will you two stop arguing? We'll be three peas in a pod; then we can all be the same."

Lil rolled her gaze heavenward. "It's two peas in a pod, and we're not the same at all."

"Got that right," Katy grumbled, thinking about the giant dishpan full of green pellets her mother had shelled. She didn't want to be a pea, either. She'd rather be a bear or a musketeer or even a stooge. What were her friends thinking?

All ten years of their lives, the girls had done things together. They sat in pews at the same Conservative Mennonite church, learned their multiplication tables at the same blackboard, and played tag with the same ornery boys. But their personalities were as far apart as the tips of a triangle. They went to all the same potlucks, but their plates never looked identical. And although Lil and Katy hardly ever agreed on anything, they loved each other something fierce. When they didn't remember that, Megan reminded them.

"Why not three strands to a rope? That's cool." Megan fingered her braid. "Like this."

Lil crossed her arms and wouldn't budge. "Three Bean Salad."

Katy glared. She could blackmail her, threaten to tell Mrs. Landis about Lil's shorts, but Megan would never permit it. So because their leader chose that moment to blow her pink whistle, Three Bean Salad it remained for the rest of the week.

The campfire events *rocked*. A new word Katy had learned. As the highlight of each day, it opened Katy's eyes to a world that existed beyond her sheltered home life. She didn't miss how Megan leaned forward with starry eyes during the mission stories. When they lay in their bunks at night, while Lil and their leader, Mary, did sit-ups on the cabin floor, Megan chatted about Djibouti and Tanzania.

For Katy, the singing rocked most, even though she knew she sang off-key. The words expressed her heart, and she felt like she might burst with love for Jesus. She wished the world could share her happiness. It saddened her to watch Lil mimic the other girls from their cabin.

She glanced sideways now. Lil's freckles practically glowed in the firelight. She was happy, but Katy wished she could hug her friend to her senses. Lil pulled her blue sweater tight around her shoulders, her gaze wistfully trailing the kids now breaking the circle, some heading toward the cabins. "I never want this week to end," she murmured.

"Me either," Katy whispered.

Lil glanced into the shadows where their leader stood talking to another camp counselor. "She's so beautiful."

Megan and Katy leaned forward and looked to their right at Lil. "Who?"

"Mary."

"Oh." They leaned back. All three girls had fallen under Mary's spell. She was kind, patient, and told great Bible stories. To Lil's fascination, she was also beautiful and planning a wedding.

Lil clenched her fists. "I know how we can make this last. Let's make a vow tonight that when we're Mary's age we'll all move in together. It'll be like camp. Only forever."

Katy furrowed her brow. "We'll probably get married."

"Just until we marry. And we'll be each other's bridesmaids, too! Oh, swear it!"

Feeling sad that Lil caught so little of what camp was really about, Katy frowned. "You know Mennonites don't swear or take oaths."

Lil placed her head in her hands and stared at her borrowed jeans.

Megan, who was seated on the log between them, reached out and clasped each of their hands. "The Bible says where two or three are gathered and agree on something, that God honors it."

Twisting her ponytail with her free hand, Katy frowned. "What?"

"Sometimes my parents remind God about it when they pray."

"Really?" Katy asked, amazed.

Megan nodded, and her voice grew grave. "We can agree, but we must never break a promise."

Katy swallowed. Her heart beat fast. Lil's gaze begged. "I promise." Katy squeezed Megan's hand. "And I already know who I'm going to marry."

The other two whipped their gazes to the left. "You do?"

"Jake Byler. He always lets me cut in front of him in line."

Over the next decade, Katy wondered if Lil had made a second oath that night. She must have vowed to never let them break their promise to each other.

CHAPTER 1

Ten years later

Katy Yoder skimmed a white-gloved finger across the edge of the fireplace mantel. The holiday decorations, such extravagance forbidden at her own home, slowed her task. It wasn't just the matter of working around them; it was the assessing of them. Feeling a bit like Cinderella at the ball, she swiped her feather duster, easing it around the angel figurines and Christmas garland. A red plastic berry bounced to the floor, and she stooped to retrieve it, poking it back into place with care.

Her mother, like most members of her Mennonite congregation, shunned such frivolity. Gabriel of the Bible, the angel who visited the Virgin Mary, probably looked nothing like these gilded collectibles. Nevertheless, the manger scene caused warm puddles to pool deep inside her heart, a secret place of confusing desires that she kept properly disguised, covered with her crisp white blouse and ever-busy hands.

The pine-scented tree occupying the corner of the room moved her with wonder. Not the ornaments, but the twinkling white lights, little dots of hope. The cheery music jingling in the background was not forbidden. She mouthed the words to "Silent Night." In December they often sang the hymn at her meetinghouse. But her singing was interrupted mid-stanza as her employer's gravelly voice brought her out of her reverie. Instinctively, she lowered her arm and whirled.

Mr. Beverly's lips thinned and his white mustache twitched. "Katy. We need to talk." Bands of deep wrinkles creased his forehead. "I have bad news," he said. His petite wife stood at his side, twisting her diamond ring.

Apprehension marched up Katy's neck. Could it be a terminal illness? In their late seventies, the couple kept active for their age, always off on golfing vacations. Katy had grown fond of them. Smiles softened their conversation, and their hands were quick to hand her trusted keys and gifts. They even bought her a sweater for her birthday, made from some heavenly soft fabric. Katy gripped the duster's handle with both hands. "Oh?"

"We're going to have to let you go."

Her jaw gaped. Never had she expected such news. "But. . .but I thought you were pleased." Her mind scrambled for some slipup, some blunder.

Mrs. Beverly rushed forward and touched Katy's white sleeve. "No. No. It's nothing like that. Our son wants us to move to Florida." She glanced at her husband. "At our age, it's overdue."

Katy propped the duster against an armchair and smoothed the apron that covered her dark, A-line skirt. "But is this what you want? Is there a problem with your health?"

Mrs. Beverly glanced at the beige shag carpet and back to Katy's face. "Just the usual, but we're not getting any younger." Mr. Beverly squeezed his wife's shoulder. "We'll give you a good reference."

Katy didn't need a reference. She needed a job. This particular job. Her best-paying, two-day-a-week job. To Katy, the tidy, easy-to-clean house classified as a dream job fast becoming a nightmare, if she was to lose it just when the doddy house came up for rent. Forcing a smile, Katy nodded. "I appreciate that. When will you leave?"

"Right away. We're turning the house over to a Realtor. Our son is coming to help us sell some things. There's really no need for you to come again. I'm sorry we couldn't give you more notice. But we are giving you a Christmas bonus."

Katy patted Mrs. Beverly's manicured hand. "Thank you. You have enough to worry about; don't concern yourself with me." She bit her lip, thinking, *I do that well enough for the both of us.*

"We'll leave you to your work, then," Mr. Beverly cut in. He nudged his wife's elbow, but she looked regretfully over her shoulder at Katy. "Come along, dear," he urged. Then to Katy, he called, "Your money's on the counter as usual. Please leave us your house key."

"Yes sir," Katy replied, watching them depart through an arched entryway. Mr. Beverly paused under the mistletoe to peck his wife's delicate cheek before they headed out for the mall. The tender gesture gripped Katy. It never ceased to amaze her when folks who never went to church loved like that. At least she assumed they didn't go to church, for she dusted their wine collection, R-rated DVDs, and sexy novel flaps without noticing any evidence of Christianity in their home except for one solitary Bible. It always stayed put, tucked between *Pride and Prejudice* and *Birds of Ohio Field Guide*. That's why the Beverlys' consistent kindness and loving behavior was so disturbing.

As usual, anything romantic always reminded Katy of Jake Byler. Growing up, she was sure they'd marry, and because of his daring, often reckless behavior, she had dreamed of sharing an adventuresome life with him. In their teen years, he stared at her with an ardor that melted her toes through her black stockings. He'd give her a dimpled grin or a wink, never embarrassed. Every autumn at the youth hayride, he'd claimed her hand. And after he got his own truck, he took her home from fellowship functions and stole kisses at her back door. She'd always loved him.

Just before he'd graduated from high school, their relationship had started to wilt. Katy grabbed a watering pitcher and marched to Mrs. Beverly's poinsettia. Her employer was as clueless about plants as Katy was about relationships. Had she caused him to become restless and distant?

Without addressing the status of their relationship or so much as an apology, Jake had enrolled at Ohio State University and moved near the campus in Columbus. After that, he often skipped church and always avoided her. Then one fateful evening—the night of the incident—he finally stopped coming to church altogether.

Even though rumors circulated that he drank and dated a wild girl with spiked short hair and a miniskirt, Lil continued to defend her cousin. But Katy deemed Jake Byler spoiled goods. Lumping him in the forbidden pile along with dancing, television, and neckties didn't remove the sting and sorrow, but it did help her deal with the situation.

She heard the Beverlys' car purr out of the drive and glanced out the window at a gray sky that threatened snow. It distressed her that the Beverlys could love like that and not know love's source. Love like the many times since Jake had dumped her when the Lord had noticed her wet pillow and sent her comforting lyrics to a hymn so she could sleep.

"While life's dark maze I tread and griefs around me spread, be Thou my guide. . . ."

The Beverlys had the nativity set; she'd give them that. Her hand slid into her white apron pocket and retrieved a small Christmas card she'd purchased. It had a picture of the nativity scene on the front and a Bible verse inside—John 3:16, her Christmas favorite. But was that enough? She could write something more on the card. Smiling, she drew a pen from a rose-patterned cup.

Katy used her best handwriting. *Your love reminds me of God's love.* She complimented them on their beautiful nativity set. *It reminds me that Jesus died for our sin so that we can spend eternity with God in heaven.* If that piqued their curiosity, they might open that dusty Bible. Surely they pondered eternity at their age, especially as they flew south toward their retirement nest.

She set the card in plain sight beside her house key. Then she put the feather duster in a utility closet and returned to the kitchen with paper towels and a spray bottle.

She spritzed the counter with her special homemade solution and polished, musing over her sudden job predicament. What would Lil say if she backed out of their doddy house plans because she could no longer afford it? She buffed a small area until it mirrored her clenched lips. She relaxed her grip. It wouldn't do to rub a hole in Mrs. Beverly's granite countertop right before a Realtor plunked a sign in her yard. Surely the poor old woman had enough to worry about.

Katy loosened the pressure of her seat belt with her left thumb and flicked on her headlights to stare through the Chevrolet's windshield at the silent twirling flakes. Since the news of her job loss earlier in the day, her stomach had worked itself into to a full boil. She veered off the country road onto a crackling driveway, where golden light streamed through the lacy windows of a white two-story.

Megan lived with her parents on the weekends and during school breaks. Otherwise, she lived on campus at the nearby Rosedale Bible College. As an only child and a tad spoiled, she had her own room where the Three Bean Salad could always meet in perfect privacy.

Katy swept up two identically wrapped gifts, stepped into the bright gray night, and slammed her car door. With her face bowed against the wet onslaught, she watched her shoes cut into freshly laid powder. She climbed the porch steps, giving her black oxfords a tap against each riser. Before she could knock, however, the front door opened.

Megan stood in the doorway, her straight blond hair shimmering down the back of her black sweater, and her blue eyes brilliant and round as the balls on the Beverlys' Christmas tree. Katy stepped into her friend's hug. "Hi, green bean. Merry Christmas."

"Merry Christmas, Katy."

After being stirred in the same pot for so many years, Katy and her two friends resembled Bean Salad more than any particular bean. Yet of the three girls, Megan's nickname stuck, because it suited her style, tall and beautiful and prone to type term papers on world peace or ecology.

"Look. Lil's here, too."

Sure enough, Katy recognized the cough of Lil's old clunker, a thorn in her friend's pride and due for a trade-in as soon as she could afford it.

Katy followed the aroma of gingerbread and ham through the house to the country-style kitchen. She hugged Megan's mom, Anita, and removed her wool coat. "So where's the blues man?" It was Bill Weaver's nickname because he restored Chevy Novas for a little extra income. But the unusual thing was that he painted them all his favorite color, midnight blue. Some Conservatives drove plain cars, and although they

16

weren't supposed to idolize their vehicles, his lucrative hobby fell within what the church permitted. Anita Weaver started calling him the blues man, and Katy had picked up on it. Since Bill Weaver was a good sport and loved jokes, she never felt she was being disrespectful.

"Bill's at an elders' meeting at church," Anita explained.

"Oh yeah. I think my dad mentioned that."

"Since Bills' gone and you girls are spending the evening together, I thought I'd get a jump on Christmas dinner. We're having all the relatives over." She swiped at a wisp of hair that had escaped her crisp white covering. Anita Weaver spoiled Katy and Lil like they were her own daughters. Fun at heart, she was the most lenient of all their parents, and she didn't sport dark circles under her eyes like Lil's mom.

"Smells good. We're hosting all our relatives Christmas Day, too." It was a marvel that Lil, Megan, and Katy were in no way related, as many from their congregation were in the small farming community. Their family trees might intersect in the old country since they shared the same European Anabaptist roots, but they'd never dug into the matter.

Megan swept into the kitchen with Lil, whose snowy-lashed eyes sparkled when she spotted the plate of gingerbread men. Katy bit back a smile, watching her friend pull up her mental calorie calculator and consider her options.

"Hi, Lil." Katy squeezed her friend. "You can diet tomorrow."

"Nope." She flipped the hood of her coat back, revealing shiny, nut-colored hair pulled back at the temples and fastened with a silver barrette beneath her covering. "Not a day until January."

Megan picked up the plate of temptations and motioned for them to follow her up to her room. "Not the whole tray," Lil moaned, shrugging out of her coat, but Katy knew she didn't mean a word of it.

"I'll bring up hot chocolate," Anita Weaver called up the stairwell after them.

When they'd sprawled across the Dahlia coverlet Megan's grandmother had quilted, Katy felt the butterflies in her stomach again. A night purposed for celebration, set aside for exchanging simple gifts and planning their future in Miller's doddy house, now pressed her secret heavily against her heart.

"Let's open our gifts," Megan suggested. They shifted and jostled until they each sat cross-legged with two gifts in front of them. Lil tore into hers first.

Shedding the dignity due her age—she was the oldest of the three by a few months, Katy followed suit. Gifts always stirred up a vestige of childlike excitement that stemmed back to her first store-bought doll. "It's gorgeous." She worked the hinge of the walnut recipe box.

"A cousin made them for me," Lil quipped.

Jake? Katy's protective instincts reared. She cast Lil an apprehensive glance, but she was tossing crumpled wrapping paper across the room, aiming for the trash can. Surely not, Katy dismissed. Inside was a handwritten recipe for Three Bean Salad, a twist from the norm with Lil's special ingredient. She always tweaked ingredients, especially intrigued by spices and herbs. Recently graduated from culinary school, Lil had been working for a month at her first real job at a small Italian restaurant. This set the course for the girls to consider renting the Miller's doddy house. Emotion balled up in Katy's throat.

"I'll keep adding to the recipes," Lil promised.

"Perfect," Megan clapped. "Now open mine."

She had embroidered pillowcases for them with roses and a Bible verse. Ephesians 4:26 read, "Let not the sun go down upon your wrath."

Katy smiled. "A good reminder." *If any of us ever got married.* She watched them open the gifts she'd made. "They're lame," she apologized.

"No they're not." Megan jumped off the bed and tied the apron's strings, sashaying across the pine floor and sliding her hand in between each row of decorative stitching. "Wow. Six pockets."

Katy wished she'd done something meaningful or clever. Always the practical one. This was the third year they'd exchanged gifts for their hope chests, another reminder of the vow to be each other's bridesmaids. At the moment, the first part of the vow—the moving in together part—worried her most. She hated to ruin their doddy house dreams. It couldn't be helped. Katy swallowed. "I need to tell you both something."

Lil and Megan turned expectant gazes toward her.

"Did you girls pray for a white Christmas?" Anita Weaver interrupted, carrying a tray of hot chocolate into the room. Lil dove into the treat, and the conversation turned to the snowfall and how special it would make Christmas, drawing everyone to the window.

Anxious thoughts disquieted Katy's mind, but she pushed them aside. Her personal problem was small stuff compared to the miracle of Christmas. She followed the others to the window and made a spur-of-the-moment decision that she wouldn't ruin the spell of Christmas. The news could wait.

Outside, the flakes swirled like little, white feather dusters, turning everything sparkling white. Lil pressed her forehead against the cold windowpane and knocked her prayer covering askew. "Remember when we used to make snow angels?"

Involuntarily touching her own covering, Katy grinned. "I remember."

CHAPTER 2

At four o'clock, Katy was late. The Three Bean Salad had agreed to look over the doddy house as soon as possible after Christmas. Squinting from the glare of sun and snow, Katy hurried around the east side of the Millers' farmhouse and headed toward the little doddy house.

Doddy houses were built for the older Amish folks after their younger family members took over the main house, what the outsiders called guesthouses. She doubted the Beverlys' son had such a sweet arrangement waiting for them. Katy sighed, and a visible puff of breath dispersed into the cold air. This one, a miniature version of the larger house, was picturesque with a snowy porch railing and a glazed blue roof. In shades of white and gray, the doddy house and its surroundings created a peaceful aura similar to a black-and-white photograph of an older era. It probably wouldn't remain that way long, once renovations began. If renovations began, Katy corrected herself.

A window with dark green window shades, partly rolled up, revealed activity inside. She stepped onto a little porch and up to a door cracked ajar. Taking another visible breath, this time for fortification, she pushed the door open.

"Hey, Katy." Lil waved with a joyful bounce.

"Hi, Lil." Trying to act enthused, Katy nodded at Megan and the newly married couple from their church. This was a mistake. She didn't want to get the Millers' hopes up and waste their time.

Aged hardwood planks creaked as Katy joined in the tour of the quaint little house. Ivan Miller explained, "It's been boarded up for years. We've been busy updating the main house and didn't get to this one yet. We figured if somebody was game to fix it up, we'd let them live here rent free for a while."

The girls exchanged hopeful glances.

"When you say fix it up, you mean electricity?" Lil clarified.

A sudden thrill tingled Katy's spine at the idea of painting the walls a cheery color and choosing modern appliances and furniture. But could they swing it? Her pulse quickened. Could she still convince her parents to approve the idea now that her income had fizzled? Her dad took his role as leader of the household seriously. She'd have to convince him she could handle the responsibility.

Ivan nodded. "Whatever you want. Paint, indoor plumbing—"

"We'd like to keep the wood floors, though," Elizabeth said. "We think it adds to its charm."

"I agree." Megan dusted the floor with the toe of her shoe. "Just needs a little sanding and polyurethane."

The kitchen contained a green sink hutch with a hand pump. The refrigerator and stove required propane gas. Elizabeth explained, "You can share the wash room with the main house. It's updated with a dryer, and there's room to hang some clothes inside, too." Katy had noticed a sidewalk connected both houses to the small building.

The bathroom was equipped with a toilet and a hand pump. A large tin tub hung on the far wall. Elizabeth shrugged, apologetically.

Katy made light of the inconvenience. "There's plenty of room to add a shower or tub in here." They moved into the hall, and Lil scribbled furiously on a small pad.

The wind groaned through a broken windowpane, and Ivan fiddled with some loose plywood. Elizabeth rested an arm across the small mound of her pregnant belly. "There's only one bedroom, but it's spacious."

They all stepped into the center of the bare, windswept room. Katy made a slow circle, assessing damages and imagining three twin beds and dressers in the room. "We could build a walk-in closet."

Pointing her pen, Lil added, "Three twins would fit along that wall."

"Or bunk beds," Megan added. "Twins would be tight."

Katy objected, but Lil and Megan volunteered to share a bunk bed and give her a twin.

"We'll leave you girls to talk," Ivan suggested. "Just stop by the house when you're finished here."

Still acting like a newlywed, Elizabeth clasped her husband's hand and, with a parting smile, told the girls she'd put on a pot of fresh coffee.

"Thanks." Katy watched them depart.

"What do you think?" Lil asked at once, her bright gaze indicating her own approval.

"I love it," Megan replied. "I only wish I could move in with you guys. It's hard to wait until graduation."

"But you can stay over on weekends. . . ." Lil started dreaming aloud then broke off when her gaze met Katy's face. "You're scaring me. What are you thinking?"

"It's perfect. Only—" She shrugged and suddenly had to fight a rush of tears.

"What?"

Her mouth contorted uncontrollably, and she fanned her hand in front of her face.

Lil and Megan rushed to her side. "What's wrong?"

She raised her hand to stay them. Her voice broke. "I'm not sure I can afford it."

"Oh." Lil's gaze darted around the weather-damaged room. "Ivan said we wouldn't have to pay any rent right away. We'll need to make a list of what we want to fix and get bids for the work. But we can do it in stages."

"You don't understand. I didn't want to spoil your Christmas, but I lost one of my jobs."

"What!"

Megan pulled her into a hug, patting her back. "I'm so sorry."

Hovering, Lil asked, "What happened?"

Megan dropped her arm, and Katy shrugged. "The Beverlys are moving to Florida."

Lil's eyes widened. "Aren't they the ones who pay you so well?"

With a nod, Katy sniffled. "Yes, and the job will be hard to replace." "Wow," Lil muttered.

"But you're a good worker," Megan reminded her. "You just need to get the word around that you're looking for more work."

Lil stomped her feet and blew out a puff of cold steam. "We already planned to dip into your savings. And we knew this place needed renovation. Until I repay you the cost of the renovations, I'll be paying the larger portion of the rent anyway. And like Megan said, you'll get more work."

Was Katy overreacting? She rubbed her coat sleeves and shivered. She'd gotten used to a cushioned bank account. And besides the expense of the renovations, there would be food to buy and other necessities.

Megan pulled a tissue from her purse and shoved it in front of Katy's face. "Here. Use this before your tears freeze."

"A heater would make this place more livable," Lil observed. "We should probably get a quote for wiring the whole house. Don't you think?"

Katy nodded, stuffing the tissue in her coat pocket. "I guess it won't hurt to find out if we can afford it. But keep in mind, we'll need new appliances and plumbing and furniture and who knows what else."

"You'll need beds and bedding, too. But my mom would donate some furniture," Megan offered. "It'll work out. You'll see."

"Sure. I want this to work." Katy met their hopeful gazes. "But I planned all along to use my income to sell Dad on the idea. And now. . ." She shrugged.

Lil crossed her arms. "You're of legal age. You can do whatever you want."

Katy shot her a stern look. "I won't go against their wishes."

Raising a palm, Megan stepped between them. "Let's not get ahead of ourselves. We'll talk to the Millers first. My folks won't agree to anything until I graduate and find a job. But out of all our parents, they are the easiest to persuade. If your parents agree, I'm sure they will, too."

"I guess we'll see if it's the Lord's will. I just can't go through with it if my folks are against it," Katy reiterated.

Lil snatched Katy's hand. "I want this so much. Come on. Let's go get warm."

—⸾—

Later when Katy left the Millers, it was with the assurance that Lil would get the construction bids. Katy needed to obtain her parents' permission and find another job. Not easy feats. Generally speaking, girls from her congregation didn't leave home until they married, unless they attended Bible college. Over the years, her parents had often snickered at her dream, but they had never forbidden it. She had the impression they thought she would outgrow it.

When she reached home, Katy hung up her coat. In the kitchen, her mom poked a long-handled fork into an oblong roasting pan of pork tenderloin done to perfection. Katy's mouth watered. Stepping up to the sink, she washed her hands. "Hi, Mom. I'm home."

"Just in time to help."

Katy took a stack of plates and set one at each place setting: for her parents, herself, and the three siblings who still lived at home. "Just the family tonight?" Often her married brothers joined them.

"Just us. Guess everybody's staying put since Christmas is over."

Katy maneuvered around the pine table her grandfather had crafted in the woodworking shop he'd passed down to her dad. If they didn't have company tonight, it would be a good time to approach her parents about the doddy house. She silently prayed for God to direct her future.

Placing the forks on the left and the knives and spoons on the right of her mom's pink Depression-glass plates, she thought about the renovations and how they would eat up her savings account. When they had first discovered the little house was up for rent, it had seemed like a divine gift. Now she wasn't sure. Maybe it was too soon. They could wait another five months until after Megan graduated. It wasn't like they planned to get married right away.

If they missed the doddy house opportunity, though, they might need to take a city apartment. Already working for outsiders, she fought off a constant onslaught of worldly ideas and temptations. Sometimes at night in the bed she shared with her fourteen-year-old sister, Karen, the darkness would pull up disturbing images from Mrs. Beverly's paperback novel covers. Katy's pulse raced with shame. She tried not to glance at them when she dusted, but inevitably her gaze would photograph the detestable images. Her cheeks burned, and she moved to the other side of the table.

And hadn't the outsiders' Christmas decorations enthralled her? She pressed her lips together and straightened a fork. She hadn't even felt ashamed. Then she relaxed. Her mind was just occupied with this doddy house problem. But she didn't want to live among the outsiders, too. She liked the idea of a safe little place tucked in among her own people. She wished she could find a job with another Mennonite family.

"Katy!" Her mother's sharp tone invaded her rambling thoughts.

"What?"

"I asked you before. Do you want to mash the potatoes or go round up your siblings?"

"Oh." She glanced about confused.

"Karen helped me get supper started and took some clean laundry upstairs. She was going to work on a school report. Your brothers are out in the shop with your dad." The woodworking shop, which now specialized only in cabinets, was located at the end of a long, piney lane. They owned one of the five-acre lots on a Plain City rural road where a farm had been subdivided. Mom wiped her hands on her apron and placed them on her hips. "Are you fretting over that job you lost?"

Katy nodded.

Glancing at the wall clock, Mom said, "The potatoes can wait another five minutes. Let's sit a spell and talk."

Katy sank into the closest chair with a sigh of relief. "It's more than just the job."

"Go on."

"You know how I've been saving to move in with Lil and Megan?"

"Oh that crazy idea." She gave a brush of her hand. "Go on."

"Did you know Ivan Miller's renting out their doddy house?"

"That old thing? There's not even any electricity. Are you so eager to leave us that you'd live like your Amish cousins?"

"You know my friends and I have been planning this since we were little girls."

Her mom poked at the pins securing her prayer covering. "I wish you were more concerned about finding someone to marry. If I know my daughters, and I do, then marriage will make you happy. That Miller boy keeps asking you out. He's such a nice young man. What's his name?"

With a sigh, Katy replied, "David. I can date even if I move into the doddy house, but you're missing the point."

"Okay. What's the point?"

"Lil's been working now for a month at a good job. I've got money saved, too. If we're going to do this like we always dreamed, now's the time. Before one of us does get a boyfriend and gets married." She nibbled on her lip. "Only what if I don't get another good-paying job? That's what worries me. I need Dad's permission, and I want this so much."

Marie Yoder's naturally bright eyes softened. "I see you're serious about this."

"I'm afraid if we don't get this doddy house, Lil will push me to rent a city apartment."

Her mom's brown eyes widened, for she not only knew her daughters, but she knew a lot about their friends, too. "Well, if you are stubbornly set on it, I wish you'd take the doddy house. That is, if your dad agrees."

"Me, too."

With a shrug, her mom said, "I'll mash the potatoes. We won't want them lumpy if you're going to ask your dad about this after supper."

Katy flew out of her chair and threw her arms around her mom's neck. "Thanks." Then she rushed to find her siblings.

Supper lagged forever with Katy forcing down smooth potatoes. A shame she couldn't enjoy the flaky pork, but her stomach was no longer interested in food. She let the rest of her dark-haired siblings chatter while she mentally rehearsed her speech. After dinner, her mom surprised her by shooing the younger children off to do the dishes.

Katy settled on the sofa beside her mom. Her dad took his favorite chair beside the little side table that displayed a worn checkerboard game.

"What's on your mind, dumplin'?" It's what her dad called both his daughters.

"Ivan Miller's doddy house." Katy's words spilled out in a rush. "Since Lil and I both have jobs, and I've been saving for over a year now, and with no marriage prospects, we'd like to rent it. Move in together."

His brows shot together. "Like a bunch of old maids?"

"No—o," Katy drew out the word. "Like girls who are particular about whom they date." Katy tried to tell if he was serious or joking. Sarcasm was part of Vernon Yoder's way of speech.

"And how will I be a good dad to you if you're not living under my roof? Have you thought about that? How can I protect you from the world?"

Moving to the edge of the sofa cushion, Katy straightened her posture and replied, "Of course, I will honor your final decision, but I'm nineteen. I think it would be good for me to learn responsibility. I think the Millers' doddy house would be a safe place to do this." In talking to her mom, she'd happened upon her most persuasive point.

And to Katy's relief, her mother added, "Better than some apartment in the city."

Dad rested his gaze on Mom, who dipped her head. He folded his hands on his lap and turned a stoic face toward Katy. "What are your plans for the doddy house?"

"To renovate it with part of my savings—"

"Hah!" he interrupted, with a wave of hand. "More like all your savings."

Her face heating, Katy ran her palms down the front of her dark skirt. "Lil made a list of our ideas, and she plans to get construction bids on the work. Ivan Miller said we could deduct the renovation costs from rent unless they exceed one year's rent; then he will start to charge rent anyways."

"And what about the job you lost?"

Beads of perspiration collected on Katy's forehead. "I will look for work. I want to work."

He rubbed his slightly shadowed chin, his gaze indiscernible. Finally he nodded, and Kate held her breath. "I will agree on three conditions."

"Yes?" Katy was too pleased to move lest she hinder what could only be a blessing from the Lord.

He thrust one finger in the air. "First, I will look over the bids and the financial arrangements and see if I think they are feasible and fair."

"Yes." She took several quick breaths. "I welcome your advice."

"Second, I will go and speak to Ivan Miller to see if he is willing to keep an eye out for you girls."

Embarrassed because their ages weren't that far apart, Katy frowned. But she gave her head a reluctant nod.

"And third, you must go on three dates with David Miller before you move into this doddy house."

"What!" Katy almost toppled off the couch, and her mouth wouldn't close.

"It would please your mother." He patted her mom's hand. "Her feelings matter in this, too."

Katy stared at her mom, whose eyes widened and then twinkled.

Silence prevailed while Katy tried to tell if he was joking. Her dad cracked his knuckles. Katy swallowed, still mystified over her father's unusual request. Finally, unable to prevent a hint of disrespect from tainting her voice, she asked, "And do I have to report to you after these dates?"

"You can report to your mom."

Still struggling with disbelief, Katy watched her siblings burst into the room. They skidded to a stop when they saw all the serious expressions. Her sister Karen tilted her head. "We're finished, Mom."

"You may go work on your report."

"Dad promised to play checkers," Katy's youngest brother reminded them.

Dad picked up a checker and rolled it between his thumb and one finger. "We're not finished with our talk. I'll call you." The trio shuffled back out, and the checker pinged back onto the game board, bounced, and rolled onto the floor.

Katy quickly retrieved it and placed it back on the board, returning to her seat.

"Where were we?" he asked.

Katy's cheeks heated again. "About David Miller. If after these three dates, I don't like him. Then what?"

"Then you are free to quit him."

"But you must agree to give him a chance," her mother interjected.

Dad patted Mom's hand, as if reminding her who was in charge.

But Katy thought her dad was losing his mind. "Isn't there something you're forgetting?" He bunched his mouth considering but didn't come up with anything.

"I've turned David down twice already. He probably won't ask me again."

Her father's face broke into a satisfied grin. "I have it on good authority that he will. Perhaps as soon as the New Year's skating party."

CHAPTER 3

That night Marie Yoder folded back her star quilt. She'd been restless all evening, anxious to get her husband alone. "Vernon. I can't believe I had to wait all night to find out what you're up to. Spill it."

He chuckled and stepped up behind her to touch her loosened hair, dark like his and streaked in gray. "Ingenious, wasn't it?" he asked.

She turned to face him. "I never would have taken you for a matchmaker. Especially for your own daughter."

His voice turned gruff. "I'm not."

"Then why?"

"You liked the idea, admit it."

She fiddled with the tie to her white nightgown. "Yes, but what are you cooking up?"

With a sigh, he moved to his side of the bed and sat. "Jake Byler is coming back to the church."

Marie's heart pounded with fear. "What? Where did you hear this?"

"At the elders' meeting. He came to talk to us. He's turning over a new leaf. Of course I'm happy for his soul, but I don't trust him. And I don't want him turning Katy's head again."

Marie skirted around the bed and touched his shoulder. "Oh, I don't either. I'm afraid he'll hurt her again. He was so wild. Our Katy

30

needs a gentle man who is strong in the faith like her."

They remained silent a moment. Marie stared at the plain oak headboard Vernon had fashioned with his own hands before they got married. Then she remembered the rest of her questions. "How did you hear that the Miller boy was going to ask Katy out again?"

Vernon removed his shoes. "Through his brother Ivan."

"What? He told you about the doddy house? You already knew of Katy's plans?"

"Of course." His voice held a hint of pride, and he found her hand. "Settle down, Marie. Ivan talked frankly, concerned that the girls would renovate and then get married. He didn't want to cheat them out of their money. He told me of his brother's interest in Katy."

"And what if Katy does spend her savings and then decide to move out and marry David? What then?"

"Then she's learned a valuable lesson. But that's something I need to work out with Ivan. Just in case. He's a kid himself, but he wouldn't have come to me if he planned to cheat them."

Marie nodded and went to her side of the bed. "Seems like you've thought of everything," she said, before flicking off the lamp.

⁓

Inching along in line at the church's monthly potluck spread, Katy and Lil each grabbed plastic silverware rolled in napkins and a paper plate.

"So what did you bring?" Katy asked, trying to tamp down her excitement until the perfect moment.

"Stew and broccoli corn bread."

"Hope there's some left." Everybody in church knew Lil and her mom were the potluck queens, a matriarchal honor passed down for generations in their family. Katy plunked baked beans on her plate, the serving spoon suddenly fumbling and splattering beans onto the tablecloth. They both reached for it at the same time. "Wish Megan could've come."

"Yeah. Too bad she's got the flu."

"At least she's still on break and has her mom to take care of her. Is that it?" Katy pointed at an empty pot, wondering if it was the stew.

31

"Yeah. But it looks like it's all gone."

"Your dishes always are. Aha!" Her enthusiasm on eyeing the nine-by-thirteen dish beside the empty pot was overplayed even for one of Lil's recipes. Using a spatula, Katy scooped up a small piece of Lil's corn bread. It missed the empty spot on her plate and plopped on top of her beans. She shrugged. "Clumsy today."

They carried their filled plates down a center aisle, glancing at the rows of long tables at either side of them. "How's that?" Lil asked, nodding her head toward a few empty folding chairs.

They settled in, and Lil glanced over at Katy. "You're acting weird. Jittery. You talked to your folks, didn't you?" Katy opened her mouth, but before she could reply, Lil gave a little squeal. "And they said yes?"

Raising her palms to calm her friend, Katy wavered, "Yes. . .no."

Lil poked her arm with her plastic fork. "Quit."

"Okay. I talked to them. But here's the deal. Dad agreed." She had to pause when Lil bounced and nearly collapsed the gray metal chair. "But he put conditions on it."

"Of course. Parents always do that." Lil shoveled down several bites of tossed salad. "So we just meet those conditions."

Katy shook her head. A part of her wanted to grab Lil by the arms, squeal, and dance with her in a circle as if they were a couple of kids, or at the least do the garbanzo shimmy. But if she didn't tamp down her friend's enthusiasm, Lil would never understand the gravity of the stipulations. And if Katy had to bear this trial, she wasn't going to bear it alone. She pointed a carrot stick at Lil. "Three conditions, to be exact."

Holding her fork at eye level, Lil stared at a chunk of gooey brownie. "Give 'em to me. One at a time."

"First, he wants to see the bids and the financial stuff."

"Easy enough. What else?"

"He wants to persuade Ivan Miller to keep an eye on us."

"Yuck. Oh fine. We can deal with it, I guess."

"You think that one's bad, listen to this." She leaned and whispered, "I have to go on three dates with David Miller before Dad will agree to it."

Lil's lips spewed brownie crumbs, and she slapped her palm over her mouth until she could spit into her napkin to keep from choking. After blotting her face, she stared at Katy. "No way!"

"You heard me."

"*Your* dad came up with that? Your dad, who's on the elder board?" Lil never missed an opportunity to rub it in that Megan and Katy's dads both served on the elder board. Lil's dad was too busy farming.

"With the help of my mom. They're real smug about it, too."

"But are they serious?"

"Dead serious. That's why you've got to come up with those bids fast." Katy lowered her voice to a whisper again, "Because if this whole doddy house thing isn't going to fly, then I for sure don't want to go through with all three dates." She worried her lip. Mostly, she didn't want to hurt David's feelings.

"But. . .then you're going to do it?"

"Well yeah. He's actually a sweet guy. Good-looking, too."

Lil stared at her with stricken eyes. Her face paled. "You like him?"

Feeling uneasy at her friend's unwarranted fear, Katy replied, "No. Of course not. But he's been asking me out for a while."

Lil crumpled her napkin into a ball and tossed it onto her plate. "Well, he's not your type."

"What's that supposed to mean? Wait a minute." Katy narrowed her eyes. "Do you like him?"

"No–o. You just need somebody with more spunk. Since you're so. . .inflexible."

Katy instantly bristled. She wasn't a goody-goody like Lil always insinuated. And she was tired of hearing that she was stubborn, too. Lil pushed sometimes just to see how far she could push. Like the time she actually wore a toe ring to foot washing. Katy still cringed over that. She'd covered it with her palm and slipped it into her pocket while Lil snickered. Giggling at foot washing was a sin in itself. Katy often overcompensated to keep Lil in line. But this wasn't the time to make a case of it, so she turned the heat back at Lil. "Did you ask your folks?"

Lil pushed her plate back and took a sip of her soda. "I did. Round one down. About two more to go, and then we're good. Honestly, Dad seems preoccupied for some reason. And Mom's lost her fight lately.

Now I can tell them what your dad said"—she lowered her voice—"without the David part. So don't worry about them. You know that even if they don't agree, I'm going to do this. "

Dread rippled through Katy's stomach. She hoped Lil didn't end up in a fight with her parents, although that had happened often enough in the past. Their relationship seemed to survive somehow. It was good Lil wasn't the oldest in her family. Her folks at least had practice before she came along. She glanced sideways.

Lil was rubbing her temples, staring down at the table. "I guess this can work."

Thinking of David's feelings again, Katy's meal turned sour. She whispered, "It doesn't feel fair to David. Think I need to tell him what my folks are up to? Warn him up front and see if he'll just play along? That way I don't hurt his feelings. He is a really nice guy."

"What if he won't? Then you won't meet your dad's criteria. Or what if that's even more humiliating for him? You better wait and tell him on the last date that you're not interested and hope that he doesn't ever find out." She gripped Katy's arm. "Wait. Did he even ask you out?"

Twisting away, Katy replied. "No. Dad said he was going to ask me to the skating party this afternoon."

"How would he know that?"

Katy shrugged. "I have no idea. The grapevine, I guess."

"The elders' grapevine," Lil added another dig. "But he didn't ask you yet?"

Katy shook her head. "You think I need to go flirt with him or something?"

Lil suddenly grinned. "I'd like to see *that* happen."

Lil's taunting attitude raised Katy's hackles again. She wasn't afraid to flirt with a guy. Katy just hadn't been interested in anyone since Jake. And she loved to prove Lil wrong. Slanting a brow, Katy scooted her chair back.

Lil clapped her hand over her spreading smile.

During their conversation, Katy had kept tabs on David, scoping the situation. He'd been watching her, too. In fact, he'd smiled once when their gazes had met. Now he loitered by the trash can, the sole of one shoe propped against the wall's baseboard. Her pulse raced with indecision.

David swiped a hand through brown hair that fell neatly back in place—shiny hair a lot of girls would envy—then took a swig of soda pop. *Trying to act cool,* she thought. Normally, the idea that he intentionally waited for her to dump her trash so he could pounce on her would be pathetic enough to make her leave the table empty-handed. But under the circumstances, she decided to put him out of his misery.

She set her shoulders and maneuvered through the crowded room, lifting her plate once to avoid a rowdy child. She reached the gray plastic can and plopped her trash in its black liner. Casually, she stepped aside and allowed her gaze to rest on David. "Oh hi," she said.

"Hi, Katy. Good food, huh?" Even though his trim physique was hidden beneath his plain brown suit jacket, overeating didn't seem to be a problem for him.

"Yes. But you're used to that. Your mom's a good cook."

His hazel gaze darted to the table of casseroles and empty platters. "What about you? Do you like to cook?"

"I can cook, but being friends with Lil, I'd rather not compete in that area. I guess that's why I like to do housekeeping. A girl wants to shine someplace." *That was a stupid pun,* she thought.

He grinned. "I like that about you. You're considerate."

Feeling the light-headed zap that follows an untruth, Katy studied the ground.

"Modest, too," he said.

"No I'm not." She raised her chin. "I'm not as good as everyone thinks."

She didn't know why it bothered her so much today. She wanted to be good. Still, it hurt when Lil called her inflexible or old-fashioned. The paradox confused her. One thing was certain: David didn't suspect her ulterior motives and didn't deserve them, either. She felt herself shrinking back from her dad's plan.

He quirked an eyebrow. She allowed herself to study his pleasantly

35

angular face. He gave her a confident grin, but not presumptuous. "I better not go there. You going to the skating party this afternoon?"

She swallowed. She absolutely wouldn't go through with this.

"If you are, can I take you?"

His eyes pleaded and twinkled at the same time. He widened his smile, and his cheek creased on the left side of his mouth. She'd never noticed he had dimples. And he really was a nice guy. And a great skater. But she had no intentions of stringing him along, doddy house or not. So much rested on her decision. Finally she determined, she'd go with him, but at the first opportunity, she would tell him about her dad's deal.

"Sure."

His shoulders relaxed a tad. "Great. How about three o'clock?"

"Perfect. But you'd better wear knee pads and a helmet. I'm not that good."

"There you go again. I've been watching you, Katy. I know if you can skate or not. You make a pretty picture on the ice."

A spurt of pleasure surprised her. "Thanks, David."

She glanced around and saw that the crowd was starting to disperse. "Guess folks are leaving. I need to put something on the bulletin board before they lock up. See you later." She spun, feeling his gaze on her back, and fought to deny the strange pleasure it brought her.

After she pinned a paper to the church bulletin board that would let others know she was looking for more work, she made her way toward the exit. The moment she stepped into the parking lot, Lil grabbed her arm.

"You did it, didn't you?"

She shrugged away. "Shh! He might be following. Walk me to the car."

"Well?"

"He's taking me to the party." Katy reached for her Chevy's door handle. "Get those bids fast, Lil. Okay?"

"Of course. I can't believe this is finally happening. I'll see you at the party."

Katy started to get in the car, but thought better of it. She jumped back out and leaned against the roof. "Lil!"

Her friend turned, and Katy motioned her back. "Be careful how you act at the party. Don't give me away. And don't tell anybody about this except Megan."

"Duh. I'm not stupid."

"Fine. See you later."

Katy slammed her car door and looked in the mirror to straighten her covering. Her scheming reflection caught her off guard. Was she becoming a stranger to herself? What was happening? She reached up and gave the mirror an angry twist so that it only showed the rectangle of the back windshield. And there was David Miller walking behind her car.

She fastened her seat belt and started the ignition. When she backed out, David was already sitting inside his shiny black sedan. She edged her car onto the street when an angry thought shot through her mind. *It's all your fault, Jake Byler. You've ruined me for everybody else.* She allowed a ball of resentment to expand in her throat. Yes, it was all his fault.

In Plain City, she braked for a red light. Jake was a rat, but it really wasn't all his fault she hadn't moved on with her life. Maybe this date was a good thing, and her dad was doing her a favor. It was time to test the waters and see if she could date somebody besides Jake.

If she gave David a chance, he might even grow on her. Maybe they'd marry and tell their children the funny story of how their mom tricked their daddy into a date. They'd laugh and say the joke was on their mom, because their daddy wanted the date all along. Wouldn't that make a happy story?

Honk! The blare of a car's horn brought her back to her surroundings, and she placed her foot on the accelerator. She needed to get home and get ready for her foolish date.

CHAPTER 4

Dashing toward the door before the bell disturbed her dad's nap, Katy snatched up her skates. She didn't need her dad telling David to take care of his dumplin'. As she passed, her mom looked up from her quilting frame and mumbled, "Have fun with that nice boy."

"Sure." Katy's black, quilted snow boots pattered across the wood flooring. It was bad enough that earlier in the week she'd caught her mom staring at a double wedding ring pattern. Gratefully her siblings, who liked to tease, were sledding out back. Her pulse accelerated. She gripped the handle and swung open the door to be instantly thrown off balance by David's hazel gaze—part warm and part mischievous, as if it held some secret.

David tilted his head, his wind-ruffled hair accentuating his boyish appeal. "Hi Katy." When his mouth quirked at the corner, she realized he was waiting on her, probably expecting to get invited inside.

"Just a moment." She ducked back inside and dove into her wool coat, throwing a scarf around her neck. David held the door for her as she stepped onto the porch. The crisp air nipped her cheeks, and she crunched down the walk with David toward a rumbling, black sedan puffing steam from its exhaust.

"Wow." The word slipped from her mouth unbidden. *Impressive,* she kept to herself. She could have sworn the car was even shinier than it had been at church.

He grinned and opened its passenger door for her, and she slipped into its warm interior. While he went around the outside, she stroked the plush seat with her thumb, inhaling David's intimate ride of leather and aftershave.

He hopped in and paused before placing a gloved hand on the gearshift. "You're stunning in that white scarf."

When she had opened the hand-knitted Christmas gift, her mom had mentioned it would make a nice contrast with her black hair. Usually her mom didn't compliment her children's outward appearance unless it was to affirm neatness or modesty.

Katy had been taught that a woman should be more concerned about her inner beauty and not prideful about the outer, which was fleeting anyway. But Katy couldn't help but be appreciative when she looked in a mirror because her face didn't need the forbidden cosmetics. She had been blessed with good features, and the plain Conservative hairstyles she wore only emphasized them.

Thin like her figure, her face was a perfect oval, and she had dark prominent brows and black-lashed brown eyes that were more exotic than plain. Her mom told her that a missionary ancestor married into Spanish blood. Her nose even protested her Conservative lifestyle for it appeared aristocratic, thin and long. Her lips must have come from the Spanish ancestor, too, because they were full and expressive. She knew that her striking eyes and mouth caused people to imagine more intensity in her emotions than she usually felt or meant to display.

Self-consciously flicking her ponytail out from under the scarf, she said, "Thanks." She dropped her skates on the floor mat, careful to keep her eyes from flirting. With a fluid movement, he put the car in reverse, and they backed onto the country road. "How do you keep your car so clean?" She motioned toward the snowy countryside. "In this?" His cheek muscle twitched as if she'd touched upon a sensitive subject. When he didn't have an immediate comeback, she asked, "What? Am I embarrassing you?"

He shot her a warm glance. "I'm just wondering how you are with secrets."

"Really?" Involuntarily, she leaned toward him. "I'm great with secrets."

His raised brow challenged, "Never knew a woman who could keep secrets."

"Try me."

"I haul buckets of hot water to the barn and wash it, towel dry it."

"How often?"

"Once or twice a week."

Katy rested her head back on the headrest. "Wow. Does your dad know?"

"Yeah. He thinks it's prideful."

"I think it's great."

He cast her an uncertain glance. She leaned forward again and jutted her chin. "I feel flattered to ride in a clean car. I think every guy should take note and learn from you. And I don't think it's prideful to take good care of your stuff. You know Megan?"

"Megan?" He seemed confused at the sudden turn of the conversation. "Yeah."

"Her parents are always harping on stewardship. And it's rubbed off on me, too. It makes good sense to take care of your stuff." He beamed, and she relaxed her shoulders. "All I mean, is I understand. I like things sparkly, too. I clean houses, remember? I just never carried it over to my car in the winter." She troubled her lip. "Maybe I should."

"Maybe I should do it for you."

She glanced over. It was a generous, flirtatious offer. "Ah. I don't think so." She snuck another sideways glance. But was this guy her clone or what?

He shrugged and concentrated on the narrow gravel road lined by low snowbanks and ditches. But the simple offer hung in the air. David Miller had ingratiated himself in only five minutes. She liked him.

He pushed a button and classical music flowed through the car's speakers.

"Can I use your mirror?" she asked.

"Sure."

She lowered the visor and pulled a soft beanie out of her pocket. Staring into a gleaming mirror, she placed it over her covering and pulled it snug over her ears. When she finished, she flipped up the visor and glanced sideways.

He grinned. "And a matching hat. Even more stunning."

"I figured I'd ease you into it, you know, so I didn't knock you off your feet or something."

"You practically ran us into the ditch. Took my brute strength just to keep us on the road."

Lowering an embarrassed gaze to the floorboards, Katy noticed her skates. "You're pretty good on the ice, aren't you?"

"Yep."

Katy sank back against the seat, listening to the music, enjoying the thrill of masculine attention that purred along her spine.

Ten minutes later, David turned into the lane next to the Stuckys' mailbox and drove to the back of the property. Several cars were already parked there. He helped her out, and they trudged over the frozen clods of a dormant cornfield toward a patch of box elders that banked the Big Darby Creek. Lil wasn't among the dozen other young adults already milling down by the ice, and Katy remembered Megan was home sick.

He pointed out a fallen log where the surrounding ground was littered with boots and shoes. "Shall we put on our skates?"

"Sure." Katy dropped to the log, trying to hide the excitement that washed over her. She bent over her gray wool culottes and removed her quilted boots, quickly slipping her black stocking-clad feet into white skates. As she laced, she glanced at David, who was already finished. His elbows propped on his knees, he was watching the skaters. The rink was a wide patch of ice about 150 feet in length, most likely cleared by the Stuckys' red snow thrower that now sat parked against the far bank.

"Ready?" she asked.

In response, his masculine grip warmed her hand through their gloves. At the bank, he glided backward and dug his toe pick into the ice, then skated forward. With surprise, Katy allowed him to clasp her by the waist and lift her down onto the ice.

"Easy. There you go."

At first they stroked forward, hand in hand, and after one circle of the rink, he pulled her into a Kilian position. The back of her left shoulder pressed against the front of his navy jacket, and his hand rested at her waist. She didn't feel uneasy at the intimacy of his touch because skating was one of the permitted group dating activities that allowed such familiarities. Several other couples skated in the group of teens and young adults.

Their skates cut the ice sending sprays of white shavings. The bumpy, air-pocketed river ice didn't hinder their skating; it was all Katy knew. But relying on David's superior skill, she quickly relaxed, their skates crossing in sync and bodies leaning and drawing across the ice as one, even when they dodged in and around other skaters.

When they'd tired of that, he drew her to the middle where a few skaters practiced spins. He twirled her, steadying her when she lost balance. Once she sailed into him, practically knocking his breath away. They laughed, visible puffs of air separating their faces. When she looked up, she saw Lil ahead on the bank, frowning at them. "Oh look, David. It's Lil." Katy waved. "Can we go talk to her?"

Whispering against her soft hat, he replied, "You can call me Dave."

The suggestive tone of his voice sent a startled warning. No, she wouldn't be doing that or anything else to lead him on unnecessarily. He drew her close again, and she felt a bit self-conscious as they glided toward the bank where some of their friends conversed around a big bonfire.

With ease, David jumped to the low bank and pulled her up with him. Then they tiptoed to the fire. "Hi, Lil." Katy beamed. Lil's hands were stuffed in her coat pockets.

"I'll get us some hot chocolate. Want some, Lil?" David offered.

"Sure."

"What's wrong?" Katy demanded. "You're looking at me like I have broccoli stuck in my teeth or something."

"You usually do." Lil chuckled. "Looks like you're having a ball."

"Why not? He's a good skater. Want him to take you a couple spins?"

"Don't you dare pawn off your date on me," Lil snapped.

Katy felt her face heat when David stepped up behind them with steaming drinks in Styrofoam cups. Had he overheard Lil's remark?

Lil thanked him and took one of the cups. "Good thing Megan's not here to see these."

David shrugged a brow. "Because?"

Katy explained. "These are not easily recyclable."

"Oh. Usually we use the thick paper cups, don't we?"

Katy frowned at Lil before she sipped the warm chocolate. "Anyway. This is good."

As they finished drinking and mingled with the rest of the group, Katy felt self-conscious over the curious glances she and David provoked. At least he hadn't hovered or marked his territory. Instead, he'd been considerate and chummed with some of his friends, giving her a chance to visit with Lil. When he asked if she was ready to skate again, Lil waved her away.

When they returned to the ice, he asked, "What's up with Lil?"

"I'm not sure." Katy glanced back at her friend and saw her tapping away at the buttons of her cell phone. Must be preoccupied over her new toy—the elder board had been divided over the issue of allowing its use. With disgust, Katy asked, "You have a cell phone?"

"Yep. Why?"

She shrugged and was saved from getting into a debate when her blade hit a root protrusion. She tripped and David caught her. But the minor incident left them skating face-to-face, with David skating backward.

"Here, put your palms flat against mine," he urged. Then she forgot all about Lil. He even taught her to skate backward, and Katy felt more happy and carefree than she had in months. Within another half an hour, however, her ankles grew tired and her toes frigid. She glanced toward the bonfire, and David was instantly perceptive of her need. "Ready to go in?"

"I am." She scanned the bank for Lil and found her talking to some tall, well-built guy who sent an odd flutter through her stomach. A warning flashed through her mind, and she looked closer. Her stomach clenched. Jake Byler? How on earth—at that instant, her world spun. Her skates tangled, too. David tripped and skidded on the knees of his jeans, pulling her down on top of him. With a grunt, her breath was forced from her lungs, and her elbow slammed the ice. When finally they quit sliding, she rolled over on her side with a groan.

She felt David scrambling out from beneath her, then leaning over her, his hand on her shoulder. "Are you okay?"

"I think so." She tugged at her culottes, but only wanted to curl in a ball and escape the humiliation, escape Jake.

She stared into David's concerned hazel eyes. He apologized, "I don't know what happened."

She did. She also knew she needed to get up before they drew even more attention than they already had. She saw his mouth quirk. "This isn't funny," she warned. "You get up first." Surely his knees were bruised, if not cracked.

With a grimace and some clumsy movements, he was soon standing on his blades. Then he grabbed her under the arms and pulled her to her feet. All his concern was directed at her, and he even brushed awkwardly at her snowy coat.

"I'm fine," she snapped, rubbing an aching elbow.

"Guess we should have quit sooner." He draped a supportive arm around her waist, and they skated toward the bank.

Feeling guilty for snapping at him, she admitted, "It was my fault. I tripped you." She drew in a quick breath. "Is he still over there talking to Lil?" As David glanced over his shoulder, she felt his body tense.

"So *he's* what happened."

"Sorry."

"So you want to talk to them? Or shall we slink off to the car in our humiliation?"

"Definitely slink."

"Sit down then, and let me help you with your skates." She lowered herself to the log. With another grimace, David went down on his knees.

She placed her hand on his shoulder. "You're in pain. I'm so sorry."

"I'm fine. Now smile. Pretend to have fun." He winked. "That'll get him."

44

She removed her hand. "I was having fun. Now I know why Lil was acting all weird on us. But until he ruined everything, I was having a blast."

David grinned and squeezed her hand. "Me, too, Katy."

⟿

A few minutes before the spill, Lil had explained to Jake Byler, "She doesn't really like him, but David's crazy about her."

Burning with jealousy, Jake Byler glanced down at his cousin, then back out at the ice where David maneuvered Katy around like some ballerina. Her slim form and fine-boned features gave her a fragile appearance, but Jake knew from experience a man couldn't force her to do anything, unless she allowed it. And it hurt to see the way she moved in sync with David. "Since when?"

"I didn't notice until he asked her out. Now it's obvious."

The Miller guy was younger than Jake, and they'd never been close. They'd played some basketball and hockey together. David's brothers were older than Jake so he'd never hung out with them, either. He didn't know what made the guy tick. Except for Katy, that is. And why wouldn't she?

She'd captured his own attention long before he'd acquired any skills to fend off female charms. Katy was younger than Jake, too, but at recess he let her cut in line just because he was intrigued with her bouncy ponytail. After he'd touched it, she'd reeled him in with her black flashing eyes.

Jake had always loved to watch her hands dance when she talked, admiring her tiny wrists and long feminine fingers. But her greatest asset was her face. There was an intensity in her dark eyes that could move mountains. They were deep, dark, and expressive. Her nose was thin and long, merely a gentle slope that drew the eye down to her best feature, those full, sulky lips. The combination of lethal eyes and pursed lips stopped a guy in his tracks. A man instantly sensed the stubborn spirit behind the face. Lesser men shrank back. She wielded her feminine weapons without chagrin, swathing her path through life, unawares that most people did not have such natural charms at their command. She had a hauteur about her that warned others she wasn't used to losing. She probably didn't realize that she could get her way without uttering a word.

As if reading his mind, she turned her brown gaze toward him. Her eyes were naturally so dark that they almost smoldered, causing a man to want to read something sexual in them, when really they were unfathomable. But it caused Jake to feel jealous now that it was David's arms around her.

His stomach clenched when recognition hit her expression and that smoldering gaze riveted upon him. His gaze pleaded with hers. But she denied him. Her eyes glittered, and her expression darkened with repulsion. Her entire body reacted. She actually stopped skating.

David toppled forward, and Jake watched helpless as the couple wiped out on the ice, Katy tumbling on top of David.

Jake lunged forward, but Lil caught him by his coat sleeve.

She grimaced. "Ouch. That had to hurt. You see how both his knees smacked the ice? At least he cushioned Katy's fall."

His jealousy reared again as David untangled himself from Katy and hovered over her. "You sure this is their first date? They seem mighty cozy."

Lil waved a glove through the air. "It's the skating. He's had his hands all over her. That's why I called you. So what are you going to do?"

He knew now this group setting had been a mistake for his first encounter with Katy. He should have waited and gone with their original plan. Lil's plan. She'd hired him to modernize the doddy house. He'd be there when Katy came over. He would apologize in privacy. Beg, if he had to, for her forgiveness.

"Well?"

"I can't go rescue her. I didn't bring any skates. But it looks like they're coming in off the ice." He glared at David. "I've got my work cut out for me."

She put an elbow in his gut. "You deserve it, chump."

"Hmph." He glanced away from the irritating scene where David was now unlacing her skates. Lil had one glove on her hip, looking miffed. She never should have told him all those years ago that Katy

46

meant to marry him. Maybe it wouldn't have made him so confident she'd always be there. Maybe it wouldn't have scared him away. But Lil had meant well. They'd always been close as if she were his sister. In fact, when the family got together, she hung out with him instead of his younger sister Erin. That's probably how he noticed Katy. She and Lil and Megan had always been together.

"They're leaving. I can't believe she's not even going to say good-bye," Lil huffed.

A hand clamped Jake's shoulder, and he turned. "Hey, how's it going?"

"Good to see you, man." Chad Penner held out his hand. Though they had once been best of friends, their relationship had become estranged when Jake had left the church.

Grasping it, Jake replied, "Better get used to it. I'm back to stay."

Chad swung an arm over Jake's shoulder. "I knew you'd be back."

With relief, Jake allowed himself to be drawn into the group of skaters warming up at the bonfire. Everyone seemed happy to see him, forgiving of his sudden absence and eager to accept him back into the group. Meanwhile, he glimpsed Katy and David disappearing into a stand of box elders. But as the group enveloped him, some of his heaviness fled. He roasted a hot dog and caught up with Chad.

Jake wished he'd never left, but all he could do now was prove how he'd changed. He was earnest in his desire to fit back in with his old friends.

When the group began to disperse, Jake walked Lil to her car then squeezed her shoulder. "Maybe this was for the best. It'll give Katy time to digest the idea that I'm back. We'll have to trust God with this, okay?"

"I've been praying for you for a long time, chump."

"I know. Thanks."

Head bent in thought, he strode to his truck and climbed in. Although he'd jumped his first hurdle, facing the group again, he knew the worst was still ahead of him. He'd never forget the incident, the night when he'd been drunk. Furious, Katy had hissed that she wanted him to go away and stay away. But this afternoon, when their gazes latched, he'd felt hopeful for an instant. Then when she'd left without even saying good-bye to Lil, he'd gotten the impression she loathed him.

He drove out onto the gravel road. Nobody had ever loathed him. Wait, hadn't he once heard that love and hate were closely related? For his sake, he hoped so. His mind traveled back to the time before he'd grown restless. He flicked on his headlights and started toward home, involuntarily scanning the snowy ditches and fields for deer and other wild animals that sometimes leapt in front of vehicles.

The farm made him restless. Jake's dad had died years earlier. His mom still lived in his childhood home, but his uncle and brother Cal managed the farm. Jake had never been interested in that, though he'd helped his uncle a lot over the years. He had been interested in construction, seeing buildings erected, swinging a hammer. He didn't regret his vocation decision, but he regretted losing Katy.

Suddenly his vision caught something that made his pulse race. Was God answering his prayer so quickly? There alongside the road was David Miller's disgustingly shiny car. A grin spread over Jake's face; then a chuckle erupted in his throat. A flat tire. Just what the woman-stealer deserved. Trying to tamp down his delight, he pulled in behind the stranded vehicle. Maybe he was going to be able to rescue her after all.

He opened the door and jumped down, leaving his headlights on for Miller. "Hey, got a problem?" David looked up. Even in the dim light, Jake could see the guy's embarrassment. "Need a hand with that?"

"Nope." David jerked the wrench, twisting the lug nuts of the left rear wheel. "Got it under control."

Jake stuffed his hands in his pockets and gazed at the car, where he could see Katy's dark silhouette.

"Don't need your help," David repeated sharply.

"Think I'll just say hi to Katy." Jake strode past his angry opponent and around the back of the car right up to Katy's door. Her face was looking straight ahead. He knocked on her window and startled her. She hit the window's inoperative button. He took that as an invitation and opened her door. It hurt to see her inside another man's car, but he gave her what he hoped looked like a contrite smile. "Hi Katy."

Her chin jutted upward. "What do *you* want?"

Her face was so lovely, flushed and pink, her hair messy under the white knitted beanie. But her gaze smoldered. He'd learned that her gaze could be dark or cool, but one thing it never did was shrink back. Still, he yearned to scoop her into his arms until she no longer despised him. "Need a ride?"

"Not hardly."

"You look kinda lonely and cold."

Just then David jerked the driver's door open and slid in. "Not lonely." He started the engine.

"And warm as toast," Katy added with a shiver.

Jake gave her a salute and eased the door closed, backing away from the car just before it spit gravel in his face.

CHAPTER 5

On Monday morning, Katy took her normal route to work, using routine maneuvers to blend in with the freeway traffic that skirted the west side of Columbus. As she drove, she puzzled over the mystery of Jake's unexpected appearance at Sunday's skating party. It didn't surprise her that he'd come home for the holidays, since like Megan he was probably on break. But why had he come to the river when he hadn't mingled with church friends for over a year now—ever since the incident between them in the church parking lot?

She probed at the matter, furious at herself for gawking at Jake like a lovesick fool. In that one weak moment, his features, wind-ruffled hair, and masculine physique had been burned into her memory all anew, more vivid and arresting than ever. She felt as if months of working to get over him had been destroyed in an instant. He'd stood on the icy riverbank and beckoned her with dark, hooded eyes so scorching and brooding and out of place in that winter playground. It had been all she could do to pull her gaze away. No wonder she'd faltered.

She reached out and flipped the car's heater off. With a glance at the green, overhead sign, she changed into the exit lane. And when David's tire had gone flat, the rat had the gall to butt in where he wasn't wanted. While David had worked on the tire, her nemesis had stepped out of her imagination and appeared in flesh and blood outside her window, wearing a crooked smile and a smug expression.

David had handled the evening's humiliation with more grace than she would have imagined possible, coming to her rescue. Twice.

Leave it to Katy to trip up the best skater at the party. But David had been a great sport—given that Jake had knocked her off her feet, David had played the hero by whisking her away to safety. Only, poor guy, his efforts had backfired.

With the pride he took in the care of his car, she knew that its flat tire probably embarrassed him the most. The tension that sizzled when David slid into his driver's side and glared at Jake would have been intense enough to ignite a forest fire in the dead of winter. Thankfully, Jake had backed away.

After all the drama Jake had caused, she hadn't wanted to humiliate David further by bringing up her dad's stipulations. Her mom had been right. He was a great guy, and she'd had a lot of fun with him, too. Although with the aggravation he'd suffered on their date, including a set of bruised knees, he probably wouldn't ask her out again.

Just when she had started to entertain thoughts of David as a real boyfriend, Jake had returned, sending her heart, mind, and body into a crazy spin. He still wielded tremendous power over her. And she resented him for it. Even if he slipped back into oblivion, his brief appearance had caused her irreparable damage.

Lil could probably explain why Jake had shown up at the party, but Katy hadn't been able to ask her yet with the way their schedules clashed.

As she pulled into the driveway of the Brooks' residence, Katy cringed. She hoped Lil hadn't told Jake about the three-date stipulation. She certainly didn't want him to think she had to buy her dates. Sometimes when it came to Jake, Katy wasn't sure whose side Lil was on. Flipping down her visor, she checked to see that her covering was straight. When she saw her grim lips, she wet them and forced herself to relax.

Moments later, she used her key to enter the house, taking a quick scope of its usual disarray. By the time she hit the kitchen, she'd already scooped up two sets of newspapers and several pink glittery items of clothing.

In the kitchen, her steps faltered. "Oh. Hi, Tammy. I didn't realize you were here, or I would have knocked."

Tammy Brooks snapped her briefcase closed and slipped into its shoulder strap. "No problem." She grabbed a designer purse off a bar stool. "I'm glad I can at least count on you."

Katy took the newspapers to the recycle bin and set Addison's clothing on a bar stool. Her slim, high-heeled employer made a turn toward the door, and Katy knew that she couldn't waste such an opportunity. "Do you have a moment?"

"Sure. I'm already late so what's a few more minutes?" Katy felt her face heat, but before she could reply, Tammy asked, "You aren't going to quit on me, are you?"

"Of course not." She hurried into her explanation so that she didn't take up Tammy's precious time. "I just wondered if you knew of anyone who was looking for a housekeeper? One of my employers moved to Florida, and I could use more work."

Tammy smiled and plunked her purse back on the counter. Her briefcase, stuffed with real estate fliers, slid to the ground. "Why don't I fix us a pot of coffee? We never get to chat. You drink coffee?"

Feeling apprehensive, Katy folded a size 7 sweater. "I'd love a cup."

Tammy flung a wet coffee filter into the garbage, and some of the grounds splattered onto her suit skirt. "Ugh!" she moaned, tearing off a paper towel and blotting at the spot.

"Can I help?"

"Nope." Tammy brushed the air with her hand. "I've got it. Good as new. See?" Then she bent over, and Katy cringed to see a cross nestled in her employer's cleavage, accentuated by her immodest neckline. "What hours do you usually work?"

Slipping onto a bar stool, Katy explained, "I work for you on Mondays and Wednesdays. I clean for an elderly woman who lives in a retirement community every other Friday. The couple that moved to Florida I worked for on Tuesdays and Thursdays. That's the job I need to replace."

The aroma of a popular Starbucks blend filled the kitchen as coffee dripped into a carafe. Tammy moved into a bar stool and swiveled to face her. "I think we can help each other. I need a nanny."

Instantly recoiling, Katy shook her head. "I don't think so. I've never babysat before."

Tammy swept off the stool and got the liquid creamer from the refrigerator. No wonder Tammy was treating her like a guest instead of a servant. The other woman returned with two steaming cups, placing one in front of Katy. "It's not really babysitting. My kids are old enough to take care of themselves. But they need somebody to haul them around and help them with their homework, field problems. Mostly keep an eye on them."

Katy took a sip of coffee, then asked, "What happened to their nanny?"

With a deep sigh, Tammy said. "She quit. Claims her classes are too full next semester. Look, she really left me in the lurch. That's why I was late this morning, arranging for a ride for the kids this afternoon. Tanya didn't even tell me to my face. She just called me last night. I was furious. I can tell you she won't be getting any references from me. In fact, I've a mind to call one of her professors or something." Tammy crossed her long slim legs and forced a smile. "Think about the benefits. A few hours every afternoon until their dad or I get home from work. You'll end up with more hours that way and still have a couple of days off to sleep in, run errands, or read a book. I wish I had that luxury."

Katy felt her face burn. Tammy assumed her life was luxurious? She seldom lounged around reading books. There was plenty of work to be done at home, helping her mom. Her mind raced, looking for a way to politely turn down the offer. When nothing came to mind, she stalled. "How old are they? It's Addison and Tyler?"

"Yes. Addy is seven, and Tyler's an eleven-year-old adult."

Katy smiled. The children seemed well behaved the few times she'd met them. It was Mr. Brooks she didn't care for. Most often, she'd encountered him on his way to the liquor cabinet or sprawled out watching television, both forbidden indulgences in Katy's mind. His drinking reminded her too much of Jake, making her distrust the older man. Maybe he was the reason the nanny quit. She found herself tapping her fingers on the counter.

"Please say you'll do it until I can find another nanny? I like you and know you'll be great for the kids. You'll help me out this once, won't you? I've got several clients this week, and I can't leave them hanging. And you admitted yourself, you need the money."

"You'll look for another nanny?"

"Yes. Oh thanks, so much." Tammy flew out of her seat. "You're such a sweet thing. And I'll ask around and see if anyone needs a housekeeper. Thanks again, honey."

"So when do you want me to start?"

"Tomorrow afternoon. Here." Tammy scribbled the addresses of her children's schools on a yellow sticky note. "Addison gets out of school at 2:30 p.m., and Tyler gets out at 3:00 p.m. Works out great." She picked up her briefcase and left like a whirlwind, leaving Katy to ponder what had just transpired and to stew over the way Tammy had so effortlessly manipulated her.

⸺ᴄ⸺

The Brooks' home was located in the west side Columbus suburb of Old Arlington. The affluent neighborhood sprawled between two rivers, the Olentangy and the Scioto, giving it a parklike feel. Many of the houses were Tudor style. With Tammy's yellow sticky note stuck to her steering wheel, Katy followed the street signs through meandering, tree-lined streets to a brick elementary charter school and eased into a slow-moving lineup. She noticed teachers lined along the walkway, helping the students into their cars. On Katy's rearview mirror hung a yellow card with a number that would identify her as Addison's ride.

Addison stood in line on the sidewalk with her classmates. The blond second-grader wore a purple coat and pink boots and had a princess backpack slung over one shoulder. Katy pulled up to the curb, and a teacher opened the car's back door. Addison started talking before she'd even buckled her seat belt.

"I'm surprised to see you, Miss Yoder. Why are you picking me up?"

"Didn't your mommy tell you I'd be watching you for a while?"

"Yes, but I forgot. I've got dance class today."

"You do?" Katy asked, easing the car back into the line of traffic. "Well, I'm not sure you'll be going today. Your mom said she'd leave me instructions at the house." Katy felt tense. Dance lessons? She turned west onto another suburban street. "We're going to pick up Tyler now."

"Okay, but where's my snack?"

"What snack?"

"Tanya always brings me a snack so I don't get bored. Sometimes she brings gummy bears or granola bars. But sometimes she brings me pop. I don't like apples. I'm really tired of apples. So don't bring me any apples. Without my snack, it's so boring waiting for Tyler. Today's going to be a boring day, isn't it?"

"I hope not," Katy replied, glancing at the sticky note again and watching for the street signs. "Do you know how to get to your brother's school?"

"Sure, I know where it is. He thinks he's big stuff just because he's in sixth grade, but they don't do anything fun. I don't know why he brags about it."

"Well, tell me if you see where we're supposed to turn."

"Okay. So why don't you just take me to my dance lessons now? I can hang out with my friends, and then I won't be bored."

"Don't worry. We'll figure that out."

"That was the street back there. You just missed it."

"Ugh!" Katy wheeled into a driveway and waited for the opportunity to turn back. Soon she was in another lineup but feeling less apprehensive about the pickup procedure. When Tyler got in the car, he threw his pack on the floorboards and slammed the door. Then he looked at his sister and said, "Hi, brat."

"Stop calling me that. Make him stop calling me that. He thinks he's big stuff. But he's not."

"Be kind, Tyler. I'll soon have you both home."

"Put on the radio," Tyler demanded.

"I don't listen to the radio," Katy explained. "Why don't you look out the window and see how many snowmen you can find?" Such driving games always entertained her little brothers.

"Why don't you listen to the radio?"

Seemed the car games weren't as fun for Tyler as they were for her siblings. She sighed. "Some of the lyrics aren't godly."

"What's that mean?"

"They talk about bad things."

"No they don't. Turn it on. Come on. My mom lets me."

"Sorry, Tyler."

She heard his seat belt unbuckle and then heard him rustling through his backpack. Katy glanced in the mirror nervously. "What are you doing, Tyler?"

"Duh. He's getting his iPod," Addison said. "He thinks he's big stuff because he has an iPod."

"Oh. Well, you need to keep your seat belt fastened." Not that it mattered as they had already reached the children's street. She'd barely pulled into the drive when both children barreled out of the car. While Katy fumbled in her purse for her house key, Tyler walked to the garage door and punched some buttons. The door opened and both children let themselves into the house. Snapping her purse closed, Katy hurried after them. She closed the garage door behind her and followed them into the kitchen, despondent to see empty microwave popcorn bags and bowls on the counter and a stack of dirty dishes in the sink. How hard was it to load a dishwasher?

Tyler jerked open the refrigerator door and stared into it. Addison pushed him and jerked open a bin.

"Stop it."

Their bodies tugged for position, and Addison came out of the scuffle with string cheese, but her brother latched on to it, too. "Let go," she demanded.

Katy walked over, taking each child by a shoulder. "Move aside, and let me see if there's more."

"This was the last one," Addison said, jerking it out of her brother's grip and quickly peeling back the plastic.

Katy glanced at the counter. "How about some fruit, Tyler?"

He gave his sister a glare but moved toward the fruit bowl and took a banana. When he peeled it back, he stuck it under Addison's nose. She squealed. "Stop. Make him stop."

Katy placed her hand on Tyler's shoulder and said sternly, "You sit in that chair." When he hesitated, she sharpened her voice. "Now." The child sulked into the chair. "Addison you sit in that one." Addison bounced into the chair, giving her brother a victorious look. "Now listen up. When I'm watching you, I expect you to respect each other. I have two brothers and a sister at home. Don't think I don't know how to make little children behave." She narrowed her eyes. "Because I do. Do you understand?"

They both gave nods. Tyler's eyes, however, darkened rebelliously. Katy moved to the counter and looked for her instructions. Sure enough, she was to take Tyler to his friend's house and then take Addison to dance class at an Upper Arlington address. She was supposed to walk her inside, watch practice, and afterward relay the instructor's parental information to Tammy.

"I'm done with my snack. Can I go play?" Addison asked.

"Yes. We have a half hour before I take you to your lessons. Tyler you'll be going to your friends'—"

He punched his fist in the air. "Awesome!"

"You may go to your rooms and change clothes, and I'll call you when it's time," she called after Tyler who was already halfway up the stairs. "Tyler, stop! Come back here and take that banana peel to the trash. It's only polite to clean up after yourself." It was no wonder the house always looked like a tornado had hit it.

He turned and marched back, like a bull eyeing a matador and snatched up the peel with a scowl. "I'll do it, but you're the maid. There." He plunked it in the trash. "Satisfied?"

"I'll be satisfied when you can do that with a smile on your face."

"Fat chance of that." He glanced at her covering. "Pilgrim lady."

Katy's jaw dropped, and she found herself speechless. Meanwhile, Tyler took the steps two at a time and disappeared.

So much for the misconception that the Brooks' children were polite. Though it was probably useless and would probably go unnoticed, Katy went through the house, picking up things that were out of place: Barbie dolls, video games, princess socks, and wineglasses.

She had threatened the children by telling them she knew how to handle her brothers and sister, but the truth was, she'd never had to deal with an adolescent boy's smart mouth. The woodshed prevented that sort of rebellion at her house. She would need to speak to Tammy about the appropriate methods of discipline.

Her more immediate challenge, however, would be taking Addison to dance lessons because dancing was forbidden in the Conservative Mennonite Church she attended. In her imagination, the word *dancing* conjured up smoky dens of drink and lust. She'd never given this type of dancing a thought. If she took Addison, as her employer expected, would she be enabling an innocent child to do something sinful?

On the other hand, Addison would continue her lessons regardless of whether Katy continued to be her nanny or not. And if Katy refused to take the little girl to her dance lessons, Tammy might get angry and fire her. Then her doddy house dreams would be ruined for sure.

Considering the options available to her, she placed the breakfast dishes in the dishwasher. Mom would probably tell her to quit her job and remind her that she could live at home until she got another one. Lil would insist that as long as Katy wasn't dancing, she wasn't doing anything wrong. Megan was adept at handling sticky situations. She would advise Katy to use this as an opportunity to witness to the children. So far that tactic hadn't worked with Tyler when he wanted to listen to the radio. But then she hadn't made Christianity sound very enticing, had she? Nevertheless, Megan's imaginary advice was the best.

She gripped the edge of the sink. She wanted to please her employer, but she didn't want to displease God. She definitely believed that bars and nightclubs were not God-honoring places. Lil had watched enough television and passed along enough steamy details for Katy to make valid conclusions about those devil houses. But that wasn't really the issue.

The Bible talked about King David dancing. Katy had wondered about that when she came across the Old Testament passage. She did little joy dances herself when she was alone. Lil had perfected the garbanzo shimmy. Nothing wrong with those. But to move your body seductively, unless it was with your husband, of course, was definitely wrong.

She had picked up Addison's dance costume off the floor several times. It was skimpy, yet how seductively could a seven-year-old dance? She turned on the faucet and watched the water rinse the sink. She washed her hands, dried them, and carefully folded the hand towel, even though she never found it that way.

She didn't want to overreact. Tyler already thought she was a pilgrim. She wasn't sure where he'd come up with that idea. Was he confusing her with Quakers? Still, it was meant as an insult, and she hadn't enjoyed his wisecrack.

A glance at the clock told her she needed to decide now. With a sigh, she opted to follow Tammy's instructions and evaluate the experience. This wasn't a permanent position, anyway. Maybe Tammy had already found a replacement for her. And God knew her heart, that she didn't want to sin against Him.

Church restrictions were put in place to keep a person from falling into situations of temptation that could lead to sin. She would be very careful not to allow temptation in. She pushed the dishwasher's START button and hurried to the stairway.

"Addison. Tyler. It's time to go. Are you ready?"

CHAPTER 6

Katy followed Addison through a lobby decorated with modern chrome furnishings. A bright ballet poster graced one wall, and a rack of glitzy costumes hung from a corner rack, but no one staffed the desk. Katy followed as Addison skipped down the hall and into a cloakroom. Next Addison went into a practice studio where she greeted her enthusiastic friends. Katy hovered by the door tentatively taking in the assortment of girls and a few jean-clad moms.

The girls ranged from about six to ten in age. They chatted and giggled with each other as they did warm-up exercises, reminding Katy of a physical education class. Only these girls were like little princesses. Most wore tights and leotards. A few had frilly tutus, and some wore skin-fitting slacks and glittery tops.

Soon the instructor walked into the room, speaking kindly and clad in a black second skin. The striking young woman intrigued Katy as she floated in and out among the girls, like a breath of fresh air that touched here, repositioned there, causing smiles and looks of adoration on her little students. When she had everyone's attention, she demonstrated a few movements that they all tried to imitate.

Katy bit her lip, amused. Although the little girls looked the part, they were hopelessly out of sync. But the instructor's youthful body and graceful air fascinated Katy. She could almost imagine Megan using her svelte body in such a way. Megan was the most graceful person Katy knew. As she watched Addison, she wondered what it would be like to be a participant and be encouraged to mimic the instructor's movements. As a little girl, it must be great fun.

She remembered learning to skip rope and the satisfaction that came with mastering the little ditties that went along with it. She found herself rooting for Addison to get the movements, and Katy felt a surge of pride when the little girl did them correctly.

As Katy glanced around the studio for a place to sit and quietly observe the class, she had to wonder if her own slim body was flexible enough to bend and stretch like the instructor's. Her gaze rested on a group of moms, and with embarrassment, she realized she'd caught them staring at her. Instantly, she jerked her gaze away. She felt like the guilty party for invading their world.

Even if she never grew accustomed to stares, the odd looks she often drew from outsiders served to ground her in her faith, reminding her of her true identity. She was a citizen of a higher kingdom. She walked in the truth. Outsiders had no idea that the heavenly kingdom was more glorious than the earthly one. It put Katy in an awkward position to be both out of place and right about life. And being right never kept one from being scorned.

She reminded herself that hers was an everlasting kingdom where thieves didn't steal, weather didn't erode, and age didn't wrinkle. At times like this, she wished she could tell the outsiders about her glorious kingdom, but would they listen to someone they considered plain and odd like a pilgrim? What could she say to make them desire her world over theirs?

"Pardon me, miss." a petite blond in jeans and a tight-fitting striped T-shirt jarred her from her thoughts. "Are you Addison's new nanny?"

"Yes, temporarily."

"Oh. Well, we were wondering. Are you European?"

"No ma'am. I'm Mennonite."

"Oh." Another woman with long hair twisted in a messy topknot burst into the conversation. "That's right. You drive buggies and stuff?"

Smiling at their naive curiosity, Katy gently corrected, "I brought Addison in my car. You're thinking of the Amish."

The second woman's face fell, and the blond snickered at her friend's gaffe. "Well, we were going to go watch the older girls. They're practicing for a Valentine's Day performance. Want to join us?"

"Sure." Katy appreciated the kindness of their unexpected inclusion, and with a backward glance at Addison, she followed the two glamorous ladies down the hall. They stopped in front of a glass window to peer into another studio.

Even before Katy looked through the glass, the sudden terrible blare of a worldly song invaded her body, hitting with thunderous force and clapping the forbidden beat through her veins. Her heart leapt wildly from the unexpected assault, and she scudded breathless to a halt. Just as unexpectedly, the music quit, but it left her quite shaken.

With caution, Katy peered through the window. Her eyes widened at the bosomy, witchy-looking creature with wild, coal-black hair, who sashayed about the room. This instructor had dark-lined eyes with fake lashes. The lids were dark lavender even from a distance. Her lips were bloodred and drawn with exaggeration outside the lines. Her skintight top was dangerously low. She wasn't slim and graceful like the other instructor, but embarrassingly curvy and provocative. And old. Katy pitied the woman who must have thought her painting and primping made her appear younger and attractive. It was a wonder her students didn't have nightmares. It was a wonder they ever returned.

The petite blond touched Katy's arm, and she started.

"This dance is so cute. They're going to perform at the mall on Valentine's weekend. Isn't that fun?"

With a slight nod, Katy looked over the girls in the class, junior high age and maybe older. She noticed dancers came in all sizes and shapes, her heart going out to the chubbier ones, the clumsier ones who at this age stuck out in a disparaging way. She heard the instructor—a Mrs. Tenny they called her—tell the girls, "Let's go through the whole thing from the top. Remember to stay in sync with the lead girls."

Mrs. Tenny started the loud, offensive music again, and it assaulted Katy's body just like it had the first time, only it wasn't quite as startling the second time around. The girls started prancing forward then backward, and Katy saw that, as a whole, they moved in sync better than the younger girls. But all of a sudden the dance changed. The girls locked their hands behind their heads and shook their torsos, gyrating their hips seductively.

Katy sucked in a shocked breath.

As if transported into a lower universe, the music changed its cadence to accentuate the girls' sensual movements. Katy felt appalled and violated. With a gasp, she reached out to support herself against the glass, unable to resist the bass that pulsated throughout her entire body, invading where it was not welcomed.

"Are you all right?" the blond asked.

"No. I don't feel so good."

"You'd better go sit in the waiting room."

The blond cast a disappointed look toward the glass as if she'd really wanted to watch every wiggle of her older daughter's performance, but took Katy's arm as if to guide her to the waiting room.

"I'll be all right."

"Well, if you're sure. Just down the hall to the right. You can't miss it. There's a drinking fountain, too."

Katy nodded. "Thanks." She fled for the hall. She would be sure to stay away from the mall on Valentine's weekend—a glaring reminder of why she shopped at the mart discount store. In the hallway, the music finally waned, but her temples still throbbed to the beat. When she reached the sanctuary of the waiting room, she dropped into a purple vinyl chair with cold metal armrests, feeling spiritually raped.

As her breathing slowly returned to normal, she kneaded her temple. Long after her heart quieted from its onslaught, her hands still trembled. She closed her eyes. "Lord, forgive me. I didn't mean to end up here, to witness that. I didn't mean to impress upon those other women that I even go along with dancing. I don't belong in this place. Forgive me for my greed for ill-gotten money. Help me get out of this awful mess."

Katy determined to confront Tammy Brooks about her duties. Knowing Tammy's temper, she'd probably lose her job. Good riddance.

God would provide another job. Unless, of course, He didn't approve of her to moving into the doddy house.

Still rubbing her sore temples, she bargained with God. But as she prayed and then tried to regain her peace, she also struggled with what Lil and Megan would think if she backed out of the doddy house arrangement. And truthfully, she hoped God didn't take it away from her because it wasn't just their dream. It was hers, too. And if she was a Christian, wouldn't a lifelong desire be from God? It had initiated at church camp, after all.

She picked up a magazine and leafed through it. With disgust over a lewd advertisement, she slapped it back down on the side table.

～෴～

Back at the Brooks' home, Katy dropped pasta into boiling water, rehearsing her resignation speech to Tammy, all the while listening for her car to rumble into the garage just off the kitchen. Five minutes later, her employer entered the room.

Tammy slung her jacket over a bar stool and dropped her briefcase and purse on the counter. "Smells good. How'd your first day go? Any news from school or dance?"

"I'm not sure."

Tammy lifted the lid off the spaghetti. "Something wrong?"

"Yes." Folding her arms, Katy lifted her chin. "I didn't know I'd be taking Addison to her dance lessons. Dancing is against my religion, you know."

Tammy's jaw dropped. "I didn't even think. . . . Did you take her?"

Nodding, Katy kept up her resolve. "I went inside because you wanted me to hear what her instructor said afterward, but the music and the dancing. . ." She closed her eyes to resist the painful image and shook her head. "I can't do that anymore."

Tammy scooted onto a stool in her short tight skirt. "Wow. They're just little girls. It teaches them grace and poise. It's not like they're strippers or anything."

Katy felt her face heat. "That's what makes it so sad for me. That they're just little girls being exposed to that kind of music."

An angry flush colored Tammy's cheeks.

Katy couldn't believe she'd spoken up to an outsider like that. She remained silent, waiting for Tammy's explosion.

But Tammy removed her designer glasses and pinched the bridge of her nose, then replaced them.

Katy shot up a prayer. *Help me, Jesus. I'm doing this for You.* She lifted her chin, while mentally making plans to apply at an agency.

"What if you just dropped her off and picked her up afterward?"

The oven timer went off. "Bread's ready." Katy shot to the oven, avoiding Tammy's gaze and especially her question. She grabbed a padded mitt and removed the garlic bread. When she turned back again, Tammy was amazingly calm, her eyes pleading.

"I need you, Katy. It's only temporary."

She wanted to help. And if Tammy was willing to accommodate her wishes and respect her beliefs, then maybe she could hang in there for a few more days, just until Tammy found another nanny. "All right. Just until you find another nanny." She moved toward the coat closet. "You could apply at an agency."

Tammy flinched but didn't object.

Katy quickly waved. "I'll see you tomorrow night."

"Okay. I'll leave you a note again, and by the way, Sean will get home tomorrow night before I do."

Dread bubbled up in Katy's throat as she slipped her arms into her coat sleeves. "It's not that I don't like your children, but cleaning is what I do best."

"I understand. I'm sorry about today."

Katy left the house, and although she'd won the battle, she knew she had been outmaneuvered again.

⁓

In her room that night, Katy prayed her evening prayer with an extra dose of humility and several more entreaties for forgiveness. When she unpinned her covering, one of the pins dropped and rolled under the chest of drawers. Katy bent from her waist to retrieve it and found herself almost in one of the positions she'd seen at the studio. The instructor had told the girls it was a cambre. She liked the sound of it. Gripping the edge of her dresser as if it were a ballet barre, she touched her heels together bent at the waist and swept one arm through the air. She heard her sister giggle and went rigid.

Ashamed, she quickly bent, felt under the chest of drawers, and retrieved the pin. She placed it through the organdy and stared at the head bonnet. She wasn't the woman who had been in the dance studio and moved with wondrous grace. She was the woman who kept herself separate from the world. Her sister Karen had already climbed into her side of the bed and was reading *Little Women*.

Katy removed the rubber band from her ponytail and shook her head. Her thick hair fell down the center of her back. Gently, she massaged her scalp. What a day. Premonition told her that the Brooks job was headed toward disaster. She hated when things got out of control. She had been too ashamed to tell her mom about the dance studio. When she asked how the nanny job went, Katy had replied it was unpleasant and she didn't wish to talk about it. But the whole experience left her feeling like she had a sinful secret. She'd asked God for forgiveness now at least six times, so why wouldn't the sad feeling go away? Maybe it lingered because she'd lost a piece of her innocence. That's what the simple life was all about, keeping separate from the world, from temptation, keeping themselves pure.

She should have just quit. But Tammy needed help, and she could put up with it for a few days. Wanting to do what was best, she weighed aiding and abetting the sin by dropping Addison off at dance class against abandoning her employer in her time of need. The church forbade dancing, and the Bible talked about giving every job your best, doing it as unto the Lord. She didn't like gray areas where she couldn't decide what was wrong or right. She liked living above the fray in a place above reproach. She gained much pleasure in following rules.

She tried to block the image of what the next day might bring. Sean Brooks coming into the kitchen and popping the top of one of those beers he kept in the refrigerator. She worked her fingers through her hair and then picked up her brush. What would she do if he got drunk? Like Jake?

She'd only had one experience around a drunkard. The incident had happened during a dark time in her life when she hadn't seen Jake for several months. Megan had let it slip about the rumors that he'd gone wild at college. About the worldly girl he was dating. Then Katy had pressed Lil about it. Lil had yelled at Megan for letting the cat out of the bag, and it had been a big fiasco. But in the end, Katy had found out that the rumors were true.

Jake. . .dating an outsider. Katy jerked the hairbrush through her tangles. Her name was Jessie, and she had short, spiked, black hair. She wore miniskirts and tall boots. Thinking about Jake and that woman brought back the sick feeling in the pit of her stomach that she'd felt at the dance studio. She'd learned Jake had started drinking, too. She'd experienced that firsthand. And who knew what else he'd done? At that point, she always forcefully disengaged her imagination.

She'd been so angry when she'd found out about Jake's behavior, that the next day she'd thrown the dusting can and cracked her bedroom window. She'd been ashamed afterward, but her parents had understood her hurt and never confronted her about her angry fit. In fact, they encouraged her to forget about Jake Byler.

For many weeks after that, she hadn't been able to sleep. That's when she had started keeping a journal of cleaning tips, even going to the library and studying about home remedies. She'd put her energies into her work, but she'd never gotten over Jake.

His shame was her shame. Then one day she wrote his name on a sheet of paper. Beneath it she wrote Leviticus 4:27—"If any one of the common people sin through ignorance, while he doeth somewhat against any of the commandments of the LORD concerning things which ought not to be done, and be guilty." Then she wrote in large script across his name: *guilty and forbidden.*

She drew a line. Beneath it, she listed the qualities of the man she hoped to one day marry. She kept this paper in her Bible so that she could refer to it on those days when she thought she would die from the ache in her heart. It stirred up her convictions to forget Jake and hope for someone who was worthy of her love.

After that, Jake had stayed away from church for several months.

Until the fateful incident. It happened one weekend when he'd come home for his mom's birthday. Katy had come out of church on a Sunday night. She had been standing beside her car when she saw his truck enter the parking lot. He pulled up alongside her car and jumped out to talk to her. He'd told her he'd come to pick up his mom. His breath stank from beer, and she'd tried to get in her car to avoid him, but he'd grabbed her arm and pinned her hard against the car. She asked him to stop. But instead, he'd pressed his body against hers. She'd screamed at him to go away, but he'd forced his rank mouth against hers, pinned her head to the car's window, and kissed her.

Afterward, she'd slapped him. He'd stepped back, stunned. She'd yelled at him to stay away. And crying, she'd left him standing in the parking lot, staring after her. Honoring her demand, he had never returned to church.

She'd felt ashamed and violated. Yet now that time had passed, she also felt guilty. She worried that if he never returned to the church, it was her fault. Mennonites were supposed to be nonresistant and forgiving. But she didn't know how to do that when her heart felt so broken. When the man she loved had treated her with such disrespect.

And now he was back? She felt like the unknown would choke her. She slapped her brush down hard on the dresser.

Karen lowered her book. "What's the matter with you tonight?"

"It's just been a hard day."

"What are those kids like?"

Drawing back the quilt, Katy climbed in bed. "They squabble a lot."

"That's normal." Karen clicked off the lamp.

The image of the older girls dancing flashed in Katy's mind, chased by a Bible verse in 2 Kings: "They followed vanity, and became vain, and went after the heathen that were round about them, concerning whom the LORD had charged them, that they should not do like them."

CHAPTER 7

Somehow, Katy survived the rest of her week without any major setbacks. She had cleaned under Tyler's cluttered bed again so that he could find his BB gun, and she had glued the plastic palm trees to the artificial turf for his science project without getting called a pilgrim. Tammy had kept her word so that Katy hadn't had to enter Addison's dance studio. Katy also survived Sean Brooks. He'd been polite and had even surprised her by seeking out the children instead of the beverage shelf of his refrigerator. To her further astonishment, he'd acted much like her own father might with her siblings, tossing Addison in the air and tussling with Tyler.

On Friday morning, she'd gone to work her half day for Mrs. Cline at the Plain City retirement home, where her most challenging job had been changing the ceiling fan's lightbulbs without falling off the rickety ladder.

"I'm sure it was as old as its employer," Katy now joked to her family over the noonday meal, but nobody laughed because their attention was riveted upon Lil's unexpected appearance. Katy noticed that Lil had a glint in her eyes that warned of trouble.

"Hi, second fam." Lil scooted into a vacant chair.

"Hi Lil. What's cookin'?" Katy's dad asked, as he had every time he'd seen her since she'd started culinary school.

"Fix yourself a plate," Katy's mom invited.

"Thanks but I already ate. Baked a cake to celebrate." She removed the plastic cover to reveal a double-layer chocolate cake, one of Vernon Yoder's favorites. "Just thought I'd drop by the bids for the doddy house."

At her offhanded announcement, Katy's heart flip-flopped. In spirit, she shook Lil for not showing her the bid first. Sometimes Lil didn't have an iota of common sense.

Lil must have read her mind, for she winked at her. Her impetuous friend, as always, seemed in full control of the situation. Lil knew the sum of Katy's savings account as well as she did, so the bid must be reasonable. Still, as owner of that savings account, shouldn't Katy have had the first say in the matter? Then again, Lil had been smart enough to catch her father resting with a full belly.

Katy jumped up and looked over her dad's shoulder. She was unable to mask her widening smile as he shuffled through the paperwork. It was a surprisingly low bid. "We can handle that, Dad." Katy moved back beside Lil to watch his expression as he silently read through the contract again, more meticulously the second time.

Lil's hand clutched hers, and Katy squeezed, perhaps loving her friend more fiercely than ever before.

Her dad tapped the papers on the table, straightening their edges, and handed them back to Lil. "I hate to see the way the world is changing. Now more than ever, you need to learn responsibility. But I have to wonder if this venture will take away from your purpose in life."

"What purpose?" Katy asked, before Lil could blurt out that her purpose was to become a famous chef.

"Marrying and raising a family."

Of course. That purpose. Katy wet her lips. "We hope to someday marry, but we don't even have prospects." She saw her dad's brows arch and had to backpedal, "Oh. There's David. But you know what I mean."

"He's a nice young man," her mom interjected. Suddenly Katy wondered how her mom knew that.

Then her dad went on. "It pleases me that you both have jobs that are preparing you for marriage. You cook and clean and babysit. Suitable occupations for single Mennonite girls." Then he pointed his carpenter-rough finger at them. "You are both good catches. And Megan, she's a good girl, too."

Katy felt Lil tense and hoped she wouldn't blurt out an objection. Lil hated any hint of female suppression or submission; in fact they often joked about the *S* word even if it was a major part of their beliefs. Women were supposed to respect their husbands and allow them to be heads of the household. Many times, that wasn't practiced, but the principle had been ingrained into Katy growing up in the Mennonite culture. Now she increased her pressure on Lil's hand, hoping her friend would exert some of that self-control that allowed her to fast for a day at the onset of every new diet and to adhere to a regimented exercise program.

"I needed to get some saw blades sharpened today anyways, so I'll stop by and have that chat with Ivan Miller on my way home. See if we can seal this deal. Now let's cut that cake. You know it's one of my favorites."

―◦―

Early the next week, Katy slid into the ripped seat of Lil's Chevy Blazer, unconsciously poking the stuffing back into place so that it didn't stick to her dark, freshly pressed skirt. "I can't believe this is really happening."

"I know. What do you think I should save up for first? A new car or one of those commercial stoves like they had at school?"

"I wish we could've bought one of those, but—"

Lil reached over and patted her hand. "Oh stop. I'm just dreaming out loud. But someday I will have both of those. You wait and see."

Katy wondered if Lil would ever realize her dreams, for they weren't normal dreams for girls who were born and raised in the Conservative Church. Must have been some other blood in her family line somewhere, too, she mused, thinking of her own Spanish ancestor. Beside her, Lil rambled on while Katy painted her own fantasy of whipping the house into order, clean and inviting, making it a place where she would be proud to—

Her thoughts jarred to a stop. Pride was the sin of the devil. But Mennonites did take pride in the work of their hands. The irony of the plain people had never occurred to her before. Everyone knew the Mennonites were hard workers and honest. They bragged about it among themselves. She tickled the inside of her mouth with her tongue, looking for a different word that would describe her feelings, one that would be acceptable. Responsible? A good steward? That worked.

When they pulled into the Millers' farm, Lil drove to the back of the property and parked in front of the doddy house. For the first time, Katy realized there wasn't any garage or barn to park the car inside. That would be cold in the mornings. Why, she'd have to scrape frost off her windshield. She supposed there were worse things. Next she noticed a truck that resembled Jake's. Lil started to open her door, but Katy reached over. "Wait."

"What?" Lil seemed impatient to go inside.

But the truck reminded Katy that Lil had been avoiding the subject of Jake's sudden appearance. "That looks like Jake's truck."

Lil rolled her gaze heavenward. "You want to sit here and talk about Jake? Or do you want to go inside and see our dream coming true?"

"It's just. . .you've never answered my question about Jake. I saw you talking to him at the skating party. I just want to know why he was there. Did you invite him?"

Lil closed her door again and fiddled with her gearshift. "Okay, here's what I know. He's moved back home. He's coming back to the church. But the important thing is he's changed. He doesn't drink anymore or chase girls. He's over all that wild stuff." She shrugged. "He's changed, and actually he's an improved model from the old one. You'll see."

Kate absorbed Lil's flippant explanation with shock. She released a moan. "No way. He's not back to stay?"

"Yep."

"But I can't face him week after week."

"He told me he's really sorry for hurting you."

"That's so humiliating. I hope you never told him how I moped over him."

"If it's humiliating, he's the one who's ashamed. He regrets his wild fling. He's the one who feels foolish. Just keep your chin up. Take it one step at a time. Now, let's go inside. I've got my list. We need to double-check everything and then go shopping." Lil let out a squeal and bumped her shoulder against Katy's. "Shopping for our own place. Can you believe it?"

Giving in to Lil's coaxing, Katy couldn't help but grin back. "Alright. Let's do it."

She slid out and slammed the door, her boots squishing through the slush caused by several days of higher temperatures. She cast another sideways glance at the truck. If Mennonites swore, she'd swear that was Jake's truck. According to Lil, she was mistaken. Still, the truck brought out a melancholy longing in her, one that gnawed at the pit of her stomach so that her excitement over shopping receded again.

When they entered the house, she heard loud ripping and pounding noises. She stepped onto the plastic flooring protection and started toward the kitchen. "Let's go see what's going on."

Lil stopped and bent to reposition some tape and a portion of the plastic. "I think he's tearing out the plaster and replacing it with drywall. Go on, I'll be there in a minute."

With a shrug, Katy stepped into the country-style kitchen onto more plastic flooring, and saw the backside of a man whose physique made her heart trip before her mind understood the reason. The air between them crackled. The worker must have felt it, too, for he froze, then turned.

His mouth curled into a lopsided grin. "Hey, Katy. You've got a great little place here."

Confused, horrified, and standing in disbelief, she opened her mouth and closed it again. But she could not deny the truth for more than a few seconds. With it came a sudden fury, and she marched forward to throw him out on his ear, or at least demand to know why he was invading her privacy.

"What—" She stopped. *He* was the contractor Lil had hired. She fought for control, not wanting to humiliate herself any further. She wouldn't show him she still cared about him. "I think so." She took a deep breath and coughed, and in the process, accidentally sucked plaster and drywall dust into her throat. She fought the tickle, then got saliva down the wrong track and choked uncontrollably.

Jake moved quickly. He cradled his arm around her and led her to the water pump. Her coughing caused her eyes to water so that she could hardly see, but she soon caught on that the water was frozen. Blindly, she fanned her face and struggled to breathe, coughing and gasping. He left her but quickly returned with a cup of water from his personal water jug. She took a sip, and he lightly rapped her back. When at last she could breathe again, she wheezed, "Stop, please."

"I should have warned you about the dust. Lethal stuff."

"Yeah, lethal," she croaked. Then grudgingly added, "Thanks."

He nodded, and her vision returned enough for her to catch a rare moment when Jake looked uncertain, even vulnerable. But that wouldn't stop her from demanding that Lil fire him. His lips moved as if to speak. Fearing what he might say, certain it would be something personal, she blurted out, "I wish you hadn't come back."

He quickly recovered from her insult. "I wish I'd never left."

Katy rolled her gaze heavenward.

"I couldn't forget you," he added.

She felt uncomfortable in his presence and wanted nothing more than to run. But before she did, she needed to fix something that had plagued her ever since the incident. This time she didn't want to have those nagging regrets. She took another deep breath, careful not to inhale drywall dust. "You remember the night I told you to stay away?"

His eyes softened regrettably. "Yes, I remember. Even though I was drunk. And I want to apologize for that night."

The memories of the incident flooded over Katy, hardening her heart. But she forced herself to continue. "I've felt guilty, thinking my words kept you away from the church."

"I understood it was personal." He grinned, sheepishly. "I didn't think you had the authority of the elders behind you."

She felt her face heat, glad the elders hadn't witnessed that incident, even though she wasn't the one at fault. "As long as you understand that I don't want you to go to hell, I just. . .don't want you."

His brows lowered, creating a dark hood over his eyes as though to shield himself from her cruel remark. A heavy silence loomed between them. Then his mouth quirked to the side, and he grinned. Before, his smile had always charmed her whenever he needed forgiveness. But then his misdeeds were only playful. Still, she had to fight to resist it. Her own lip trembled, and she pulled her gaze back to his eyes. They pierced, searched her blushing face.

"Hi, guys," Lil entered the room, acting as though nothing was irregular, as if this reunion were an everyday occurrence. She wasn't apologetic over Jake's presence. Her behavior disregarded the significance of the awful trick. "Wow, look what you've got done." Lil gazed at the wall, which had jagged plaster and exposed wood.

Katy took her eyes off Jake and stared at the demolition. Yes, he was good at tearing down. And Lil's nonchalance—her play-acting—infuriated her. Sucking in her lower lip, Katy grabbed Lil's arm and pinched hard, pulling her toward the hallway. "Let's go over that list now."

Once they were out of the kitchen, Lil shrugged her off. "Ouch."

"You deserve that and more. Traitor," Katy hissed.

Rubbing her arm, Lil said, "Lower your voice. Jake's going to hear us."

But Katy didn't comply. "You're ruining this for me, you know." She threw up her arms. "Some dream! This is a nightmare! Do you even get it? You're going to fire him. Today. Now. I don't want him here. I don't want him." She crossed her arms. "Go on. Do it. Tell your cousin to pack up his tools."

Lil's arms waved emphatically. "Get a grip. Obviously, you're not thinking straight. He's the reason we're able to remodel cheaply. Nobody else would give us a bid that fit our budget. Don't you see? His guilty conscience is paying off."

Katy narrowed her eyes. "That's despicable."

"Let's go in the bedroom."

Katy stomped after Lil then slammed the door behind them. "This is the most underhanded thing you've ever done to me. You knew that was his truck outside, but you claimed it wasn't."

"I didn't lie."

75

"You didn't warn me."

"Because you wouldn't have stepped inside."

"You got that right!"

"Look, I know Jake's hurt you, but he's really changed. He wants to make amends at church and with you. You don't have to date him or marry him. Just let him make his peace. Accept him as another human being living in the same universe. That's all."

The wind whipped through a cracked windowpane, blowing pieces of sandpaper and bits of wood splinters across Katy's shoes. She stared at the floor. It hurt so bad to see Jake face-to-face again. And she felt betrayed that Lil had allowed it to happen. That her best friend had arranged it, opened the door, and invited her enemy in. She raised her face. "This place was our dream. I looked forward to fixing it up. Now I won't even want to come over here."

Lil pulled her coat tighter. "I'll tell him to leave you alone. How's that? But we need him to get the work done at the price we can afford. Think of the prize at the end of the race, okay? It is our dream."

With a groan, Katy used her foot to grind debris into the floor. "Does he even know what he's doing?"

"Yep." Lil looked like a proud mama. "He graduated with a bachelor's degree in construction systems management. Most of his classes were on campus at the Agricultural Engineering Building. Anyway, he needs some jobs for his résumé so that he can get his license and start up his own construction company. So this will help everyone in the long run, even though it's a bit awkward now. And you can deal with him here in private, not at the meetinghouse with everyone watching you guys."

The image of her wiping out on the ice with David flashed in Katy's mind. She probably would have made a fool of herself at the meetinghouse if she hadn't been forewarned of his appearance. And she hated pity. "I guess I'll deal with it. Get over it." She'd never get over it—him. She could still feel his arms sheltering her, as they had in the kitchen. If she didn't hate him so much, she'd be running right back into his embrace.

"Guess what? Jake said he'd throw in the beds for free."

"What?"

"He can make furniture."

Katy shoved her finger in Lil's face. "He is *not* making my bed!"

Ducking away, Lil backed down. "Fine."

"You don't get it, Lil." Katy lowered her voice then. "Just having him here is going to cause me pain. Just remembering him standing in the kitchen or looking at a piece of furniture he's made. I'm going to have to work through forgetting him all over again. Especially if he's here at the doddy house. At church." Her voice trailed off. "Everywhere I go." *I see his face.*

"That's just it. He's back to stay. So why not deal with him on your terms? You can heal faster that way. I'm doing this for your own good."

Face-to-face. Those dark mournful eyes, that crooked grin. A mouth she'd once kissed, cherished, owned for her own. No, she wasn't falling for it. "It feels like you're treating me like a child. Giving the contract to my dad before you let me see it, and now this. Why the big surprises? Why couldn't you just be straightforward?"

"Because you wouldn't have been able to see clearly in this situation, to see what's best for you." Lil pulled out her list and made a poor attempt at diversion. "We can talk about this later. We're wasting shopping time. Let's go over this and hit the stores. It's going to be fun."

"I'll tell you what. You go over the list. I'll wait for you in the car, having the time of my life." She heard Lil sigh as she stomped down the hall without even looking in the direction of the kitchen.

—⌒—

Jake swung the sledgehammer, and a chunk of plaster caved in, some of it crashing to the floor and filling the air with white powder. After Katy's rebuff the night of the skating party, he hadn't expected her to give him an open-armed welcome as her surprise contractor, but her rejection still hurt. He'd overheard much of her ranting and raving, wanting Lil to fire him. Mennonites might be antiwar and noncombatant when it came to flesh wounds, but his fellow brethren could wield weapons that slashed through flesh to the soul. What was the term he'd learned in college? Passive-aggressive. Yeah, that described his Katy. He'd rather she'd just come at him swinging. That he could handle. But when she employed her smoldering eyes and pouty lip, he'd rather scoop her up and kiss her to her senses. Only he'd tried that. It hadn't been successful at all.

Still, her reaction to him today, treating him like he was some lowlife, was a twisted blade to his heart, reiterating the very words she spat at him the night of the incident: *Stay away.* Those words had hardened him then, but now that he'd let God back in, they just plain hurt. And she'd added even more meaning to them today. *I don't want you to go to hell. I just don't want you.*

He knew a few things about Katy. She took life seriously, categorizing everything in labeled cubbies. Six out of ten of these cubbies she labeled off-limits: lying, missing curfew, stealing crackers from the church cupboard marked COMMUNION, watching movies through his neighbor's window when he was mowing, driving over the speed limit, and kissing in the church parking lot.

But being stuffed into a cubby didn't suit his style, and he had no intentions of staying there. The thing was, he knew the real Katy, the little girl he'd teased who loved a good adventure and thrilled at life. She'd always pretended she didn't, but he knew the truth about her. And he intended to bring that inner woman to the surface—the wonderful, vivacious one—then claim her as his own. He wanted to nurture that part of her, not stifle it.

His cell phone jangled in his pocket, and he propped the sledge-hammer and yanked down his dust mask. "Hello."

"Hey, it's Lil."

"So she still mad at me?"

"Yep. But we knew she'd be ticked. That only goes to show how much she still cares about you."

"That love-hate thing?"

"Right."

He sat on the rung of a ladder and stared down at the feminine footprints remaining in the drywall and plaster dust. Tracks that led away from him. "Look, you know how important she is to me. I don't want to drive her away. And I don't think she appreciated the setup. She's not stupid. About our next plan, she's not going to trust us."

"She already doesn't trust you. Just don't go chicken on me. We've got a great plan. You have to show her a little at a time that you've changed. You can't do that if you don't see each other, and she's going to avoid you, so we have to set up some planned meetings like this. And once we move into the doddy house, I'll be able to put in lots of good words for you. She'll come around. I'm sure of it. She loves you, Cuz. Even if you are a chump."

"She tell you that?"

"Yep."

"Lately?"

"No but—"

"You just saw it in her wild eyes? Or maybe you caught that from her sweet talk?"

Lil chuckled. "She's intense, all right."

After their call ended, Jake stuffed his phone in his pocket, stood up, and pulled up his mask. Lil was right. He had to allow Katy the right to voice her anger. He'd just cling to the hope that her anger was evidence that she wasn't dead to him, that their love could be revived. Picking up the sledgehammer, he looked at the demolition he'd accomplished, feeling satisfaction that he was making good time.

He lifted the hammer, and another chunk of plaster met its demise.

CHAPTER 8

Saturday morning, Katy submerged chapped hands in soapy dishwater and looked through a frost-webbed window. Between snowballs and horseplay, her little brothers hand-shoveled the sidewalk, while nearby her dad steered the snowplow through fresh snow.

Was the doddy house blanketed in snow, too? Or had Ivan cleared the drive so that Jake could work? Maybe he didn't work Saturdays. She tried to pull her thoughts away from Jake Byler, but once again they stubbornly fixed upon their unexpected meeting. Every time she went over it, she felt coerced, boxed in, and smothered, clawing to strike out at him and Lil. Katy smiled wryly, remembering how she'd vetoed the patterned dinnerware for plain white plates, just for the sake of defiance. And for once, Lil had backed down. Would they survive as roommates without Megan living with them to keep the peace?

In spite of Jake's return and Lil's manipulations, Katy felt a sense of accomplishment and personal freedom over her anticipated move into the doddy house. She might be trapped in a nanny job she didn't want and forced to accept Jake's return to the community, but she was moving into a new season of life where she could find her own niche in the community. She'd be washing her own dishes from now on, not her folks'. She'd be living out her faith, not theirs.

She dried her hands on her apron and startled. Then pressing her face to the window for a closer look, she watched a familiar automobile turn into the newly cleared lane. The shiny black car that braked next to the snowplow could only belong to one person. At that instant, she was glad she prayed over the little paper she kept in her Bible—the one where *forbidden* marred Jake's name. The husband qualities below it reminded her of David. His smiling face was just what she needed.

Slathering on some lotion, she ran to a hall mirror and checked her hair, straightening her head covering. Then she answered the door. "Hey, you're out and about early."

"Dad sent me out to run errands. I ended up trapped behind a snowplow and thought I'd stop in to stall."

Backing up, she held open the door. "Come in. I'll make coffee."

He glanced down at his snowy boots. "Actually, I can't stay that long. But I wondered if you'd like to go on a sleigh ride tonight?"

Feeling a trickle of mounting excitement, not only because of the time she would spend with David, but also because she'd never gone on a sleigh ride before, Katy nodded. "Sure. That sounds fun."

He brushed back a stray strand of hair and displayed his dimple. He hadn't shaved, and she liked the rugged look. Usually, he looked so perfect, but this natural side of him brought out his masculinity.

"Great. I'll be over about seven. Dress warm. And wear that scarf that makes you so stunning."

Involuntarily, her hand fluttered at her waist searching for her apron pockets, but she'd removed it earlier. "Aren't you sweet?"

A golden glint danced in his eyes. He straightened and rolled his shoulders so that his chest swelled and his coat brushed his chin, drawing her attention back to his intriguing hint of a beard. "We'll see how long I can keep up the charade. Usually after about the third date, most girls dump me."

Katy flinched. Was he flirting or was that a challenge? Had he somehow heard about the three-date deal she'd made with her dad? Her heart raced with confusion.

He touched her cheek with his glove. "See you tonight."

David Miller was an intriguing riddle.

The huge horse, a blond Belgian draft with white feet and mane, was borrowed from David's Amish neighbors. The animal quivered with impatience.

"Is the sleigh the Beachys', too?" Katy asked.

"Yep," David replied. "Ever since I can remember, they've taken me on at least one ride each winter." He helped her up onto the seat of the simple box sleigh. "Now that the Beachys are getting up in years, the horses don't get enough use. The Beachys usually get someone to drive them to town these days. You know they sold Ivan's property to him?"

She nodded. The sleigh heaved under his weight as he climbed up next to her and took the reins.

"Last year, I took their grandkids out a time or two. Now they trust me with their horses. He pulled out a lap blanket and placed it over Katy's skirt. "You might need this till you get used to the cold." He gave the reins a flick. "Giddyup, Jack!"

A full moon gave the snowy evening a pristine glow and provided a soft backdrop for the black goblins that reached from dark trunks toward the passing sleigh. The silent world painted with only black and white seemed unnatural without color, the black so stark against the white. Lil would probably argue it was the other way around. Katy had to wonder if David had felt a bit creepy driving over alone through the lonely countryside. She'd always been a little afraid of the dark herself. Thankfully, the sounds of beast and human made the night less eerie, the soothing clopping of hooves, the creak of leather and wood, and the companionable timbre of her male companion's voice.

The glittering sky, however, gave her an awareness of her insignificance, and the feeling balled up unwelcome in her throat. She wondered if he felt it, too. Glancing sideways, she said, "It's different out here like this. Almost like the night could swallow us up."

"It's pretty." He cast her a glance. "Like you."

"No. It almost feels like we shouldn't be here, like we're trespassing in somebody else's world." She shivered then, not sure if it was from the cold or the idea. It was a familiar one, feeling like a foreigner in an outsider's world. Oftentimes, she felt insignificant. The outsiders' world was confusing. The Conservatives' world was constrictive, yet comforting because it was the most familiar. It was where she fit in best.

His hand slipped over her shoulder. "Come closer."

She inched over so he could still shelter her from the wind, yet their bodies weren't touching, and adjusted the blanket. "Do you ever think about how the Amish live? What it would be like?"

"I've thought about it. The sleigh is nice tonight, great for a date, but I can't imagine life without my car. I don't think I'd like that much. Aren't very many Amish buggies around Plain City anymore, but my dad's good friends with our neighbors, says it's a shame most of the Amish moved out of the community because just having them around added a missing element."

"What's that?"

"The desire for a simple life. Even if we don't choose to follow their way, it's nice to know it's still possible to make a stand like that. It takes courage not to follow the crowd."

She thought about her predicament with her nanny job. "You're right." She warmed her nose with her glove. "I have some Amish cousins."

David burst out laughing. "Doesn't everybody?"

They both laughed.

He drew his sleeve across his eyes and then glanced over to study her, allowing Jack to keep to the road on his own for a bit. "I hear Jake Byler is remodeling the doddy house."

She flinched. Of course he would know because his brother owned the property. "That was all Lil's doing," she clarified. "Jake and I have a history, and she thinks this will help us get past the awkwardness, since he's back to stay. They're close, being cousins, and she thinks we all have to be one big merry family, I guess." Katy gave him a contrite smile. "Plus, he gave us a really cheap bid."

"Is he? The big-brother type?"

"He's the type to avoid. Lil hired him behind my back. I'm still ticked. But he does need the work, too."

"Sounds like you're making excuses for him."

She tilted her head. "I don't mean to. Guess I'm just repeating what Lil said, trying to deal with the situation." She suddenly straightened. "We're headed in that direction, aren't we?"

"Yep. You have a key?"

She grinned. "In my purse."

"Then let's check out his work. Maybe we can get something warm to drink from Elizabeth before we head back."

"I'm not sure that's a good idea." She knew she should avoid dark, secluded places with a date.

"Just a quick look. Elizabeth will see us turn in the drive and be expecting us."

That was almost like having a chaperone, and it was considerate of him. She stole several long, contemplative glances at him. "Okay."

At the doddy house, David worked the key in the lock while she held a lantern they'd found inside the sleigh. She felt a naughty elation, checking out the place alone after Lil and Jake's conniving. Well, not exactly alone.

"Watch out for the plastic on the floor," she warned.

He took the lantern from her. "I see it and a few other obstacles, too. Don't worry, I don't plan to trip you like I did on our last date." He skirted her around a pail filled with a few tools and nails and a roll of electric wire.

Sweet of him to take the blame for that. If it weren't so personal, she'd ask him if his knees still bore bruises. If he'd limped the next day. She bit back a smile. If he'd gotten a new tire.

Jake had torn off most of the kitchen's old plaster and started the wiring. As they walked through the house, she noticed holes in the other walls and some in the ceiling.

"He'll drop the electric down through the walls and put switches and outlets there." David set the lantern on the floor. They stood in the center of the darkly lit room. It grew quiet, the seclusion of their surroundings conducive to a feeling of intimacy. He captured both her hands, and she warmed inside. His voice was low and kind. "Do you know when you'll move in?"

Her breath caught at the intensity of his hazel gaze that bore into hers, drawing her in as though he meant to kiss her. She felt embarrassed when her voice sounded too breathless. "I don't know how long the work will take." She wet her lips, glanced at the walls. "Doesn't look like they started the plumbing." She looked into his eyes again. "Guess I was too angry to ask the important questions."

His thumb caressed her hand through their gloves. "Can I help you move?"

She swallowed, nodding. "Thanks." She drank in his quiet confidence and floated to a higher plane. Not that she was needy. But her toes tingled with anticipation of what he would do next.

He kept caressing her knuckles. It was almost like he was waiting for her to make the next move, but she wasn't sure what he wanted from her.

Finally, he said, "Katy Yoder, will you"—he paused, showed his dimple. His face was now freshly shaved, and he looked younger than he had earlier that morning.

"What?"

"Share a hot chocolate with me?"

He really was a tease. She bit her lip, caught up in the flirtation. "You're practicing for the day you pop the big question to some lucky girl, aren't you?"

"Yep."

"Yes, I will. I'm so thrilled you asked," she played along. "Only, that wasn't as smooth as it could have been. You definitely need more practice. Aren't you supposed to go down on one knee or something?"

"Already did. Both knees. In front of all our friends, too." Grinning, he released one of her hands and scooped up the lantern.

A cup of hot chocolate and a shared blueberry muffin later, they were headed back down the snowy road. "The horses always go faster on their way home, don't they?" she asked.

He squeezed her shoulder. "Wish they'd go slower. Will I get to see you again?"

"You did offer to help us move."

"Before that."

Moved with guilt over her three-date deal—he was making this far too easy—she made a mental note to at least date him four times just for the sake of. . . She looked away from him to the eerie landscape.

"Tough decision?"

"Yes. I'd like to get to know you better." She placed her hand on his arm. "Only I'm not really looking for a relationship. Anything serious."

"I wasn't out looking, either. I just felt attracted to you." Silence pervaded for several moments. "Are you worried my feelings are stronger than yours?"

She dropped her hand and smiled. "So you're a guy who talks about feelings?"

"I'm glad you're good at keeping secrets 'cause that's another one to add to your list."

She laughed. "I won't spread the word that you're a mushy guy."

"Oh man." He shook his head.

She took pity on him. "I enjoy spending time with you. Yes, I'd like to see you again before I move into the doddy house."

His cheek twitched. "How about next Saturday then? We could drive into Columbus and have dinner at a nice restaurant."

"Want to go to Lil's place?"

"Do we need reservations?"

"I don't think so, but if we do, I'll take care of it."

She was pleased because all their dates had been fun, and it appeared the next one would be, too. She'd been wanting to see the restaurant where Lil worked, anyway. They rode in amiable silence except for the soothing horse noises and the creaking of harness and sleigh. When they reached Katy's house, he walked around the front of the sleigh and patted the horse's velvety nose before he helped her down. At the door, she turned to face him, but he was so close, she nearly bumped into him. A nervous giggle escaped her lips, and she saw the dimple dance in his left cheek. She glanced up.

He swallowed.

She winced. He had a prominent Adam's apple. Or was his neck too skinny? Her budding attraction died on the spot, and there wasn't a thing she could do to stop it.

He tipped her chin, lightly brushing her lips with his. "Good night, Katy."

"Good night," she whispered, overcome with the desire to put distance between them.

Inside, she reached the second-floor landing before she realized she'd forgotten to hang her coat in the downstairs hall closet. When his lips had touched hers, not only had it felt strangely cold, but she had envisioned Jake's face, leaving her feeling guilty and ashamed.

As nice as David was and as fun as the sleigh ride had been, she hated herself for using him. She hated how in the end, she would hurt him, because Jake's return had shown her the truth. She wasn't ready to start a relationship with anyone else. No matter how nice of a guy he was or how much her dad desired it.

CHAPTER 9

The churchwomen threw a baby shower in Elizabeth Miller's honor, and since Elizabeth was Katy's new landlord, she felt obligated to attend. The night of the shower, however, Katy had to go alone because her mom needed to stay home with her little brothers, who had caught winter colds.

When Katy arrived at the meetinghouse, the gravel parking lot was already filled with cars. She turned off the ignition, and an unexpected shiver passed through her body, most likely only weariness from a tedious day of cleaning and babysitting and hopefully not the beginning of a cold. When she flicked off her headlights, the dark, moonless night sent prickles along her spine, and she quickened her steps across the parking lot.

Inside the fellowship hall, the buzz of female voices floated to her through the narrow hall, easing her inexplicable jitters. Moving toward the source of the din, she stepped into a large, multipurpose room, and Megan instantly waved her over.

"Hey, green bean. You feeling better?"

Megan looked great, clad in a navy pencil skirt that hit below the knees and a white crewneck sweater. Megan reached up and tucked some hair behind one ear, the rest of her straight blond mane shimmering well below her shoulder blades. "I am. I came home for the shower." Her voice grew animated. "Lil says there's progress at the doddy house."

"Where is she?" Katy involuntarily glanced toward the kitchen.

"Working." She followed Megan's glance and located Lil at one of the two pink-clad tables, stabbing homemade pickles, easing them out of their canning jar, and arranging them on an oval serving platter. "I heard about Jake. Dad told me he came before the elder board to make things right with the church," Megan said.

Katy's head whipped back toward her friend, her mind racing. "You're kidding. My dad didn't tell me about that."

"Probably wanted to spare your feelings."

She remembered her bedroom's broken windowpane. So her dad had withheld important information from her while Lil barged in to control the situation. She clasped her chapped hands together, hating such manipulation.

"They meant well, I'm sure."

Bless Megan's heart, she understood the reason for Katy's rising anger. And as usual, if Katy dug deep enough, she could see that her friend was right. For when it came to Jake, no matter how her friends and family responded, they wouldn't be able to please her. Jake deserved her anger, not everyone else. "You're right. Let's go look at the cake."

When they reached the table, Lil waved a slow-cooker lid. "Hi, guys."

The cake had tiny pink bows for decoration and was scalloped with ribbon. "Cute cake," Katy commented. "Can you do that ribbon thing, Lil?"

"Sure. That looks easy."

As they spoke, a loud crash resonated from the kitchen, followed by an interval of heavy silence. Inez Beachy, an older woman whose head covering still had Amish strings, hurried to the front of the room and used the lull to get everyone's attention. She said a quick prayer over the food, and at the *Amen*, a wave of women started ambling toward Katy and her friends.

Megan elbowed her. "Quick. Let's head up the line."

They grabbed pink plates, and Katy filled hers with a whoopee pie, some nuts, and a meatball.

Katy and Megan found seats near the front, where they could watch Elizabeth open her baby gifts. The party launched and was soon in full swing, with the church sisters losing themselves in the wonder of tiny, hand-knitted booties and doll-sized dresses.

"Make you want to play house?" Megan asked with a smirk. "I heard you're dating David Miller. I miss one Sunday and when I come back, you've already had two dates in one week."

"Hush!"

"You went with him to the skating party. It's not a secret."

"No kidding." Katy pulled an exaggerated frown then with her next breath caught a faint whiff of something abnormal. Perhaps because of her earlier apprehension in the parking lot, she furrowed her brow and inhaled more deeply. She caught it again, only stronger. Touching Megan's wrist, she asked, "What's that funny smell?"

Megan sniffed. "I don't smell anything."

With Megan's allergies, that came as no surprise. Before Katy could disagree, a feminine shriek filled the air, and somebody shouted, "Smoke! Kitchen fire!"

A chaos of activity followed the pronouncement. Women gasped. Chairs scraped and clattered. Aghast, Katy jumped up, too, thrusting her finger. "Look!" Small puffs of smoke wafted through the kitchen's pass-through window. She couldn't hear Megan's response above the mass of feminine hysteria.

Inez flew to the front of the room, her covering strings flying behind her. The older woman clapped her hands until she had most of their attention. Her curt voice shot orders to the nervous crowd. "Everyone. Move out to the parking lot! Move orderly. But hurry!"

Now the women started to act with purpose, crowding toward the entrance, all the while casting worried glances toward the kitchen.

But Katy remained riveted, her mind scrambling for ways to help before exiting.

"What about Lil?" Megan shouted.

Snatching up her purse, Katy unclamped her lips. "There's an exit in the kitchen. She's closer to the door than we are." Starting down the aisle between the rows of vacating chairs, Katy took a final glance behind her and stopped. "Elizabeth!"

Megan swung her gaze around.

The pregnant woman sat stunned, glued to her metal folding chair like a queen ruling over a sea of packages and tissue paper. Quickly running back to her, Katy urged. "Elizabeth! We have to leave the building."

Elizabeth cupped her palms over her swollen stomach and nodded, but still didn't budge.

Katy stepped over gifts and bent over her. "What's wrong?" Surely she wasn't going into labor?

"The baby's gifts. I—"

Understanding, Katy gripped Elizabeth's arm and pulled her to her swollen feet. She glanced toward the jammed exit and made a quick decision. "We'll help you get them."

Katy swept a few gifts off the floor and handed them up to the dazed woman.

"Megan, what are you waiting for?" Anita Weaver suddenly loomed over them with a frightened expression.

Katy shoved a pink gift bag into the older woman's hand. Then Megan and her mom hurried to gather as many gifts as they could.

"Let's go," Anita urged.

The three women juggled gifts and pushed Elizabeth toward the exit, all of their gazes fixed on the thick smoke billowing into the back of the room and the bright flames now visible as well, flickering up through the pass-through window.

"We waited too long," Anita cried. "Hurry, girls."

They tried to run, but the area next to the exit was filled with stifling smoke. Worried for Elizabeth in her pregnant state, Katy yelled, "Hold your breath."

After that, they didn't speak. They reached the rear of the frantic bodies packing and blocking the exit where the smoke-filled multipurpose room narrowed into a hall. A handmade receiving blanket slipped out of Elizabeth's arms and fell to the floor. With a shriek, she halted.

Anita whipped it up off the floor.

The line steadily moved, and as soon as they stumbled outside, they all took welcome draughts of the fresh air. Katy found herself coughing much like she had with the drywall dust, but with each inhalation of uncontaminated air, her breathing became more normal.

Inez urged, "Keep moving so others can come out."

"We were at the end of the line," Katy informed her. The woman nodded with relief and ran toward the other door, which was the kitchen's exit.

Katy instantly remembered Lil and lunged after Inez, but Ivan Miller blocked her path. He moved around Katy and swept Elizabeth into a quick embrace that knocked several gift boxes to the ground.

"Thank God, you're okay." The young husband's voice was husky with worry.

Feeling a touch at her elbow, Katy turned. David gave her a worried nod, his gaze darting nervously to the building and back at Ivan. He moved past her and stopped beside his brother. "We'd better check inside."

Ivan reluctantly released his wife. "Go wait in the car, honey. The smoke isn't good for the baby."

Elizabeth nodded but stooped to pick up the packages her husband had recklessly knocked to the ground. Involuntarily, Katy stooped to help as her worried gaze followed David and Ivan into the smoky building. Torn with which entrance to use to go search for Lil, she watched them until they disappeared.

"No!" Elizabeth lunged, belatedly, after Ivan.

But Anita snatched Elizabeth's arm. "Don't," she reprimanded. "Let the men go."

Megan interrupted her mother. "Do you think Lil and others are trapped in the kitchen?"

Alarm sprinted up Katy's spine at Anita's stricken expression, and she quickly pressed, "Can you take Elizabeth to the car?"

The older woman clamped her lips together for a moment, then replied, "Only if you both stay put, out of danger's way." At Anita's stern look, Megan nodded for the both of them. Katy couldn't promise anything until she knew Lil was safe. Anita draped her arm around Elizabeth, moving the distraught woman toward the parking lot.

Katy's fingers imprinted the soft gift boxes she still clutched. "Oh Lil. Where are you?" She whipped her gaze to Megan. "She must be inside."

Flames now flickered through the kitchen exterior windows. Megan clenched her fists at her side. "We have to go get her."

In the distance they heard a siren. Somewhere along the kitchen's exterior wall, Katy had dropped the gifts. Outside the door, she shrugged someone's hand off her shoulder and grabbed the door handle. But she quickly released the hot metal. Her shoulder jerked back under a firm grip. She glanced back. Inez warned, "Don't do it!"

Frantically, Katy looked around. She needed padding to open the door handle. For the first time, she realized none of them had bothered to fetch their coats or gloves. Hysterically searching her body for something to put over the door's handle, she cried, "But Lil's in there."

Inez clamped her arm on her shoulder again. "I hear the fire truck."

Before she could resist, Megan cried, "Look, Katy! Lil's safe!"

Katy whipped her gaze around, and saw Lil and Mrs. Landis standing by the opposite exit with David and Ivan.

Katy ran to them with relief, her voice laced with fear-induced anger. "Where were you?"

"I don't know. The men found us. We couldn't get the fire out. It blocked the door. When we left the kitchen, it was so hazy we couldn't see."

"Are you all right?"

Lil nodded. "I think so."

A red fire truck screamed into the parking lot. Three men in dark-blue uniforms barreled down and rushed to the building.

Mrs. Landis turned away to speak to Inez. Shivering, Lil rubbed her arms, and the three girls huddled together, watching.

One fireman swung an ax thru the kitchen window. A second stuck a hose through it while the third man ran to them and questioned Ivan.

"What happened in there?" Katy asked.

"Did you hear that crash earlier?" Lil asked.

Katy nodded.

"We dropped a punch bowl. There was a huge mess. Anyway, we all chipped in to clean it up. I think somebody forgot what they were doing. The fire started from the area where there was a slow-cooker and a big coffeepot."

"But how would those start a fire?"

"I don't know."

"I hope it wasn't my fault," Mrs. Landis moaned, stepping into their circle. "Somebody could have been killed."

"It's nobody's fault. It was an accident," Megan assured her, but the older woman looked stricken.

David returned from speaking with some firemen. He looked glum, disheveled, and sooty.

"Everybody out?" Katy asked.

"As far as we know. The firemen are checking now." They both glanced over where one of the professionals was wetting down the meetinghouse.

"You think the meetinghouse will catch on fire?"

"I don't know. The fellowship hall's ruined."

"But you found Lil." Katy's emotions suddenly overwhelmed her. "What if you hadn't been here?"

"I just came to help Ivan pack up the gifts. We came early to sneak some cake. When we got here, we saw women rushing out of the building. Then we saw the fire. While Ivan looked for Elizabeth, I called the fire department." He glanced toward the parking lot. "How is she?"

"I don't know. Anita Weaver took her to the car like Ivan requested."

A crashing noise commanded their attention. They stared at the fire in riveted horror. Part of the roof had caved in, and a new flurry of flames and smoke drove them farther away from the building.

As they stood dazed, more help arrived. A barricade was soon erected. At some point, David removed his coat and placed it across Katy's shoulders. She heard him say, "They want those cars moved. If you give me your keys, I'll move yours."

She dug into her purse and handed him the keys. "Thanks."

"Dumplin'?" Katy nearly broke down at her dad's touch. She turned into his sturdy embrace, clinging to him for a long while.

When she drew away, she asked, "How did you find out?"

"Lil called her dad. Will started the prayer chain." He motioned behind him. "I parked down the street. I had to make sure you were all right. Your mom's real worried."

"I think everybody's okay."

"According to Will, Rose is pretty upset. She's worried she may have been the one who started the fire. She remembers setting a roll of paper towels next to the coffeepot."

"Poor thing. But it was just an accident," Katy replied.

"She feels responsible as head of the hostess committee."

"A punch bowl broke," Katy protested, as though that would explain everything to her dad.

He pointed, "That your car?"

Katy nodded. "David's moving it for me. He and Ivan came to load up Elizabeth's gifts. They were the first men on the scene."

"I'm going to go ask the firemen if there's anything I can do to help. We don't want the sanctuary to burn."

Katy noticed other churchmen who had heard about the fire were starting to mill about the parking lot. "Okay."

"I'd feel better if you'd go home. Your mom's worried."

She realized that even with David's coat, she was shivering. "Okay. But be careful, Dad."

Off to the side, Will Landis was helping his wife to their car. Katy hurried over, asking Lil, "Your mom going to be okay?"

"I think so. It hit her when the firemen checked us over."

"You didn't get burned?"

"No." Lil crossed her trembling arms.

"You in shock?"

"Just cold. My throat's raw, too."

"Want me to take you home?"

Lil's teeth began to clatter. "No. I'm going home with my folks."

Katy watched Lil get in the car. Turning her back to the surreal scene, Katy hugged her arms against the cold and trudged to her own car. Behind her, another crash sounded. When she looked over her shoulder, she saw more of the fellowship hall had caved in. Fire illuminated the winter's night sky. She gripped her car's door handle and instantly flinched at the pain. How would this fire affect their small congregation?

CHAPTER 10

A few nights later, Katy was rebandaging her hand when the telephone rang. From the living room, where she lay on the couch buried to her chin in a quilt and nursing a box of tissues, Mom called, "Git dat?"

Tearing off the medical tape and pressing it in place, Katy hurried to the phone and cradled it in the crook of her neck. David's voice tumbled into her consciousness, low and masculine. "You busy?"

"No, I just finished the dishes."

Her stomach did a little somersault until she remembered the coldness of their kiss. With his bravery at the fire, she had forgotten about that. She brought her attention back to what he was saying. He wasn't saying anything particularly personal, he was just talking about the fire.

"Elizabeth's fine"—David's voice held a hint of hesitance or despondency—"fretting over some handmade blankets that got ruined in the fire, but otherwise good. She told me you got most of the gifts out of there."

Twisting the phone cord, Katy replied, "I just reacted. It was weird."

"You're an angel. Elizabeth thinks so, too. Now she's embarrassed about the way she acted, obsessed over the gifts. She's going to apologize."

"That's not necessary. I'm sure it was just a mixture of shock and probably had something to do with being pregnant."

"That's what Ivan told her. But about the fire, the men are having a cleanup day this coming Saturday. It'll be a long day, and my dad asked me to help with the chores afterward to make up for the time away from the farm. Guess what I'm getting at is, can we postpone our dinner date?"

Disappointment rushed over her. "Of course. We can do that anytime." Unless. . .was he trying to break up? "Or we don't have to go at all," she added.

"Hey, I want to see you. It isn't that."

She didn't reply because everything had become so confusing with David that she didn't know what she wanted anymore.

After some silence, he asked, "Did you do your nanny thing today?"

Leaning against the wall, she worked the kinks out of the phone cord. Maybe he knew about the three-date proposition and wasn't going to give her the third date. Maybe he was going to dangle it. She'd deserve that. "Yeah. Addison broke Tyler's iPod."

"How'd she do that?"

"I have no idea, don't even know how they work, but there was some kind of struggle going on in the backseat on the way home from school. Tyler can be a real imp."

"Boys will be boys. Maybe you need to pack Addison a bigger snack." Katy couldn't help but grin. David's listening abilities amazed her. He really understood and remembered when she'd talked about work. "Did they get in trouble with Tammy?"

"Big-time."

"Oh yeah? She take away his BB gun?"

"She promised him a new iPod. A better one. And Addison is getting her own so they don't have to fight over Tyler's."

"That's a little harsh."

"I know. But I'm sure you've got better things to do than talk about a couple of spoiled kids."

"Nothing's more important than talking to you. Why haven't we talked on the phone before?"

So maybe he wasn't breaking up with her? Unless he was baiting her so he could dangle the third date. She hated to end the call until she knew exactly where they stood. "I made the mistake of asking Tammy what kind of discipline I should administer. She got all white-knuckled and said I should just tell her when they misbehaved, and she'd deal with it."

"By rewarding them?"

"Exactly. Now my hands are really tied. I asked her if she's looking for another nanny. She said the agencies were too expensive. She was thinking of arranging her schedule differently and asked if I could babysit two days a week, on the days I come anyway. She's a pro at getting her way."

"That's not something you want then?"

"Hardly. I told her I'd think about it. If I hadn't stalled, I'd have ended up manipulated into a yes on the spot, and—" She dropped the phone cord, twirled her ponytail, and sighed.

"Guess you need to practice all the ways to say no. There's a lot of country songs on that subject."

She remembered his car radio, although he'd only turned it to classical music on their date. "You like country music?"

"I listen to it sometimes. Anyway, don't practice your no on me, okay?"

"If you're a gentleman, I won't have to."

———

Later that night, Vernon Yoder found Marie asleep on the sofa. He leaned over her and lightly shook her shoulder. "Wake up, honey."

"What? I'b just sleeby. How was your meeding?"

"Mennonite Mutual will cover the fire, and we've decided to rebuild, and while we're at it, to add those Sunday school rooms we've been needing."

She sniffled. "Zounds like work."

He grabbed a tissue and handed it to her, easing onto the couch beside her. "We're forming a committee so the elders don't get bogged down."

Dabbing her nose, she asked, "Who's on the gammittee?"

"Maybe your lovely daughter."

Marie jerked to a sitting position. "Why Gaty?"

"First they tried to get someone from the hostess committee. Lil's mom is feeling low right now, so then Lil's name came up. We called her from the meeting. She said she couldn't because she works nights, but she suggested Katy. For some reason, the elders thought she was a good candidate. We tried calling, but the phone was busy."

"Dabe Miller called; then I vell asleep."

"I didn't want her on the committee."

"Why not?"

"Because Jake Byler will be the project superintendent. They called him, and he's already agreed."

"Oh no."

"Talking to David, huh? I guess that's a good sign."

"Dey sounded habby."

"We'll just have to keep praying about it. You have sick eyes, honey. Let's go to bed."

⁓

Later that week, Katy caught lingering whiffs of a smoky odor as she hurried past a yellow ribbon that fenced off the charred disaster. She shouldered the door to the meetinghouse. Low laughter floated to her from the sanctuary, where the building committee was scheduled to meet. She had never served on any committees before and wasn't sure what to expect. She figured she was here as Lil's proxy, but that seemed fair since the elders had asked Lil first.

Curious to see who else would serve on the committee, she stepped through the open double doors that separated the foyer from the sanctuary and made her way down the gray-carpeted center aisle. Dark-stained pews flanked her on either side. She had almost reached the front of the room when her steps faltered.

Her shoulders drooped in utter disbelief. Not Jake again? As if on cue, he turned, meeting her stricken gaze with his own contrite one, the ever-so-charming grin that infuriated her these days. She forced her attention to the elder presiding over the meeting. Her dad had told her he was thankful he wasn't chosen for the position. Instead Megan's dad had received the honor. "Hi Mr. Weaver."

"Hi Katy." He stepped into the aisle and took her hand, but when he saw the large Band-Aid, he treated it with care. "What happened?"

"A few blisters from the fire. But it's healing."

"I'm sorry. We miss seeing you since Megan's away at school."

"I miss you guys, too." Trying hard to ignore Jake's presence, she asked, "Got any midnight blues in the works?"

He held a finger to his lips, pretending nobody else knew that his favorite pastime of restoring cars and painting them midnight blue, but everybody knew.

She took stock of the seating arrangement, and Jake's eyes dared her to sit beside him, but she opted for the painter's pew. Still, Jake's presence beckoned her. He certainly didn't look repentant, coming to church with shaggy hair and wearing a T-shirt. She struggled harder to disregard him, giving her full attention to observing the other committee members.

Besides the blues man, the group included representatives from the finance committee, the grounds committee, and the church council, as well as a layperson who was a painter by trade, Katy as a stand-in for the hostess committee, and obviously Jake as construction advisor. That made seven. To Katy, there were only two people in the room, and that made her want to flee, but she couldn't do that. She'd have to endure the torture of putting in her time at the meeting.

It started with the groundskeeper reporting on the scheduled cleanup and answering questions on easements.

"What if the congregation doesn't want to spend the money for the additional Sunday school rooms?" the painter asked.

"The finance committee will head up the bids, and we'll have all that information before we take it to the congregation for a vote," Mr. Weaver explained.

"What if they think we're trying to push it through by getting on this so quickly?"

Katy hadn't known the painter was such a pessimist.

"There are always a few rumbles, no matter what direction leadership takes. We'll deal with the problems as they arise. We're not trying to trick anybody, just get all our facts together at this point."

As the meeting progressed, Katy's neck stiffened from being held in one position so long to avoid Jake's gaze. Hearing the low rumble of his Dutch accent—his mother's family came from an Amish background—was trying enough, for it brought back yearnings she'd hoped to have stifled by now. Putting a hand to her neck, she twisted to ease the tension. Of course her traitorous eyes sought the most desirable man in the room.

And he knew the moment she looked at him. His brown eyes caressed her, and she found it hard to turn away. Then those sensuous lips of his gave her a private smile, and she remembered how she used to always make him smile. He had once delighted in her, in their relationship. He had that look now, that darkened gaze that clung to her every breath. He probably only wanted her now because she was unobtainable. The thought was enough that she was able to break their visual contact.

She made a show of rubbing her neck and focused once more on the agenda. She gleaned that she needed to speak to the present hostess committee and collect their input on an updated kitchen and get the information to Jake as soon as possible. He needed the details before their next meeting. He was in charge of getting a blueprint drawn, collecting bids for the congregation's approval, and submitting the plans to Plain City's Planning and Zoning Commission.

Now she knew why her dad sometimes returned from elders' meetings looking frayed and worried. Bill Weaver prayed and dismissed them, and finally she could flee. She lurched to her feet and hastened down the aisle, confident that as the only woman present, no one would detain her. She planned to escape before Jake got the opportunity to engage that lethal gaze of his again, the one that made her heart revolt against her will. But she'd not even reached the double doors before a touch sent a shock through her shoulder.

With a frustrated sigh, she stopped. Turned.

"I need to get your ideas before I draw up the kitchen."

So he didn't have anything personal to say to her. Good. That was the way she wanted it, too. "I need to talk to Lil first. I'm sure the hostess committee has ideas."

He raised a brow. Perhaps he hadn't realized Lil was asked first and would be giving her input. "As far as the blueprints go, the plans for the new kitchen are major. Think we could get together sometime soon to discuss it?"

Were those ulterior motives or was he only taking care of business? She troubled her lip. "To be honest, I didn't know I'd be working with you. Otherwise I wouldn't even have accepted this position. I'll have to resign if it includes private meetings with the likes of you."

"That's right. You don't want me. I get that, but if you back out of this committee now, it will just delay the preliminary process. For the congregation's sake, we can surely put our personal feelings aside long enough to get this job done." He gave her a crooked, albeit contrite smile. "Think of all the little Sunday school kids. How would you like to listen to adult sermons without getting any David and Goliath stories afterward to make up for it? And think of all the starving bachelors who count on the church potlucks. And think of—"

"Okay. I get it." She bit her lip to keep from smiling and raised a brow. "What about the doddy house?"

He squinted those intimidating brows. "You're afraid of me, aren't you?" He lifted his arms to show he wore no weapon. "Come on, Katy. I'm just a harmless Dutchman. Totally defenseless."

She ignored his comment and rephrased her question in a voice she might use with Tyler. "Is your work for the church going to slow down your progress at the doddy house? This is a major project."

She saw his eyes darken; anger and lust with him looked so similar, she couldn't tell what was going through his thick, tousle-haired skull. "I'll work overtime, if that's what it takes. I'm not a slacker. I need both jobs to get references for the construction business I plan to start." The painter walked by, giving them a once-over.

"They want to lock up," Katy observed.

"Let me walk you to your car," Jake whispered in reply.

She started to put her coat on and resented the way Jake helped her shrug into it. She moved toward the door. "Regarding the new kitchen, what kind of information do you need?"

He gave her the quick version, one that fit into the distance between the church and her car, and she realized he could be precise and intelligent when he chose to be. He wasn't a boy any longer. He was a stubborn, irrepressible man. When they reached her car, she had a vivid flashback of the incident. It shook her. She only wanted to get rid of him. "I'll make some calls. Talk to Lil and the rest of the committee. Maybe I can stop by sometime at the doddy house and go over it with you." She reached for her car door handle.

"Wait. Do you have paper and a pencil? I should give you my cell phone number so you can call before you come." She frowned and slid into her seat. As if she'd ever call him. But he continued to explain. "I'm usually there, but sometimes I have to run after materials. Sometimes I have to sit with Grandma, too."

Her emotions flickered with instant sympathy, remembering his grandma who now had Alzheimer's. Minnie had been her favorite Sunday school teacher, a vibrant part of their congregation, but now the elderly woman fell asleep the moment her skirt hit the pew, her snores embarrassing everyone within hearing. He must have misread her expression, because he quickly added, "I can always stay late, if I have to do that. But it's one of the reasons I moved back home. To give Mom some support. Sis is staying at a dorm at OSU." He rammed his hands in his jeans.

Trying to tamp down the sympathy she felt for him, she started rifling through her purse. Her bandage caught, and she jerked it free. "I'm sorry about your grandma."

"Thanks."

She handed him paper and pen. "I don't mean to sound like a slave driver. I'm sure you'll do a great job. I just have a problem with you."

He shed off her insult and scribbled seven digits on the paper. Then he started rambling about something totally off the subject, and Katy struggled to follow.

He was saying something about God dividing time into days? "Every morning is a new start. He gave us a new birth, too. There's not much without the hope of new beginnings, Katy."

Getting his drift, she snatched the paper away. "There's always endings."

He stepped back and stuffed his hands in his jean pockets again.

She shut her window.

He turned his back to her and walked toward his truck, and rats if she didn't feel sorry for him.

CHAPTER 11

Parked outside Addison's dance studio, Katy sat in her car and sulked. Tammy Brooks was one stubborn woman who wouldn't get her red-painted claws out of Katy's usually well-ordered life. Surely she wasn't becoming a pushover? Why was everyone interfering with her plans? She had her own ideas of how things should go and didn't like the obstacles she'd been encountering at every turn. She'd had it at home with her dad's matchmaking, in her personal life with Lil hiring Jake, and now at work. She banged her head back against the padded headrest. She was definitely becoming a pushover.

Bored and restless, she opened the glove compartment and withdrew a small testament she kept there, opening the Bible and leafing through it at random. Just as her luck would have it, every verse her gaze fell upon had something to do with newness, reminding her of Jake's oratory in the parking lot. She frowned at God's sense of humor. In the book of Lamentations, she read God's compassions are new every morning. She read passages about new spirits, new hearts, a new commandment—the commandment to love one another—new creatures, and in Revelation how God makes all things new.

Newness? Why couldn't things remain the same? What was wrong with old and boring?

105

She felt confirmation in her heart that Jake had received God's newness, but that didn't mean she had to let him worm his way back into her affections. More restless than ever, she snapped the testament shut and returned it to the glove box. She glanced in the rearview mirror, involuntarily straightening her covering while she scanned the parking lot. Addison should be out any minute. Not wanting to argue with God about Jake, her fury transferred to Tammy again, who had insisted that Katy try babysitting just two days a week and wouldn't take no for an answer.

Tapping on the steering wheel, she prayed, "Lord, I feel like nothing gets resolved. Like I'm losing control of my life. I need Your help." *I need to be more assertive. Okay, and loving.* She accepted the thoughts that came into her mind as inspiration.

Tap, tap. She jerked her gaze to the passenger's window and saw Addison's bubbly smile. Her small palms were pressed against the window. Her blond hair was piled on top of her head, and sweaty tendrils stuck to her cheeks in spite of the cold temperature outside. Her purple coat was open, revealing a pink tutu beneath it. Feeling a flash of fondness for the little girl, Katy quickly unlocked the doors and allowed her young charge to climb into the backseat.

"We're going to the ballet!" Addison chirped, hopping into the car.

"That's nice," Katy said. "Fasten your seat belt, sweetie." She heard the click and then the shuffling sounds of Addison's dance bag, probably because the girl was retrieving her new, pink iPod.

They swung by Tyler's friend's house to pick him up and then drove to the children's home. Katy had a garage door opener of her own now, and she pulled into an empty stall. The children sprang out and ran inside for their snack. By the time Katy got inside, they were fighting over the last can of soda pop. Tyler snapped it open, and fizz spilled over his hand and onto the freshly mopped floor.

Addison planted her tiny hands on her tutu hips and did a little dance move, posing and gloating over Tyler's sticky mishap.

He burped, grinned, and headed for the stairway.

"Pick up your backpack," Katy called after him.

"I know. I know."

Katy smiled inwardly that he didn't seem quite so resentful, hadn't called her a pilgrim. She gave Addison a faint smile. "How about some orange juice?"

"Okay." The little girl ditched her pose and climbed onto the bar stool, propping pink-clad elbows on the bar, adult-style. "I'm excited about the ballet. It's *Cinderella*."

A brief wave of nostalgia hit Katy, for she'd loved that fairy tale when she was a little girl. But that's all it was. A fairy tale. Pouring the juice, Katy said, "That's nice." Then she wet a paper towel to clean up after Tyler. She was glad it was Thursday. She wouldn't have to come back to the Brooks' until next Tuesday. The coldhearted thought zipped harsh in her own mind, especially after agreeing with God in the car that she needed to be more loving. She slid into the stool beside Addison. "I have some time if you want to play that tea-party board game you have."

"Okay!" Instantly, she abandoned her drink, bounding off the stool and running up to her room.

"Better change first," Katy called after her, wondering if she should follow her up and check on Tyler. When she'd decided to do just that, she'd gotten partway up the stairway when she heard footsteps. She whirled. Sean Brooks was home.

"Oh hi. You're early," she said, retracing her steps so that she could speak to him.

"Tammy told me you needed a break."

"She did?" Katy glanced up the stairway and back with hesitance. "Tyler's in his room. I was about to check on him. And Addison's changing out of her dance costume. We were just going to play a board game. I'm afraid she's going to be disappointed."

"I'll do that with her." Sean started toward the kitchen.

Katy waited with hesitance. To her relief, he didn't grab a beer but returned with an envelope in his hand. She had cleaned around it earlier that day. "Tammy wanted me to give this to you."

It hit Katy that Tammy must have sensed her frustration. She'd misjudged her employer after all. The envelope probably contained a token of apology. She felt a tinge of guilt over her ugly thoughts earlier in the car. The envelope felt like it might hold a gift card. They still needed many things for the doddy house. "Thanks." She took her coat off the bar stool and shrugged into it. "Tell Tammy I really appreciate it."

"No problem. Our treat. Just enjoy."

Nodding, Katy replied, "Tell the children 'bye for me. I'll see them on Tuesday. Thanks again." In the garage, she got into her car and started the engine. But her curiosity couldn't be ignored, and she ripped open the envelope. Inside were two tickets. Not what she'd expected. Furling her brow, she pulled them out far enough to read the print. Tickets to the *Cinderella* ballet! She lay her head against the headrest, pinched her eyes closed, and rapped her forearms against the steering wheel. The horn honked.

⁓

By smooth maneuvering on Katy's part, Lil was joining her at the doddy house to talk with Jake about the new church kitchen. Katy refused to meet him alone.

Still, as she approached the front porch, her nerves bristled. Inside the tiny house, Jake turned and gave her one of his crooked grins. She drew in a deep breath at his dark good looks and willed herself to stir up some of those Christian attitudes God had impressed upon her in her recent car devotional. . . . She needed to act lovingly. No, that was just too strong for this circumstance. Arguing inwardly, she substituted the word *sisterly*.

"Hi." For a Christian attitude, it left her feeling a bit breathless. "See you've got a whole crew here today. Where's Lil?"

"In the bathroom, talking to the plumber. The electrician is installing lights. But the rest of the house is ready to start painting."

"Awesome." Now she was talking like Tyler.

Jake caught her slip of tongue. "Somebody's in a good mood."

Maybe being nice wasn't such a good idea. Looking at him wasn't, either. He definitely wore his jeans too tight for a Conservative boy. It made her wonder how much he'd changed or if she even knew him anymore. She sucked in a breath when he looked down at the buckle on his low-slung tool belt, worked the clasp, and dropped it on the ground beside him. *Breathe*, she told herself, *pull up your gaze.* The view wasn't much safer there. His logo-free T worked to his advantage, the black material emphasizing the black, wavy hair that fringed his baseball cap.

"I don't suppose that means you've decided to tolerate me?"

Of all the nerve, after she'd specifically told him she didn't want him and that he bothered her. Truth was, he probably sensed how well she tolerated him—desired him. But trying to act nonchalant, she replied, "Actually, I have." Unconsciously, she fiddled with the shoulder strap of her purse. "I thought about what you said about new beginnings. I'm sure God wants that for you. I want that for you."

His deep-hooded brows relaxed and his brown eyes lit with more enthusiasm than they should have as he bounded toward her, his voice thicker than ever with his Dutch accent. "I won't let you down, Katy. I—"

Throwing both palms in the air, she quickly interjected, "Don't"— and he stopped—"misunderstand. This has nothing to do with us."

His expression wilted, making him seem boyishly vulnerable. He hooked his thumbs in his slim jeans and studied her with tilted head. "You saying you want to be friends?"

She rolled the question distastefully around in her mouth. "More like what you said at first. I'm just trying to tolerate you. It's the decent thing to do. Sisterly."

He made a face. "Sisterly?"

"Christian. Sisterly."

"Oh." His stupid grin returned. He moved forward again. She froze, not sure what he was up to, but thankfully she must have presented a formidable presence, for once again he hesitated. Still, he stood too close. He looked down at her with his dark gaze, and she hoped he said something, did something soon, before she passed out from lack of oxygen. Then he did. Reaching out, he wrapped his forefinger in her ponytail, like he had so many times over the years. He gently untangled it from her purse strap. She lowered her gaze, making it eye level with his neck. He had a handsome Adam's apple. He swallowed as if the gesture affected him the same as it did her. But neither of them would admit it.

"Thanks," he murmured.

"Hey, Jake"—the electrician broke off his sentence when he saw he'd intruded on an intimate moment.

Jake, never one to act embarrassed, slowly turned without dropping his hand.

But she jerked away.

"Yeah?" Jake asked, if anything showing only irritation at the interruption.

"When you get a minute, I'd like to show you something."

Jake turned back to Katy with furled brows, and she knew their business wasn't finalized, but it had gotten more personal than she'd hoped. She was grateful for the interruption.

"Go on." She motioned with a wave. "I'll go find Lil and check out the new shower."

"Okay." His gaze roved over her in a leisurely manner. "Meet me back here in five minutes, and we'll go over the church project." He gave a mocking tip of his ball cap and strode away.

She stood still for a moment longer, both mourning and exulting over the leap their relationship had just taken with its flirtatious undercurrent. It had all happened so quickly that she feared where it might lead in the future if she kept melting a little each time she was in his presence.

She found Lil in the bathroom, flirting with the plumber. Ignoring that, Katy snapped, "You abandoned me." She lowered her voice. "You knew the plan. You were supposed to back me up, so I wouldn't have to talk to him alone."

Lil gave an offhanded frown with a small toss of her hand. "I didn't even know you were here. But now that you are, check out the shower." She opened and closed a glass door. Stepped in and out. "Don't you love it?"

She did. The shower compartment wasn't fancy like the travertine walk-in shower Lil had cut out of a magazine. It was an unpretentious white, but it was new and would serve the purpose. Well, after they scraped the stickers and handprints off, Katy thought, grinning. "I call the first shower." The back of the plumber's neck reddened, and she clamped her hand over her mouth, backing out of the room. In the hall, they both burst out laughing.

"He's kinda cute, don't you think?" Lil asked.

"Married?"

"I don't know. Either that or just shy. I'll have to ask Jake."

They met Jake back in the living room and settled down on the plastic-covered floor for their meeting. Over the next ten minutes, they discussed all the pertinent details of the future fellowship hall's kitchen. Jake asked plenty of questions and scribbled notes on a legal pad, even sketched. While they were at it, he gave them the dimensions they would need to shop for appliances for the doddy house, which was where they were headed next.

"You driving?" Lil asked, popping to her feet.

"Sure," Katy replied.

"Good. I've gotta go find my purse." She winked, and Katy thought it was an excuse to flirt with the plumber again. "Then I'm ready to go."

Jake pinned Katy with his dark gaze, and as soon as Lil left, he jumped right in where they'd left off before his cousin joined them. "You could probably tolerate me better if you'd let me tell you my story. I need to tell you exactly what happened to me the last couple of years. How it's changed me."

She shook her head. "Nah. I don't want to get involved in your personal life."

"Come on, Katy. You already are."

She started to stand, but her foot slipped on the plastic, and he lunged forward and caught her arm, steadying her. Their faces were close, mere inches away, and he whispered. "I hate the word *never*."

When he drew back, she asked, "What?"

"You'll never forgive me, and I'll never forget you. And never's a miserably long time."

Lil popped back into the room. "Found it." She hooked her arm under Katy's coat sleeve. "Let's hit the shops. See ya later, chump."

Katy forced a smile for Lil. At the doorway, she hesitated, but Lil went on outside. Katy glanced back at Jake.

He winked.

Hoping to wipe the smirk from his face, she said, "One thing before we go. I was wondering, is your plumber married?"

His brows furled. "Very."

Katy shrugged and started through the doorway.

But behind her, the amusement in his voice couldn't be denied. "Tell Lil the electrician's single."

Straightening her shoulders, she didn't reply.

CHAPTER 12

B arely able to contain her excitement, Katy grinned over at Lil, whose car was filled with painting supplies. In response, Lil did a little shoulder shimmy. They were both anxious to get started. In a few short weeks, the doddy house renovations had nearly been completed. New purchases were stored in Mr. Landis's barn. Now came Katy's favorite part: cleaning up the place and making it livable.

Lil turned the car into the Millers' drive and honked just as Jake strode out of the doddy house. With a wave, he headed directly to the back of the Blazer. It amazed Katy how those two read each other's minds. They were more like twins than cousins.

Ever since Katy and Lil's spat over hiring Jake to renovate the doddy house, Katy had kept her feelings and frustrations over him private, aware that information somehow magically passed between the other two.

Sometimes Katy's escalating problems seemed overwhelming. She hadn't told anybody about the ballet tickets either. That problem continued to fester, frustrating her peace. Once she would have shared all her job-related problems with her mom, but now that she was operating in a gray zone, she didn't think her mom would understand. With time nearing her move into the doddy house, she didn't want her mom to worry that she was getting pulled into worldly ways.

Katy watched Jake easily tote a five-gallon paint can in each hand—shabby chic yellow for the kitchen and tropical turquoise for the bedroom—jaunting to the doddy house without speaking to her. The sly rat knew how to turn her head, showing off his muscles and ignoring her just the way she wanted him to, all very unfair. Was this something he'd learned at college? How to Win an Old Girlfriend 101?

"Want me to get the white can?" she asked Lil.

"Nah. Too heavy. Let Jake get it. But together we can manage the ladder." Lil struggled to extract it from the back of her car. Katy caught the end just before it dropped to the ground. They did an awkward, baby-step shuffle all the way inside the house with it. "Bedroom or kitchen?" Lil tossed breathlessly over her shoulder.

"Bedroom." *Jake can work in the kitchen*, she hoped, *far away from my work area.*

Lil nodded as they maneuvered the ladder through the hall. Next they struggled to set it upright in the center of the bedroom, next to the paint cans.

"Whew!" Katy said. She removed her coat, taking in the metallic, new-heater smell. Filled with pride and amazement, she thought, *Our heat from* our *new heating system.* Suddenly she had something to show for her hours of housecleaning. Stoking her feeling of satisfaction, she headed for the new closet. "Wow. Have you seen this, Lil?"

Her friend followed at her heels, then did a slow circle inside the large walk-in. "Um-hm. Shoe racks, shelves, clothes bars. It's perfect."

"Which half do you want?" Katy asked, imagining her dark skirts spaced apart in perfect half-inch increments, her long-sleeved blouses classified by colors, sweaters by color, too, in perfectly folded piles on the shelves. With her meager wardrobe, there would be room to spare. She could keep other personal items here, too: some cleaning supplies that she purchased by the gallon, her sweeper bags, her childhood dolls, scrapbooks filled with school papers, and her collection of the *Young Indiana Jones Chronicles.* No, she'd leave those for her little brothers. But she had a stack of unread Christian novels she'd purchased at the Shekinah Festival in September.

Lil pointed at the far wall, the one more visible from the bedroom. "You'd better take that side since you're neater. And we can put a dresser on this wall. I'll take the bottom two drawers."

"That's kind. Thanks." But Lil's reminder that she wouldn't be the neatest roommate sent a tremor of foreboding into her future fantasy vision. When they stepped back into the room, Jake had already started masking off the baseboard.

He looked up. His shaggy black curls flipped out under his hat. The brim had been knocked off-kilter, and he didn't seem aware of how attractive he looked at that moment. Both masculine and boyish. "This wall's ready to go," he offered.

"Now it's your turn to pick. Cut or roll?" Lil asked.

Katy tore her gaze from Jake and stared at Lil, until she could concentrate on the question. It certainly wasn't a difficult one. In the closet, Lil had chosen first. She had given Katy the best, the higher drawers. So Katy chose the chore she thought Lil would least want. "Cut in."

Katy pried off the paint lid and stirred the white swirls with a wooden paddle until she had a solid color that resembled a pale tropical sea. Grabbing a tray and brush, she went to the can, and Jake jumped to her assistance.

"Let me lift that for you." He poured, then placed the can back on the plastic flooring. "Nice color."

She imagined there would be nights when sleep would fail her for remembering his tight jeans-clad form in the center of their bedroom. He was a nuisance in them. Without thanking him, she took the tray to the wall and knelt, straightening her skirt beneath her and then teasing the color along the top of the stained baseboard. She glanced over, "Yes, I love it." His eyes darkened, and then he turned away, filling Lil's tray.

"Me, too," Lil said. "Reminds me of summer." After a few minutes, she called, "Whoala. Look at this."

She'd painted two stripes on the wall with the old green color showing between.

Looking up from her painstakingly straight handiwork, Katy pointed out, "If you don't do it right, it's going to look streaked."

"You think? Okay, if you're sure stripes wouldn't be cool?"

"Crooked stripes are not cool. Neither is that green color. We both agreed on that."

"Your call. Here goes, plain turquoise wall. Love it." She glanced over at Jake. "We'll do the kitchen next, if you want to prep it."

"I can do that, but the closet needs a primer. If I do that first, it might be dry enough for you to paint before you close up the can."

Lil glanced over at Katy. "How does that sound?"

She might as well give in to the fact that with Megan having to finish a school project, Jake's help was allowing them to get more work done, even if it kept him in alarmingly close proximity. "Fine."

Jake tossed her a rakish grin, then disappeared to get the primer.

"He's behaving, don't you think?" Lil asked, her gaze hopefully skittering to Katy.

"Probably up to something."

"Just wants you to believe he's really sorry. . .for everything."

"He has done a good job with the place. Fast, too."

"And cheap."

"Cheap isn't always good," Katy quipped, thinking of the little outsider he'd dated and giving a different meaning to the word.

"In our case it is. Shush. Here he comes."

Jake trudged back through the room, sporting a gigantic grin and barely missing the upturned paint lid. Then he disappeared in the closet.

Out of sight was good, Katy thought, pulling the ladder next to the wall and balancing herself on the top rung to edge along the ceiling. "How's work?"

Lil replied, "Anybody can boil pasta and stir sauce. But it'll pay the rent. The way I figure it, I need to get a good reference and move up to a better restaurant at my first opportunity. Mark my words: I will someday be a top chef."

Katy climbed down and moved the ladder. "David wants to take me out to dinner the next time we go out. I suggested your restaurant."

"Tonight?"

"Nope. He's helping at the church today and has to help his dad do chores afterward."

"One more date, right?"

"Shh!" Katy hissed, nodding her head toward the closet. Jake appeared as if on cue, and Katy fought back a grin at the globs of paint on his hat and in his hair. His cell phone tight to his ear, he walked through the room.

"How's babysitting going?" Lil asked.

Katy's hand paused, unable to shoulder her problem alone any longer. "You're never going to believe it. Tammy tricked me into accepting tickets to the ballet."

"How'd she do that?"

Happy to vent for the next five minutes, Katy explained the details.

"I can't believe she did that, knowing how you feel about dancing," Lil muttered, wearing a mama-lion-protecting-her-cub expression—endearing to Katy that somebody was at last siding for her, and cute, too, given the turquoise freckles. Like her cousin, Lil was wearing the paint. Lil was much prettier than she realized. "It's a test." Lil pushed her hair back with her forearm and some wisps escaped from her ponytail. "She's trying to break you."

Then Katy noticed a clip had been holding her hair in place and not the ponytail rubber band. "You cut bangs!"

Lil grinned, pushed more paint into her hair. "Cute, huh?"

"Has your mom seen them?"

Laying down the roller, Lil clamped her hands on her hips, getting paint on her clothes, too. She faced Katy, directing that mother bear attitude to thwart her now. "When are you going to get it? We've the same as left home. We're adults on our own. We can do whatever we please."

Climbing down off the ladder, Katy felt a rush of fear that one more piece of life was crumbling away. "And what pleases you?" Was Lil going to go crazy wild on her?

"Cutting bangs."

"What else?"

Jake strode back into the room and, noticing the tension, drew back a step.

Katy shook her head and turned away. "I'm done here. Is the closet ready?"

"Nope, wanna help me prep the kitchen?" Honestly, she didn't know which cousin was more frustrating. She followed him into the other room, fretting that Lil was going to pull her further into the gray area or even the black.

Jake stepped close, a tape contraption in his hands. "This is a little tricky. Works like this." As he demonstrated, and they bent over the dispenser, she wanted to reach up and pluck the globs of paint from his black curls. But at least her anger at Lil was easing away. His nearness commanded all of her attention. "Wanna try it?"

"Sure." She took the contraption then mumbled sulkily, "I think you ruined your hat."

"What's a hat compared to a day spent with two lovely ladies?" Then he grinned and, referring to the dispenser, told her, "That's backward."

Katy tried to remove the tape that she now had stuck between her fingers. "Uh-oh."

"No problem." He took her hand, taking his time removing the twisted ruined tape. Their gazes locked.

"I see your hand has healed."

She jerked it away. "It's fine."

"Here, try again."

She nodded and leaned across the counter, running the contraption along the wall seam, amazed at how sweet the tape went in place when she did it correctly. Then she got a prickly sensation that he was still watching her and paused. Sure enough, his hand touched her shoulder and then rested at her waist.

"You got it."

She opened her mouth to reprimand him, but he'd already moved away. Then she heard the sound of tearing tape from across the room.

After that, it went smoothly, the dispenser gliding along seams. They worked at opposite sides of the room, and just when she'd relaxed, his voice whispered, "I miss hanging out with you, like this."

Her hand flinched. She could smell him, faint sawdust and stronger soap. She redid a crooked strip, not daring to glance at him. "Did you know I'm dating David Miller?"

There was silence, and then he replied, "I heard. Is it serious?"

118

"Now that would be personal, wouldn't it?"

"Hey, you brought it up."

"Only because I want you to back off. Give me some space here. I'm trying to tolerate you, remember?"

"Oh. Right."

—⌒⌐

Later that evening, Jake opened the back door and stepped into his mom's kitchen. His grandma Minnie sat at the table, and the sight squeezed his heart with tenderness. He strode over and placed a gentle hand on her shoulder. "Hey, Grams."

"Sit down and see what I made," she replied.

Jake dropped into a chair and pointed at the picture in a magazine the older woman was viewing. "You made that quilt?"

"Yeah. I made it for my little girl." As usual since she had developed Alzheimer's, Grams was living in her past memories, believing that Jake's mom was still her little girl.

"That's pretty. I'll bet she loves it."

"Oh, she does. But she's playing now." Then the elderly woman started to her feet. "I need to make supper before the children come in."

He glanced at his mom by the stove. "Mom wants you to enjoy your quilt. She's going to make supper for you tonight."

"She is? How thoughtful. Are you sure, dear?"

"Yes, Minnie," Jake's mom called. "Fried mush, your favorite."

"No, you were always Dad's favorite," she rebuffed. For some time, she'd been thinking that her grown daughter was her sister Martha. Usually Jake and his mom just played along. The only time her confusion really bothered him was when she mistook him for her departed husband, and Jake's grandpa, but the resemblance couldn't be denied.

He kissed her on her cheek. "I need to go change before supper."

"Hurry back. I want to show you what I made for my little girl."

"Okay, Grams. I'll be right back." He looked over at his mom, and she gave him a nod so he hustled up the steps to his room. After his shower, he speed-dialed Lil while he finished dressing.

119

"So did she say anything about me?" he asked.

"She's not talking to me about you. Except about your work. She's pleased with that."

The compliment gave him a great deal of satisfaction.

"But I can tell by the way she looks at you that she still cares. It's like she's afraid to be around you."

Jake leaned against the wall and crossed his arms. "She told me she's dating David. That she's only tolerating me. She's warming up, but too slowly. I'm almost done at the doddy house."

"There's still the building committee."

He straightened. "She's smart. And you're right about her keeping her distance. I'm scared this isn't going to work. I can't stand the thought of that Miller guy and her together."

"I have an idea. What do people do when somebody's in the hospital or there's a death in the family?"

Jake shrugged and moved to his window. "I don't know."

"Think, chump."

Jake looked down over the flat fields, clumps of snow still evident. "They send cards and take casseroles."

"Exactly. Well, you're going to take her a casserole."

"I know you think a lot about food, but that's pretty stupid."

"A good-deed casserole."

"Go on."

"She's under pressure at work. Her boss gave her tickets to take Addison to the ballet. To her this is a stressful thing. You're going to hold her hand."

"I'm taking her to the ballet?"

"Sort of. Here's the plan."

Jake listened and realized that Lil was a genius at more than cooking.

CHAPTER 13

February brought Katy a reprieve—clear skies and melting snow—with no storms on the personal front, either. Although she still had the ballet tickets tucked inside her cleaning journal, work had been uneventful. The doddy house was progressing nicely in spite of Jake's presence, and the weekly building committee meeting had been postponed.

Also David had asked her out again—date number three, which fulfilled her father's stipulation. But she wasn't a fool. A person couldn't count on a winter's reprieve to hold out much longer than a week.

Katy and David eyed each other over a plastic red rose. The cozy Italian place with its white vinyl tablecloths was the type where waiters could be heard calling out their orders and the clinking of dishes filled any break in the music, a place where David didn't look out of place in his jeans and button-down shirt.

He snapped open his menu and asked, "Know much about Italian food?"

"I know spaghetti and lasagna. Love them both." Katy relaxed in the soft black booth and cast him a smile.

"Lasagna. . .number three on the menu." He set the menu aside. "Since this is our third date, that sounds like a good fit, don't you think?"

The pulse-pounding question caught her off guard, and she peeked at him above her own menu. Was he goading her? His eyes shone with something she couldn't quite read. Straightening, she set down her menu and took a sip of her water. Only she choked. Clutching up a red napkin, she struggled not to send water spewing across the table at David. Quickly she unrolled the napkin and dumped the silverware, pressing the cloth to her face. When she finally could breathe again, she peeped at him through watering eyes. Was he goading? Or just naive?

He looked concerned. "You okay?"

"Fine."

The waiter came, and David gave him their orders. When they were alone again, he asked, "So you love lasagna? What else do you love?"

"Clean black cars," she said.

"Is that why you go out with me? Because you like my car?"

"No. I'm here because I wanted to see where Lil works." When she saw her teasing had hit its mark, she grinned. "And because you're a really nice guy."

His gaze told her he didn't believe that for a moment.

"So what do you love?" she asked him, but instantly knew what he would reply.

"Shiny black cars," they said in unison and then both laughed.

"What about farming?" she asked.

"I like driving the big machinery, but it's pretty dull in the winter. Ivan and I get along good, though. If it wasn't for him, I'd probably be doing something else by now." He studied her a moment, then ventured, "It's not the farming I like, it's the driving. You know, anything with a motor. *Brrrm-brrrm.*"

She smiled.

He leaned close, and his aftershave wafted over her, warm and inviting as his secretive hazel eyes. "I like engines. Speed. You ever go to the races?"

When he leaned back again, the scent was gone but there remained a more vivid impression of the workings of the man across the table, one that might explain the mischievous glint that often appeared in his eyes. Was it a desire for something more than the ordinary, and might that be fast cars? In her imagination, she saw David yanking his

gearshift down and racing his shiny black beast down some country road. "No. You drag race?"

"Now that would be breaking the law," he grinned. The smell of garlic, and the appearance of their salad and a basket of buttery breadsticks instantly commanded their appetite and attention.

He passed her the basket then said offhandedly, "How's the doddy house coming?"

The warm bread melted in Katy's mouth. Savoring it, then swallowing, she said, "We're moving in next weekend."

"We missed your friend Jake last Saturday at the cleanup. Was he working at your place?"

She couldn't miss the jealous tone of David's voice and felt instantly defensive. "He did help us paint last Saturday." She tried to make her tone cheerful. "And we finished that today."

A glance across the table caught David's jaw tensing. He'd always been so kind and attentive that she found his resentful behavior unsettling. In fact, he was ruining her appetite. She dangled a fork. "You still want to help us move in?" She pushed her salad, hoping he would redeem himself.

"Yeah, maybe we can make a contest of it."

She pushed her plate aside, no longer able to disregard his barbed comments. He was obviously ticked at her. "What do you mean?"

"See who can carry the most boxes. Me or Jake."

Her face burned. "That would be fun." She slid out of the booth. "You'll excuse me a minute?"

"Sure." He ran a hand through his hair.

Katy slapped her napkin on the table and headed for the restroom, but just as she rounded the corner, Lil appeared, slightly breathless and her face slick with moisture. Her hair was plastered into a smooth brown knot with a hair net securing it, and her newly cut bangs were bobby-pinned. She wiped her hands on a long white apron that protected her white blouse and black skirt uniform. "I wanted to come out sooner, but I couldn't get away."

"Great place." Katy shouldered open the door to the restroom.

Lil followed her. "Hey, what's wrong?"

"Oh, David. He's acting weird tonight." Katy didn't miss the little light that danced in Lil's eyes. "I guess you're happy about that."

Lifting both hands in the air, Lil objected, "Whoa. Don't get me involved in your lovers' spat."

"I'm sorry. This really is a great place. We ordered lasagna. Did you make it?"

"Cooked the noodles and stirred the sauce." She put her hand on Katy's shoulder. "Look. Everything's going as planned. Don't lose sleep over David. If he blows it now, at least you had your three dates. And he had his chance."

"I'm so sick of hearing about *three* dates. One more time and my head's going to explode. I think I'm just going to go back out there and tell him the truth."

"Fine, except please taste the lasagna first. Tell me my noodles are perfecto and not sticky."

Grinning, Katy said, "Okay. And I mean it. I really do love this place. We've got to bring Megan sometime on your night off."

"It's kind of a dead-end job. But it's fun. Did you see how cute the waiters are?" Lil went to the sink and washed her hands, then hit the electronic dryer, raising her voice over the blowing air. "I'll call later."

"No, it'll wake up the household."

The blower shut off, and Lil left.

Katy washed her hands and caught the image of her brooding eyes in the mirror. She fiddled with her covering, wishing she'd brought her purse to the restroom so that she could refresh her lipstick, the only makeup she ever wore. Then it hit her. Lil hadn't had her prayer covering on. She bit her lip. That didn't surprise her much.

When she felt like she could face David's interrogation again, she left and returned to her booth, relieved to see that their meals had arrived. As if they weren't in the middle of a spat, she slid into her seat and took up her fork. "Looks good."

David reached across the table and touched her hand. "I'm sorry for making you mad."

She nodded, avoiding the impulse to shy away from his touch. It was warm and assuring, and her anger melted away. "I wasn't back there sulking. I met Lil in the restroom."

He drew his hand away with a nod. Then he tasted the mild, creamy dish, studying her. "Mm, good. She make it?"

Grinning, Katy said, "She boiled the noodles. And she wants our opinion on their consistency."

He grinned back, holding her gaze until she blushed. The rest of the meal, he reined in his jealousy, and afterward, they even lingered over coffee. She was relaxed, enjoying herself, when abruptly, he started in again. "So what happens after date three? You going to go out with me again?"

He hit the nerve dead-on, jarring her out of her complacency. The dreaded question now hung in the air between them. She tensed. If she didn't go with him again, then she was a user. After her second date, she had already known that she was not romantically interested in him. Her hands clasped her cup, its soothing warmth her only bit of comfort. "Why do you keep bringing up date three?"

"I think you know why. I was allotted three dates to prove myself."

Holding back a moan because her nightmare had come true—he was aware of her despicable behavior—she asked softly, shamefully, "How long have you known?"

His clipped response barely contained his anger. "Before date one."

She sighed, placing her hands on her lap. "So you've been playing me." Her anger suddenly flared, too. Just like everybody else in her life, he'd been manipulating her. She looked at him through the blur of pain-filled eyes. "Why?"

"I wanted to follow the course. See where it led. Are you a user, Katy? Using Jake, too? To get the doddy house fixed up cheap?"

Katy folded her napkin and placed it neatly on the table in front of her. "You figure it out. I'm ready to go now."

David didn't make any moves to leave the restaurant. He had more to say. "Ivan told me about the deal he made with your dad. I'd hoped that after the first date, you'd go with me because you liked me, not because you were using me. I hoped you'd tell me the truth."

"What I told you before is still true. I never intended to look for a guy, but I like you, and I was willing to get to know you. I opened myself to the possibility of falling for you."

"A win-win situation for you, wasn't it? So back to my question. What did you decide? Is there going to be a date four, or are you finished with me?"

"Wow, you are so romantic. So persuasive." She reached for her purse. "Probably not, David."

He took care of the check, and drew his lips in a tight line. "Let's go."

The car ride was dreadful and quiet, except for a country song on his radio about some forlorn man who'd just been dumped by his girl. From the sounds of it, Katy figured the guy in the song deserved it. There was a hint of smoke in the air, emanating from the jacket that David had loaned her the night of the fire. She had returned it earlier, and it now was on the backseat of his car, reminding her of his heroics the night of the fire, heaping more coals to her shame.

When they pulled into her drive, he spoke again. "I guess I could have gone along with the game, but my pride wouldn't allow it any longer. One of us needed to address the issue. Make a new start if there's ever to be a date four. Something real to go on, you know?"

She nodded. "It's been wearing on me, too. I'm sorry for using you. Although you did use the situation to your advantage, too."

"Guess I was willing to settle for scraps."

She gave him a weak grin.

He said, "A promise is a promise. I'll help you move in next Saturday."

"No, please. You don't need to."

"You want to get rid of me?"

"No. I—"

"Good. There probably will be a contest between me and construction cowboy. After all, it's almost Valentine's Day."

"Cowboy?"

"His holster. The tool bags."

She guessed she wasn't the only one who'd noticed Jake wore his pants too tight, and his tool bags only added to his attractiveness. But what had David meant about Valentine's Day? Was he still going to pursue her? The idea of date four had been left hanging. She felt confused but remained quiet.

He walked her to the door, drew her close, and kissed her forehead. Then he tilted her chin up and kissed her mouth, slow and sensual, but he broke it off abruptly. She hadn't wanted to kiss him at all, but she hadn't wanted to humiliate him further by rejecting him. The kiss was calculated, the kiss of a bitter man.

With a sigh, she watched him go, sorry she'd hurt him. She stepped inside the dark interior of the house.

"Do you love him?" came a startling voice out of the darkness.

Katy clasped her heart. "Karen! Don't scare me like that. Why are you still up?"

"To answer the phone. It was Lil." Karen offered, pulling back the curtain and looking outside. "I told her you weren't home yet, and she didn't seem happy."

Katy pushed her sister's hand away from the curtain. Hadn't she told Lil not to call? Maybe she hadn't heard her above the din of the hand dryer.

"So do you?" Karen repeated.

"No. Why are you standing in the dark?"

"I—"

"Were you spying on me?"

"I—"

Suddenly Katy thought better of having this conversation so near their parents' bedroom door. "Come upstairs."

"If you don't love him, then why were you kissing him?" Karen whispered before they'd even reached the landing.

CHAPTER 14

O n moving day, ominous purple clouds swallowed the sky. Everyone involved in the move met at the Landis farm, where the furniture was stored in the barn. Katy's car was packed to the roof with clothes, and the rest of its interior resembled a bag of puzzle pieces vying for space. Her new upright vacuum cleaner rode shotgun, and stacks of bedding filled the seats. She crawled out, careful that everything remained wedged in place, and eyed Megan. "I can't believe that leather couch your mom found at a garage sale. What can we do to thank her?"

"Just let her come see the place sometime."

Lil strode away from the place where David and Jake were loading furniture and joined Katy and Megan.

"Maybe we should have a parents' night and make dessert or something," Katy suggested.

"Nah!" They all protested, giggling and then shivering when a fierce gust whipped through the yard. It forced the girls into a huddle then rolled on across the farm's barren fields.

Katy straightened her covering, watching the swirling snow and debris. "Wow, glad my car door wasn't open."

"Careful," Jake yelled.

Looking over to see if the warning was for them, Katy saw Jake nod at David to move slightly to the right as they maneuvered a table onto the bed of his truck. Jake must have felt her gaze, because he glanced over. "We've almost got it, if you girls want to go on over and meet us at the doddy house in a few minutes?"

The scene drew her curiosity, Jake and David working together. Jake winked and brushed his gloves before heading back to the barn. David trailed behind. When he saw that Katy was watching them, he made sport of Jake by mimicking his walk for a few strides, probably to get even for Jake's ordering him around like a hired lackey.

As if David didn't know how to keep things nice, she thought, having always admired that part of his personality. But so far, the two were at least remaining civil enough with each other to have packed their first load of furniture. Katy dismissed their antics and looked back at Lil, thinking about the day's work. "It was great of Jake to take the appliances over earlier this week."

"I love that stainless steel GE stove." Lil did the garbanzo shimmy.

Katy didn't know the difference between a GE or a Viking, but as long as they had sparkling drip pans and working ovens to cook Lil's mouthwatering dishes, they suited her. Grinning at Lil's enthusiasm, she started toward her car. "See you over there."

When everybody reached the doddy house, the unending trips to the cars began. Katy started with the boxes in her trunk—kitchen and household odds and ends her mom had donated—and was sweating by the time she had to struggle with the piles of clothing still on their hangers. Nearly colliding with Megan on the path of freshly laid plastic floor covering—her genius idea—she cried out, "Look out, green bean, or I'll squish ya."

Megan's arms had just been emptied, and she pointed. "Here come the beds."

Every time the guys appeared, Lil became the moving director, which was fine with Katy because Lil had an eye for furniture placement. In this case, Lil's job was easy because the girls had already imagined and reimagined it together many times.

"Last load," David informed her, setting some long pieces of bed

129

support at his feet so that he could take a break. "Feeling pretty excited, huh?"

Jake tried to pass them while balancing similar bed braces on his shoulder. With an irritated huff, he said, "Blocking the way, guys, for us working fellows."

Ignoring him, David smiled at her. "I'll put the beds together next."

"Great."

Just then Jake reappeared. "I'll help you unload your car if you want."

Glancing uneasily at David, she told Jake, "Sure, my sweeper's out there yet and one box in the trunk that was too heavy for me."

"Done."

"Show me which bed's yours," David said, vying for her attention. "Want to help hold the rails in place while I fasten them together?"

"Sure."

After following him into the bedroom and hanging up their coats in the closet, she pointed at a white headboard. "Start with that one. My dad made it. And my little brothers painted it." She'd always admired the white iron set Mrs. Beverly had in her guest room. She tried to get a similar look using wood. Excitement bubbled up inside her that her dream was coming true. But she covered it by saying, "Guess they were eager to get me out of the house."

"I doubt that." She did, too. In fact, the parting with her family after breakfast had been emotional and had left Katy, her mom, and Karen all teary-eyed. David set the frame in place. "Okay, hold that piece."

She knelt next to her hope chest on the warm, restored-wood flooring and involuntarily smoothed her gray skirt around her. To dispel the intimacy of the situation, she blurted out, "You know how to use that tool?"

Working the screwdriver, David grunted, "I've worked on a lot of farm equipment."

"You like fixing stuff? Working on equipment?"

"Nope, like driving—"

"Fast cars," she finished for him just as Jake strode into the room and witnessed the flash of familiarity and ensuing laughter that passed between her and David. She glanced up at Jake's face, and his disapproving sneer pierced her with shame. But a flash of anger quickly followed her guilt, because it was Lil who'd asked Jake to help them move, or maybe he'd volunteered. Either way, if Jake and David hadn't helped, their dads could easily have done the work. She didn't need to *use* them. The remembrance of David's accusation from the night at the restaurant made her eager to finish with the bed assembly.

With her free hand, Katy tugged Jake's sleeve. "Hey, can you hold this for David?" As soon as she touched him, an awareness of his masculinity surfaced old memories and emotions. "I'm going to go help the girls organize the kitchen," she mumbled, backing into her hope chest.

"Don't you think Lil will want to do that?" Jake protested, as he reluctantly replaced her hold on the sideboard.

No ready reply came to her mind so she just fled the room. Let them glare at each other. She bit her lower lip, knowing Jake wouldn't appreciate serving as David's helper. Thankfully, the moment she stepped into the kitchen where Lil and Megan were unloading boxes, the atmosphere lightened.

"We have food, too?" Katy couldn't believe how much their parents had chipped in to make their empty doddy house a real home.

"We'll need some groceries, but we won't starve, either." Lil lifted a small carton. "There's cocoa mix and popcorn, here. The guys have been working hard all day. Should we bust some out?"

"Let's unpack that last box first," Katy replied. "Maybe then the boys will be done with the beds. Gotta make sure we got a place to sleep tonight." *Using them again? They volunteered,* she snapped back at her conscience.

"We can always sleep on mattresses." Lil turned to Megan. "And you have to stay over our first night."

"You sure? I didn't bring any bedding."

Lil gave Megan a playful shoulder bump. "We'll squeeze you in."

"Awesome."

Katy glanced fondly at Megan. Guess Tyler wasn't the only one who used that word. It must be common at the college.

Megan flipped through the microwave's instruction manual, and by the time the last box was unpacked, she had it figured out and was explaining the workings to Katy, who gave Lil the joy of operating the cookstove first.

"I smell popcorn." Jake's thick Dutch accent preceded him and David into the kitchen.

"Sit and enjoy our first meal," Katy motioned toward the drop-leaf table by the window. The boys and Megan settled in, allowing Lil and Katy to serve them. Katy passed out small wooden bowls, old ones that had been made on her father's lathe, then took a chair between Jake and Megan.

When Lil was finished serving, and there weren't enough chairs for everyone to sit around the table, David jumped up and offered, "Sit here."

"Katy can sit on my lap," Jake urged, reaching over and tugging her sleeve.

"Stop it," she hissed, jerking her arm away and glancing up at David, who was acting the gentleman. His expression, however, had darkened.

Lil solved the problem by plopping uninvited on Jake's left knee. "Thanks, chump."

He grinned, supporting her with a hand at her waist, and David slid back into his seat by the window. He glanced out under the dark green, Amish-style window shade. "It's snowing. A storm's been brewing all day. But I'm in no hurry to go. I can always stay over at Ivan's. 'Fraid you girls are going to have to get used to looking at my ugly face. I'm at Ivan's a lot."

Sensing the silent tension coming from Lil and Jake's chair, Katy dipped her smaller bowl into the larger, then offered, "More popcorn, anyone?"

Lil jumped up, "I'll put on more water."

Jake tipped back his chair and stretched his arms lazily. "Let it storm. I'm too tired to move. You gals are slave drivers. I'm ready to hibernate for at least a month. The living room floor will do fine. I'll just roll up in that rug over there and be snug as a bear."

Noticing with worry that the snow really was blanketing the ground, Katy said, "Oh no, you don't. We won't be getting any of that started here."

"Well, you're letting him hang out," Jake lowered his arms, and his chair snapped back to the floor. "And I'm family."

"Your truck too wimpy to plow through a few snowdrifts?" David baited.

"Yeah, pretty wimpy. Maybe in the morning when you go out to do your daily car washing, you can start my puny engine for me. You know, warm it up."

He sneered at Jake. "Puny like its owner?"

"I worked circles around you today, and—"

Katy stood. "Stop it. Both of you."

Megan snatched the empty popcorn bowl from the table and placed her hand on Jake's shoulder. "I'm sure you guys both know that we won't be having either of you stay over. But we can't thank you enough for all your help today." She speared Katy with a warning look.

"Megan's right. We do appreciate your hard work today, but you guys need to quit the bickering. As far as I'm concerned, it's juvenile."

Lil flicked a dish towel at Jake's chest. "Hey, juvie, I'll wash. You dry."

Katy rolled her gaze heavenward. So much for herding the guys out. She could tell Lil was giving Jake an excuse to be the last male to leave. Doing her part to get them both out the door, Katy started toward the bedroom for David's coat. With frustration, she heard him clomping down the hall behind her. He followed her all the way into the walk-in closet.

"I'm not leaving before he does."

She flicked on the light and wheeled to face him.

"I don't trust him." David abruptly pulled her close.

She wiggled free and placed a hand on his chest to separate them. "Stop it."

The golden star in his eyes flickered. "Why?"

She shrugged completely out of his embrace and looked at the floor, rubbing her palms over her arms. "Because we're not—"

"I'm sorry," he interrupted. "It's just that jerk out there acting like he owns you."

"Forget about him."

David's shoulders relaxed, and he nodded.

She saw that as a good sign but wanted to make sure he wasn't getting the wrong idea. "I don't want you to get your hopes up." She hurried on before he could interrupt again. "I'm not looking for a relationship with either of you. Otherwise, I wouldn't have moved in here."

David rubbed his chin, studying her.

"Katy?" Lil strode into the bedroom and stuck her head in the closet. "Oh whoa." She quickly exited.

Katy whipped David's coat off its hanger and flung it at him, scurrying after Lil. "Just getting David's coat."

In the few moments she'd spent in the closet, the house had grown darker. She snapped on a light in the living room. "Thanks again for helping," she told him.

David shuffled to the entry. "See you girls at church tomorrow?"

Katy opened the door and peered out. "As long as we're not snowed in."

"And if we can find an alarm clock," Megan added.

Jake pulled on his coat. "Use your phone." He glanced down the hall where Katy and David had just emerged, then looked at Katy. "We have an extra coatrack I think my mom will donate. I'll bring it over."

She blushed at his insinuating observation.

"Thanks again, guys." Megan waved as they departed.

Just before she closed the door, Katy thought she overheard David challenging Jake to a race. Surely not on these slippery roads? Nah, impossible. Even for those juveniles. She leaned against the door, only rousing from her thoughts when Megan asked, "Wanna make up the beds?"

That night they used Lil's extra set of pale blue flannel sheets for Megan's top bunk, and Katy loaned her a hand-sewn comforter. She snuggled under white crisp sheets and turned on her side to face the bunk bed, a night-light softly illuminating the room.

"Can't believe you sleep with a night-light," Lil teased.

"Don't want Megan falling out of bed," Katy shot back.

Lil looked overhead. "This reminds me of summer camp that first year. Remember?"

Feeling a lump in her throat, Katy murmured, "How could we forget?"

"And this is just the beginning," Lil purred.

But caution ruffled Katy's already exhausted nerves. For so long, they had pushed for this day, for the big prize. It seemed strange to think of it as a mountaintop where they would step off into the unknown. Lil's normal walk—on the Conservative Mennonite edge—filled Katy's spirit with uncertainty. She was tired. Tired of fighting Lil's outlandish whims. They were adults. Living on their own. Would it backfire if she gave in and just allowed Lil to be Lil?

"You think David's gonna keep hanging around?" Lil asked.

"Probably some. Like he said, he's over at Ivan's a lot. I hope Jake doesn't think this is a place for *him* to hang out."

Megan asked, "You going out with him again?"

"Jake? No way."

"No, David."

"Not him, either. I pretty much told him so tonight." Then Katy thought about how her sister had caught them kissing. Though Karen's curiosity had been mostly about boy stuff, it had been a sticky situation. The kind of circumstance a Conservative girl shouldn't be caught in. She needed to set things right. Maybe living in the doddy house could be her new beginning, to be a better person. One who didn't get pulled into the outsiders' world. Lil could be Lil, and she would be the Katy she had always wanted to be. Better than before.

"That what you were doing in the closet?" Lil mocked.

"Pretty much. That and fending him off."

"You should send your scraps my way," Megan complained between allergy sniffles. "Better yet, how about I set you up with a guy in my Bible class?"

"No thanks. I'm going to go solo for a while. Enjoy my freedom."

"That'a girl." Lil handed a tissue up to Megan. "Me, too. Unless that cute waiter with blond hair asks me out."

Giggling, Katy warned, "Better get your beauty sleep then." Nobody but Lil would entertain thoughts of dating an outsider.

CHAPTER 15

The next morning, to Katy's delight, the wind had pushed the storm out of Madison County, and Ivan was able to dig out the drive in time for the girls to attend church. Afterward, Lil made them spaghetti, complaining about using store-bought tomato sauce. It was a given that Lil would cook and Katy clean, although she hadn't envisioned herself hand-carrying all of Lil's empty diet soda cans to the recycling receptacle that Megan had supplied them. And she hadn't decided what to do yet about Lil's unmade bed.

In the afternoon, Megan headed back to her Rosedale dorm, leaving Katy and Lil to experience their first taste of what normalcy at the doddy house might resemble. When the day wound down, they tossed bed pillows in the middle of their tan leather couch, lying head to head with their legs slung over opposite armrests, and allowed the wonder of the moment to settle over them.

"We need throw pillows," Katy remarked, leery of placing her pillowcase on a secondhand couch.

"We need more furniture."

"Maybe we need to invite Anita Weaver over so that she can take pity on us and find us a couple of armchairs, too." Worrying her lip,

Katy mumbled, "I'm such a user."

"Why? Just because you have chapped hands?"

"What?" With a giggle, Katy waved her gloved hands above their faces and corrected, "Not loser. U–ser." She had smeared a home remedy on them, something she did a couple times a week, sometimes sleeping in the goo. It had become an ongoing experiment, trying to find the perfect combinations of ingredients to rectify her occupational damage. She stared at the white gloves, one of several pairs.

"There's so many things I want." Lil sighed. "A new car, a computer."

"Computer!"

"Well, yeah. Someday."

Katy pinched the bridge of her nose. "What else?"

Lil suddenly sat up. "I think I'll make a list in the back of my journal. Anyway, I learned that marjoram adds more flavor to pasta than oregano. And I need to jot down a penne recipe before I forget it."

"Under computer, you can write. . .new roommate."

"Ha, ha, very funny. You want me to bring you anything?"

Katy kept a journal of cleaning tips, but she wasn't in the mood to think about work or which hand-cream concoction worked best. "Grab one of those inspirational novels for me. I have a stack on a shelf in the closet."

"The same closet where you were kissing the moving guy?"

"Stop."

"So when's your next building meeting?" Lil taunted, skipping off before Katy could throttle her.

─────❦─────

The meeting was held in the sanctuary again, and Katy passed by the lobby's bulletin board to stare at her unfruitful advertisement. As much good as it had done, she might as well take it down. Yet there was always that distant chance. . .

"Still no job?"

Startled, Katy looked over her shoulder to find Jake standing behind her. "Lil told you I was looking for work?"

He stuffed his hands in his pockets. "Yeah, I'm looking, too. I'll

137

need something after the fellowship hall is done."

Katy moved to find a seat for the meeting. Jake slid into the pew beside her.

"Must you sit so close?" she asked, shrugging her shoulder away from him.

"Mm-hm."

She glanced at the meetinghouse's plain spackled ceiling and back.

The painter settled in on Jake's other side pinning him in place, and Jake grinned.

"You're impossible."

"That often goes hand in hand with juvenile behavior."

She remembered calling him juvenile the day of the move. Was that his subtle way of reminding her that she owed him? "Yes, it does."

Leaning against her—so that she nearly fell off the end of the pew trying to avoid his touch, not to mention his soap and sawdust scent—he dug something out of his tight jeans pocket and flipped it onto her lap.

"Maybe this will make up for it."

She pushed away something that resembled a pair of tickets. "Whatever you're up to, no thanks."

"Come on. They're ballet tickets."

"What!" She snatched them back and stared, her gaze so smoldering it could have turned the offering to ashes. Two tickets to *Cinderella*? Slapping them back at him, she narrowed her eyes into stormy slits. "How did you get these?"

He shrugged. "At a ticket office." When she continued to gawk in disbelief, he added, "At the mall."

The painter leaned forward and stared, too, and to her further aggravation, she noticed they were attracting a small audience. Why did Mr. Weaver have to be late this night, of all times?

"How did you know?" she hissed.

"I'm not uncultured. I thought you might actually enjoy it."

"A kid's ballet?"

"It is?"

She glared at him, not fooled by his feigned act of innocence. "No thanks."

He gave her a lopsided smile and winked. "Let me know if you change your mind."

Bill Weaver, breathless from running into the meetinghouse, strode down the aisle and took his place in the front of the sanctuary. He quickly called the meeting to order. But other than recognizing the welcome distraction of his opening words, Katy became oblivious to the proceedings of the meeting.

The tickets to the same performance couldn't be a coincidence, and the only way he could know she was going to that ballet was through Lil. But why a pair of tickets when she obviously already had hers? Just to keep up the pretense? Why would he think she'd want him along at an already-dreaded event? As the evening wore on, she mulled over the details and poked it from every angle.

Slowly, Lil's part in the incident became glaringly clear. She recalled that Lil hadn't wanted her to date David from the beginning. Because she wanted her to date Jake instead. Lil must have warned Jake about David, and that's why he came to the skating party. Katy's mind rushed on, working out the scenario. That night at the skating party, Lil had been acting cranky. She'd called someone on her cell phone, too. Then she had hired Jake to remodel the doddy house. Katy widened her eyes in further revelation. And Lil had talked Katy into serving on this committee. And just the other night on the couch, Lil had teased her by asking when her next committee meeting was. What a conniving little matchmaker.

"Katy?" Bill Weaver asked.

She felt Jake's elbow in her ribs. "Huh?"

"You look like something troubles you. You don't agree with the size of the storage room?" All gazes turned toward her, eyebrows raised in expectancy.

"No. I mean, yes, I agree," she fumbled, feeling her cheeks heat. Lil was going to pay.

That night after the meeting, Katy waited up for Lil to come home from work. She rehearsed her angry speech as she emptied the trash, the night air nipping her flushed cheeks. She scrubbed toilets and scoured sinks and wrote furiously in her journal about removing unwanted scents from clothing. And when Lil's clunker coughed into the yard, Katy was ready for her, standing five feet from the entry, legs planted and fists on her hips.

The door opened and Lil halted. "Whoa."

"I can't believe you," Katy ground out.

"What? You didn't have to wait up. I'm exhausted. I had to stay and close."

"You told Jake about the ballet," Katy accused.

Flinging her purse on the table, Lil shrugged. "You didn't tell me it was a secret. I only wanted to help."

Katy followed her to the table. "You think I want the whole church to know that I'm participating in a dancing event?"

Shrugging out of her coat and dropping it over the back of a chair, Lil said dryly, "Where's Megan when we need her?"

"This isn't funny. I figured out your matchmaking schemes."

Lil leaned wearily against a chair. "So that makes me a terrible person?"

"Just the other day when you cut your bangs, you told me that we were adults. So why are you trying to run my life for me? Did you ever stop to think that I might like to be treated like an adult, too?"

Lil shot both hands in the air. "Look. Can we discuss this tomorrow after you've cooled down? Like I said, I'm really tired. I just want to go to bed."

"I'm tired, too. Tired of you interfering with my life. You're always trying to change me. I'm sick of it, and I don't think this"—she flung her arms in the air, gesturing at the room—"is going to work out. Us living together."

Lil froze. Her freckles paled. Then she became angry, too. "You don't get it. Jake is like a brother to me. He loves you. If you weren't so stubborn, you'd admit that you love him, too. Because of your pigheadedness, I have to help you guys along."

"You can't decide what's right or wrong for me. Even God gives people free wills."

Lil's eyebrow arched. "Don't go bringing God into this. As if He's on your side. As if I'm not a Christian. You're always doing that for me with your goody-goody attitude. But look at you yelling. What happened to your Mennonite upbringing now? Ever hear of nonresistance?"

"And do Conservative girls go around without wearing their coverings?"

Lil's hand went to her head, then slid back to her side. She raised her chin. "At least I don't pretend I'm something I'm not."

"No you don't," Katy whispered.

"But you do." Lil snatched her coat and purse and flung open the door.

"I do not."

Lil shook her head, then strode out and slammed the door behind her. Shocked, Katy stared at the rattling door. She heard the engine of Lil's car cough to life and then sputter off the property. Katy flicked the dead bolt with such force it popped back open. She slid it the second time, more deliberately, into the locked position. Good riddance.

She marched to the couch, plopped down, and stared at the floor, virtually panting with outrage. What did Lil mean about pretending? She was serious about living a holy life. Sure she fell short, but she didn't pretend.

With crossed arms, she went over their argument, even embellishing it with what she should have said but hadn't. But as much as she tried to justify herself and her anger, Lil's barbs kept darting back. Especially the idea that Katy wasn't honest or real.

Slowly, she came to realize that Lil hadn't been referring to her actions, but her feelings. And specifically her feelings toward Jake. As much as she tried to cover her pining for him, Lil had easily read her. As Katy sat with clenched hands, she allowed the enormity of what had just transpired to flood over her.

Had she really shouted that living together wasn't going to work? Where had that come from? Some hidden fear? She hadn't planned to say any such thing. She thought about all the hateful things that had spewed from her mouth like an uncontrollable and unrecognizable force. She couldn't erase the image of Lil's shocked, pale face.

She sat for a very long time in her desperation. The timbers of the old house began to creak. She felt alone. And just as that angry force had come unbidden earlier, so did another intruder. Fear. She'd known this enemy all her life, the fear of darkness.

Katy heard another bump, and jerked her glance over her shoulder. Though it was the wee hours of the morning, she would never be able to sleep if she went to bed. Miserable, she rose and put a kettle of water on the stove. Lil's stove. She waited for the whistle, blinking back her tears. When the tea was ready, she flicked off the kitchen lights and hurried through the dark hall to the bedroom. The thought shot through her mind that something invisible followed her, but she didn't look back. Heart racing, she shut her bedroom door. The house became a silent, lurking monster that she tried to ignore.

She flicked on her bedside lamp and set her tea on the nightstand. She pulled the drapes and tamped back her panic. Sitting on the edge of her bed, she removed the pins from her covering and placed them on her nightstand. Lil's messy bedcovers flagged her attention, and she couldn't look away.

Calmly she padded across the floor and made Lil's bed. When the last wrinkle was smoothed away, she sat on her own bed again and sipped her tea. What would happen to the doddy-house dream now? She hadn't considered Megan's feelings at all.

Eerie shadows danced in the closet. Strange house noises emphasized her loneliness. Would she have to slink home and admit to her dad she wasn't ready to live on her own?

CHAPTER 16

The next morning upon awakening, Katy groaned and pulled the twisted bedcovers over her tangled locks and bleary eyes, trying to dispel her fragmented dreams and the reality of the mess she'd created. During the night, she'd not only dreamed but woken to fits of unreasonable panic over every creak and moan of the doddy's ancient timbers. Though daylight brought relief in that respect, the promise of future terrifying nights stole from the welcome respite.

Lonely and somewhat isolated, the doddy house was located down a long lane on a rural road, yet received a fair amount of morning work traffic with men gunning their trucks to punch in their time card at Ranco Incorporated or yellow school buses screeching their brakes and picking up students. Most of this noise passed unnoticed by Katy, but one clunker didn't, causing her to throw off her covers at its faintest din before it even rumbled into the Millers' drive.

Thank You, God! She hit the bare floorboards running and fumbled with the dead bolt. She swiped a matted clump of hair from her face, the entire black bramble bush tumbling over her shoulders and tickling her waist. She peered through the frosty window, quickly rubbing a visible circle with her palm. Sure enough, there was Lil stepping out of her Blazer. She had her head bowed and her coat pulled tight. Lil walked toward the doddy house!

Every nerve at alert, Katy turned to face the entryway, waiting for Lil just as she had the previous evening, only her emotions came from a different place now. The door cracked open, and Lil stepped inside with the widening eyes of a burglar caught in the act of breaking and entering. Eerie quiet filled the room with only the memory of bitter words crackling between them.

"Lil," Katy finally managed, unable to form redemptive words with healing power but stupidly muttering the obvious. If she couldn't think how to patch matters up, then she feared to say anything. Had Lil returned to pack her bags or to win another of a long string of arguments that had transpired over the course of their friendship? Katy hoped her friend stood there because the doddy house was their home.

"You're back?" Katy finally asked.

Nodding, Lil blurted out, "I was wrong. I'm sorry."

Overcome with relief, Katy cried, "I didn't mean to push you away. I've been miserable. I had a terrible night."

They flew into each other's embrace and awkwardly swiped at burning eyes. When they drew apart, Lil sniffed the air. "What? No coffee?"

Katy sucked in her bottom lip; her attire, a cotton nightgown that hung to her ankles, vouched for her when she protested, "I just got up. I was in bed with the covers over my head."

Lil gave her a gloating smile. "I forgot you did that."

"I didn't think I did anymore."

"I just got up, too." Lil flung off her coat, still dressed in yesterday's clothes, and started toward the coffeepot.

"We need hooks or something for our coats," Katy mumbled, taking cups from the cupboard. Then she remembered Jake was bringing them a coatrack.

"I got up early 'cause I didn't want to have to explain to my mom why I spent the night. She doesn't need something else to worry about. Anyway, I felt childish afterward."

Katy waited until they stared repentantly at each other over steaming mugs before she ventured upon the delicate subject. "I'm sorry I yelled at you last night. I've been stuffing my feelings." Remembering Lil's accusations, she owned up to her actions with as much honesty as possible. "I just couldn't handle another disappointment. I felt betrayed. But I don't know where all that came from. The terrible things I said."

"I'm sorry you didn't feel like you could confide in me. I called Jake last night."

Conflicting emotions gnawed Katy's insides, fearing to talk about him because a part of her still didn't trust the cousins' intimacy, yet knowing that the problem wouldn't get settled until everything was exposed. At work, she'd never dream of sweeping dirt under a rug, yet lately she'd done that with her emotions. It had resulted in an angry explosion. She didn't want that to happen again.

"I told him I was wrong to get involved. That I didn't want it to ruin my friendship with you. That I loved you both, but I wouldn't be doing any more matchmaking. That he's on his own." Lil held Katy's gaze. "I mean it. I won't interfere again. I want you to know I only did it because I love you both. But I see now I was wrong to stick my nose in where it didn't belong. Like you said, you're an adult."

With a warm smile, Katy acknowledged what this must have cost her take-charge friend. "Thanks."

Lil nodded and quietly drank coffee.

With her anger completely dissolved, Katy thought about Lil's use of the word *matchmaking* and couldn't help but wonder who had initiated that idea, Lil or Jake? Katy's rebellious heart hoped it had been him, but she couldn't be sure because the cousins had similar personalities. It shouldn't matter because the point she was trying to make was that she wasn't going to take him back, regardless. That she was mad about the matchmaking. Yet the question niggled her curiosity.

"What?" Lil asked, peering over her cup and then setting it down.

"Oh, it doesn't matter. But whose idea was it to begin with?"

A sudden glint lit Lil's eyes. "The ballet tickets?"

Katy thumbed small circles on her mug. "I know that came from you. But you know"—her neck heated—"the matchmaking part?"

"Jake came to me. He asked how to win you back. I knew how

much you'd grieved over your broken relationship. I just wanted you both to have a happily-ever-after."

Fighting back unwelcome tears, Katy softly asked, "What if I can't be happy with damaged goods?"

Lil didn't blink at the embarrassing question that had haunted Katy ever since she had heard about Jake's fling with an outsider. "You don't know *that* happened."

Katy raised her chin. "Do you know if it did?"

"No." Lil spit the word out as if it tasted bitter in her mouth. "Guys don't talk about that kind of stuff to girls."

"Exactly." Feeling a mounting resolve that she had every right to brood over the question, she asked, "Don't you think I'd always wonder about him and that other girl?"

"Jessie."

Katy's jaw dropped.

Lil shrugged. "Her name is Jessie, and she's probably not as awful as you picture her."

"If they'd only dated, it would be one thing, but Jake and Jessie went to drunken parties, and I'm thinking"—Katy's lip began to quiver, but she couldn't quit until she'd exposed her imaginations—"she probably went to bed with him." Afterward, she stared at her cup, unable to look Lil in the eyes.

But Lil's voice was soft and sympathetic. "Maybe that's something you should ask Jake. It might change things if you learned the truth."

Swiping a hand across her eyes, Katy protested. "I can't."

"Do you want me to ask him?"

"No!"

"Even if your future depends upon it?"

Katy stared at her, wondering if it would be better to know. If he had kept himself pure, it would make a difference. She opened her mouth to ask Lil if she would do that for her when Lil suddenly waved her hand through the air, as if to erase the offer.

"Sorry. I'm overstepping my bounds again. I promised not to interfere. Let's forget about Jake for a moment. I did a lot of thinking last night. What you said about him being damaged goods, sometimes it feels like you lump me in the same dough as Jake, thinking I'm wild and don't have any scruples. Like I'm not a Christian." Her voice broke. "Like. . .I'm no good."

Hot shame rushed over Katy's face. Lil had never allowed such vulnerability to surface before. "Oh Lil. That's not true," she denied. "I love you."

Lil raised her hand again. "Let me finish. I pride myself on being an open book. What you see is what you get. But here's the thing. I hate being different from everybody else."

Leaning forward, Katy softly probed, "You mean the outsiders?"

"Yeah, everybody." Lil's gaze pleaded for understanding. "I don't like being plain or weird, having people whisper about me when I walk into a room. I don't like being told how to act or how to look by sour-faced men, either." Katy had to swallow her gasp when Lil alluded to the elders, including her own dad, with such disdain. "For once, I'd like to be noticed in a good way. The church discourages dressing in the latest fashions and frowns on focusing on outward beauty. That's why I've just got to be a good chef. I can make food beautiful. There's no sin in that, is there? Jesus made wine out of water. I just want people to respect me. Can you understand that?"

She met Lil's earnest gaze and felt her pain. "Yes. I don't like being different, either. Mostly, I just want to be invisible. Like when I took Addison to her dance class and stepped into a room of glamorous women in jeans with glittery belts. I wanted to disappear through the floorboards. Not to stand out like some oddball. But I swallowed my pride and told myself that following Christ is not an easy thing."

"But we're not supposed to be invisible. We're supposed to let our lights shine."

"Well, the light of God," Katy corrected. At Lil's crestfallen expression, Katy wished she'd refrained.

They both grew contemplative, and the ticking of the wall clock that Lil's mom donated to the doddy house reminded Katy that soon she would need to get ready for work. "I think we both try to express our true selves through our work. I'm thankful we have that."

"Yeah, I obsess about food, and you go around picking up after everybody. What's that say about us?"

Katy shrugged. "That we're weird?"

Lil giggled. "Too bad Megan's not here to get in on this deep stuff. It's right down her alley."

"She's probably smarter than us. But we've got to learn to get along together without her."

"Exactly. More coffee?" Lil got up and brought the pot over.

Katy glanced at the clock again but decided one more cup wouldn't make her late. "Another thing I want to bring up. You're right about us being adults. I'm going to quit preaching at you and just let the real Lil shine."

Lil glowed as if she'd been handed the world. "And I'm not going to try to change you, either. Except it wouldn't hurt if you combed your hair. It looks pretty bad." She lifted her coffee cup. "This calls for a toast."

Rolling her gaze heavenward, Katy relented, "Fine." She mimicked Lil and raised her cup, biting off the urge to ask Lil where in the world she'd learned to toast.

"To adulthood, womanhood, and sisterhood."

Katy felt awed. "And friend-hood."

"Clink your cup against mine, silly."

Clink and *clink* sealed the deal between them.

"Now what are we going to do with our coats?" Katy asked. "We can't just keep hanging them over the chairs. And if we hang them in our bedroom closet, they smell up our clothes."

"I'll ask Jake about that coatrack again. Otherwise, he could make one or put up some hooks for us behind the door. I'll set it up for some day while you're at work."

CHAPTER 17

On Sunday morning, Katy and Lil chatted as they passed a row of cars and headed toward the rectangular shaped—soon to be L-shaped—meetinghouse. A young couple directly in front of them reined in their tiny children, who had spotted the playground and had tried to veer off toward it.

"No. Maybe after church for a few minutes," their mother corrected. "But it might be too cold."

"And no talking in church today," their father added. "Children are to be seen and not heard at times like this."

Katy's eyes, however, lingered nostalgically on the side lawn, now snowy and covered with worn playground equipment. There she and her girlfriends had often sung their ditties. She and Lil had always vied for control on the teeter-totter. Lil, who had weighed more at the time, had often kept Katy airborne at her protest. It had been an act, however, for Katy had always preferred the loftier position.

Now, at last, she hoped the contention was gone between them. She hoped the manipulative games were finished. She didn't wish to be a fraud. She wondered if Megan could sense the change in their relationship or if they would revert back to their old behavior in her presence.

Wrestling with that disturbing thought, she tentatively glanced at Lil, who had moved on from the head chef's ridiculous requests to describe a certain waiter's distracting eyes.

"Speaking of distractions," Katy cut in, "I hope when Megan comes over today, we don't revert to our old style of bickering."

At first Lil's expression blanked, lost in the sudden twist of the conversation; then she smiled. "We won't let that happen." They entered the lobby, and Lil's family called out to her. "Save me a seat, okay? I want talk to my mom."

"Sure." Inside the sanctuary, Katy veered to the left, where the women sat, to locate her favorite pew. Her sister, Karen, spied her and hurried over.

"Hi, sis. I miss you. The bed stays cold all night. And it's no fun being outnumbered. I never realized how much you stuck up for me around the boys. And Mom hasn't gotten me a new night-light yet. Anyway, she says I can sit with you, if you don't care."

"Yes, sit with us." Katy clamped an arm around her sister's shoulders and squeezed. "I miss you, too. After all, you are my only sister."

"Exactly. Please come for dinner today. Mom said to ask you. Please. Please."

"Oh I'm sorry. Lil already has lunch planned. Megan's coming over." At Karen's crestfallen expression, she quickly added. "Tell Mom I'll come next Sunday for sure."

"Promise? It'll be fun."

"I promise."

Lil and a few stragglers shuffled in. Brother Troyer and the song leader strode to the front, causing a hush to fall over the congregation. There was no raised platform. Void of stained glass or unnecessary grandeur, the architecture and interior were plain, reflecting the humble mind-set of the worshippers. But after the singing, the sermon was anything but ordinary.

"Sometimes an unrest blows across a congregation. Like the wind before a storm. Every generation or so, this happens. It has happened again. I believe it's time to address some hard issues like submission and the prayer covering."

If possible, the congregation became even quieter. "In the coming month, I will preach on husband-and-wife relationships, discussing how marriage symbolizes the relationship between God and the church. We will also review the scriptures on the prayer bonnet, which sets us apart from the world."

Katy felt a jubilant little thrill and forced herself not to glance at Lil, whose face must have turned scarlet.

"Rumblings of discontent can destroy a congregation. We've already amended the custom from our Amish friends by allowing our women to take the strings off our bonnets. It's time we take a fresh look at the symbol and explore its relevance to this generation. While it sets us apart from the outsiders, it's starting to divide us as insiders. I don't know if you've ever noticed, but right below the scripture regarding the prayer bonnet, the Lord commands the church not to allow division over unimportant issues."

Katy joined the collective gasp that roused and then hushed the congregation. Was he insinuating that the bonnet was an unimportant issue? Right before that, he had stated the matter was not to be taken lightly. She stirred uncomfortably.

"Some would argue that the covering's not necessary because it was merely a custom in the apostle Paul's time. Others may think it is appropriate for church and prayer but not everyday life. We'll get into all that. And after the series is over, we'll hold a meeting and listen to the congregation's input. We'll encourage the women to participate freely at this meeting. Afterward, a vote will be taken on how we will adhere to the custom. Then I pray that our congregation will abide by the decision, and we can move on at peace with one another. For if we are not at peace with one another"—he raised his arm toward heaven and lowered his voice to a near whisper—"how can we exemplify our Lord?"

Countless questions churned in Katy's mind. Who had complained about the head covering? Was it possible the church would outvote something so vital? Her pulse sped, and her body threw off enough heat to warm the sanctuary.

She knew there were sects of Mennonites who had already abandoned the head covering, but she'd never dreamed the Conservatives

151

would even consider it. Or wouldn't they be Conservatives any longer? Would they move into a higher conference? Was that the ulterior motive of some, bringing televisions and regular clothing into the church, too?

She stared at the elderly preacher. Surely not while Brother Troyer was shepherding the flock. Tension crawled up the back of her neck. As the service wore on, she fought the urge to go out for fresh air. She rubbed her aching temples and glanced across the aisle at the clock near the exit sign.

Fifteen more minutes. She ran the scenarios through her mind again. And only when Karen nudged her, did she discover that she'd been leaning forward and staring at the men's side far too long. But just before she straightened, she met Jake's amused gaze. And he had the audacity to wink at her.

She straightened her spine and looked back at the preacher, then at the plain wooden cross that graced the wall behind the pulpit. Its larger counterpart marked the exterior of the meetinghouse as a house of God, but Katy wondered how pleased God was over the bonnet controversy.

—❦—

The ride home from church was subdued, neither Katy nor Lil having the courage to bring up the bonnet issue and risk a potential argument. They talked about how good it was to see their families and agreed to spend the following Sunday with them. Lil was worried about her mom, who had been declining ever since the church fire. "I think she's blaming herself, ashamed over all the trouble and expense the fire's caused," Lil explained. "Although even before the fire, Mom was acting depressed."

"But nobody accused her?" Katy asked.

"No, but the fire marshal went to the house and questioned her."

"Because she's chairman of the hostess committee?"

Lil nodded. "Dad told me she felt like a criminal. He's real worried about her. Dad seems more stressed than usual, too."

"Maybe the sermons Brother Troyer has planned will help her."

"No," Lil shook her head. "I don't think it has anything to do with their marriage."

Katy fell quiet, not knowing how else to help. But she determined in her heart to pray for Mrs. Landis.

When they reached the doddy house, David was just getting out of his car, too. As soon as Lil parked, he strode toward them. Before she opened her door, she turned to Katy apologetically. "Do you care if I go on in and start lunch?"

Katy cast a reluctant look in David's direction but relented. "That's fine. I'll be right in." She swept her purse off the floor and stepped out of the car.

David waved. "Lunch ready? I'm starved."

"Well. . ."

He chuckled. "Just kidding. I'm eating at Ivan and Elizabeth's." Before Katy could respond, he added cheerfully, "But I'm available for dessert."

Katy placed her hand on her hip. "I'll just bet you are."

"So is that an invitation?"

Katy thought about the devil's food cake that Lil had baked and hesitated, thankful when she recognized Megan's car pulling into the drive. David's gaze followed the blue Ford, then returned to Katy to wait for her answer.

She finally offered, "You can stop in this afternoon if you're not afraid of the odds."

"What odds?"

"Three to one."

He watched Megan get out of the car. "You've got to be kidding. Those are great odds. Even if they weren't, you should know better than to dare a guy."

She countered, "It's not exactly a dare."

He flashed his dimple. "What is it?"

Katy shrugged, giving in to his good-natured teasing. "We're just hanging out. Drop by if you want. Lil usually makes popcorn mid-afternoon."

He chuckled. "You sure it wasn't a dare?"

Katy smiled, not sure why he was laughing but finding his amusement contagious. "Yes, I'm sure."

"Thanks. Maybe another time."

She waited until David had turned his back and rolled her gaze heavenward. She watched him stride toward Ivan's, seeming more mysterious than ever.

Inside the doddy house, the smell of flank steak and honeyed carrots roused Katy's appetite.

"Wow, look at this place. You guys are all settled in." Megan made a slow circle of the combo dining and living area, then went through the doorway to the kitchen. "This is nothing like my dorm. You guys seem domesticated."

Katy tied her apron. "We are." Then she teased, "Hey, Lil, I'll peel the potatoes if you pitch your own soda cans today."

"Deal."

Megan pulled potatoes from a bag and washed them in the antique kitchen sink. All the while, Katy could feel her quietly observing them. She peeled and plopped the potatoes in a black kettle.

After several minutes passed, Megan spoke her mind. "You guys have jobs and are making this happen. But what about me? What am I going to do after college?" It was a question they couldn't answer since none of Megan's job-hunting pursuits had ever been successful.

Once Megan had applied at the Plain City Laundromat, but when she had been offered a position, she had asked for time off to teach Bible school. They had hired someone else instead. She had checked out the recycle plant in Columbus, but thought the application process was too complicated just for a summer job. Her longest job had been delivery girl at a flower shop. But that fizzled when her allergies worsened.

Katy had hoped Megan would find her niche before she graduated, but Megan's dreams flitted about butterfly-style, matching her personality. While she made the world around her a beautiful place, she flew from one pretty flower to another, never finding a place to employ her special talents. Katy wondered if butterflies ever remained still unless they were pinned to a collector's board. She'd never want to destroy Megan's spirit.

At present it was engaged in praising Rosedale's mission opportunities. "In Nicaragua, people line up to get in the eye clinic," Megan explained. "I was talking to a guy who went last year. He said they had cobblestone roads with palm trees and lizards in the hotels and papayas at every meal and dogfights that woke them at night."

An image of Tyler's science project popped into Katy's mind.

"I can picture you there," Lil said. "Let's fill our plates at the counter so Katy doesn't have such a mess to clean up."

"Hey, thanks," Katy said, giving her friend a little hip-to-hip bump, then forking a serving of tender meat onto her plate. "We can't wait for you to join us here, green bean, but you need to go for your dreams. Maybe God's destined you to be a missionary."

"You think?"

The wistfulness in Megan's voice touched Katy.

"I think you should try a mission trip. See how it goes."

"Even if it keeps me from job hunting? From moving into the doddy house right after graduation?"

"We're doing fine here," Lil replied, shooting a meaningful glance Katy's way. "Committing to a job is a tough thing. Especially a dead-end job. Maybe you're not ready for that yet."

It amazed Katy that Lil would release Megan from their vow so easily, and she wondered if Lil would have been able to do that if they hadn't just had their big argument. They were changing, all of them. It blessed her. And she hoped it would continue for their betterment.

But she could only take a little change at a time. And the one happening at church was too dramatic. As they settled in at the kitchen table, where she and Lil had bared their souls with each other earlier in the week, Katy glanced at Megan. Striving to keep her voice sounding nonchalant, Katy ventured, "What's the deal about the head covering? You guys know anything about that?"

"Not me," Lil quickly replied.

"My dad says we're losing some members to higher churches"—the girls all understood the Mennonite lingo for more liberal churches—"and that although it's up to a husband to be a spiritual leader, the women usually have the most influence behind the scenes. Giving them a chance to express themselves on this matter might appease more of our members in the long run."

"So it's just an offensive tactic? There's not really a group of dissenters?"

"I think there is, but Dad didn't name any names."

"Wow," Lil muttered.

Katy said, "I'm glad Brother Troyer's going to teach on the subject. Like he said, maybe it will help everyone see its relevance."

"Or irrelevance," Lil countered gently.

"Well it's relevant to me," Katy said in a softer tone than she normally would have used.

Megan eyed them carefully. "My dad says it could save the church, but it could also split the church. But if it does, then it probably would have happened some time, anyway. So it's worth a try."

Katy set down her fork. "This is awful."

"Some churches require bonnets at services but allow the people to decide whether they're worn at other times," Megan offered.

Feeling the color drain from her face, Katy strained to keep her poise. "Is that what you think should happen, green bean? Is that what your dad thinks?"

Megan nodded. "Yes. It would be good if everyone agreed to disagree."

Naturally. That had always been Megan's goal. She and her family lived and breathed peace, the fiber that kept the Mennonite church grounded in its nonresistant stand. But Katy didn't get it. "How can it be both ways when it clearly states in the Bible that women should cover their heads?"

"In church and in prayer," Lil clarified.

"Maybe we need to hear all the teaching before we discuss this," Megan suggested. Then she asked, "Is there dessert?"

"Devil's food cake," Lil said, seeming happy to change the subject, too.

But Katy thought keeping the peace came at too great a price. She didn't want the elders to mess with her bonnet. Why, it was almost as sacred to her as her Bible.

CHAPTER 18

In her closet, Katy sighed and scraped hangers across clothes rods, searching through her wardrobe for something appropriate to wear to the ballet. When Addison had shown her the pink confection Tammy had bought her daughter for the performance, Katy's heart had sunk to a deeper level in the downward ballet spiral of doom. Would they even allow her inside the magnificent theater, or would they turn her away at the door? Or worse, would they hand her a broom and point her to the janitor's supplies?

Lil stepped into the closet. "What are you doing in here so long?"

"Barring a miracle, I'm still taking Addison to the ballet, and I don't know what to wear. Do you have any ideas?"

"Yes! I do." Lil dove into her side of the closet and came out holding a black outfit. "Here it is. You can wear this." She held it against her own form, doing the garbanzo dance.

Katy touched the slinky black skirt and its matching top. "It's gorgeous. Where did you get it?"

Lil colored slightly and shrugged. "I had to attend a formal affair at school. Try it on."

"Oh I couldn't. It's way too glamorous. You know I've never worn anything like it. No," Katy protested.

"Is that what you're going to say on your wedding day? There are certain occasions when you need to raise the. . .ah, notch a bit. You don't want them turning you away at the door, saying, 'Sorry, ma'am, the performance hasn't started yet. Cleanup starts at 11:30. Come back then and don't forget your bucket.' "

Katy burst into laughter. "I was thinking the exact same thing." She held the skirt in one hand and the hanger with the top in the other. It is modest, except for. . ." She hung the skirt up and examined the top closer. "I've never worn this type of neckline before."

"It's not a low neckline. Try it on."

Katy faltered, wondering what it would feel like to wear the slinky expensive fabric against her skin. She was thankful the color was basic black. With her dark hair, she'd probably just fade into a shadowy corner somewhere. Yes, every eye would be on Addison, and this might help her maintain a respectability, the invisible air she sought when operating in the outsider's realm. "All right."

Lil helped her slip into the dress. "We need a full-length mirror in here." Impulsively, she said, "I'm splurging on one this week. Then you'll have it in time for the ballet. I'll get Jake to install it. I've got an idea." She left and then toted a kitchen chair to the bathroom. "Climb up on this so you can see yourself in the mirror."

Katy's pulse slammed in her throat when she saw herself. Her figure had transformed into a pleasing hourglass. But the formal attire also maintained a sophisticated modesty. Lil urged, "Hold your hair up." With a nervous giggle, Katy piled her hair atop her head. It flopped to the side, smashing her covering, but she'd fix that later. "Some red lipstick and my black nylons and nobody will ever notice you," her friend teased, reading her mind. "It really makes your eyes smolder."

Ignoring the eye comment, for folks had always raved about her eyes, Katy whispered with awe, "It'll be perfect."

"Not quite." Lil grabbed a fistful of material at the waist. "It needs just a little tailoring. And we definitely need to go shoe shopping."

"Oh I don't know. That looks too tight, doesn't it? I don't want to ruin it for you."

"We can baste it, and we'll remove it afterward."

"Surely I have some shoes that will go?" But Katy's voice trailed off for she knew she didn't have anything worthy of the occasion.

"We'll find you some shoes you can wear to church, too. And afterward, we'll drive downtown and locate the theater and check out the parking situation. Forewarned, and all that."

Feeling a catch in her throat, Katy climbed down and hugged Lil. "Thanks. You're the best. This has just been eating at me, terrifying me. Maybe now I'll be able to endure the whole experience."

"And you won't have to join the cleanup committee," Lil added with a glint in her eyes.

Katy held Addison's hand and stared at the scrolled billboard. *Cinderella*. "This is it," she announced to Addison, feeling as if she'd swallowed a glass slipper. A street policeman standing on the corner raised his hand to stay the traffic, and Addison plunged them into a jostling, crowded crosswalk that whisked them directly in front of the Ohio Theatre. They took their place in line, and the touch of Addison's enthusiastic hand was somewhat comforting. Everyone wore smiles and eager expressions, and she forced herself to feign a similar countenance for Addison's sake.

But she didn't have to pretend long. She was awestruck from the moment she stepped inside the marble entry and viewed the high, arched ceilings, gilded and frescoed, from which hung a huge stained-glass chandelier. Spanish Baroque architecture gave the theater a medieval flair, palatial in rich red and gold.

Its splendor was so breathtaking that Katy struggled for comportment, yet Addison took her surroundings in stride and suddenly jerked her hand away. "There's Samantha," she cried and dashed off toward another girl from her dance class.

With a gasp, Katy lunged, but only caught a satin sash that untied and slipped through her fingers, dragging on the ground behind Addison like a pink tail. Involuntarily, Katy clamped her teeth on her bottom lip and helplessly watched the two little girls separate to skirt an elderly couple and join together again laughing. Linking arms, they next burst through a group of teenage girls and vanished. In the blink of an eye, Addison had disappeared. Panic tamped up Katy's spine. She vied to get another glimpse of Addison's pink frothy outfit.

"Hey, Katy."

Startled, she whipped her gaze around to the tall male figure clad in a plain black suit. In all the excitement, she'd forgotten about Jake.

His sister Erin smiled. "Hi Katy. This is my first time here. Great, isn't it?"

Erin's presence momentarily dazed Katy. But the dark-haired girl's enthusiasm and winning smile reminded Katy of her manners. There was no excuse to be rude to Erin Byler just because of her brother, so she took just a moment to engage in some necessary small talk. Then Katy bit the corner of her mouth with frustration. "I lost Addison."

"You want me to help you look?" Jake asked, lines of concern framing his eyes.

Considering that the lobby was filled with children and Jake didn't know what Addison looked like, she wasn't sure he'd be much help. "She's wearing a pink frilly dress."

Jake frowned. Half of the girls were clad in pink or princess outfits.

"What's her name?" Erin asked.

Before Katy could answer the question, the youngster under discussion had returned and grabbed her by the waist. Without missing a beat, Addison urged, "Let's go in."

"Addison!" Katy clutched the girl's hand. "Sweetie, wait. You need to calm down and stay with me. I met some friends." She reeled her charge in and introduced her to Jake and Erin.

Erin bent down and began to tie Addison's bow. "Are you a performer? Are you the dancer who is Cinderella?"

"No, but I take dance lessons."

"Are you sure? You look like a princess."

"That's just because. . ."

"That was unnerving," Katy whispered to Jake.

"I guess she didn't lose you; that's the important thing. Shall we go find our seats?"

"Ours?" Katy raised a brow.

He gave her his notorious lopsided grin. "We're in the row behind you."

Naturally. "So you admit to a conspiracy."

"Yeah, that's old news." He touched her elbow. "Ready?"

With a nod, Katy tugged Addison's hand. "Let's go, sweetie."

"I like Erin. She thinks I'm a princess."

"You are, aren't you?" Katy teased, and the little girl shrugged. Katy held tight so that she didn't skip away again at the first glimpse of someone else from their dance troupe. All the while, her gaze took in the auditorium. More gilt and arches, even more elaborate than the lobby, a perfect fairy-tale setting. They found their seats, and Addison entertained herself by talking to her friend Samantha, who was seated next to her. Katy relaxed and stared overhead at the lighted, coffered ceiling and enormous, tiered chandelier.

Jake leaned forward and whispered, "It's something else."

"I think God must live here," Katy replied.

Soon the lights dimmed, the curtains opened to an elaborate set. Amidst the magic lights and changing colors, a ragged-clad Cinderella appeared on stage, dancing with a broom. Instantly enthralled and swept into the performance, Katy laughed along with the children, enraptured with the ballet movements of the story. When the wicked stepsisters danced onto the stage in bright costumes, Addison whispered, "Look at their funny hats."

In a mere twinkle, it seemed to Katy, it was intermission. "Can we get something?" Addison instantly begged, swinging Samantha's hand.

Katy put off the question momentarily, standing to let others in their row pass. Meanwhile, Addison was skipping impatiently from toe to toe. Katy turned and glanced toward the lobby.

Erin offered, "I'll take the girls. I need a drink myself."

"All right, but stay with Erin," she warned the children, and Addison nodded.

"You want something, too?" Jake asked.

"No thank you. I just want to sit and drink in the splendor." Katy slid back into her seat and Jake climbed over the one next to her and plopped himself down in it. They shared an armrest and spoke about the performance and the costumes. She glanced down at the orchestra pit. "I was nervous about tonight."

"That's understandable. So how does this story end, anyway?"

She spent the next several minutes insisting that he had read far too few books in his childhood and spent too many hours getting into trouble.

At the end of the intermission, Addison squeezed into the row, stepping on Jake's feet, and he reached out a hand to stay the little one. "Can I sit with Erin?" Addison asked. Katy drew in a ragged breath. Addison begged, "Please."

"Me, too." Samantha echoed.

With a shrug, Katy changed places with Erin and trailed Jake back to his row, sliding in beside him. And that's when the afternoon really became enchanted. When the glittery carriage rolled onto the stage, pulled by white-wigged men wearing tights and doublets, she felt like she was living inside the fairy tale. Her shoulder pressed against her prince's, she allowed her guard to melt away for one afternoon and indulged in what it might be like to be Cinderella, or at the very least, an outsider.

When the performance ended, Jake whispered, "We'll walk you to your car." Behind them, Erin kept up a charming dialogue with Addison. Katy was having too much fun to replace her guard. There was always tomorrow. She had until midnight before the spell ended. While Jake opened her door, Erin moved around the back of the car with Addison.

Jake whispered, "I wish this didn't have to end."

Her pulse quickened. She felt the same way, reluctant to ruin a magical afternoon.

He kept his voice low. "I know I don't have any right to ask, but I'd like to take you to dinner tonight. To tell you my story. You did say I need to have more interest in stories with happy endings."

"You're twisting my words."

"Please say yes."

She started to protest. "No. I—"

But he wouldn't have it. "It's not a date. Just two old friends. We're all dressed up." He winked.

She didn't want to remove Lil's dress just yet. *Until midnight, and then I'll get back to reality.* "All right. I need to take Addison home first."

"I'll drop Erin off at her dorm and pick you up at your castle, say around seven?"

She smiled. "Okay."

—☙—

Jake stood statue-like, watching Katy back her car out of its parking spot and steer it toward the garage exit.

"Good job!" Erin exclaimed.

He let out a sigh. "I can't believe she said yes. Did you see her, Erin? She's so"—he shook his head unable to express his feelings—"and she's giving me another chance." He stuffed his hands in his pockets. "I can't believe it."

"You've got it bad."

He grinned. "I know."

They walked past a row of cars and stepped into an elevator. "You think she considers this a date?" he asked.

Erin's brows knit together. "What did you say to her?"

"I asked her to go to dinner"—he inwardly groaned as he recalled his exact words—"as two friends."

"That was lame."

He flashed Erin a frown. "It just popped out. While I was begging her."

Erin's mouth gaped. "You begged, too?"

They stepped out of the elevator and went toward his truck. "I guess it's not a date. But it's a chance. She's giving me a second chance, right?"

"When did you get so insecure?"

He reached out and ruffled her hair. "I'm not. Get in." Erin wasn't nearly as helpful as Lil, but his cousin had made it clear that she couldn't help him with Katy anymore because Katy had forbidden it. He was on his own now.

They climbed into his truck, and he put the gears in reverse. Erin's phone rang, and he tuned her conversation out, losing himself in his own thoughts. The ballet had been a new experience for him, and although he had mostly endured it, Katy had been the one enraptured.

When he'd first seen her in the foyer, his heart had nearly stopped. Her eyes were so alive and her lips slightly open; she'd been awestruck with her surroundings. And he'd been awestruck with her, so plain yet elegant in her black gown. He had never seen her so lovely and yet vulnerable. He'd stood and stared, unable to move until Addison momentarily slipped away. When Katy's expression became troubled, he'd come to his senses, snatching at the opportunity to approach her.

He shot Erin a tender gaze across the cab. She had been a natural with Addison, providing him an open door to talk to Katy. When she was off the phone, he thanked her for her help. "I couldn't have done it without you."

"Don't let her get away this time," Erin replied. "By the way, Jessie says hi."

Her remark was just what he needed to bring him back to task. He'd promised Katy to share his story tonight, the one that included Jessie, and he didn't even know where to start. He only knew he needed to express his genuine sorrow over his falling away. Katy wasn't the only one he'd hurt. Now Erin was following his path of folly. "Tell her 'hi' for me." Near Erin's dorm, he pulled his truck to the side of the road. "And be careful. Stay out of trouble, won't you?"

She leaned over and kissed his cheek before she hopped out of the truck. He watched her stroll toward her dorm as if she didn't have a care in the world. He had plenty. He had an hour to figure out what he was going to tell Katy over dinner.

CHAPTER 19

The Worthington Inn, a historical Victorian restaurant, provided a charming atmosphere to prolong the Cinderella spell. Katy placed a cloth napkin on her lap, smoothing the surreal fabric of her skirt, and inhaled contentment. The waiter handed them their menus and disappeared.

"Look." Katy pointed at a descriptive item on the menu. "They use Amish, free range eggs."

"We can dine in elegance and still feel right at home. But Beef Worthington for me. Never hurts to try the house dish, right?"

With a giggle, Katy marveled, "You and Lil could be twins."

He leaned forward. "We are, but our parents gave me away."

"As you well deserved," Katy teased, then folded her menu. "The garden vegetable plate for me." The waiter returned for their orders, and they relaxed over coffee.

"One time when we were kids, I asked Lil why she didn't play with Erin instead of you. She said you were more fun. That Erin could hardly keep up with you two."

"Erin always tried to keep up with me," he admitted with a hint of sadness in his voice. Then he gazed into Katy's eyes and changed the subject. "The Cinderella fairy tale suits you. Especially the pretty part.

You look lovely tonight, your hair swept up like that. Your eyes are amazing. They draw people in, Katy. Did you know that?"

His scrutiny made her uncomfortable. "And the cleaning part. I'm pretty good at sweeping cinders. But I thought we came to talk about you."

"We did. But I want you to know that you've always intrigued me. That has never changed. My problem was a spiritual one, wondering where I fit in. Our family's divided when it comes to beliefs with the whole Amish-Mennonite thing. My mom broke away from the Amish, but my dad was always Conservative. Then my brother moved to a higher Mennonite church. So I never felt like there was only one church or one way to get to heaven or to please God."

He paused when their dinners arrived, and once the waiter left, he asked, "Shall we pray?"

She nodded, pleasantly surprised. Even David hadn't prayed over their meal at Lil's restaurant.

Jake bowed his head. "Lord, we thank You for this food, but mostly I thank You for the opportunity to share my story with Katy. Amen."

The sincerity of the simple prayer touched her with tenderness. "Amen," she breathed. When she opened her eyes, Jake was watching her.

"Anyway, when Dad died, it did something to me. Made me think about how short life is and how trapped I felt. I guess my brother Cal saw my struggle, and he invited me to his Bible study. For the first time I heard about grace."

Katy clenched her fork. "What do you mean? Brother Troyer teaches grace."

"But I never heard it. Never understood."

"Oh."

"Now there was another decision to make on top of wanting to break away from farming. Cal suggested construction, and it appealed to me. So I signed up for some courses. I wanted to get through school as quickly as possible and get on with life, so I took a full load. But I was still torn about the grace thing. At the time, I thought that if I chose grace, I'd have to leave our church and join Cal's. To be honest, I enjoyed his Bible study. But I missed some of the studies and delayed making a choice. I knew that if I moved up to another church, I'd lose you."

You lost me anyway, she thought. But she asked, "Why didn't you talk to me about this? Instead you just withdrew." Remembering how painful it had been, Katy whispered, "You just left."

"I knew where you stood. You've always been rigid in your beliefs."

Rigid. She despised that word. His perception of her matched Lil's. "Was I? Then why was I drawn to the orneriest boy at church?"

"I'm just saying that's how I felt at the time. Then my surroundings desensitized me and pulled me into the world. I didn't intentionally go off to college to sow my wild oats. It just happened one step at a time. There was a new world to explore."

She felt her ears heat. "And new girls."

"I guess. Jessie was in my business class, and she liked to poke fun at me, but at the same time she helped me out, explained things."

I'll bet she did, Katy thought, jealousy rising in her spirit and stealing her appetite.

"She was fun loving and comfortable to hang out with. She convinced me to go to some parties, and the next thing I knew I was drinking. I knew that lots of Mennonite guys drink before they settle down, and I just figured it would help me figure out what I wanted to do with my life. If I even wanted to settle down. But after the initial excitement wore off, I realized that Jessie wasn't for me. I knew I'd lost my most precious gift, you. I tried to win you back that night in the parking lot, but I went about it all wrong. When you smelled the alcohol on my breath, you despised me for it. I want you to know that if I hadn't been drunk I never would have manhandled you that way. I'm so sorry about that. I hope you can forgive me."

She shrugged, not able to answer that question. "I don't know."

The waiter came and refilled their drinks, giving Katy a moment to consider everything Jake had just told her. She realized that he was right that she wouldn't have understood then what it was like to feel the pull of the outsiders. But since she'd started working in their world, she'd experienced some of that excitement, and the lure, too. Wasn't that what tonight was all about? She didn't want to condemn him—maybe a guy was drawn with even more force—but his actions had stolen his innocence. At least sexually, she assumed. And that bothered her a lot.

"When you told me off, I decided to leave the church where I wasn't wanted. The world took me in."

"Jessie did, too." Katy murmured.

"Yes. But I was miserable. Soon after that, I broke up with her. Then one night I ended up drunk on Cal's doorstep. He sobered me up, and we talked a long while. I knew I needed God so I confessed my sins and attended Cal's Bible study and even his church. Once the Lord entered my life, I viewed everything differently. I'd changed and would change even more in the months after that."

He continued. "By then, Erin had come to school and hooked up with Jessie and started following my dead-end path. I tried to talk some sense in her, but she wouldn't listen. Gram got worse, and I decided Mom needed some support at home."

"Why did you come back to the Conservative Church instead of Cal's?"

"Because I love it here. And you're right about grace. It was here all the time, but I was too wrapped up in the dos and don'ts to understood it. Now I realize that church restrictions are put in place to shield us from temptation. They don't get us to heaven. I could attend a higher church without going against my conscience."

Katy wondered how he could be content in either church. Couldn't he see the differences between them? "So you came back because of your friends, and you intend to live Conservative the rest of your life?"

He nodded. "I knew that I had to come back for you. I knew that you'd probably refuse me, but I had to try to recover my most precious loss. Aside from God. Except I don't think I was ever a Christian to begin with."

That startled Katy.

"But I am now," he quickly clarified.

She believed he had repented for his falling away, but she didn't know if she could take him back. She longed to know how intimate he'd been with the other woman, and yet she didn't know if she could handle the truth. The question tickled her lips. "I always thought we would get married. To me, it was like you committed adultery."

"But I didn't. We weren't even engaged. If anything, my experience deepened my love for you."

The admission of his love caught her off guard. She didn't know how to respond, wanting him, yet not sure she could forgive him. She wanted to trust him.

He looked so handsome in his Sunday suit, but it reminded her that this date was still part of the fairy-tale experience. He seemed caught up in it, too. As much as she desired him, she knew she wasn't ready to take him back. But how could she let him go? She felt torn.

The waiter returned to their table. "Are you finished with these?"

Katy nodded.

"May I bring you a dessert menu? We have freshly churned ice cream."

"That sounds good. I'll have chocolate." Jake said.

"Me, too."

When the waiter left, she fiddled with her knife. Jake reached across the table and covered her hand with his. She stilled.

"Thanks for listening. Please. Try and forgive me."

He must have read her mind. She could tell that his asking for forgiveness was difficult. He was such a masculine guy, and he'd pretty much bared his soul. His feelings. He loved her. She looked into his tender gaze and wanted to swim there forever, but how could she settle for less than perfect? Finally, she repeated what she'd earlier told him. "I don't know if I can."

At his crestfallen expression, she quickly added, "I'm sorry. I forgive you as a sister in the church, but as a girlfriend, I don't know if I can. I still resent Jessie. I'm angry you chose her over me. I don't know if I can forgive you for those months of. . .being with someone else." Her lips trembled, and she said, "I'm even angry over the way you and Lil manipulated me."

"You haven't forgiven her?"

"Actually, I did. We're closer now than ever."

He licked his lips and frowned. "I understand your frustration, because I'm just as jealous over your dates with David."

The ice cream arrived, and he released her hand. When the waiter left, he said, "I'm sorry I hurt you. I'll never hurt you again. Just think about it."

How could he promise such a thing? She nodded, unable to speak.

"It isn't midnight yet, and I don't want to spoil our dessert. Let's talk about something else. Addison sure is a cute little thing."

"Much sweeter than her brother, Tyler."

"Girls always are sweeter," he teased, and soon he had her feeling at ease again. When she relaxed, she could almost imagine she was sixteen and nothing had ever changed between them.

When he dropped her off at the doddy house, he walked her to the porch. "Thanks for a wonderful evening, Cinderella." His finger grazed her chin, and drawn like a moth to light, she turned her face upward. He lingered. "See you at the next builders' meeting."

She replied softly, "That's one way to bring a girl back down to earth. Look, don't expect much from me. But I'm thankful for tonight, for a good memory." One that would go far in erasing the uglier, more painful ones.

She thought he might try to kiss her, but then his hand fell away, and he left her alone to the sound of his truck rumbling down the country road and to the blackness that could only be midnight.

—⌒⌒—

Jake shifted gears. Although he'd grown up on a farm, the country road stretched out dark and lonely as his heart. He ached inside for his mistakes, for the beautiful, dark-eyed beauty he'd just taken to dinner. He ached because he was afraid to hope that she might give him a second chance.

Over dinner he'd watched her expressive eyes. He'd seen the desire in them when he admitted he still wanted her. But when she spoke, her eyes had glittered with anger, and when he'd asked her to forgive him, they had saddened with regret. Her lips also held clues. When he spoke about Jessie, they quivered. When he talked about the changes he had made, coming back to the church, she had tucked them between her teeth, showing her suspicions. And when he had wanted to kiss her on the porch, they had seemed willing. But he had made that mistake before. So he left, almost abruptly, to keep from giving in and pulling her into his arms. He knew she was not ready. With a sigh, he turned on the radio.

CHAPTER 20

Katy spent Sunday with her family. They enjoyed a meal of ham and coleslaw, and her married brothers and their wives all played the card game Rook, while Katy's oldest niece entertained the toddlers. The fireplace crackled, and Katy's heart swelled with love for her family that only weeks earlier she'd taken for granted. She considered the new confidence in Karen's behavior.

"Can I bring anyone anything?" Karen had asked between rounds.

Katy realized that Karen had become her mom's new chief helper. It sent a twinge of regret through her to be replaced, yet she knew that just like her married siblings, she would always remain a vital member of the family.

But later that evening it was good to get back to her cozy little doddy house, where Lil fed her popcorn and asked her about the ballet, assuring her that this time, whatever she said would remain confidential. Lil deserved details since she'd donated her beautiful dress to the cause.

Both girls relaxing on the couch, Katy re-spun the spell.

Lil purred, "What a fairy-tale evening."

"Probably my one and only. The church forbids dancing. Do you think the ballet is sinful? That it's wicked to watch men dance in their tight costumes? Now I know why they are called tights, too."

Lil giggled. "I have no idea. Did Jake seem embarrassed by it?"

Katy considered the question. "No. But he never gets embarrassed. I used to think any form of dancing was wrong, but it was so beautiful. Then again, at Addison's dance studio some of the girls were taught seductive moves. " She sighed. "It's confusing."

"The outsiders call it art. I suppose it depends on disciplining your thoughts."

"I was captivated by the entire spectacle. The theater, not the guys." Katy reiterated, nestling comfortably against the leather armrest. "But maybe that was wrong, too. Just basking in such wealth and splendor. Nothing humble about the Ohio Theatre." She shrugged. "I'm struggling with the whole evening."

Lil gazed at her with understanding.

Katy bit her lip then went on, "Especially since I let my guard down with Jake. I don't think I'll ever get over him. What if I turn him away, and he marries someone else? I'll be miserable. After he shared his story with me, I feel partly to blame because when he was restless, I wasn't able to help him. He didn't feel comfortable talking to me about it. He told me that he didn't even think he was a Christian at the time."

"You can't change the past. And if he wants to be with you now, then that's more important. Present definitely trumps past." Katy figured Lil must have played Rook with her family, too. But this was no game. This was her future.

⸺☙⸺

On Monday, Katy couldn't help but try out the broom for a dance partner, humming off-key to the songs she'd heard at the ballet. Feeling a stab of conscience, she changed the song to a hymn. But hadn't David danced with joy after one of his war victories? And he was a man of God's heart.

Although dancing was forbidden in her religion, nobody but Lil had ever talked to her about it. She'd never been tempted until she'd stepped into Addison's dance studio. Was it wrong to dance from joy or to express graceful movement of the body that God had created? It was hard to contain joy, and she was joyful over the news that Jake still loved her. But was love enough? That question was more troubling than the first.

Jake's testimony hung in her mind until she picked up Tammy's children from school. Tammy's note reminded her that Sean Brooks was still out of town. That was the reason Katy had taken Addison to the ballet. Now she would have to babysit late. In the note, Tammy asked her to help Tyler with his homework, especially assisting him on a school project.

"So tell me about your school project, Tyler."

"It's kinda dumb. We're supposed to watch certain TV shows and observe people's mannerisms. We have to write down what they say and what they do. Describe how they act. What their faces look like. What gestures they make. Stuff like that."

Her spirit sank to hear that television was involved in the school assignment. "Can I see your notes?"

"Sure." Tyler brought her a thin, bound notebook. Katy flipped through and saw dates on several page and the titles of television shows.

"Did you choose the shows?"

"Nope. I copied them from the blackboard. We have to write a whole page each night."

"Wow."

"But I'm not very good at it, and Mom's been helping me. I can't watch people's faces and write at the same time. That's what you need to do. Write down their lines."

Katy sat on the edge of the couch and rubbed her brow. This was going to be worse than she'd imagined if it included viewing television shows. She eyed Tyler. "You sure you can't do this alone?"

"Nope. And I'll get a bad grade if I skip a night."

"When does the show come on?"

"Seven o'clock."

It was already six forty-five. Reluctantly, Katy rose. "I'll go check on Addison. You get everything ready."

Tyler grabbed the remote and flicked on the television while Katy ran upstairs. She found Addison playing with her Barbie dolls. After explaining she was going to help Tyler with his homework project, Katy started back down, pausing on the stairway at the television's blare.

Once again duty collided with conscience. The way her babysitting responsibilities were pulling her into the life of her charges, she might as well move in and become a part of this outsider's family.

She'd only watched television in the stores a few times as she'd passed through their electronics sections and had caught glimpses of it at various times when she'd been working for her employers. Tyler often had it on in his room, and Addison sometimes watched princess DVDs. In fact, after the ballet it was all Katy could do to refuse Addison when she'd begged her to watch the *Cinderella* movie with her. But somehow, she had prevailed against that temptation.

Katy had never sat down and watched an entire television show. But this wasn't about pleasure; this was a school assignment. And she'd gotten involved in plenty of those lately. Now she considered this one. Surely Tyler's teacher would not have assigned something inappropriate, given his impressionable age?

She'd heard television debated in her congregation, and some claimed all television shows weren't bad, but that it was playing with fire to have a set in your home because it invited temptation by desensitizing you to sex, violence, and greed for beauty and material wealth. In short, it brought the outsiders' world into your own home where you could sit and dream that you were living their life.

She watched Tyler settling in on the sofa and breathed a prayer, "Lord, if this goes sour, then I'm quitting this nanny job, even if I lose my cleaning job with the Brooks. I'll take it as Your will." Then she steeled herself.

She sat next to Tyler, and he handed her his notebook. "You write down something they say, then I'll hit PAUSE. Then we'll play it back, and I'll tell you what to write down about their mannerisms."

"Okay, I'm ready." She thought, *I don't have to watch the show. But I do have to listen to the lines.*

"We have to wait until the commercial's over."

"Commercial?"

Tyler stared at her. "Are you for real?"

Katy started scribbling.

"Not yet!" he cried. "It's a commercial." He shook his head as if she was from the dinosaur era. "Just wait, and I'll tell you when the show comes on." Then he displayed an uncharacteristic gentleness. "You'll get the hang of it. I'm gonna get a soda. Be right back."

She started to protest, that he should turn off the television while he left, but her gaze went to the screen as if magnetized. She watched a seductive woman caress a car, and felt the heat rise up her neck. Then some men climbed through a refrigerator and stepped into a bar, and Katy instantly regretted the glimpse into such a dark sinful place. However, she couldn't look away. Next two guys in a truck cracked jokes about fast food, and she laughed at their silly conversation. Just when her interest was growing, Tyler interrupted, "Okay, now. It's starting."

She gripped her pencil. The show was about an Indiana family with three kids. The teenage boy sauntered into the living room in his underwear, and Katy gasped.

Tyler laughed at the actor. "He's hilarious. Did you get that?"

She shook her head, still embarrassed over the teen's bare chest and legs and low-slung boxers. "I don't know. I missed it."

Tyler sighed, then pressed the remote and to Katy's amazement it all reversed back to the beginning of the episode. "Just write what he says, okay?"

"All right," Katy stared at her pad, determined not to watch the screen again and to get it down and get this assignment over with as quickly as possible. After about three more tries, she had his line and Tyler's mannerism description, but listening was almost as bad as watching. Katy was appalled that the teenage actor would talk to his mom with such disrespect. It was eye-opening, how Tyler's behavior mimicked the teenage star's attitude.

The process took forever, and Tyler fast-forwarded through a batch of commercials. The next round of note-taking included a scene with a scantily dressed neighbor. Her eyes had strayed to the screen again, because it made it so much easier to get the lines down. "Are you sure you should be watching this?" Katy asked with concern.

"Are you kidding? My mom loves this show. Remind me not to delete it. She'll want to watch it later. She says it's true to life."

"Maybe your life," Katy mumbled.

"Yeah, well, Miss Pilgrim, what do you do at night? Clean the toilets?" He snickered and flicked the show on PAUSE. "Huh, where do you live anyway? On the Mayflower?"

"I live in a doddy house with my friend Lil."

Tyler laughed. "What's that?"

"It's like a guesthouse."

"Whatcha do there?"

"We cook, read, play games."

"What kind of games?"

"We play Rook."

"A video game?"

"No." At Tyler's confused look, she explained, "It's a card game."

"But you don't watch television and don't know anything about it?"

"Nope."

"That sounds boring to the max. I'll bet you don't even have a computer, do you?"

"No. But it's not boring. I don't like to watch things that aren't God-honoring."

"Whatever. You ready to go again?"

"Yes. . .wait a minute." Suddenly things clicked for Katy. "You can stop and start the show?"

"Duh, that's what we've been doing."

"And you just said you're going to save it for your mom. So why do I have to be doing this with you?"

"Because my mom told you to on the note."

Katy felt her anger flare. "Tyler. We're done now. Your mom can help you when she gets home, or you can finish this tomorrow."

"But my teacher checks my notes every day. I lose points, and you're gonna be in trouble. You may have to do something really crummy for your punishment like"—he looked about the house—"clean under my bed."

She already had done that, many times, and he was right about it

177

being a really crummy job. "Or maybe she'll buy me a new iPod," Katy argued.

He glared at her, not quite getting it, but realizing it was some kind of an insult.

Katy sighed. "We'll wait until eight o'clock, and if she hasn't come home yet, then we'll finish it. Why don't you go up to your room and play now."

"Okay. It's your head, lady pilgrim." He got up and charged up the stairs.

His smart mouth didn't irritate her as much as it had when she'd first started sitting for him, and although she shouldn't have, she let his sarcastic remark pass without admonishing him. She tried to imagine him raised in her own home and thought of her brothers, how they played hard outside and enjoyed working with her dad. Tyler didn't know the disadvantage life had given him.

Then her thoughts went to his mother. Tammy was deliberately asking her to do things that went against her beliefs for no good reason other than Tammy's own inconvenience. Oh, she'd claimed she'd had a workshop to attend on the Saturday of the ballet. But she was just being lazy not to help Tyler with this assignment tonight, especially given her knowledge of Katy's Mennonite beliefs. As she brooded, she picked up the room, placing Tyler's backpack on the stairway, a juice can in the recycle bin, and Addison's princess boots in the hall closet.

"What a day. I'm beat."

The unexpected comment floated within Katy's hearing, and she flinched, thinking the television must have drowned out the sound of Tammy's car. She turned and raised her chin, determining this was the night that she would be more assertive. "Yeah, me, too. Housecleaning's no breeze."

"Uh-oh. Somebody's in a rare mood. The kids acting up or what?"

Once she'd made her mental stand, her frustrations poured out. "I feel manipulated, Tammy. You asked me to help Tyler with his school project when you know I don't watch television. And you can even replay the show."

Tammy's mouth gaped; then she composed her features. "I didn't know you don't watch TV. Anyway, I thought I'd get home too late. I knew I'd be beat."

It was as if Katy had stepped out of her body and the words came from some other source. "Well, I'm tired, too. I've cleaned this entire house. And I'm constantly picking up after the children."

"But this is your job. I pay you. And a high wage."

She saw that some of Tyler's attitude came straight from his mother.

"I've made more at other places." Katy shocked herself with that remark and worked quickly to remove the angry glint from Tammy's eyes. Responding in anger wasn't God-honoring, even if it felt right. "I'm sorry. That remark was inappropriate. I don't mean to sound ungrateful for the work. But the nanny part is not working out. I told you from the start, it isn't what I enjoy doing. You've got to find someone else. I won't be picking the children up from school on Wednesday, either." Katy crossed her arms and waited for Tammy's explosion.

"Excuse me?" Tammy ground out with sarcasm. But Katy didn't budge. Then Tammy softened her voice. "You can't back out now. You agreed. I'm working long days so I can be home the other three afternoons."

Dropping her arms, Katy reasoned, "You've always known that I'm a housekeeper, not a nanny. Your kids are great, but the job doesn't suit me." She took a step toward the coat closet. "I'm sorry. I quit."

"Wait! You're not quitting cleaning, too, are you?"

Katy froze. Bit her bottom lip thoughtfully, "Not if you still want me."

"Of course I want you."

If Katy wasn't losing that part of the job, she'd been a fool not to stand up to the woman earlier. "Great. I'll be here on Wednesday. To clean," she clarified, lest Tammy think she was giving in again.

Tammy ran her hands through her hair. She glanced at the stairway and back. "Well, okay. I'll figure something out."

Katy felt a twinge of compassion for her employer, imagining the Realtor trying to show a house with two quarrelsome kids in tow. Or maybe she could handle it. Maybe they'd sit in some corner listening to their new iPods. She caught herself. It wasn't her problem. These were Tammy's children. She was a housekeeper, not a nanny. She needed to be strong, not cave in to her employer's sympathy ploys. She straightened. "Great. We only got halfway through Tyler's homework assignment. 'Night."

Walking to the car, Katy felt like King David must have after his war victories. How she could whip that broom around now! Why her feet were barely hitting the pavement. No more babysitting, and she hadn't even lost her cleaning job! She didn't know how the money would come in until she found another job to replace her loss, but she'd gone nose to nose with an outsider and just shed one hundred pounds of chains. Thank You, Lord!

CHAPTER 21

T he next day, Katy and Lil headed to the kitchen door, snatched their coats off the coatrack Jake had dropped by earlier in the week, and started outside toward the washroom. Katy was relating to Lil how she'd stood up to Tammy and gotten rid of her nanny job. Lil set her basket down to close the door behind them and froze.

"What's this? There's a red envelope taped to our door."

Katy's heart thumped. "A valentine?"

Lil tore it free from the door. "Yep. And your name's on it."

Katy dropped her clothes basket, too, and tore open the envelope. Her heart sank. "It's from David."

Lil raised her brow. "Guess he didn't get the message."

Katy opened the envelope of the store-bought card. It was blank inside, but he had handwritten: *Thinking of you and that popcorn! Or maybe dessert?* She bit her lip. When was the last time she had thought about him? She tucked the card inside her wash and picked up her basket. "I hate hurting him."

"Hey, at least one of us got a valentine. That's something, huh?"

"I guess."

They started out for the washroom again, using the sidewalk that

181

connected the doddy house to the workroom that they shared with the main house.

"About our earlier conversation, I'm glad you finally got rid of that nanny job. Don't worry. Something will turn up." Lil plunked her clothes basket on the cement floor, then rifled through it once, then a second time, more thoroughly. "I'm glad you stood up to Tammy. She'll probably treat you with more respect now."

Katy sorted her clothes, making neat piles. "We may be okay with it now, but it will catch up to us eventually. I've got to get a real job soon. Especially if Megan goes on a summer mission trip and doesn't move in with us."

Lil upended her basket until all its contents rained onto the floor, then garment by garment replaced each article with growing frustration as Katy watched with amusement. When that didn't meet Lil's satisfaction, she exhaled angrily and stared at the door as if her missing garment had sprouted legs.

Biting back a smile, Katy poured detergent in the washing machine and added her darks. Then she dangled Lil's work skirt in the air. "This what you're missing?"

Lil snatched it, casting her a dirty look that dared her to make some remark about it. They both knew that if Lil didn't throw her stuff all over the closet, she wouldn't lose things, or at least they wouldn't end up in Katy's dirty clothes basket instead of her own.

"Oops, wait a minute." Lil dug into her skirt pocket and tucked her cell phone into the hollow of her neck. "Hello?" As she talked, she tossed her darks in with Katy's and set the dial.

"Here," Lil shoved the phone in front of Katy's face as they made their way back to the house. "Jake wants to talk to you."

Frowning, Katy held the phone to her ear. "Can you meet me at the new fellowship hall? I've got a quick question about the kitchen cabinets."

"I can be there in an hour."

⸻

The fellowship hall carried the tangy smell of new lumber and in its skeletal state was as much a war zone as a construction site. Voices from the other side of a two-by-six frame wall stuffed with shiny insulation rectangles warned Katy of the presence of workers.

"Okay, boss. See you tomorrow."

"Don't let that baby keep you up all night so that you come crawling in late again."

"No sir. I'll send the wife over instead."

"Can she swing a hammer?"

"The question is, can I change a diaper?" the worker replied. "And the answer is no, I can't."

Jake's good-natured laugh echoed through the nearly vacant building, the crew heading home for the day. As Katy waited for him, she gazed around the kitchen. The island location was chalked off on the floor. Wires protruded at regular intervals through the walls. A piece of sharp sheet metal lay at her feet.

When Jake stepped into the room, like always, his dark good looks caught her unawares. When would she get used to the way the short sleeves of his T accentuated his muscles? The way his tool belt slung low, emphasizing his trim waist. "Hi. Thanks for coming over."

She jerked her gaze off him, stared at the kitchen wall, pretending the building drew her interest more than his presence. "It's like this place went up overnight. Everyone will be amazed on Sunday."

"The framing makes a big difference, but it'll still be a while till it's complete. Over here's the problem. He stepped around a stack of drywall. "We had planned on a countertop microwave, but actually we could fit one in the cabinetry right here beside the refrigerator. What do you think?"

She thought she shouldn't be here, alone with him like this, if she wanted to continue to resist him. And surely she must. Shouldn't she?

He tilted his head. Waited.

Oh! She studied the space he'd indicated and considered the options between less counter space or less cabinet space. "I think we should take it up off the counter if that works." *And yes, I want to resist him.* This could easily have been handled over the phone. Knowing that he had invented a reason to see her, a shiver of delight traipsed up her spine.

He stood so close that she could smell soap mixed with the leather from his tool bags. *Or maybe I don't want to resist.*

"Listen, me and some of the guys have been shooting hoops over at Chad Penner's barn."

Chad was Jake's lifelong friend, although Katy knew they hadn't hung around much when he'd fallen away from the church. Chad had gone straight to work for his dad on their farm while Jake was at school. She frowned. Or maybe they had stayed in touch. What did it matter? Was she losing her mind? She tried to concentrate.

"Tomorrow night, they're inviting their girlfriends to come watch. Afterward we're going to roast hot dogs. Would you like to go with me?"

Yes and no. Both. But he wanted her to decide now. On the upside, she wouldn't be babysitting. She did want to explore the possibility of a relationship since he'd explained everything. On the downside, she didn't want to do it in front of an audience. "Who will be there?" she stalled.

Jake's eyes darkened. "Not David, if you're worried about him."

"I'm not. I'm worried about you," she snapped. She knew how to keep an argument going, these days. She didn't know anything, though, about starting or ending relationships.

But her challenge was disregarded as he fixed his gaze on something beyond her. His hand went to his hammer, and he slowly eased it out of his holster. She sucked in her breath, her common sense telling her to be still. He slowly drew his arm back over his head. She closed her eyes. Then a second later, its clang caused her to shriek and open her eyes.

"Got it!"

Wheeling around, the tiny dead mouse caused another involuntary scream to slip out of her mouth, before she shivered and turned back to him. "Ew!"

He grinned and took her into his arms with a whisper. "Sorry about that. Don't think the hostess committee would want him around, nibbling on the communion bread."

"Ew!" she repeated. But she didn't shrink back from his embrace. *I can't resist him. I don't want to resist him.*

184

The room was darkening. His voice was husky against her ear. "Give me another chance?"

She stepped away. Finally she replied, "Well, you were pretty tolerable on Saturday."

But his touch wasn't, it was deadly. *Irresistible.* As if he could read her mind, he took her hands and pulled her close again. But she bumped his tool bags and the sharp edge of a square dug into her hip bone. "Ouch."

"Sorry." He fiddled with the belt and dropped into onto the floor. He reached for her again, and his touch thrilled and completed her. The question was no longer applicable.

They entered an embrace that removed the last shred of debate. It was just the two of them, and a place of contentment she'd thought was gone forever. Longing for more, temporary as the fix might be, she looked into his face and saw his desire. It wasn't a sexual one, but a soul's longing, and she knew what he felt because she experienced it, too.

He dipped his head and his lips touched hers briefly, igniting a fire that flowed through her veins. When she didn't resist, he kissed her again, more fully. It sizzled with a promise that she longed to give in to. How she wanted to trust this man. Her hands had moved up to his forearms, and she lightly pushed away, breathless.

"Will you?" he asked.

She ran her tongue over her lips then whispered. "It's wrong to claim the prize before we've taken the journey, you know?"

He nodded, rubbing his thumbs against her palms. "You can trust me for the journey."

"How?"

He studied her intently. "Are you talking about our kiss?" She nodded. "Then I won't kiss you again."

Biting her lower lip, she nodded. "Then I'll go with you."

"And I'll do everything in my power to win you."

She grinned. "But no kissing?" When they kissed, she couldn't think rationally.

"Not until you ask. But you were supposed to say, 'And I'll do everything in my power to let you win me.' "

She arched a brow. "Well, that's just not true."

He sighed. "No, I suppose not. That's all right. You'll see. It will all be all right. "

Maybe. She changed the subject. "I quit my nanny job."

"Ah," he groaned. "Addison will miss you. Believe me, I know."

She went on to confide her frustrations with Tammy, the television incident, and even voiced some of her confusion about her emotions over the whole ballet experience. He didn't interrupt her with objections or give his opinions on dancing or television, but just replied, "It's a lot to work through. The Christian walk hinges on our choices. I'll pray for you."

He'd changed. Wasn't the teenager she once loved, but had become a man who prayed and who talked about his mistakes. A man willing to wait and woo. He was the same guy with new intrigue. When she started to leave, she felt his gaze on her back; she turned with a sly smile. "By the way, you're real good with that hammer. That mouse didn't stand a chance." *And neither do I.*

—❦—

Afterward, Katy's heart thrilled over the exciting encounter so that when she pulled into the Millers' driveway, she could hardly recall the drive home. But the sight of David's shiny black car brought her out of her daydreams and sent a jolt of anxiety up her nerves. She needed to make it plain to David that she was going to entertain Jake's pursuit. That they were dating again.

The sedan's driver door opened, and David jumped out, tall and perfect as ever. He saw her at once and started toward her car. Tucking the inside of her cheek gently into her bite, she turned off the ignition and stepped outside to face him. "Thanks for the valentine."

He nodded as if it embarrassed him and that he was sorry he'd left it. "Just home from work?"

"No. Church. Going over some stuff with Jake." She carefully watched his reaction, wanting to let him down easy, knowing that was impossible. Once she attended the basketball game, news of her date with Jake would be all over church. Better to tell David in person. "We're dating."

There was an awkward silence. David tilted his head. "Guess his valentine was bigger than mine?"

She gave him a contrite smile. "Older."

His eyes narrowed, and his mouth contorted into an uncharacteristic scowl. "So you're going to give the jerk another chance?"

"I think he's changed."

He crossed his arms and glanced at the doddy house, his expression softening. "And you're not going to invite me in for popcorn?"

"Maybe sometime when Lil's home." She hoped they could remain friends, especially since he was often visiting at Ivan's, but that depended upon him.

Resignation dimmed his eyes. Then they took on a hateful glint. "Think I'll pass on that offer. Popcorn's irritating, the way it gets stuck in your teeth, you know? Don't know what I ever saw in popcorn in the first place. Not when desserts are so plentiful. Think what I want is something real sweet, creamy, and rich. Something that melts in my mouth." He turned abruptly and strode toward his brother's house, leaving her face to turn hot as a stove's burner.

CHAPTER 22

Jake's feet left the ground, his body made a smooth arc as he soared upward, and then his arms suddenly smashed down, slamming the orange ball through the hoop. Some pigeons fluttered in the barn rafters, and Katy shot to her feet with a squeal, clapping just as she had for his previous four baskets.

As the players ran to the opposite end of the court, she settled back onto the bale of hay she shared with a slim blond girl named Mandy, who was Chad Penner's girlfriend.

"He's good," Mandy commented, following Jake with her gaze. A twinge of pride warmed Katy. She glanced sideways. Mandy's eyes followed Jake up and down the court. Or was she watching Chad, who was guarding him?

Jake and Chad had been best of friends yet always challenging each other. Naturally, Jake was a showstopper with his love to perform. Most likely, the show was part of his scheme to woo Katy, but he was also attracting the attention of all the other females inside the barn.

She hated the jealousy that erupted inside her, that desire to possess and control him, even quell him. She'd first felt it when he'd started falling away. She hadn't been able to keep him then, so the familiar grinding in the pit of her stomach also carried a foreboding.

She should flee before he hurt her again. Only she had no place to go since Jake claimed he was here to stay, winning back the community. That made her a part of the spectacle, with everyone waiting to see if she would take him back, too. When Jake winked a roguish blackened eye at her, Katy wished she hadn't allowed their fragile beginnings of a relationship to go public.

Mandy caught the flirtatious gesture. "Glad to see you two back together."

"Excuse me?"

"You belong together."

Thoughts shot through Katy's mind: *If he dumps me it will be even more humiliating this time. If I lose him, the pain will be even worse than it was before. What am I doing here?* With the realization that she was a long way from trusting Jake again, she shrugged, "We'll see."

Everyone inside the barn was paired off, and some were even engaged to be married. Most of the girls were older than Katy and had never been as close to her as Lil and Megan, yet they were more than casual acquaintances. There were few strangers and even fewer secrets within the farming community of Plain City, Ohio, especially for those worshipping together in Katy's small Conservative congregation.

Her hands involuntarily worked tiny bits of prickly chaff from the bale of straw as she watched the guys pound the floor and dart from one end of the barn court to the other. The basketball bounced and flung at various levels of skill. A calico cat suddenly sprang onto her bale and looked at her as if the act surprised the creature, too. Katy rubbed its head, and it tentatively climbed onto her lap.

She wasn't fond of cat hair, and this one had a thick, partly matted coat, but the creature's need drew her and provided a pleasant distraction from the true object of her heart. She quietly stroked the cat's head, and when she eased off, he nudged her hand. Maybe she needed a cat at the doddy house. Lil adored animals, had always taken in strays at the farm. Vernon Yoder hadn't allowed cats at their place because their hair was a nuisance in the woodworking shop, hard to remove from a wet, stained surface.

"What happened to Jake's eye?"

Katy had arrived at the game after it had started and hadn't talked to Jake alone yet. She shrugged, "Probably a construction accident."

Jake commanded her attention with a flamboyant dunk. When he landed, the women heard a loud ripping sound. Katy's hand flew to her mouth in amusement, sure he was in trouble. He made the timeout sign with his hands and backed over to the far side of the barn. When he entered the court again, he had a shirt tied around his waist.

With a giggle, Mandy said, "Serves him right."

"I know." So Mandy had noticed that he wore his pants too tight. Unexpectedly, her jealousy swung to its opposite extreme, where she no longer wanted to flee but wanted to stake her claim before somebody else did. As David had implied, there were plenty of available girls willing to be sweet. But Katy wasn't playing a game, at least that had never been her intention.

The cat leapt down and rubbed its matted fur along the bales. She watched it go and brushed hair off her skirt, realizing the little creature had used her for warmth and affection and moved on.

Later at the bonfire, Katy watched Jake poke a roasting stick into the crackling flames. Their shoulders touching, she asked, "What happened to your eye?"

"Pillow fight."

She grinned. A fleeting picture of the church construction site, however, brought several real possibilities to her mind. Softly, she said, "Now that I've decided to tolerate you, I want you to take care of yourself."

His eyes caressed her. "I like that."

She dropped her gaze, then noticed the fire lapping at the hot dogs and pushed his arm. "Look out."

He jerked the stick from the fire and stared at the charred meat. "Guess these are ready. Let's go fix them." She followed him back inside the barn to a long, metal folding table laid out with buns, hot dog relishes, and paper products. As they fixed their plates, he said, "Hey, about that nanny job you lost? I found another job for you. If you're interested. It's one that might help us both."

Turning back toward the barn door, she replied, "No. I'm not cleaning your room."

He followed her with a chuckle. "I wouldn't want you to. And I'm not joking. It's a real job."

"Oh yeah? What is it?"

They sat on a bale to eat their dinner. "With my gram's Alzheimer's, she can't be left alone anymore. My mom just needs a break. Would you be interesting in sitting with her sometimes? For pay, of course."

"I'd be happy to help for free. I can organize some others to help, too. I'm sorry the church hasn't recognized the need before now."

"That would be too confusing for Gram. Mom mentioned hiring someone. I don't think she'd feel free to go out, otherwise. I'm sure she can find someone else, if you don't want to do it."

It would be good to work for someone within the church; that was what she'd been hoping for. This wasn't a housekeeping offer, but maybe it was God's provision until she found another job. She didn't miss the irony of moving from babysitting kids to babysitting grandmas. "Why don't I give it a try and see how it goes?"

"Great. I know Mom won't have any qualms about leaving Gram with you."

"I've always liked your grandmother. She was one of my favorite Sunday school teachers. Such a great storyteller, and she had so much energy, keeping the boys in line." Katy watched the cat return and rub against Jake's jeans. "Will she know me?"

"Probably not. But sometimes she remembers more than other times. We can't figure out why. The good thing is, she's usually happy."

"I'm sorry she has the disease."

He shrugged, obviously unable to express his grief. He dropped the mewing creature bits of his hot dog, and it ate greedily. "Are you getting a phone soon?"

The question startled her, and she worked it out in her mind as she spoke. "Lil doesn't need one with her cell phone, so I'd probably have to pay for it. As you know, we didn't put in a phone line."

"I meant a cell phone."

Instantly, Katy's spirit rose up in resistance against the unnecessary technology. "I don't think so."

"It might come in handy with work. Or for emergencies."

She nibbled at her lip, her mind conjuring up possible emergencies. "We'll see." Then she thought of the perfect solution. "You can always call the Millers if you can't get a hold of me through Lil."

His expression was clearly frustrated, yet he didn't argue.

—◌—

Katy's hands grew sweaty. It was the third week into the relationship and marriage sermons, and Brother Troyer had finally broached the topic of the prayer covering. He now directed them to open their Bibles to 1 Corinthians 11:3–16. Only the sound of ruffling pages broke the awesome silence pervading the sanctuary. The pages of Katy's Bible wanted to stick, but she finally found the passage where the apostle Paul clearly stated that a man should worship with his head uncovered and a woman with her head covered.

As Katy followed along, she realized the passage was not as clear as she had remembered it. The verses contained riddle-like prose, and to her great dissatisfaction, the preacher zeroed in on its most troubling portions. Was a woman's hair her covering? Next he touched on what the bonnet symbolized. Even at that point, he had more than one opinion. By the time she rose for the benediction, she felt angry that he hadn't given the congregation clear direction. Instead he had debated the meaning of the passage, playing both advocate and challenger, and had left the matter open-ended. His parting remark admonished them to consider and pray over God's intention. She thought a preacher was supposed to shepherd his flock. Surely the sheep didn't know where to go on their own.

With frustration, she moved into the foyer where another kind of confusion took precedence. Folks were fumbling with babies and umbrellas. Some women waited while their men hunkered down and made a run through the downpour to bring their cars around. Katy's focus on the sermon had been so intense she hadn't even realized it had started raining. She gazed out and sighed. Her umbrella was useless from its location on the rear floorboards of her car.

Just as she was mustering up the courage to make a dash for her car and comforting herself with visions of Lil's bean soup simmering back at the doddy house, the back of a young man's perfectly combed brown hair caught her attention. A tincture of mixed emotions drew her to a halt. She froze.

She had hoped to put off her first meeting with David since his humiliating set down, but the tiny room was too crowded for her to shrink back. She watched him determinedly weave through the foyer toward the door. When a family blocked his path, he glanced up and around. When his unfortunate gaze met Katy's, he flinched. Quite abruptly, he turned and shot through the first opening that led him out into the storm.

Katy gave a gasp. His brief shunning didn't trouble her as much as what she had just glimpsed. David's face was no longer perfect. Battered, with swollen lips, his face bore an ugly bruise on his cheek where his dimple normally played. With a sinking heart, she knew it was no coincidence that both her pursuers sported facial contusions. Why hadn't Jake told her the truth about his black eye? Mennonites didn't fight or brawl.

Already emotional over the sermon, this new revelation fed her churning stomach. Jake hadn't been at church so she couldn't question him. She had seen Ann Byler, so most likely his grandmother was having an off day and he'd stayed home with her.

Sucking in her lower lip, she nodded thanks to a considerate door tender and sprinted for her car. The rain streamed down her face in blinding torrents. The storm pelted her covering. The wind tore it loose. Her hand flew up to catch it. Rain drenched her hair, but she hardly cared. Emotionally, she was drowning. From her first job with the outsiders, she'd started sinking. In every direction, waves swelled. Wind clawed. Decisions loomed. Everyone tossed life preservers at her, but she didn't know which one to grab. If she chose wrong, she was going to drown.

CHAPTER 23

S ome smart person started the saying that time heals. Or was that in the Bible some place? Katy didn't know, but she supposed it was true because even an hour had done wonders for her emotional state. So had the heat that flowed through the doddy house, carrying with it the welcoming aroma of Lil's hearty bean soup. Dry clothing and a securely pinned covering also contributed to a better perspective.

After church, Megan had flitted in with her cheery countenance, joining Katy and Lil for Sunday lunch. Their blond friend had chatted about her summer missions options, then flown off to spend the afternoon with her folks before heading back to Rosedale College.

Now Katy lined up her dominoes. Across the table, Lil did the same. As they played, they could look out the kitchen window and watch the steady rain turn the ground into tiny rivulets.

"I didn't see Jake at church, did you?" Lil asked.

"No, but I saw his mom. He probably stayed home with his grandma." Just remembering something he'd mentioned at the basketball game, she added, "He has to bid some blueprints this afternoon." They exchanged a disapproving look, for even Lil knew they shouldn't work on Sundays. "Last night he asked me if I'd like to work for his mom, watching Minnie."

Lil's gaze softened with fondness at the mention of her grandmother. "Mom and I have watched her before. She's a handful, but I love her."

"I'd like to try it and see how it goes. It will be a challenge, but I've always loved her."

"You going to clean their place, too?"

"I don't know. I'll do whatever Ann wants. If it works out, the extra income should help us scrape by. Think Megan will ever settle down with a job?"

Lil matched a yellow domino to another yellow domino. "Hard to tell. Jobs can be disappointing. I need to find something better. Nobody ever sees me back in the kitchen, and the restaurant's not big enough to move to a higher position. No prestige. No extra money. Dead-end job." She glanced out at the rain. "I should drive into Plain City and buy a newspaper."

Trailing her friend's gaze to the dreary weather and back, Katy offered, "I'll go with you, if you'd like."

"Okay. Let's finish this game first. Maybe the rain will ease up by then." They both glanced out the window again, sharing skepticism. Several plays passed without conversing as Katy thought about Lil not liking her job. Her friend had high expectations and the grit to fulfill them. Maybe that was part of her own despair. She didn't have any goals. Just then a shiny black car turned into the Millers' driveway.

"Oh great," Katy said sarcastically. The image of David's bruised face flashed across her mind. Who needed goals when it was hard just to survive each day's handouts? "David won't be coming here."

They both leaned toward the window and watched, but the car disappeared in front of Ivan and Elizabeth's house.

Lil looked over with amusement. "Did you see him today?"

Katy rapped her dominos on the table in disgust. "Yes! How could they? What does fighting solve? Do they think I'm going to throw myself into the winner's arms?"

"I wonder who started it? Jake's been real jealous, but I never heard of him fighting before."

"Probably David. He was quietly furious the other night when we talked. It shocked me." She told Lil about his cutting remark.

"Whoa! Maybe we need to sic Megan on them. Remind them of their Anabaptist upbringing."

"They both know better. It's humiliating. And Jake is going to get an earful the next time I see him, too. When I asked him what happened, he said he'd been in a pillow fight."

Lil giggled. Then she asked, "Is it really humiliating? Or is it a little gratifying?" She slid another ivory rectangle into place. "I'd like that kind of embarrassment—having two guys fight over me." Involuntarily, she waved a domino. "Maybe the blond waiter and that one guy from culinary school that who wouldn't give me the time of day. Yeah, that'd be something. I'd want the waiter to win. The other guy was smug."

"Two things to keep in mind. First, you may be saying good-bye to your blond waiter if you find another job. And second, they aren't really available if they aren't Mennonite men, are they?"

Glancing up, Lil said, "Oh, there's the Katy I remember. Thought we weren't going to get preachy. Especially since you have it all with your dark, smoldering beauty." Lil shook her head. "Pass."

"Don't forget my lovely smooth hands and preachy mouth," Katy reminded her. Then she cocked an eyebrow. "You can't move?"

"Nope."

Making a dramatic gesture with her occupationally chafed hands, she made a winning move. Lil let out a moan and paused to write down her points. Then they turned all the colored dots over until the pile was plain ivory and worked to shuffle the pieces. "What number are we on?" Lil asked.

"Three. I've got it." They kept their peace while lining up their dominos, and then Katy gave Lil a wry grin. "You're right. It's really hard for me not to preach. But you set me up with such lovely opportunities all the time. Speaking of, what did you think of Brother Troyer's sermon? Are you going to be submissive when you get married?"

"Ah, the awful S word. You did hear him say that men and women are equal? One's not superior over the other?"

Katy nodded. "He was talking out of both sides of his mouth, 'cause in the next breath, he implied that the husband was in charge." She knew that her own mom showed deference to her dad in a lot of ways and that Lil's folks had modeled the same type of marriage, but she couldn't picture Lil settling for that type of arrangement. And to be honest, she had to wonder if she could settle for it, either.

Lil thoughtfully tapped a domino on the table. "I like what he said about it being purely an order issue. Adam was made first to reflect God's glory. Then woman next, to reflect man's glory."

"Glorious man," Katy taunted, and Lil burst into giggles. Then Katy pushed back from the table and stared out the window. "Seriously, I don't get the glory thing."

Lil glanced out the window and back. "You agree that God's creation shows His greatness?"

"Sure. Nature draws me to God."

Lil explained, "Man's the highest of his creation. When a man shows honor to somebody, he removes his hat. So Adam worships with his head uncovered. But mankind sinned. When Adam and Eve sinned, what did they do?"

Katy shrugged. "Hid and covered themselves with fig leaves."

Lil pointed to her own covering. "So when woman wears a head covering, it's a symbol of mankind's fall."

Inadvertently, Katy touched her own covering. "Wow. What a spiritual picture."

"For the angels to witness."

Katy felt drawn to Lil's depiction of equality. "So what about the angels?"

Lil shrugged. "Honestly? I don't know. I'm not *that* smart."

Katy would have laughed if it wasn't such a crucial topic. "So it's not just about the woman submitting to her husband?"

"If it were, only married women would wear it."

Katy demanded, "How do you know all this?"

"Duh? Brother Troyer preached it today. Weren't you even listening? Sometimes I get the impression you think I'm totally lost and going to hell or something."

"Lil! Don't say that. Of course I don't think that." Katy felt contrite.

"But I did think you'd be happy to ditch the covering."

"Not really. At work, but not at church. The important thing is that the church doesn't split apart over it."

Katy hoped for more than peace. She hoped nothing would change. Since their big argument, Lil had seemed softer, more sensitive toward spiritual things than Katy had given her credit for, and yet she couldn't picture Lil taking a submissive role. "So back to the *S* word. You going to submit to your husband?"

"I'm hoping to find a man who'll welcome my opinions, but right now I can't even find a man." She pushed back her chair. "I think we need a hot chocolate perk or we're never going to finish this game. And I need that newspaper." She started the teakettle, then returned to the table. "Since you've got two guys fighting over you, the *S* word seems to be more your problem than mine."

Katy cringed. She didn't like the idea of submission. Thunder cracked, and she glanced out the window at the dark sky, considering God.

When Lil returned to the table with two steaming cups, she placed one in front of Katy. "Just take your time with Jake. I don't want to lose you as a roommate."

After the game was finished, they left to get Lil's newspaper. While they drove, they discussed the benefits of Katy getting a cell phone versus a landline. Lil finally persuaded her that just because cell phones were more modern didn't make then any worldlier than landlines. A phone was a phone, and it was a safety precaution to have while driving.

When Lil brought up driving, it touched a chord with Katy. She did get nervous when she drove alone in the dark.

After they got back to the doddy house, Lil gave her a demonstration of how a cell phone worked, and Katy finally relented to the idea. After that, Lil circled two job ads that she meant to check out the following week.

"You think once you get married things get easier?" Katy asked.

"Nope. Then you get kids. That's when your trouble really starts." Lil moved to the floor to begin her regimented sit-ups, and Katy knew the conversation was over.

She opened the jar that contained her latest concoction and rubbed the greasy cream on her hands. After that, she slipped into her night gloves and jotted notes in her journal. She had an entire section devoted to her hand-cream experiments.

Since her journal had become a handy tool for housekeeping, she decided to add a spiritual section. Nibbling on her pen, she came up with a practical heading: The Prayer Covering. Below it, she copied the scripture Brother Troyer had given them to study.

CHAPTER 24

The telephone store might not have been so intimidating if it hadn't been located inside the indoor mall, which screamed to Katy *lust of the flesh, lust of the eyes, and pride of life*—all phrases from a Bible verse. Lil told her she was lucky it wasn't the weekend for that's when it became a breeding ground for weirdness. Katy didn't even want to know what that meant.

Young moms in tight-belted jeans and high-heeled boots pushed strollers and shushed babies without dropping their gaze from the window displays that carried the latest fashions. Some hurried by as if they were participating in a shopping marathon in which they wouldn't hesitate to run over stragglers. Others stared at her and Lil, their gazes sweeping over them from their oxfords to their coverings, but Katy kept her shoulders ramrod straight. She had as much right as anyone to spend her money. To own a cell phone without being frivolous or self-centered. Or so Lil maintained.

A sudden face darted in front of her. "Ma'am, try this ring cleaner?" Katy halted and stared at the teenager, who blushed when he discovered that she wasn't wearing any jewelry.

"No thank you." Katy sidestepped, bumping into Lil.

"Over there." Lil pointed.

Katy glanced at the store's sign. When they stepped inside the phone store, Katy felt more out of place than a guy at a quilting.

"I already looked the phones over and can point you to a couple of good deals," Lil advised. She pointed out various features of the display phones that rested on tiny glass shelves throughout the store. Next a sales representative explained the terms and told Katy about rebates. After Katy chose a phone, she followed him—careful not to stare at his low-slung pants—to the cash register and got out her checkbook. She wrote the check out for the amount he had indicated and pushed it toward him.

"Um, if you write a check, I need to see a debit card."

Katy glanced at Lil, then back at the young man behind the counter. "I don't have any cards." A card had come with her checking account, but she had filed it away, refusing to use it.

"Sorry." He glanced up at her covering. "I can't take this then."

She returned the wasted check to her checkbook and dropped it inside her purse, pulling out her billfold instead. "I'll pay cash then."

The young man seemed surprised and patient as Katy worked to get him the correct amount. He programmed the phone and handed it back to her. Her pulse quickened unexpectedly as she stared at the shiny rectangle in her palm. Beside her, Lil snatched Katy's shopping bag off the counter and nudged her toward the door.

"Thanks," Katy tossed over her shoulder. The clerk smiled.

"Let's celebrate. I'll buy lunch," Lil urged.

After everything happened so quickly, Katy did need to catch her breath, so she agreed to dine at a Mexican restaurant. Over the chips and salsa, Lil entered some of her phone numbers into Katy's phone and demonstrated its unique features.

"Thanks for going with me. It was pretty intimidating. How did you ever have the nerve to go by yourself?"

"I didn't. Jake went with me. Here, let me show you about texting."

"No thanks. I only bought this for practical purposes."

"That's why you need to learn how to text. Watch, I'll text Jake and tell him your new number."

"No. Wait. I'm not ready for that yet."

"What good's a phone if you don't use it?"

"Oh fine," Katy relented.

Moments later she got a reply from Jake. CAN U COME TO DINNR FRI NITE TO C HOW GRAM DOES?

Lil showed her how to reply: YES.

I'LL CALL W D TAILS.

Amazed, Katy wondered how she could have feared something so convenient and practical.

—⟶

Jake's familial home was a typical Plain City farm. It consisted of a two-story house, barn, silo, and more than forty acres of flat, tilled cornfields. Large ash and buckeyes shaded the house, and Katy recalled her first kiss happened under the huge weeping willow by the circle drive. She had been sixteen years old. Trying not to think about it, she stepped up onto the front porch that cooled the Bylers' guests in the summer and sheltered them in winter.

As soon as she touched the bell, Jake opened the door. His hair was still damp from the shower, and his face clean-shaven. For a moment he just grinned at her, looking rakish with his one black eye.

She flashed him a timid smile. "This feels strange."

"Not to me. You belong here." He took her hand and drew her inside. "With me."

She wet her lips, choosing to ignore his remark. "Where is everybody?"

"In the kitchen. Come on."

Ann Byler's kitchen reflected her cheery disposition. She celebrated sunshine, welcoming it through rows of windows dressed in perky yellow valances. The window and ledge above the sink displayed a collection of stained-glass sun catchers. An antique cupboard held a sun chime. Its soft jingle had always intrigued Katy. In the summer, Ann grew sunflowers in her garden, and in the winter, silk ones decorated the table.

Rocking in a corner stream of late-afternoon light, Jake's grandmother bowed her head over a lap-sized hoop. She didn't look up when

Katy moved closer to observe her project, watching the old hands work a needle up and down through taut material. To her pleasant surprise, the stitching was small and even. The old woman's hands were steady, and the tips of her fingers that weren't covered with thimbles were dry and cracked from the continuous push of the needle. Sympathy curled inside Katy's heart. She would bring Minnie some of her healing hand ointment.

"Mom loves to quilt pillow shams," Ann said, then returned to her stove.

"I sell them for her on eBay." Jake winked and moved to give Minnie a side hug. When he saw Katy's confusion, he explained, "An Internet store. On the computer."

Katy touched Minnie's arm. "That's very good stitching."

The older woman looked up then focused on Jake. "Who have you brought home, Jacob?"

"This is Katy Yoder."

"Oh. I taught her in Sunday school, you know. Such a lovely girl."

Katy beamed that Minnie remembered her, but sadly Minnie thought Jake was his grandfather, his namesake. "I loved your stories about David and Goliath. The way you marched around the room with a pretend slingshot."

Minnie giggled then covered her mouth, whispering between her fingers. "I should have been a movie actress."

Shocked, Katy replied, "I'm glad you were a Sunday school teacher instead."

"Dinner's ready," Ann called.

"Are you hungry, Gram?" Jake asked.

"No, I need to finish this while there's still light."

"We're having meat loaf."

"Well that does sound good. Maybe I will." He helped her stand, and then she walked to the kitchen table, confused.

"In the dining room. Since Katy's visiting."

"Who's Katy?"

Katy's heart sank.

Giving Katy a sympathetic look, Jake guided Grandma Minnie by the elbow to her place in the dining room. "What a pretty table." She stopped mid-step and smiled at Ann. "You shouldn't have gone to all this trouble."

Jake whispered to Katy, "Most of the time she thinks Mom is her sister, and I'm Grandpa."

"You always looked like him," Katy whispered.

Once Minnie was seated, Ann smiled at Katy. "I'm so glad you came tonight. I've missed you."

Katy had always appreciated Ann's gentle manner. Rumor was she didn't have any backbone, and that's why she allowed her only daughter to traipse off to OSU and why Jake went wild. With his dad gone, there was simply no discipline. Katy tried to rein her thoughts back to the conversation. Ann was asking polite questions, inquiring about Katy's work and skirting around Grandma Minnie's periodic interruptions with a practiced skill that was both sad and heartwarming. Sipping water from a sunflower-patterned glass, Katy listened to Ann's summer plans for a fruit and vegetable stand, and cast smiling eyes Jake's way, pleased with him for returning home to help his family.

Before she left, Katy and Ann planned for Katy to stay with Grandma Minnie one day a week. If that worked, they might extend it to two days and include some cleaning. Around eight o'clock, Jake offered to walk her to her car.

Taking her gloved hand, he said, "How about you start the heater, and I'll join you for a few minutes. We haven't had any time alone."

Instantly, Katy remembered times they'd sat in his truck after a date and talked. Sometimes they kissed, but he'd always remained a gentleman. Would he keep his word tonight, about not kissing her until she was ready?

Inside her car, he took her hand and leaned close. "Thanks so much for helping with Grams."

"We'll get along fine. She remembered me for an instant."

"She loved you. Back when we were in high school, she encouraged me to date you."

Resisting the nostalgic pull, Katy drew her hand away, taking hold of the steering wheel. Light shone through the living room windows. Everything inside had been faintly familiar yet different. Jake's dad was now gone, Cal was married, and Erin was away at college. Jake seemed changed, too, older and more mature. But should she trust him? It would be so easy to fall under his spell.

Take it slow, Lil had warned, in spite of her earlier matchmaking. Did Lil know something about Jake she wasn't sharing? Or was it just Lil's way to hang on to the doddy house dream?

Katy glanced over. "What really happened to your eye?"

The corner of his mouth quirked. "I just collided with something."

She arched her brows. "Did you know David had a similar accident?"

Finally he replied, his Amish-Dutch accent thicker than usual, "It's a good thing you dumped him. He's a real hothead."

"He started it then?"

"He came to the church one night after the crew left. I tried to reason with him, but in his condition it was useless. I'm surprised he even made it home without ending up in some ditch."

Her pursed lips slackened. "He was drunk?"

Jake nodded.

"But everybody thinks he's such a nice guy," Katy protested.

Jake looked hurt. "Everyone makes mistakes."

She considered his statement. David Miller had gotten drunk and started a fight because of her mistakes. She tightened her grip on the steering wheel. "I know what you're thinking. That I used him to get the doddy house. But I wanted to find out if I was over you, too. I hoped my dates with David would turn into more."

He touched her cheek. "Thanks for your honesty."

She dropped her hands in her lap and stared at him, blinking back threatening tears. Silence hovered between them, and she knew instinctively when he thought about kissing her. She saw his inward struggle, but he refrained.

Should she ask him more about his relationship with Jessie? Would there ever be a more fitting time? Before she could trust him, she needed to know exactly what she was forgiving.

But he spoke again first. "The doddy house has always been your dream. I want you to enjoy it. Although I made mistakes when I was out on my own, it helped me find my way. I want that for you, too. It will help us in our relationship."

It seemed contrived now to bring the conversation back to Jessie. Instead, Katy asked, "What if I become too independent and never marry? I like being my own boss."

"You still have Lil."

She chuckled, glad they'd lightened the tone of the conversation. "I don't get to boss her around, but we do have some great argu— discussions."

His laughter rang in her ears long after the car had grown quiet. Then he said, "You have a pure heart, Katy Yoder. It draws a man."

But it was his heart Katy wanted to explore. She needed to know if they still meshed. "What do you think about the prayer covering?"

He didn't answer directly. "If we ever married, I'd give you lots of freedom to be yourself."

She considered the implications of the *S* word as she studied his moonlit face. He seemed serious.

"You wouldn't boss me around?"

"Would you listen if I did?"

She shrugged.

He stared at her lips. "I'm finding it hard to behave."

Involuntarily, she twirled her ponytail.

He swallowed. "I'd better go." Once he was out, he ducked his head back inside. "I'll call."

As she watched him go, she had to wonder if he offered a relationship with plenty of freedom because he wasn't willing to settle down himself. If she pursued a relationship with him, even marriage, would there be more things to condone? Or worse things to forgive? Freedom was a frightening thing. Was his newfound faith in God enough to make him a faithful husband?

CHAPTER 25

Ann Byler lingered at the door, a worrisome gaze flitting over her sunny nest, and Katy sensed the other woman's reluctance to give her elderly mother over to someone else's care.

"Grandma Minnie will be fine with me. Take as long as you like." Katy knew Ann needed a break, regardless of her own niggling apprehension at spending time in Jake's home, where even in his absence, his presence permeated every corner.

Was she overly sensitive that everything about that man attracted and cautioned her at the same time? That everything about him screamed, *Tread carefully*?

The door closed and she braced herself. She owed Grandma Minnie. In Sunday school, it was Minnie who had instilled in her to color inside the lines. And taught her faces weren't purple, but legs were black. Minnie had guided generations, campaigning against prideful adornment whether it be a necktie or lipstick. Normally, Katy used a lip moistener with just a touch of shine, but in case Minnie was having one of her lucid days, Katy had avoided that luxury.

No need to vex the woman in her old age. Katy couldn't imagine the pain Minnie must have endured over the years as changes invaded their tight-knit community. It was sad, but Katy didn't know another woman in the church who could follow in Minnie's stead to keep the church from conforming to the world around them.

Minnie sat on the couch, staring across the room where her gaze was transfixed on a tree outside the window. Her quilting hoop lay discarded on the cushion next to her.

"Hello, Minnie."

The woman jerked her gaze away and squinted at Katy. "Are you here for firewood? That old tree isn't dead. Only dormant, waiting for spring." She folded her arms. "My swing's in that tree."

The homestead had been Minnie's childhood home. No wonder she was so confused now. "I'm just here to visit."

The deeply folded face belied the childlike spirit. "Then let's go swing." Minnie pushed up from the couch and started toward the kitchen with amazing agility.

Scurrying after her, Katy objected. "It's really cold outside."

Minnie's chin jutted up. "But I want to swing."

Seeing there was no stopping the older woman, Katy went to the coat closet. "Put this on first."

Thankfully, Minnie shrugged into her black, Amish shawl.

"Sit down. I'll help you put your boots on, too."

Minnie sat, a wide smile on her face.

Katy grabbed a pair of winter boots that appeared to be the appropriate size and knelt in front of Minnie. The action reminded her of foot washing service, and it humbled her and sent warm fuzzies up her back to serve the woman who had once served her. She untied the black oxfords and set them to the side, then tipped the boots. Minnie obediently poked her black-clad toes into the opening. She tilted her face to the side, studying Katy.

"Who are you?"

"Katy Yoder. A friend of Jake's. All done. Let's go." Minnie took her hand, and they went outside. For an instant the older woman braced herself, confused and blinking at the sudden glare of sunlight. The sting of cold air nipped Katy's face. "This way."

She led the five-foot-two woman around the side of the house to the old ash tree. She helped Minnie onto the swing's board seat, which was supported by two thick ropes. "Hold tight. I'll push you." Minnie pumped her legs and giggled. Her blue skirt billowed out, exposing thin, black-clad knees. Minnie was always barely over one hundred pounds, and now seemed more waiflike than ever, and as Katy stepped away to watch, a melancholy lump formed in her throat.

How many human generations would the old tree know? It was sad to see Minnie's life end in confusion. It hurt to learn that even when you colored inside the lines, life was still not a safe place to inhabit.

"I can touch heaven," Minnie said, pointing her toes. "God's smiling at me."

Katy swiped her coat sleeve across her eyes.

After they finished playing, Katy fixed Minnie the leftover chili that Ann had set aside for their lunch. Her face still aglow from the crisp cold, Minnie had the spoon to her mouth before Katy was even seated. With a smile, Katy said, "I'll pray."

She closed her eyes and, still feeling melancholy over Minnie's condition, she waited for peace to settle over her before she started speaking. "Lord, I thank You for Minnie's life, for her years of leadership and love to us. I pray that You will fill her heart with joy and peace. May she always feel Your presence. We thank You for this food. Amen."

Katy opened her eyes and looked across the table. Her jaw dropped. Stunned, she stared at Minnie.

The Alzheimer's victim had removed her prayer covering and placed it upside down in her bowl of chili. Her hair was partly unpinned, and she was struggling with its remaining pins.

Katy jumped up and fairly flew around the side of the table. She grabbed Minnie's hand, but the older woman jerked it away and knocked over her water glass. With a yelp, Katy ran to the counter for a roll of paper towels. Minnie had jumped up now, too, and was holding her apron out, staring at a giant wet spot, her lower lip quivering. Her hair was as wild as a bag woman's Katy had once observed on a Columbus street corner.

Dabbing at the puddle of water spreading across the tablecloth and dripping onto the floor, Katy soaked up as much as she could. Then she glanced at Minnie, still not believing the woman had stuck her covering in her chili bowl. But when their gazes met, Minnie must have felt her displeasure because she started to cry.

Katy set down the roll of towels and touched her shoulder. "It's all right. Let's just take off your apron and find a dry one."

The woman whimpered and eyed Katy suspiciously. She tried to keep her voice soothing. "Why don't you sit in this other dry chair?" Minnie eased into it like a frightened child. Katy smiled, pulling the woman's bowl over. But Minnie beat her to the covering and whipped it out of the food, plopping it onto the table. Katy tightened her lips at the ugly orange stain on Ann's white tablecloth. She snatched another paper towel and scooped up the covering, taking it to the kitchen sink along with the wet apron.

She quickly returned to the table and gave Minnie a weak smile, handing her a spoon. The woman clamped her hand around the spoon but didn't eat. Remembering how Jake had gotten her to the table the other night, Katy started talking about how good the soup smelled. Minnie took the bait.

Katy wanted to push the woman's hair back over her shoulder so it didn't hang in her chili, but she didn't want to frighten her again. Instead she returned to the sink and ran water through the covering, reverently patting it dry and trying to plump out its shape, setting it in a sunny spot.

Next she seated herself beside Minnie and forced herself to take a few spoonfuls of the soup, wondering how she was going to get Minnie's hair combed and the covering back on her head. She knew that if Minnie were in her right mind, she'd want to wear her head covering. She'd want someone to make sure she kept it on when she wasn't thinking clearly anymore. Katy determined to make that happen.

Eventually after much maneuvering and gentle urgings, Katy managed to get the contrite woman to her bedroom. She combed out Minnie's hair, plaited it and replaced her covering. While Minnie settled under the bed quilt, Katy read a few scriptures from a Bible on a nearby nightstand. She patted Minnie's back until the old eyes closed. Even afterward, Katy lingered outside of the bedroom door until she heard

Minnie's snoring. Then she leaned against the wall a moment to collect herself, wondering how so much damage could happen in such a small fraction of time.

Next she returned to set Ann's kitchen to rights. Katy set the dirty dishes on the counter and removed the white tablecloth, running water over the tomato spots, then dabbing vinegar on the stain. She draped it over the washing machine and returned to the kitchen to wash the dishes.

When she had the kitchen finished, she went to listen outside Minnie's bedroom door. But she only heard silence through the walls. Sensing that Minnie could get in more trouble than Addison at seven years of age could even dream of, she slowly turned the doorknob and eased it open.

Her heart leapt in her chest. Katy cried, "Stop!"

Minnie's hand paused. Orange-handled scissors interlocked a long shank of thin white hair. Hair that had hardly ever been cut. Minnie blinked. Then Katy saw a rebellious glint enter the old eyes. Was this some sort of showdown? It was becoming obvious where Jake got his rebellion.

Katy was afraid to step into the room. If Minnie jerked, she might snip off her hair. She willed her voice to calm. "Your hair is so lovely. If you give me the scissors, I'll brush it for you again."

"No! That hurts. I'm cutting it so it doesn't hurt." The woman lifted the shank of hair and dropped her gaze to it, pressing the scissors handles closed. With a gasp, Katy watched twelve inches of growth slip to the floor.

Katy flew into the room and wrestled the scissors out of Minnie's hand, all the while being sure to keep it away from her face. When Minnie saw she had lost, she curled into a ball on the bed, making a noise that sounded like an angry cat. And Katy had a moment to take inventory. Minnie's wet covering was squashed on top of the pillow. Not only was a large chunk of Minnie's hair gone, but now Katy noticed that part of the cape on Minnie's gown was shredded.

Katy pressed her eyes together in agony and regret. Had she been too rough when she'd brushed Minnie's hair, giving her charge the idea to cut it off? Then remembering she couldn't give Minnie a scrap of time unwatched, she flashed her eyes open again. But Minnie was still curled on the bed making unearthly sounds. Katy rubbed her sweaty palms on her skirt, wondering how to rectify the situation.

Suddenly Minnie sat up. "My dress is ruined."

A flash of anger shot through Katy, but she quickly reminded herself that it wasn't Minnie's fault that the cape was shredded. It was the disease. And Katy's own neglect. First, she needed to get rid of the scissors. A glance at the door told her Minnie's lock had been removed, but she still didn't trust her alone. Katy backed toward the closet, stood on her tiptoes, and shoved the scissors on a high shelf that the shorter woman wouldn't be able to reach. While she was by the closet, she saw a clean dress and removed it from its hanger. Draping it over her arm, she started toward the bed. "Let's put this on before Ann comes home."

Minnie swung her legs over the side of the bed. "Where is Ann?"

"She went to town."

"How? Did she go with her daddy?"

Katy realized Minnie thought her daughter was a child again. Taking advantage of the older woman's contemplative state, she unfastened her dress and managed to remove it from a compliant body. "May I pin up your hair? Jacob likes it that way." Minnie shrugged, and Katy used her fingers to inspect the damage. The shearing was noticeable, but could be disguised when plaited. After that she shook open the covering. "A woman should always wear her covering," Katy soothed, starting toward her.

"No." Minnie stuck out her foot and kicked Katie in the stomach.

"Ugh!" The unexpected blow took her breath away and brought tears to her eyes. But Katy quickly recovered. She narrowed her eyes. Her voice came out harsh. "Why not?"

"I'm sick of it. I always wanted to be an actress."

The words hit Katy with a force equal to the earlier kick. This was more serious than she'd thought. Katy began to perspire. She tentatively bent toward Minnie, softening her voice as though she spoke to a four-year-old. She pointed, "I'm wearing one, see?"

Then quick as a viper, Minnie's hand struck out and swiped Katy's covering from her head, taking pins and hair with it.

"Ouch!" Katy's arms flew up, but she was too late.

Minnie now waved Katy's covering, from which several long black hairs dangled.

Setting an angry jaw, Katy placed a firm hand on Minnie's shoulder and with the other tried to snatch her covering back. But Minnie waved it overhead like a white organdy flag. This was far from a truce. Katy made several swipes through the air, and the last one toppled them both back on the bed with Katy landing on top of the weaker woman.

But Minnie fought like one twice her weight and hollered like she was being murdered, crumpling the head covering and pulling it close to her body. Katy feared Minnie would scratch herself with the pins. Then in a quick flash, the wily woman stuffed it inside her bodice.

With both hands free now, Minnie started to beat Katy and kick. She landed several blows to Katy's face. "Get off!"

Katy thrust up a protective arm and tried to capture Minnie's battering fists. "Stop. Give me that! This instant!"

"What on earth!" a feminine voice wailed from the doorway.

Katy flinched then sat up, her own hair now nearly as disheveled as Minnie's. Minnie crawled to the far side of the bed and pulled the covers up around her protectively. Katy's cheeks flamed to see Ann burst into the room with Jake at her heels. Katy slid to her feet and withdrew a few steps.

Jake swept past her and fell to his knees, gently embracing his grandmother. "Grams. You all right?"

The gentleness in his voice and his total disregard of Katy enraged her. Ann wore a pained expression. How could they think this was her fault? "Just keep it!" Katy spit out. She faced Ann. "She cut her hair and her dress. The scissors are on the closet shelf. And my covering is in her bra!"

Ann's face paled, and she took a backward step, her hands going to her chest as though she might have a heart attack.

But Katy ignored it and stormed out of the room.

"Wait!" Katy heard Ann call after her.

Utterly humiliated and in spite of the footsteps clamoring after her,

Katy fled from the nightmare. She flung open the closet door, threw her coat and purse over her arm, and ran for the car. But she slipped in the gravel driveway and fell, bruising her knees.

Behind her she heard, "Oh Katy."

She struggled to her feet and didn't look back.

CHAPTER 26

As two of the most important women in Jake's life fled from the room, his mom screaming after Katy, he sat on the bed and draped his arm around his gram. On the floor lay a pile of discarded clothing and a covering with strings. His gram's.

Instantly, he understood what had happened. Gram had been removing her bonnet a lot lately, and Katy probably tried to force her to wear it. They should have warned Katy about that. But struggling with scissors? What had Katy been thinking to allow it to come to that? Headstrong and hotheaded. Maybe it was good he'd seen this side to her. He couldn't believe the image that lingered over what he'd witnessed when he entered the bedroom. Katy on top of his little grandmother, manhandling her. Unbelievable!

Minnie shivered, and Jake realized she was still recovering from the ordeal. He pulled the quilt up over her shoulders. He needed to dress her. He rose and sorted through the mess on the floor, and his hand touched the discarded head covering. Wet? How on earth? With a frustrated sigh, he let it lay and retrieved the fresh dress from its hanger. "Let's get you dressed."

"Is that awful woman gone?"

"Yes. You're safe now."

Minnie nodded obediently. "Wait." She stuck her hand through her torn bodice and withdrew another smaller covering, thrusting it forward like a great prize.

Jake blinked. She did have Katy's covering in her bra! How in the world?

He narrowed his eyes. "Grams, what did you do?"

"She's a wildcat! Do you want it or not?"

He obviously wouldn't get to the bottom of it by talking to his gram. Katy would have to explain the situation. He tightened his jaw. Her version of it. Her sanctimonious version of it. At his grandmother's contrite expression, he relaxed his jaw. "It's all right, Gram." He opened his hand, and she dropped it into his palm.

She tugged at her bosom. "It scratched me."

Surprised, he noticed the pins. He'd never paid much attention to the little caps, although he'd seen plenty in his day. For years, his grandmother had designed and sewn them for others as extra income. He dropped the straight pins in his shirt pocket, but left Katy's hair in the organdy cap and stuffed it into his jeans pocket.

"She's gone," Ann declared, entering the room with a sullen expression. "We scared her off." She swept a painful gaze across the room, like he had earlier. Then she looked at Minnie, and her eyes softened. "You tired, Mother?"

"No. I think I'll swing," Minnie declared.

Ann sighed.

Jake handed the dress to his mother and left them, intending to get to the bottom of the incident. In the kitchen, he saw the bare table, the open closet door, the wet boots. There'd been plenty of action in a few hours' time. He strode to the window and looked outside. Gone were all but the tire tracks of Katy's Chevy. He turned and scaled the stairs, hurrying into the privacy of his room. Moving to the window that gave view of the barren fields, he speed-dialed Katy. But she wasn't answering. Of course, she wasn't, he fumed, jamming his phone in his pocket and striding to his door.

—ᘒ—

Stomping into her bedroom and jerking open the drawer of her nightstand, Katy took out a fresh covering and marched to the bathroom. She was taken back momentarily when she saw her disheveled state. Her face was bruised on the right cheekbone just below the eye. Well, now she matched Jake and David! She washed her face and quickly put herself to rights, pinning on the fresh covering.

"Ouch!" She stuck her thumb in her mouth. The physical pain subsided, but not the pain over the incident with Minnie, and worst, getting caught in the midst of it.

Her stockings had a hole in one knee. She removed them and washed gravel from the wound, placing salve over it and a bandage. Then she put on her slippers and went to the kitchen.

Not knowing how to rectify the situation, when Ann and Jake so obviously blamed her for everything, she got out a pint of chocolate ice cream. Absurd images flashed through her mind. Her hands shaky, Katy licked the tasteless dessert. Shame flooded over her. How had she lost control of a petite, eighty-five-year-old woman? An innocent babe who didn't know what she was doing? And worst, why hadn't she stayed to explain her actions instead of running away like a guilty criminal?

Because Jake betrayed her. Again.

Still she could have heeded the soft warning, the quiet voice that had warned her to cease struggling. She could pinpoint the exact moment when she'd let her anger take control, overstepped her bounds, and pressed ahead in anger instead of retreating in love. She hadn't done anything wrong. Until the struggle. Then she'd chosen the same childish behavior as Minnie's. But it had all happened so quickly, she rationalized. She would have quit struggling if she'd had only a moment more. She didn't want Minnie to get scratched with the pins. But Ann had returned at the most inappropriate time.

As she thought back to the incident, she remembered Minnie's bloodcurdling screams. No wonder Jake and Ann had burst into the room with looks of horror on their faces. She jammed the spoon into the frozen mound and pushed it away.

Her cell phone rang. Jake again. She groaned and didn't answer it. He'd called at least six times now. She wasn't ready to talk to him, couldn't forget the condemnation in his eyes. She put the carton of ice cream away and got out her journal instead.

Tomato stain—run cool water until clear, then blot with white vinegar.

Next to the tip, she wrote: *Removing the stain does not remove memory of the incident. I remain in search of that particular cleansing agent that can renew thoughts.*

She remembered reading something like that in the scriptures and went to her bedroom to get her Bible. When she passed the window, however, she caught movement outside. Her spirit sank to see Jake's truck pulling into the drive.

Squaring her shoulders for battle, she started toward the door. *He just doesn't know when to give up!*

When Jake stepped inside, his face was grim. He looked around the spic-and-span doddy house with snapping eyes. "Am I interrupting something?"

"No."

"Then why didn't you answer your phone?"

"Because I saw your name on the screen."

His face flinched. He lifted his gaze to the top of her head and dropped it again, his expression burning with accusation. He swept her covering out of his pocket and slapped it on the table. "Guess you don't need this."

Her cheeks heated.

"She's a frail old woman," he admonished.

"How dare you come blaming me without giving me a chance to explain what happened?"

"You're the one who ran. You let her alone with scissors? What were you thinking?"

Katy placed both hands to her temples. "Okay, stop. Just sit down. Listen to my side of it."

He hesitated.

She tilted her head to the side impatiently, "Isn't that why you came?"

He brushed past her and strode into the living room. She wasn't expecting to win him over, but she wasn't about to let him leave without defending herself. She followed him and sat at the opposite end of the leather sofa, keeping an awkward distance between them.

She folded her hands on the lap of her dark skirt and painstakingly conveyed the entire story. Surprisingly, he didn't interrupt. His expression had softened when she told him about swinging with his grandma, but it hardened again as the story continued. "Then you burst into the room, and you know the rest," she finished.

"But how did she get the scissors?"

He was one-tracked. Katy shook her head. "I'm not a fool."

He lifted a brow.

"I don't know. Maybe she slipped into the living room. Maybe she was pretending to sleep. Honestly, it's almost like she was testing me, playing me."

He rolled his gaze toward the ceiling.

Katy insisted, "You know as well as I do that the covering was once important to Minnie. If she were in her right mind, she would want us to keep it on her head."

"You can't control the congregation's vote, so you control someone too weak to defend herself."

"Minnie may be small, but she's not weak. My face has the bruises to attest to that. And you won't find any bruises on her!"

Jake studied her face, perhaps seeing the bruises and scratches for the first time. His voice calmed. "God knows my grandmother's heart. After years of service and faithfulness, do you think He's going to reject her now when her physical mind has grown senile? She's our family. It's our responsibility to keep her safe and happy. And if she doesn't want to wear her covering, then so be it."

Were they going to encourage her to become an actress, too? She pushed the bitter thought aside and faced the truth. She had failed miserably, neither keeping Minnie safe nor happy. And she wasn't part of their family. Jake and Ann had the right to decide what was best for Minnie. Feeling the depths of her failure and desperation over what she'd done that might never be set right again, Katy slumped, resting her head in her hands. A grievous mistake. So many mistakes. Her shoulders convulsed uncontrollably.

Within seconds, she felt Jake's arms drape across them, sheltering her. She closed her eyes, inconsolable, not knowing how to make things right. Unconsciously, she curled into the comfort of his embrace.

"It's okay," he murmured again and again.

When she opened her eyes, his face hovered over hers, lined with empathy.

She squirmed then froze. When had she crawled into his lap? His hands cupped her face, caressed it. "Katy. Katy," he whispered.

"I'm sorry." She tried to sit up, but he stayed her.

"Me, too," he breathed into her ear.

She nuzzled into the crook of his neck, slid her arms around his waist, and rested there, not knowing what else to do until a creaky door and a surprised *Whoa!* brought Katy to her senses. At Lil's voice, Katy tried to leap off Jake's lap, but his arms tightened and firmly held her in place.

"Don't mind me," Lil chirped, walking past them and disappearing into the bedroom.

Katy groaned in the crook of his neck. "What else?"

"Be still," he whispered. "I'm not letting you up until we understand each other. I lost you once, and I won't do it again."

She looked into his eyes. "You're not angry?"

"No."

She gently bit the inside of her cheek. "I handled it all wrong. Do you think Ann will forgive me?"

"Yes." His voice was low and soothing.

"Minnie?"

He smiled and shrugged. "Don't know what's going through her mind."

Just then Katy remembered something. She wiggled her arm free and reached into her pocket for a small container of her homemade hand cream. "I meant to give her this. For her cracked fingers. Will you take it to her?"

With reverence he stared at the small Tupperware container in the palm of his hand. His voice grew gravelly. "Oh Katy."

CHAPTER 27

Katy watched Mr. Weaver walk to the front of the sanctuary, and her gaze went to the plain wooden cross on the wall behind him, a humble symbol of the Lord's ultimate sacrifice. She hoped today's special meeting addressing the head-covering ordinance would be God honoring.

Lil sat to Katy's right, whispering to Mandy. On Katy's left, Megan fiddled with her purse strap, no doubt nervous for her father and well informed of the many facets of the issue.

Mr. Weaver cleared his throat, and the congregation quieted. He held up his left arm and pointed to his watch. "The board of elders has elected to allow one hour for discussion, and then we will conclude the meeting with a vote. Women are invited to give their opinions on the matter. Keep your comments short. Everyone will be allowed to speak no more than twice per household to avoid any heated personal debates. Who will begin?"

A young mother stood up with a toddler straddled on her hip. He squirmed and swatted at her face, poking her eye. Blinking, she handed him down to her husband, who was seated beside her.

"Yes, Sister Irene."

"I think we should wear the covering because it's like baptism. A symbol that reflects an attitude of heart and spirit, one of love and submission and obedience to God."

The congregation remained quiet, and another woman shot to her feet.

"Sister Terri."

"*Symbol* is the key word here. But home's a private sanctuary. I don't need to wear a symbol at home. I don't have to prove anything there." She glanced fondly at the tall, thin man beside her. "Simon knows my heart. God, too. That's all that matters."

Irene stood, holding the baby again, this time patting his back. "It's not about proving anything. It's about honoring God's order. The design of the body attests to it. Men are designed to lead. Women nurture." She cradled her little boy into her arms to demonstrate her point. He reached up and batted her face. She rubbed her face into his playful arms and sat back down.

Next Mandy stood. "I'm not opposed to wearing a covering, but if we're going to be biblical, why not wear something that actually covers, like a larger veil?

Mr. Weaver recognized someone at the far side of the room, who had been trying to get acknowledged earlier. Katy strained to see who had stood. Lori was a single woman, self-educated, and rumors were that her learning included how to use the Internet for other than business purposes. Her sisters had all married into a higher church. She was also the church librarian. "I say it's all a principle. The actual cultural practice is old-fashioned and not applicable to today when women hardly even wear hats any longer. I love the people in this congregation. You are my family. I'd hate to have to move to a higher church because of this little piece of organdy."

Katy stifled a gasp, and Megan touched her hand, whispering out of the side of her mouth. "She'll leave if this doesn't go her way."

It would be sad to have to replace her in the library, and she was an excellent quilter, too. An elderly woman stood, leaning heavily on the pew before her. "I've never talked in church before. But I've prayed over the years for most everyone here tonight. Or at least one of your loved ones." She took several deep breaths. She had severe asthma, and speaking was difficult. "You probably think I'm old-fashioned, but I've seen a lot of changes in my day. And change is not necessarily good." After several wheezy inhales, she said, "The church ordinances were put there for a reason. We—"

Beside her Lil rolled her gaze heavenward.

The woman spoke longer than was necessary, as if she took to being in the limelight, making the entire congregation uneasy with her struggle to breathe and her incessant rambling. Mr. Weaver grew antsy, moved to the head of the center aisle. Eventually she got around to her point. "We know that we are not to conform to the world. Once the prayer covering goes, it's only a matter of time until we will blend in with mainstream society."

"Mainstream?" Lil whispered. "Where'd *she* learn that word?"

"Probably reads the newspaper," Katy replied.

Next a man spoke. "Just as every action we perform throughout the day is a choice that reflects our relationship with the Lord, I consider wearing the covering a personal choice, not something to be forced. Just like salvation." He sat down. For this meeting, couples had been encouraged to sit together instead of taking separate sides of the room as was customary during regular church services. Now his wife nudged him. He popped back up. "And the style of the covering should be personal choice, too." He started to sit and popped up again and grinned. "Long as it's not a baseball cap."

Titters filled the auditorium. Everyone realized that last tidbit was the only original part of his spiel.

"Anything more to add?" Mr. Weaver asked, with a teasing glint in his eyes.

The speaker shook his head and crossed his arms. His wife leaned into him with a proud smile.

Then one of Megan's professors stood. He spoke clearly, enunciating every word as he might in a classroom when he wanted to make a point. "Free choice? As in women wearing male attire like blue jeans? As in abortion? Or feminism? Or perhaps women ordination?"

A second collective gasp resounded in the sanctuary. All those issues seemed far-fetched, even to Katy, but she respected him for reminding them of the pressures of society.

Her own experiences lately had shown her how easy it was to get pulled into worldly ways. She wanted to remain in God's will. The shelter of His wings was the only place where one could find stability and safety. Minnie came to mind. God hadn't prevented her from getting Alzheimer's, but when swinging, she'd been aware of His presence, even joyful.

Katy considered her most recent encounter with Jake. When he'd held her and comforted her, she'd felt safe, yet tried to jump off his lap. But he'd clamped his arms tightly and lovingly until she'd submitted. They had resolved their problem. Was that the meaning of submission? Did it bring a woman to a better place? And wasn't the covering submission to God?

The elder in charge of the meeting looked at his watch. "There is time for a few more comments."

Katy had butterflies, yet her opinion welled up inside her and threatened to spew forth. But she didn't know if she could express what she understood in her spirit. Like many of the others who had not made the best impression, she'd never spoken up in church. She might even hurt the cause. Many of the husbands sat red-faced, grim-mouthed. But she didn't have a husband. Jake was present. Ann, too. If she spoke, would they be reminded of the recent covering incident?

The next speaker was another man. He read the long passage of scripture in Corinthians. Katy felt like he was stealing from the congregation's discussion time, for they had already covered the scripture several times in the course of Brother Troyer's sermons. She tried to calm herself, to listen. She tried to remain open-minded. To silently pray. But after the man sat down, she found herself on her feet.

"Yes, Sister Katy," Mr. Weaver said gently.

"I—" She closed her eyes a moment and swallowed, trying to put her thoughts into a short summary. The image of God's sheltering wings shot into her mind again, along with the scripture she'd just heard. "But we are to wear the covering on behalf of the angels. According to the scripture just read, they are present in this room." She paused. "Right now." Nothing else came to her mind so she sat.

Silence prevailed for a long moment. She dipped her head and stared at her skirt, thinking she had not expressed her opinion logically. Megan took her arm in support. The silence prolonged. And amazingly, nobody else stood. Her heart drummed inside her, for she wondered what everyone was thinking. Still nobody spoke. She slowly raised her head. Across the sanctuary, several heads were bowed. A rush of shivers passed over her.

Then a sweet note filled the silence, and she turned toward its source. One of the women had started to sing from her pew. Her words rang pure and sweet wafting over the otherwise silent room: *"Angels from the realms of glory, wing your flight o'er all the earth."* Katy joined her voice to the rest of the congregation's. *"Ye who sang creation's story, now proclaim Messiah's birth; come and worship, come and worship, worship Christ the newborn King."*

At the end of the song, Mr. Weaver spoke in a reverent tone. "I believe the angels are observing our meeting. In the awe of this holy moment, let us pray." His prayer held reverence and worship. A few *Amens* sounded afterward.

He looked over the congregation and explained, "If the vote to keep the present headdress ordinance does not pass, then the elders will appoint a committee to write a new ordinance. That one will be brought to the congregation for a vote of approval. Let us take our vote now regarding the original ordinance. Remember, only church members are allowed to participate. All those who wish to keep the head covering ordinance as it is, please stand."

Katy stood. Megan and Lil both remained seated. But Katy joyfully noticed a large number of men and women stood with her. After they were counted, Mr. Weaver asked them to please be seated. Then he said, "All opposed to the present ordinance on the headdress, please stand." Lil and Megan stood, and a lump of despair and unbelief filled Katy's throat when she saw that the opposing side was equally represented. Her heart drummed inside her as she waited for the count to be concluded.

"Be seated." Mr. Weaver coughed into his hand. "The opposed have it. The ordinance will be amended. This meeting is now adjourned."

Stunned to silence, the congregation slowly rose and, Quaker-like, filed out of the meetinghouse. The winning side did not gloat, and the losers did not protest. Generations of practicing nonresistance came to the fore and governed the congregation's actions. Everyone seemed to understand that it was best to just disband until everyone had time to pray over the elders' decision since it was such a controversial matter. Katy followed the suit of the others, but inside, she felt turmoil. Soon the turmoil turned to anger.

When they'd reached the parking lot, Megan said, "I want you to know that I stood because I believe the only way we can keep the congregation from splitting is to allow everyone to make their own decision. I'm sorry. I know it hurt you. I hate to go, but I've still got homework."

A black veil shuttered Katy's vision at the glib explanation. "Bye," she mouthed, woodenly.

As she and Lil walked toward the car, she was pleased Lil made no small talk, and even more pleased to note that nobody unpinned their covering in the parking lot. She had a mental picture of what Megan said happened with caps at graduation ceremonies.

"Katy, wait up."

She halted, squared her shoulders. She wasn't feeling up to small talk, even with Jake, who knew where she stood on this matter.

"I'll wait in the car," Lil said softly.

She nodded and turned, unable to fake a smile.

"I'm sorry." He took her hand.

Chapped and ungloved, she felt his touch on her bare skin. She'd been too shocked to remove her gloves from her purse. He rubbed his thumb across the top of her fingers, and she almost warmed to the physical contact. Yet she resisted, unable to give in to defeat.

"It should make Minnie happy," she said sharply.

His hand fell away at the cruel remark. The shock in his expression sent a pang of regret through her. "Katy," he said sadly.

"I'm sorry. I don't know why I said that. I just can't deal with this."

He cast a quick glance over his shoulder and stuffed his hands in his jeans pockets. "Can we drive into New Rome, get some coffee?"

"I don't think so. I'm not good company right now." She longingly glanced toward the car. "Lil's waiting." She knew she should invite him over to the doddy house, but she really wasn't in the mood. With that, she turned away from his hurt expression and walked across the crackling parking lot. Only headlights broke the darkness, each vehicle heading off to their solitary places.

CHAPTER 28

On Monday morning, Katy tossed her cell phone on the nightstand, then quickly grabbed for a Kleenex. She sneezed twice, her eyes welling up in tears. "Ugh."

Lil perched on the edge of Katy's bed. "How did Tammy take it?"

"She wasn't pleased I called in sick. She asked if I could come in tomorrow instead, if I was feeling better. I do need the money."

Lil nodded sympathetically. "Here's coffee. Maybe it will help. I'm going to make a big pot of chicken noodle soup. It'll be ready in a couple of hours, and you can sip on it all day. And I'll even clean up the kitchen."

Katy took the coffee with little strength to protest. "Thanks."

"Hey, you know how we've been hoping for a chair for the living room?"

After taking a cautious first sip of her coffee, Katy nodded.

"My mom's willing to give us her green-striped armchair. And if you agree, I can get Jake to haul it over."

"Why is she willing to let it go?"

"Well, you know how she's been moping around ever since the fire?"

Katy nodded.

"Her birthday's coming up, so Dad told her to pick out some new furniture. He wants her to get a recliner-rocker that's just her size. He's worried about her."

"I was sorry to hear that she resigned from the hostess committee."

Lil's shoulders sagged. "We're all worried about her. We've never seen her so depressed."

"I know the fire's bothering her, but do you think empty-nest syndrome has anything to do with her despondency?"

Lil's eyes widened. "You think? I guess I was her baby. Maybe I need to visit her more often."

Katy crooked her mouth in mock deliberation. "Nah. I can't imagine why she'd miss you. Can't say as I would."

Lil's mouth flew open, and she countered, "If you weren't sick, I'd make you eat those words. I know how ticklish you are."

"But I am so sick right now." She popped a throat lozenge in her mouth and glanced at the tropical turquoise wall and longed for summer. It had been a long, hard winter in her soul. And she was growing weary of it. She sighed and took another sip of coffee. "Yuck, those two don't mix."

Lil chuckled. "Dummy. So it's okay to take the chair?"

"Of course. It will add some color, too. Though without two chairs, I suppose we'll fight over it."

"You bet we will. Just like everything else." Lil studied her a moment, and then ventured, "I haven't told you, but I'm sorry for you, about the outcome of the head-covering vote. But at least you'll be able to still wear yours. That won't change."

"It is a symbol. I feel like Megan's professor. That without it, we'll just become part of the world."

"I don't want to argue, but if it's a symbol and someone's heart isn't really in it, then it makes them feel like a hypocrite. That's how I felt. That's not good, either. You know how Jesus hated hypocrites."

She knew, because sometimes she felt like one, too. She'd felt like that after the ballet. "I know. I'm surprised you're still wearing yours."

"I figured it would break your heart if I didn't."

Katy saw the caring in Lil's eyes. It brought back a memory flash.

That first summer at camp. In one of the group games, Lil had taken a different trail from Megan and Katy. They'd needed to pair off, and Lil had gone with one of the Mennonite girls who wore shorts. It was a scavenger hunt and race to a designated clearing. Katy didn't remember who won, but what she remembered was the reunion and excitement at the clearing, and how they'd each shared their adventures.

She saw that's how it was with them. How it always would be. They were always going to go at the goal from a different path. Her throat thickened, whether from the cough drop or her emotions, she wasn't sure.

She whispered, "Bend down."

"Huh?"

"Just do it."

Lil bent, and Katy reached up and unpinned Lil's covering. Lil straightened, her eyes round. In a sudden rush of emotion, she hugged Katy.

"You're going to catch my cold."

"I don't care. I love you."

"I know. But I expect to see that covering on at the church meetings."

"Duh."

"Okay, go start that soup. I need something to get me out of this bed."

Lil started toward the door, then looked back. "Thanks for understanding."

Once she was gone, Katy spit the cough drop into a small trash can and turned onto her stomach. Her own covering sat on her nightstand beside her cell phone. She punched her pillow and released her sobs.

⸻

That afternoon, Katy lay on the couch, reading an inspirational romance novel, but she was jolted out of the story when the heroine used the phrase *sensational solo woman*. The heroine was bragging that she didn't need a man to find happiness. Since it was a romance novel, she assumed the heroine would change her mind somewhere in the plot. Still, she paused to toy with the idea. Could she remain single and be happy?

It was the Mennonite way for a woman to prepare herself for marriage and children. It was presumed that every woman sought fulfillment in wifely duties and motherhood. She'd always gravitated toward that end herself, dreaming of one day marrying Jake or after they'd broken up, some other godly man.

Much like the heroine in Katy's story, Lil scoffed at the idea of a man fulfilling a woman. Lil liked guys, all right, but she was super-independent for a Conservative girl. During the church's recent series on relationships, Brother Troyer had made it clear that fulfillment came from the Lord, not marriage. Perhaps that's where this story was headed. Her interest piquing, she turned the page and started reading. But seconds later, she was interrupted again, this time by a knock at the front door.

"Come in," she croaked, then clutched her neck. Realizing that nobody could hear her raspy voice and that Lil had locked the door, she stuffed her feet into slippers and shuffled off to see who was calling.

"Jake," she said, staring through the cracked door with surprise.

Dressed in his work clothes, a dusty T, and sweat-stained baseball cap, he said, "Yikes, you okay?"

Katy mumbled, "Fine thing to say to a woman," and turned to shuffle back to the living room. They'd only talked once since she'd been rude to him in the church parking lot. The phone conversation had been another attempt to patch their tempestuous relationship. She sank back on the couch, and looked up at him. "This is a house of germs, you know."

He gave a wave. "I never get sick. Too ugly."

She couldn't resist the grin that belied that preposterous remark. "Real ugly," she added.

"I've got the chair from Lil's mom."

She sat forward, "Great!" Then, involuntarily, her hand clutched her neck again.

"Can I leave the door open for a minute?"

"Sure. You need my help?"

"Nope."

She soon heard a *plunk* in the kitchen. Then the door closed. Then a shuffling, and he manhandled the green-striped armchair into the room, lowering it in a vacant place off to her right. "Where you want it?"

"Move it about three feet to your left. Though we both know Lil will change it later."

He chuckled, moved the chair, then flung himself down. "Nice," he said, leaning back and making himself at home. Then suddenly he jumped up. "Oh sorry. Forgot how dirty I am. I came straight from work."

"You're fine," she said uncharacteristically, too weak to bother with protecting the chair. "I could use some company."

He glanced at her novel and sat more tentatively on the edge of the chair. "Wish you weren't under the weather. I'm playing basketball later. Could use a fan."

She thought about his flamboyant dunks. "Yes, I suppose you could."

"Next time." He took off his hat, set it on his lap. His wavy black hair stuck up in disarray, and she figured with her bed head, they made a pair of bookends about now. He fiddled with its brim. "We're good. You and me. Right?"

She gave him a wry smile. "I'm tolerating you pretty good, yeah."

He grinned. "Here it is, then. Mom wanted me to ask you if you'd like to clean for her."

Katy grew serious. "Yes, but. . ." Her voice softened. "As you know, watching Minnie is a full-time—"

"She'd take Minnie with her. She knows Gram is a handful and thought that arrangement might work better. Mom could use the help."

"Of course, I'll do it. I'm just relieved that Ann would still want me."

"She does." He grinned. "So do I."

CHAPTER 29

The elders of the Big Darby Conservative Mennonite Church came up with their revised head-covering ruling and took it to the congregation for a vote. The new decree stated that a woman should wear a head covering of an unpretentious style to public meetings of worship and prayer. It was approved. Outside of that, the wearing of the head covering was a personal matter for a woman. Or if married, between a couple.

The new ordinance held no surprises, and neither did Katy's interpretation of it. Since she'd became a Christian at church camp all those years earlier, prayer had become a natural habit for her whether it was congregational prayer, devotional prayers, or one-word prayers of praise or agony shot heavenward at various unplanned moments throughout the day. And she wasn't going to be caught uncovered and unable to commune with God whenever she pleased or needed. The only time she removed her covering was when she showered or slept. She figured the water would be her covering in the shower, and her bedding would serve at night. She'd taken to heart her own mother's advice on those two exceptions. As far as Katy was concerned, she was covered. The Lord knew her heart, and she was set on doing her part to please Him.

After the official vote, she determined to put the painful issue out of her mind. She didn't want to stir up coals of anger against her church family who had disappointed her by voting down her precious tradition. There was nothing left for her to do but tamp down her feelings. It was the nonresistant way, the Mennonite way.

Even though Katy had initiated that moment when Lil quit wearing the covering around home, sometimes Lil's uncovered head still shocked her and caused a niggling of anger to resurface. When that happened, Katy rehashed their conversation and forced herself to consider Lil's point of view. She didn't want her friend to wear it hypocritically. But as the days passed, Katy found it easier just to stuff her feelings.

Even so, the first time she went to clean the Byler residence, she primed herself to be ready for the unexpected. If the female members of Jake's family were bareheaded, she would simply disregard it. Jake had already explained how they felt about Minnie, and as for Ann, it wasn't Katy's place to fret about her decision. She needed to let it go so that it didn't interfere with her fragile relationship with Jake. She determined to allow nothing to go wrong like it had the last time she'd watched Minnie. This day would be all about mending bridges and restoring relationships.

It was a pleasant surprise then, when upon Katy's arrival at the Bylers, both Ann and Minnie wore their head coverings.

Ann acted first, hesitantly drawing Katy into a quick hug. "Thank you for coming. I'm happy we didn't scare you away."

"I'm sorry it ended so badly, the other day. I guess I wasn't prepared for"—she glanced over at Minnie, whose head was tilted, intently trying to follow their exchange.

"Let's just put it behind us." Ann suggested. Then she brightly added, "Today Mom and I are going shopping at the discount mart and then meeting Erin for lunch at Der Dutchman."

Minnie spoke up, "I'm having raisin pie."

Katy smiled at the older woman's enthusiasm.

As they slipped into their coats, Ann cast Katy a final glance. "I feel guilty going off to have fun and leaving you to do my work."

"Don't. You need to do something fun. I'm sure Minnie does, too."

Ann gave her a few quick instructions, and once they'd gone, Katy brought her own cleaning supplies in from the car. In most instances, she preferred her homemade mixtures to anything store-bought. She took a quick walk through the house before she decided where to start. The kitchen was all Ann, but as soon as she left that room, the house carried Jake's presence. A pair of his jeans lay folded beside an armchair, waiting to be mended. She forced her mind away from his tight jeans and the man who wore them.

She noticed a handmade magazine rack. In it was a *Fine Homebuilding* magazine. Her heart warmed to think of Jake's love for building things. He was like her father in that regard. When Jake had brought their new chair to the doddy house, he'd ended up staying much longer than either of them had planned. In fact, he'd almost forgotten about playing basketball. They'd eaten chicken noodle soup, and he had even joined her in a game of Concentration, Jake denying he'd get sick. She wondered now if he had.

He'd talked about his dreams of starting his own business and getting his general contractor license. He told her he was going to be a hands-on boss, doing some of the work himself. At least while he was young and able. He thought it would allow him to keep better tabs on the construction process and cut down on mistakes and wasted materials. This, in turn, would allow the job to be more economical for him and the customer. It was his desire to put out a quality project. He thought that by hiring other Conservative men, who weren't money greedy, they could build at a fair price. A quality house at a fair price. And when he got older, he wanted to design new homes. He'd explained about the software that helped with home design, and her distrust of computers had lessened one notch. She smiled, dusting the magazine and replacing it.

After cleaning the bathroom and kitchen and then dusting and sweeping the downstairs, she moved into more dangerous territory, the upstairs bedrooms. Jake's room wasn't on the list, and she remembered him once teasing her that he wouldn't want her cleaning his room, yet she felt drawn to it as powerfully as she was to the man himself.

In all the times she'd been at his home, she'd never been inside his room. She ventured up now. She noticed a bathroom and another room with a closed door. Feeling the prickles of wrongdoing, she glanced over her shoulder then turned the knob. When would she ever get another opportunity to learn more about him? She pushed.

Stepping into the room, she smiled and closed her eyes, letting the scent of sawdust and soap waft over her. After a moment of basking in his scent, she opened them and surveyed his domain. His bed was made, yet the blue-and-white quilt lay uneven and lumpy. Definitely could be a twin to Lil, she smirked.

He had a desk beside the window. She moved to the blue-draped panes and peered down at the fields below. A crow flew down and landed on a furrow, poking at something with his beak. He looked in her direction and cawed.

They were fields that Jake hadn't wanted to farm, glad his brother Cal and his uncle had taken over that responsibility, yet this was the view that Jake had gazed upon ever since he'd been a little boy. She took it in now, the barren fields, the barn, the road. She imagined his truck leaving the drive, heading to—she broke off her thoughts because she didn't want to remember his falling away. Not while they were mending their relationship.

No, she didn't want that. But what did she want? She wanted to trust him. To love him. To marry him and raise a family that never veered from God's truth. That was what she wanted. She'd always wanted that since she could remember. But she'd been denying it for the past couple of years. She'd been denying her innermost longings. No wonder she'd been miserable.

There were deeper facets to his personality now. She hoped with the new Jake her dreams could come true, after all. She wondered how many times he'd stared out this window, thinking about his dreams. Hadn't Jake talked about new beginnings? And with God, all things were possible.

The crow flew off, and she turned away from the window. Some rubber-banded blueprints were propped up beside his desk. She skimmed her palms over them. A laptop computer was open on his desk. His screensaver flashed galactic patterns, galaxies, and stars. It was beautiful. Another surprise. She hadn't known he was interested in astronomy. Her curiosity suddenly piqued. What else didn't she know about him?

She glanced at the door, feeling a bit guilty for snooping, but crossed the room to his nightstand. Her breath caught. He had a Bible, one she recognized, and sitting on top of it was a framed picture of two girls. She froze. Then slowly, she picked up the photograph and looked closer at the two young women. Across the bottom of the picture was cursive writing:

Love always. I'll never forget those steamy, starry nights. Just Jessie

Feeling hateful thoughts toward the girl with her arm around Jake's sister, Erin, Katy stared long and hard at the woman who had caused her such grief. She resembled pictures she'd seen of fairies, petite, slender. Her hair was black with white-streaked bangs. It was short and spiked. Her eyes were bright blue and lined with black pencil. So different from Katy's own dark ones. She wore bright lipstick. While Katy was plain and natural, this woman was worldly. Katy drew the photo closer, and her jaw fell open. She wore a nose ring. Katy's eyes narrowed, taking in the tight jeans and slim, yet appealing silhouette. A black lacy tank top revealed a tattoo on her upper arm. The other arm was wrapped possessively around Erin. A wide belt emphasized her figure. Both girls were exhibiting a seductive pose.

Katy felt stricken, as if she couldn't breathe, would never breathe again. She felt as if Jake had taken a spike and driven it through her heart and all her will to live had poured out the open wound.

She read the inscription again. Every word held intimate implications of what had passed between them. Romantic nights under the stars. Steamy even. She tried not to envision what those nights might have entailed. She couldn't stand the thought of this stranger touching Jake, kissing him, embracing him. And *Just Jessie*. What did that mean? It insinuated a lot of time spent together, a relationship so cemented that it didn't need further explanation.

She turned the despicable photograph around. Nothing was written on the back. But he kept her picture on his nightstand, on top of his Bible of all places. He probably read his Bible every night, and first he picked up the photo and looked at her. The last image he saw before he closed his eyes at night.

Jake's betrayal fell over her afresh. Darker than anything she'd ever experienced because this time there was no window left for renewed trust. No chance of making things right. No hope. He cared about this awful woman. He'd lied. He would never change. There was no future with him. And she would never be able to love anyone else. All these truths swept over her like a storm with no warning and no escape. She thought she would die. Or worse, she might live.

CHAPTER 30

Katy drove blindly, the tears streaming down her face, her car headed for the Rosedale Bible College. She had to find Megan. She couldn't face Lil yet. She had to do something to make the pain go away.

At the college, Katy hurried straight to Megan's room. The door was unlocked, but the room was empty. Katy let herself in. Impatiently, she studied the posters on the wall. The one over Megan's twin bed had bare hands stretched up, most likely toward God. It read: *He is able.* Swiping her cheeks, she wished it were that simple. She climbed into Megan's bed and curled up in a ball. Nothing was simple any longer.

"Katy? Katy!"

Katy felt something shaking her shoulder. Slowly she came out of her stupor, feeling as if she'd slept for one hundred years, but when she took in her surroundings, her memory returned along with her sense of Jake's betrayal. She met Megan's gaze. "It's over."

Megan plunked on the edge of the bed. "What? Did something happen at the doddy house?"

"No." Her voice trembled. "It's Jake."

"What happened?"

"He loves Jessie."

Megan's usually serene face furrowed around her blond brow. "Who's that?" Then before Katy could reply, Megan's eyes narrowed. "That girl from OSU?"

"Yes."

Megan looked aghast. "He told you that?"

"No. But he has her photo on his nightstand. On top of his Bible."

"I don't believe it. Wait a minute. Why were you in his room?"

Katy knew that Megan was only questioning her so that she would know how to help. "I was cleaning their house. And it's true. Jessie has her arm around Erin, like she's wiggled her way right into the family. Don't you see? He keeps her picture on his nightstand. He has feelings for her. Yet he had the nerve to tell me he loves me. He's such a rat, chasing me and acting like it's me he wants."

Megan sat in quiet thoughtfulness. Then she asked, "You love him, don't you?"

Katy nodded and looked at the floor.

Megan stood. She began to pace. "Then you're going to talk to him about this. And you're going to ask him why he has Jessie's picture on his nightstand. Maybe there's some simple explanation. The last time you guys broke up, you never talked it out. It tore you up afterward. You have to confront him and listen to his explanation."

"So he can squirm out of it?" Katy demanded angrily.

"Something's not right about this. I feel like you're missing some of the pertinent facts."

"Believe me, I discovered more than I wanted. Now her picture is etched in my memory. Tramp." Katy clenched her jaw and gripped the bed covering, allowing her jealousy to consume her.

Megan pulled up a chair and sat facing Katy. "Just because she's an outsider doesn't make her promiscuous."

Katy's mouth flew open. She'd thought of all people, Megan would understand. "You didn't see her."

Megan leaned forward, imploring, "But you can't just accuse him and ruin your relationship without knowing for sure that he loves her. Sometimes things just aren't the way they look."

"Yeah? Well, it's too late for that." Katy felt her face heat. "I left him a note."

Megan moaned. "You didn't."

Katy stared at the green comforter. "I was so angry that he betrayed me again. He told me he didn't like her that way."

Megan patted Katy's knee. "But there has to be an explanation. You said Erin was in the photo. You want me to tell you what I honestly think?"

Looking up into Megan's gaze, Katy replied, "Of course. That's why I'm here."

Megan's pink cheeks indicated that she knew Katy came because she needed a caring shoulder more than someone who would lecture her, yet she was going to do it anyway. "I think you've never forgiven him. That you'll never be able to move forward in your relationship until you quit judging him for what he's done in the past. You live in fear because you can't control the situation, and you don't want to get hurt."

"Of course I don't want to get hurt!" Katy cried in her own defense.

"It's not your job to control everything. It's God's."

Katy trembled with resentment. "That's a terrible thing to say. Especially when I'm hurting."

"But it's the truth. You don't trust God in this."

Katy stood and moved away. "Maybe."

Megan followed her. "There's something else."

Katy crossed her arms. "What?"

"You and Lil are like night and day. I've been mediating between you two for years. But did you ever stop to think that it isn't Lil who starts the arguments or works herself into a huff?"

Katy hung her head. "That really hurts."

Megan's hand pressed Katy's shoulder. "I'm sorry. I'm tired of watching you pull the world down crashing around you. It's just that you get so fired up, when a soft word could ward off so much of the distress you bring upon yourself."

Katy shook her head. "I'm not wrong about this one. Jake loves Jessie."

"Maybe so. But you need to give Jake a chance to explain the photo before throwing him into the discard pile."

That illustration gave Katy pause. Not only discarded, but *forbidden* in big bold letters across his name on a paper in her Bible. She narrowed her eyes. Maybe Megan was right. She needed time to think about it.

"Do you want me to call him?" Megan asked.

———

Freshly showered and wearing boxers and a T-shirt, Jake padded down the hall in his bare feet. The cold medication he'd taken the moment he'd gotten home had made him drowsy. His sinuses ached, and all he desired was a tissue box and bed. Finding Kleenex in a linen closet, he plodded into his room and crawled under the covers with great relief. *Too ugly to get sick.* Yeah, right.

Earlier he had tossed his cell phone on his nightstand, and he remembered he still needed to plug it into its charger before he fell asleep. With his eyes closed, he reached over and patted the top of the nightstand. But his fingers touched something out of the ordinary, something out of place.

He propped up on his elbow and frowned at a piece of paper stuck between his Bible and the photo of Erin and Jessie. The only items on his nightstand should be his Bible, the photo, and his cell phone. He kept his watch, billfold, and change on his desk, so it couldn't be a sales receipt. He didn't remember placing any paper on his nightstand.

He brought it up to his face. *We are through. I hate you. Just Katy.* He frowned, turned it over, and saw his mom's cleaning list on the other side. A shudder of dread struck him. His mom hadn't told him that Katy was coming. His pulse quickening, he read it again. He closed his eyes in agony, knowing it was about the photo that Jessie had signed similarly.

A long time ago, when he'd asked Jessie her name, she'd told him it was Jessica, but she was just Jessie. So he often teasingly called her Just Jessie. Now he picked up the photo, and although he had the inscription memorized, he read it again, flinching at her pun, using the word *steamy*, and easily imagining how that had sounded to Katy. *Love always, Don't forget about those steamy, starry nights. Just Jessie.* He wasn't a fool. He understood exactly the images and insinuations that would have gone through Katy's mind. And she thought he kept the photo there because he still cared about Jessie. He moaned, shoved everything back on the nightstand, and turned his back to it. He heard a crash. *Women. Way too much trouble.*

Jake awoke to music from his cell phone. With a groan he rolled over and swiped the nightstand for it, knocking it onto the floor. As he came to his senses, he remembered that Katy was mad. Was that her calling? Muttering at himself, he stumbled out of bed, bringing half the bedcovers with him, and scooped the phone off the floor. He glanced at the phone's rectangular face, noting that the caller wasn't Katy or anybody else he had in his address book.

"Hello," he growled.

"Hi. This is Megan."

"Yeah?" There was silence on the other end. He tried to sound more civil. "Megan?"

"I thought you should know that Katy came to see me this afternoon. She was really upset. With you."

"I figured."

"You sound weird. Is this bad timing?"

"No. I've got a cold."

He could hear a feminine sigh. "I'm sorry. Anyway, I told her she needed to hear your explanation of why you keep Jessie's photo on your nightstand. I'm hoping you have a reasonable explanation?"

"You bet I do. It's not what she thinks. Thanks for sticking up for me. So. . ." He looked at the ceiling and sent up a quick prayer. *Please, God.* "Is she willing to listen to reason?"

"Maybe. You're not going to hurt her again?"

He sighed. "No. Is Katy there? Can you put her on?"

"Just a minute."

Listening to feminine protests, he grabbed up an armful of blankets and tossed the soft ball back onto the bed. Fortunately, Megan was trying to patch things up for him.

Finally, a familiar voice snapped angrily, "This is Katy."

She acted like he'd called her instead of them calling him, waking him up, too. He really wanted to snap back at her for snooping in his room—for getting him sick—but he knew that when he felt better, he'd regret it. He gentled his voice. "I got your note. But I think you jumped to the wrong conclusions."

"I thought she didn't mean anything to you." Now she sounded pouty. He could visualize her sulky lips, her smoky eyes. "I trusted you." Now she sounded heartbroken, definitely vulnerable. That clenched his heart because he knew how much it cost her to reveal her jealousy.

For weeks he'd worked at earning her trust. Now if he wasn't careful, he would lose her over a stupid misunderstanding. "Remember when I told you that Erin and Jessie became friends? That Erin was going down the same path I went? That I'd give anything to prevent that?"

"Anything, huh?"

He lay back on his pillow, disregarded her heated barb, and continued to speak softly. "I love my sister. And I worry about Jessie, too. I keep the photo on top of my Bible so that I remember to pray for them every night. It's simple as that. There's no attraction there. It's you I love. Not Jessie. That's the truth." There was a silence, and he waited.

"You love me?" He'd told her that the night at the restaurant, too.

He quirked his mouth. "Yes I do."

"But the inscription on the photo was so intimate. I was jealous."

"You love me, too?"

She paused too long.

"Sorry. Dumb question."

"I want to."

He swallowed his disappointment. He'd just lost major points on trustworthiness. Her anger and jealousy revealed that she cared deeply for him. She said she wanted to love him. That probably meant she did love him but couldn't trust him. If she wasn't ready to do that, he shouldn't push her. He might scare her away. Instead he needed to convince her of his sincerity. He needed to win her over, but not now when he felt so sick. "I wasn't too ugly after all."

"You're sick?"

"Yep."

"I warned you."

"It was worth it." Losing his battle against the drowsy side effects of his cold medicine and starting to shake with a fever, he pulled the rumpled covers up around his sore throat—that was getting more painful with talking—and off his bare feet. Shivering, he curled them up under the covers.

"I didn't know you liked stars."

He closed his eyes and managed, "Took a class in school."

Her next sentence was long, distorted, and dreamlike, and then his mouth and hand went slack.

CHAPTER 31

Katy stood in the open doorway and glared at Jake. Then she slammed the door in his face and strode through the doddy house into the living room. Behind her, the door creaked open. She heard heavy, intruding footsteps.

"That was rude." Jake's voice was laced with irritation.

"Yes, I'm rude and obviously boring," she replied. Then dropping to the sofa, she pulled a pillow onto her lap and hugged it to herself.

She felt the couch sink, and his shoulder brushed hers. "It was the cold medicine. I can't even remember what I said to you yesterday. When Megan called, I was sleeping."

She jerked her shoulder away from him. "We were discussing our relationship. Our crumbling relationship. I was baring my heart, and you started snoring. Or was that just an excuse not to have to talk about steamy, starry nights?"

He didn't speak, and finally she glanced over at him. His face was pale, stricken. He still looked sick. "You told me you loved me?"

"No, I did not!"

"Well that's a relief. I wouldn't want to miss that." He rubbed his jeans with his palms. "I vaguely remember telling you—"

"What?" She arched a brow.

He shook his head. "Never mind about that. Just tell me again why you're mad. So I can make it right."

She gaped at him. Then she spat out. "It hurt to see Jessie's photo on your nightstand. And you didn't care. You fell asleep on me."

"What is the big deal about Jessie? I told you she's just a friend."

Hugging her pillow, Katy corrected, "*Girl*friend. With whom you shared steamy, starry nights!"

"Like David was your *boy*friend. Come on, Katy. This is childish."

She felt heat rising up her neck and into her cheeks. "You know there wasn't much between David and me."

"Did you kiss him?" he demanded. Katy pressed her lips together. "And did you skate in his arms?" he asked. Her eyes narrowed painfully. Jake's voice softened. "I know how you felt when you saw the picture because I felt that way when I saw you with David."

"But I wasn't emotionally involved with him."

He eyed her skeptically. "So you want to hear about Jessie?"

She nodded.

"Fine. I'll admit to some flirting, some dancing, a few kisses, toying with the idea of a relationship, and then dismissing it. Because I knew I was in love with you. It was the whole idea of exploring the world that she was part of, but it was only a fleeting attraction."

It hurt to hear him admit what was between him and Jessie, fleeting or not, yet she also understood because it had been similar with her and David. There had been moments when David caused her pulse to race, and she had entertained a deeper relationship. Though she had wanted the relationship to deepen, it was always Jake who she loved. But had there been more between Jake and Jessie?

She needed to know. She felt her blush returning. She searched deep in his eyes, wanting to watch his facial reaction to the question. Then her heart fluttering like a caged bird seeking freedom, she asked, "Kissing? Was that all that happened between you two?"

His eyes didn't dart away in fear, but softened and pleaded for her to trust him. "Yes. That was all. I'm saving everything else for you. If that's been bothering you, I wish you'd asked me sooner."

With relief she admitted, "Me, too."

"And for the record, the steamy, starry thing was just a pun about a dud of a field trip. It was nothing romantic, just a joke because a group of us got stuck in a flash rainstorm."

She gave him a skeptical look. "Everybody knows you don't go stargazing on a cloudy night."

"Now everybody knows."

She couldn't help but smile.

"Just a class project. That's all it was, Katy. Nothing at all for you to worry about."

He pulled her close, embraced her, and whispered, "I'm yours. Whenever you're ready."

She nodded against his shoulder. "Thanks." Then she pushed away. She gave him an embarrassed smile. "So tell me about your astronomy class. And don't fall asleep this time."

─◌─

Katy stood beside Jake's truck, staring at the bejeweled sky. "So that's the Milky Way?"

"The galaxy where our solar system is located," he explained. His arm was draped across her shoulders. "You're shivering. Want to go inside?"

She glanced up at him and troubled her lip, uncertain. His invitation included the use of his computer to post an Internet housekeeping advertisement.

By unanimous consent, Katy and Jake had decided it would be better if Ann got somebody else besides Katy to help with the cleaning and with Minnie. They just didn't think their relationship could stand any additional drama. But this left Katy missing a chunk of income again. And the church bulletin board had been unfruitful.

Earlier in the evening, she'd watched Jake play basketball at the Penners. On the drive home, they had discussed a popular website where people could post free ads. Since the Byler farm was on the way to the doddy house, they had pulled in and parked in the circle drive to continue their conversation.

"It's not forbidden." He repeated the same argument he'd been using all evening. "The church permits computers for business purposes." Jake's Dutch accent grew thicker when he was adamant about something, as he was now.

She had already relented that the computer was necessary for his future as a businessman. He was right that the church allowed its members to use the computer for business purposes but strongly discouraged its use as a social outlet. They frowned upon browsing the Internet just for the sake of entertainment for the same reasons they discouraged owning televisions.

"Let me show you the site; then you can decide."

The light shining through the kitchen window assured her they would not be alone in the house. "I guess."

Inside the house, there was an awkward moment when Ann acted surprised to see Katy. It grew even more awkward when Jake explained, "Katy needs to use my computer."

Ann glanced at the clock. "I guess it's not too late."

Katy felt the other woman's disapproval. "We can do it another time," she protested.

But Jake grabbed her hand and started leading her toward the stairway. "It won't take long."

"You want to come with us?" Katy threw over her shoulder.

"Sure. Let me just get Minnie situated. I'll be right up."

"Chicken," Jake whispered.

At the top of the steps, they turned right, and he opened his bedroom door and motioned her inside. She forced her gaze to his desk rather than across the room to his nightstand.

Behind them, Ann called up the stairwell, "I'll bring cookies."

"Is she nervous about us being up here alone? Or is she mad at me?"

"Just playing the chaperone."

Katy nodded, hoping that was true while Jake slipped into the chair and booted up his computer. While he was fiddling with his mouse, she couldn't resist the urge any longer and glanced over at his nightstand. To her glee, the photograph was gone.

"What did you do with it?" she asked.

He knew what she meant and quickly replied, "I took it out of the frame and stuck it in my high school yearbook."

"What about praying for them?"

"Funny. After our spat, I realized it had become such a habit to pray for Erin that I didn't need the photo to remind me."

"Of course you can pray for Jessie, too." She couldn't be that controlling. Could she?

He gave her a lopsided grin. "Thanks. Here's the site I was telling you about." He pushed back from the desk. "You sit down."

Feeling a tad nervous, for she hadn't used a computer since high school, which made it a couple of years now, she took his chair and stared at the unfamiliar screen.

"You just type your ad"—he hovered behind her and pointed at a blank space—"there."

"I see. But I'm still considering if I really want to do this." She brought up a new argument. "By using the computer, it's pretty certain anyone who replies to the ad will be an outsider."

"The church bulletin board hasn't helped you," he reminded.

"I know. I just hate using the Internet."

"If you get work with an outsider, you can always quit if you get a better position."

She worried her lip. "Oh fine." She started typing, surprised when her keyboard ability returned easily:

Need housecleaning jov,

"Oops." She backspaced and typed again:

job, one or two days a week. Experienced with references.

She paused and glanced over her shoulder. "Now what?"

He rested his hands on her shoulders. "You need to type in my e-mail address."

"You have e-mail?" she snapped, instantly regretting her judgmental tone when she felt his hands tense in frustration. "Never mind. Give it to me." She typed it into the appropriate space. "Guess you're now my agent."

He gently kneaded her shoulders and whispered, "That and anything else you allow me to be."

His patience struck her. He was waiting for her to express her trust, her love. He was also waiting for her to initiate their next kiss. He could have stolen one earlier when they were stargazing, but he hadn't. For years, Jake had carried the knowledge that Katy wanted to marry him—she had blurted it out to Lil at age ten—but now he had become the uncertain one.

She grinned. "I like that." Katy filled in a few more spaces and took in a deep breath, hovering the mouse over the SEND button. "You're sure I should do this?"

He squeezed her shoulders. "Yes."

"Here goes." She hit SEND. "I did it!" She threw up her arms.

"And now the job offers will come rolling in," he teased. "So will the money."

"Ready for cookies?" Ann asked, stepping into the room.

Katy turned and rose from the chair. "Yes, they smell delicious. But do you mind if we eat them downstairs? We're finished here."

"Those look delicious," Jake said, then leaned over his computer and placed it in sleep mode.

"Yes, let's go downstairs." Ann gave a relieved smile.

As they followed her down the stairs, Katy basked in the approval she'd seen in Ann's eyes. It wasn't that Jake's family was hard to please, but just that she'd already made so many mistakes. She prayed that placing that ad on the Internet would not be another one.

—◌

Katy was cleaning at the retirement center for Mrs. Kline when she felt her apron pocket vibrate. Setting aside her dusting mop, she punched a button and placed her phone to her ear. "Oh hi, Jake."

"You want to be a working woman?"

She chuckled. "I am one. I'm working right now."

"I mean every day."

Excitement coursed through her veins and quickened her pulse. "Someone answered my ad?"

"You have three replies. Want me to read them to you?"

She gave a happy sigh, as she imagined him sitting at his computer, his broad shoulders bent over his desk while working on her behalf—a rakish agent with his tousled hair and lopsided grin. "Yes."

" 'Elderly woman needs a housekeeper for two days a week. Small house. Can pay $12 an hour. Barbara White.' And she leaves her phone number."

Katy found a pen and pad on Mrs. Kline's desk and scribbled the information. "Interesting that she needs two days with a small house. Okay next."

" 'Can hire for one day a week at $10. Widower with three children. Harry Chalmers.' "

"Not as appealing." But she jotted down his information anyway. "Go on."

" 'Looking for housekeeper. Can pay good.' No phone number. You'll have to e-mail that one back to get more information."

"Great, thanks," Katy said. "So what are you doing home in the middle of the day?"

"Figuring a blueprint. Pricing a job. A referral from Mr. Weaver."

"That's good. Guess we better both get back to work. Thanks for the information."

"You bet."

As Katy slipped her phone back inside her apron pocket, she read over her notes. She would start with Barbara. In her mind's eye, she envisioned someone sweet and kind like Mrs. Beverly, who had moved to Florida.

CHAPTER 32

Katy stared at Barbara White's tiny home in a downtown section of Columbus. The weeds thrived, but the grass was scarce. Nothing like Mrs. Beverly's picture-perfect, country club home, but Katy tried not to judge Mrs. White by her home's exterior. Maybe she was too old to do any gardening.

Through burning eyes, Katy observed that, indeed, Mrs. White was stooped, and her overall impression of the job didn't improve when she was bombarded with a strong odor of cat urine.

"Come and sit. We'll have tea." A large-boned, top-heavy woman led her across the living room's dirty carpet. The coffee table was laden with stacks of glued jigsaw puzzles. Boxes of unsolved puzzles filled every corner. A calico cat sat in a sunbeam, using its claws on a threadbare sofa.

Wide-eyed and venturing with trepidation into the kitchen, Katy was motioned toward a chair. The table had puzzle pieces spread over its surface. The sink held unwashed dishes.

Katy's stomach clenched at the idea of taking tea in the midst of such filth and rank odor. Trying to keep her nose from wrinkling, she asked, "Have you had a housekeeper before?"

Barbara straightened a few inches from her bent position and let out an uproarious bout of laughter. Then she brushed at the air in front of her face. "Does it look like it? I wouldn't be looking for one now except my kids threatened to put me in a retirement center if I don't"—she twisted her lips in a snarl—"meet their high and mighty expectations." Then she smiled, again. "Chamomile or Licorice?"

"Chamomile."

Barbara eyed Katy's covering. "Figured you for that sort."

The older woman lifted a grimy teapot from a white cookstove cluttered with pots and crusty spatulas, allowing time for Katy to assess the room. Besides the dirty dishes, filthy hairballs covered the floor, and her chair felt sticky. Something touched her leg, and she jumped. Then she heard a purr and looked down at a Siamese cat that wove in and out between her chair and her legs. She gasped when a large white Persian jumped from the floor onto the counter.

"Stay away, Goblin. Stove's hot." Barbara scooped up the cat in her arms, patting its fluffy head, shuffled a few steps, and dropped the cat. White hair floated down over the stove and teapot. "She's white like a ghost, but I liked the sound of Goblin better. Catchy, don't you think?"

"Scary." Katy nibbled her lip. She nudged the Siamese away from her ankle and, making a spur-of-the-moment decision, stood. "How many cats do you have?"

Barbara's gaze skittered nervously from the Siamese to Katy. "Only three. And Sergeant spends most of his time outside. They're sweet little kitties. You'll see."

"This isn't going to work out for me."

"I expect it's the smell scaring you off, but if you keep up the litter box more regular than I do, that should fix that problem. I can't smell it, but my daughter says it's bad."

"I'm sorry." Katy shook her head and started toward the door. She wasn't going to get herself in a fix like she had with Tammy. She would nip this disastrous job opportunity in the bud.

Barbara clambered after her, huffing by the time they reached the entryway. "You didn't even give me a chance to ask you any questions. I thought the one doing the hiring was supposed to ask the questions.

I ain't so sure I want some Amish person working for me anyway. You didn't mention that in the ad."

"I'm Mennonite. Don't forget about your teapot, Barbara."

With that Katy turned and opened the door. With a gasp, she reached down and caught the white cat just before it escaped and pushed it back inside. Behind her, she heard Barbara say, "What a shame. I liked her, Goblin. The kids ain't gonna be happy about this, either."

Katy regretted not being able to help Barbara, but there was no trying to fool herself. She was too fussy to fit in with the woman and her cats. And this had seemed like the best opportunity of the three replies.

———

Katy glanced across the truck's cab at Jake and gave a tremulous smile. After a few e-mails, they had discovered the third response to Katy's ad was a dud that ended up flooding his computer with spam. This added to her apprehensions about the entire Internet process and also about her interviewing with complete strangers.

Playing it safe with the widower, they had scheduled the last interview for a Saturday so that Jake could accompany Katy. Now his truck braked in front of a multilevel house in a nice neighborhood with huge lots.

"Wow." She leaned forward to look past Jake. She'd never cleaned such a large, beautiful home. Surely Harry Chalmers could afford more than ten dollars an hour. She determined right then she'd ask for more. Then she remembered how Jake wanted to build better homes at more affordable prices and felt ashamed over her greed. But she quickly rationalized that, after all, she needed to be able to afford her expenses.

They opened an entry gate and walked up a long brick sidewalk flanked by camellia bushes with white blooms. Jake rang the doorbell.

They heard rattling on the other side of the door. Then little footsteps and a youngster yelling, "Daddy! Daddy!"

When the door opened, a tall, good-looking man in jeans and a polo shirt greeted them. One of his hands rested on the red head of a preschool-age boy. Harry Chalmers glanced at Jake and then at Katy's covering. His eyes crinkled. "You're Katy?"

She made the introductions, explaining that she'd brought Jake along as her escort.

"With the way the world is today, I totally understand. Come in."

The entryway was impressive, two stories high with an iron-and-glass chandelier hanging from a domed ceiling. There were two armchairs, a table, and a large mirror. She looked up at the chandelier and wondered how she'd ever clean it. They went into a large great room and sat in dark leather furniture that was grouped around a fireplace and entertainment area. Katy had never seen such a huge television. The room was dusty, but not as cluttered as Tammy's home usually was.

Her gaze rested on the little red-haired boy who was still plastered against his dad. The child's stare had never left Katy.

She placed her references on the coffee table that separated them and folded her hands on her dark skirt. Harry Chalmers briefly scanned the page and nodded. "I just need the normal stuff. I don't even know what that is. I haven't done any cleaning since—" He broke off. "I'm a bit of a perfectionist, so I hate the house like this."

It seemed his loss was recent. Katy gladdened to hear that he was the type who would keep things orderly. "I could clean your house in one day, but it would be a long day, and I'd need to rotate some of the cleaning. But $10 is low for this size of house."

He studied her, his gaze slowly raking over her entire body as if trying to decide if she was worth the money. She tensed, instinctively knowing that he was using the wrong gauge. The uncomfortable moment was broken when an older girl, about Addison's age, called down from the stairway, "Is Mommy here yet?"

Harry's face colored. "Not yet, sweetie."

The little red-haired girl started down, one small hand gliding along the wood hand railing, the other dragging a wheeled, pink-handled backpack behind her, allowing it to bump awkwardly on each step.

Katy considered the implications of the little girl's question. Had her interviewer been married twice? She searched his face and then quickly scanned the room for photos, trying to piece the puzzle together.

Next, the doorbell chimed.

"Excuse me." Harry Chalmers rose. His son took a fearful look at Jake and churned his little legs, running after his dad.

Once the family had left the room, Katy looked at Jake and shrugged. He seemed as uneasy as she. From the entryway, angry voices carried into the great room. Jake patted her hand. The voices escalated.

"But I want to go with Mommy, too," the little boy begged.

"No, it's not your turn today."

Then an older boy, whom they hadn't seen yet, entered the room from the direction of the entryway. He was almost as tall as his father and wore jeans and a black T-shirt. He was using an iPod and halted when he saw them sitting on the couch. Then he hitched up his backpack and strode past them with a curious look. Once he reached the stairway, he bounded up to the second level and disappeared, but Katy heard him slam a door.

The situation grew increasingly uncomfortable with Harry and the children's mother still arguing in the entryway. The little boy increased his cries whenever his parents allowed a silent moment. It seemed Harry wanted her to take all the children at the same time, and she wanted to spend quality time with each one. Harry claimed she just wanted to make it hard for him to have any time to go out with his friends. He accused her of being jealous of his secretary and trying to control his life. He didn't sound like a grieving widower. Their youngest son's cries suddenly drowned out their conversation.

Jake squeezed her hand. "Sorry," he whispered.

"I'm so glad you're here," she whispered back. "We can't leave; they're blocking the entrance."

"Let's wait." His Dutch accent thickened. "Maybe Chalmers will enlighten us about his personal situation. Otherwise, this is not the job for you."

Before Katy could decide if Jake was overstepping his bounds by saying the job was not for her, Harry rejoined them, carrying his son. The little boy struggled in his father's arms, his face tear-streaked. When the boy calmed a bit, Harry gave Katy a sheepish grin. "Sorry about all that." Then his voice hardened. "She's such a—" But his voice broke off, as if he suddenly realized he didn't want to speak harshly of the woman in front of his son. Or perhaps in front of strangers, for the couple had been arguing in front of the children. Shoulders slumped, he tenderly patted the little boy's back.

When she felt Harry intended to let the matter drop, Katy withdrew her hand from Jake's and squared her shoulders. "Normally, I don't pry into personal affairs, but under the circumstances. . .well your ad stated you were a widower."

Harry placed his son on the floor and ruffled his hair. "Your brother's home. Why don't you scoot up and say hi?"

The boy nodded and tramped partway upstairs. Then he turned back and jutted his lower lip out. "I wanted to go with Mommy." He swiped his forearm across his eyes and sullenly went up the stairs.

With a sigh, Harry sank back onto the sofa. "Okay, look. I'm not a widower. I'm divorced. I haven't been having any luck getting a housekeeper. I just thought if I implied I was a widower, it might help. I can't afford an agency. The divorce really cost me. I'm a good guy. You'd be safe working here. We need help. But I can only pay ten dollars."

Katy met Harry's gaze, unswayed by his sentimental act. "Implied? You gave me false information."

"I just thought that once you met me, you'd see I was a good guy."

She narrowed her eyes, wondering if that was what his secretary thought. Then she snatched her references off the coffee table and stood. Jake quickly jumped to his feet, and reassuringly, touched her elbow.

"I can't accept the position," Katy said. "It's not about the money anymore. But if you lied to me once, I don't feel I can trust you."

"But you can trust me."

Did all men think trust could be earned so flippantly? She wanted to add that she didn't like the way he'd looked her over, either. Instead, she said, "I'm sorry, Mr. Chalmers."

He rose, following them to the door. "You're sure? I wouldn't even be here. The kids, either. You'd have the place entirely to yourself."

She hesitated. That did sound inviting. Her gaze swept over the grand entry, taking in the elegant furnishings and marble floor, but her heart sank when she felt uneasiness in her stomach and recognized the little warning voice. This time she listened to it. "I'm sorry."

Chalmers opened the door, and they stepped into the sunny March afternoon. Jake matched her hurried strides.

"Good choice. I didn't like him," he said. "I didn't like the way he looked at you. Especially after what his ex said about his secretary." So she hadn't imagined that. But while Jake intended to show his support, he made her feel worse, reminding her of how deceptive a man could be. This new peek into the outsiders' ways disturbed her peace of mind.

Jake opened the truck door for her, and she climbed up into the cab. As soon as he jumped up and seated himself behind the wheel, he went on, "We'll put another ad online. I know there's the perfect job out there for you."

"No. This isn't working out."

―⌒⊃

Jake turned the key, and his truck rumbled to life, but he let it idle while he studied Katy. There was an edge to the tone of her voice that insinuated more than disappointment. She had shot the remark at him as if she were speaking of their relationship and not the computer ad service. As soon as she'd gotten inside the cab, she stiffened her shoulders and clenched her jaw, not looking his way but straight ahead out the windshield. No doubt, she blamed him for owning the computer that set up the failed interview.

How illogical. He'd only wanted to help her see that she needed to come out of the Dark Ages. He pulled onto the suburban street and glanced over again. Her shoulders had relaxed a bit so he tried to put it as logically as he could manage. "The point of job interviews is weeding out the undesirables. The right one will come along. There was no way of knowing that man was a liar."

She turned glittering, brown eyes in his direction. "I should have known. He's an outsider."

Again, her frustration seemed personally directed at him. "That's rather harsh."

"Is it? Or are you so close to. . .them. . .that you can't see the difference anymore?"

How did Katy always manage to turn everything inside out and hurl it back at him? "But you like your job at the Brooks. There are a lot of good outsiders, Katy. Good jobs waiting for you."

Her jaw dropped open momentarily. Then she flew into a passionate protest. "Surely you know how many struggles I've had with the Brooks' job? It's tested me in every aspect of my faith."

He quirked his mouth, trying to lighten her mood. "And that's a bad thing?"

"Of course it is," she snapped.

Her narrow-mindedness was increasingly irritating. "I disagree. It's how I found my faith."

"At the expense of others. Your little fling caused damage, Jake. How can you be so flippant?"

Her retort cut deeply. He braked for a light, hurt that she felt the need to continually punish him. He lived with the pain of his sister's rebellion and of the damaged relationship with Katy. He had already bared his past like an open book, hoping she would understand that he hadn't intentionally set out to hurt her. But Katy wouldn't forgive him or believe that he'd changed. She kept ripping open the old wounds. She would never let them heal. It was unfair.

He slapped the steering wheel with both palms, and then gripped it firmly. "You think you are so perfect, living your self-righteous life. But I'm not your puppet, and I don't want a mean-spirited woman."

Her eyes widened and her sulky lower lip dropped. Then suddenly her nostrils flared. "Right. I remember your type."

"At least Jessie was an honest person. She didn't pretend. She was kind and fun to be around. You may look good on the outside, but you have an unforgiving heart."

"Don't try to put the blame on me. You *are* just like Tammy, trying to get your own way and not caring how it affects people around you."

Jake laughed out loud in disbelief. Katy crossed her arms and jerked her gaze to stare out the passenger window. He shook his head. No use in talking to someone so stubborn and deceived. They drove in charged silence until they reached the doddy house.

He hurt bad inside because he knew this time there would be no reconciliation. They'd spoken words they could never retract. He needed to say something before she jumped out of the truck. He reached over tentatively and touched her arm.

She looked up at him, the stubborn set of her face slackened lightly, and he glimpsed something vulnerable. Somewhere in there was the woman he had once known. That was the woman he loved. He wanted nothing more than to lean over and kiss her. But she'd forbidden that, hadn't she? She'd kissed David, but she refused him. His pride swelled, and his resolve hardened. This woman was impervious, and he just didn't have the heart for it anymore, so he told her what she'd been trying to tell him all along. "You're right. It's not going to work between us. We've both changed. I'm sorry."

She yanked her arm away. "I'm sure it won't take you long to find a woman on *the Internet*. Somebody who understands you. Or maybe Jessie will take you back." Tears streaming down her cheeks, Katy jerked the door handle and jumped out. In her wake, the door slammed and shook the cab.

He refused to watch her walk away and kept his gaze straight ahead. It was all he could do not to spin his tires in the gravel. In his mind's eye, he could see her marching to the doddy house. Stubborn, foolish woman who made him furious. If he had a hammer in his hand, he would surely demolish something.

Jake drove, hardly noticing the traffic signs, his mind churning with anger and guilt. Finally he pulled over, his wheels partly on the road and partly on a sloped embankment. He no longer felt like swinging a hammer; he felt like crumbling. He couldn't talk to Chad or Cal. Guys didn't take much to weakness, weren't good at helping a guy deal with a broken heart. He'd never had one before, but he felt like he'd explode if somebody didn't help him. He tried calling Lil, but she didn't answer. For several minutes, he sat with his phone against his forehead. He tried again. Still no answer. Then he tried his sister. When she answered, he blurted out, "Katy and I broke up. Can I come over?"

"Sure. I'll meet you outside the dorm."

"Twenty-five minutes?"

"Okay."

When Jake reached the southern edge of the manicured lawns and red-bricked university buildings, he calmed a bit. It helped just to get away from the country and everything that reminded him of Katy. He pulled to the side of the road in a no-parking zone and glanced at Canfield Hall, wondering if he should text Erin.

But then he saw her standing on the sidewalk near the residence halls. When she started running toward him, he jerked his gearshift in PARK and jumped down out of the cab. Erin pulled him into a firm embrace.

"I'm so sorry," she said.

He didn't say anything. Erin knew how much he loved Katy. She'd conspired with him the afternoon of the ballet, jumping in to entertain Addison so that he could spend time with Katy. He clung tight to his little sister, leaning his head on top of hers. Just feeling the beat of her heart brought him a sense of assurance. Finally, Erin drew back, touched his cheek. "You can't park here. Can we go someplace? Wanta go get coffee?"

"No." He shook his head. "Someplace private."

"Let's go down to the lake."

He agreed, and at Mirror Lake, they found a vacant bench, but the location probably wasn't ideal. Many lovers strolled through the park, reminding him of his great loss.

He slunk forward. "It's over."

"You want to tell me what happened?"

"She'll never forgive me. She thinks I'm contaminated. Says my falling away has done irreparable damage to others." He looked at Erin, and her face had paled. Yet he needed to get it all out. "She's right. Because of me, she's changed. I've ruined her."

Erin sucked in a deep breath. "No. She's responsible for who she is. She can't blame you for that." Erin brushed his hair with her hand. "I don't understand why she can't see how you've changed."

He shrugged. "You're the one taking psychology. The thing is, I want the old Katy. It's hopeless. All we do is fight when we're together."

Erin rubbed her forehead with a ringed hand. She lifted her gaze out across the water. "This is awful," she said. "I thought Katy would take you back."

He stared at his sister, who had changed so much in the past six months. She dressed in jeans and wore jewelry and makeup. Although her hair was still long, in many ways she resembled Jessie. He grabbed her by her upper arms. "The Bible's right about one thing."

"What?" she asked, widening her eyes.

"We reap what we sow. Erin, don't let the same thing happen to you. Promise me, you won't let your falling away ruin your life."

"You're scaring me. Your life's not ruined." She cupped his face with her hands. "It's all reversible, right?"

He gently pushed her hand away. "Once I thought it was. Now I don't."

"Sure it is. Before you know it you'll be reaping the good stuff. The blessings."

"Maybe. But it's too late with Katy. And that's something I'm going to regret the rest of my life."

―⁂―

Katy flung herself on her bed. Jake had dumped her. He'd begged her to forgive him, and then he'd dumped her. The cruel words he'd tossed at her burned through her mind: *Self-righteous, mean-spirited, unforgiving.* If she was any of those things, it was because he'd caused it. Still, it hurt so bad to know he felt that way about her. She hated him for putting the blame back on her. She hated herself for giving him reason to do it.

She had known from the start that she was wrong to blame him for the bad interview, but still she had gone down that destructive path. And to what end? She'd left him with no way out because she wanted to punish him. She'd brought this on herself because she couldn't forgive him. She thought she had, but she must not have, because she wanted to punish him again and again for his rejection, his betrayal. Now she disgusted him. She disgusted herself.

He wouldn't care that he'd lost her, but she would. And she would never get over him.

She bunched up her pillow and released pent-up pain and anger. She punched it and moaned. She hated him. She hated herself.

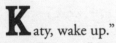aty, wake up."

"Go away." Katy pushed at Lil's hand. She didn't want to wake up. "I'm staying home."

Lil laced her voice with concern. "But you never miss church."

Katy tried to focus her eyes through swollen slits. "Then today will be a first because I'm not facing Jake."

"But you can't stay in bed all day."

Katy turned her head toward the wall, wondering why not.

"I know you're miserable. Look, you gave it a shot. Now you can both move on. . .without regrets. No more what-ifs."

"That's easy for you to say. Nobody's ever dumped you. Twice."

Lil's hand retreated.

Instantly, Katy regretted her harshness. Her failed relationship wasn't Lil's fault. "I'm sorry. But he said horrible things to me."

Lil sighed and lowered onto the edge of Katy's bed. "He was only angry. We both know he's a hopeless chump."

"When people are angry, they say what they mean. And chump doesn't cover the half of it."

"Sometimes they try to lash out to cover their own hurts, too."

That's exactly what Katy had done. Lashed out at him for no reason yesterday, even when he'd only been kind. She had lashed out because of her own fears.

"You can still be friends. You were great at that."

Katy tried to imagine a brotherly relationship with Jake, one built on kindness and an intimacy gained from knowing each other so well. It would never work because one of them would flirt, and then they'd end right back where they were today. But he was Lil's cousin so he couldn't be avoided, either.

"Megan's coming over for lunch. She's made her mission-trip choice. Wants to show us her Bangladesh brochure."

Katy moaned. She wasn't interested in Bangladesh. She had her own *Bungled-mess*. But weekends were the only time she saw Megan. And Katy didn't want her to think she was mad over the discussion that had taken place in Megan's dorm. "Okay, but when she wants to patch me up with Jake again, stand with me on this. You agree we're hopeless together, right?"

Lil hesitated. "I haven't heard Jake's side yet. But it does seem that way."

Katy bunched and cradled her pillow. "I can't do this if you won't help me."

"All right." Lil nodded. "I'll back you up. But Megan won't push you."

"She might. Seems to have some honest streak going."

"You think so, too?" Lil tapped her freckled cheek. "The other day she lectured me about self-respect. Had the nerve to say that if I didn't chase guys so hard, they'd be chasing me. Like that would ever happen. She said some other stuff, too. Brought up my mom's depression. Gave me a bunch of advice." She dropped her hand. "Usually, she's not so pushy. I thought she was acting weird, too. Maybe it *is* an honesty thing."

Katy rose up on an elbow. "I'll bet she's taking some psychology class and testing it out on us."

Lil's voice grew animated. "Yes. I'll bet that's it."

Nudging Lil with her hand, Katy snapped, "Move off my bed. I've gotta hurry if we don't want to be late."

Lil jumped up and smiled brightly. "Great, I'll be in the kitchen."

———♋

The sermon was on spiritual seasons. The preacher brought up Dutchman's breeches—little, white, spring flowers that resembled a row of upside-down breeches on a clothesline. They represented summer's promise. He compared spring and summer to God's love and blessings. Winter symbolized the hard times. He stressed the beauty of faith in winter. Katy recalled the beauty of the barren wintry countryside when she took that dark sleigh ride with David. How long ago that seemed.

Applying the concept to her situation, she figured she was experiencing the bleakest winter of her life. Her latest fight with Jake must be dead winter. According to Brother Troyer, spring was around the corner. He claimed the key was trusting God. She thought about God and wondered if it really was that easy. Did God take a personal interest in her? Was He planning a spring and summer for her? Or was it all wishful thinking? Was He a judge, watching to see how she handled adversity?

Normally, Katy didn't like change, but living in bitter cold forced her to welcome it. She jotted down a few notes on her bulletin, thinking she should start a spring-cleaning section of her journal and incorporate the spiritual season theme.

Brother Troyer ended the sermon by challenging his congregation to trust a loving God with their winters. The idea invaded the core of Katy's heart like a live coal. As it burned deeper, she prayed, *I want to believe, Lord. Please help me.*

Before she knew it, Megan and Lil were singing on either side of her. She felt glad Lil had urged her to come to church. The sermon had given her hope, and she couldn't wait to find some time alone to pray and ask God to give her direction and shower her with an emotional-spiritual spring. She had to believe that the burning sensation she'd felt at the conclusion of the sermon was God's drawing her, wooing her.

Time after time, she had ignored God's voice. Yet He still wooed her. That was amazing.

But after the closing prayer, Katy remembered Jake. She returned her hymnal to the rack in the back of the pew in front of her and slowly turned. Her eyes scanned the sanctuary. Thankfully, he wasn't anywhere in sight. Relief flooded through her. Either he hadn't come and was at home lying in a bed of misery like she had been, or he had shot out the back at once, dreading their meeting as much as she did.

"I'm going to go find Mom," Lil said.

Katy watched her friend depart, feeling a bit forsaken. But she understood that Lil was still worried about her mom's depression. Feigning a smile, she turned to Megan. "I'll bet you're excited about your trip."

Megan's blond head bobbed. "So excited. I don't know how I'll ever wait until June."

They moved down the center aisle, maneuvered around clusters of farmers eager to get in the fields and discussing disking and planting.

Megan added, "The sermon was awesome. I kept applying it to my life. Graduating and my trip. I can't wait for summer to come so I can get to the good stuff, you know?"

Awestruck that God could use a sermon to speak to an entire congregation in a personal way, Katy nodded. "I feel the same way."

Megan gave her a curious look. "Something's happened, hasn't it?"

"Yes, but I don't want to tell you about it here."

"All right. But I hope it's a good thing. You deserve something good."

The comment struck Katy as odd. Did she? Hadn't Jake said she was self-righteous and ugly on the inside? Sometimes she felt like she was two persons, the proper one on the outside, and the enemy on the inside. How did anyone ever get that inside woman to jive with the outside one? If only Megan knew the real her, she'd realize she didn't deserve much. No. What happened wasn't good. At least not now, while she still hurt.

They shook hands with Brother Troyer and stepped into the foyer, and then Katy's heart plummeted straight to the carpet. There stood Jake next to the exit. She had a view of his profile, and he had a happy expression. She ground her teeth. Happy to be rid of her. Happy because he was talking to two girls. Her eyes narrowed, and she tightened her grip on her purse. Then she noticed with relief that one was his sister, Erin.

She felt conflicting emotions. Katy should be happy that Erin was back in church. It was an answer to Jake's prayers. But a selfish meanness arose in her that resented any kind of happiness for him today while she was hurting. At the same time, she felt ashamed.

Erin started laughing. She was dressed in her normal conservative clothing. Had Jake made all that up about her falling away? But Erin's guest was a definite outsider. Jake was staring—or more like flirting—with a blond girl. A definite outsider, so maybe Erin hadn't changed. Jake, either.

Jealousy flooded through her. How could he be able to flirt and forget her so easily? Then the blond girl moved, and Katy saw her face. The girl wore a nose ring. Katy gasped. Her jealousy reared like a wild stallion, an uncontrollable beast. Jessie! With bleached hair. Her entire hair, not just one strand.

For an instant, she stood spellbound and incredulous. The waiflike woman wore the highest spiked shoes Katy had ever seen. Her slender legs showed way too much skin, even though her skirt swirled around her calves in some clingy, flowery material. She couldn't believe the elders had even allowed her inside the doors. Her pale hair had dark roots, not natural and beautiful like Megan's. The change of hair color was why she hadn't instantly recognized her. But her clothes had given her away even though her tattoo was covered. No, she had another one low on one leg. Katy blushed at viewing such a shocking, worldly display. Her face burned to think that Jake had been attracted to this type of woman. It seemed he still was, the way he was responding to her bright smiling lips and seductive eyes. Katy longed to turn away from the display, and at the same time felt riveted to watch it play out.

She should be happy she was rid of Jake, yet she felt like ripping Jessie's hair out at its fake roots. Her eyes narrowed as she envisioned doing just that.

Then she felt Megan's touch at her elbow. "It's Erin!"

"And Jessie," Katy ground out.

Megan's face paled as she took in the significance of the scene. "Oh. And they're blocking the door."

In case her friend didn't get the whole of it, Katy said between gritted teeth. "Get me out of here." *Before I make a scene.*

But before that happened, Jake turned his gaze in her direction. He was in the middle of a sentence and stopped speaking. He closed his mouth and tightened his jaw. When he did so, Erin and Jessie turned, too, following his gaze. All three stared at Katy, and Katy stared back, feeling nothing but hatred for the three of them.

Megan's arm shot around Katy's shoulder, and she was propelled around, probably heading back through the sanctuary and out a side door, but she wasn't sure because her surroundings blurred into a swirling green that swallowed her vision. Green movements, green people, a green cross, and green shrubbery. She felt her feet moving, but all she saw was Jake and that despicable girl.

Like a drowning person, her mind struggled. Had he run straight from her back into Jessie's arms? Slowly, Katy realized that was exactly what she'd told him to do. In fact, it was her parting jab. *Maybe Jessie will take you back.*

Incoherent thoughts shot through her mind. *Spring? Darkness. Did God cause this? Or was this His warning against testing Him? Jake loved Jessie all along. Just Jessie. Steamy, starry nights with Jessie. Maybe they'd marry, and he'd leave. Please let him leave. God's not listening. Help me, God.*

Then she saw they were standing on the passenger side of Megan's car. She looked up at her with confusion.

"You're not driving like this. Get in. I'm taking you home."

CHAPTER 34

By the time they'd reached the doddy house, Katy had tearfully told Megan all about the breakup and had recovered somewhat from the initial shock of seeing Jake with Jessie. Her thoughts still skittered chaotically, but she was able to divert some of her frustrated energy into setting the table. Aware of Megan's sympathetic glances, Katy set the plates on the vinyl tablecloth. "So much for spring," she said sarcastically.

"It will come."

Pressing a firm crease into a paper napkin, Katy remembered Megan's earlier excitement over her upcoming mission trip. "I'm sorry I've ruined your news. You were so happy before—" She fumbled with the napkin.

"Don't even—"

The door burst open, and they both turned to watch Lil enter. She plunked her purse and Bible on the counter. Then she placed both palms flat on the counter, looked at them, and burst into tears.

Katy's mouth gaped, and the napkin she had been holding floated to the floor.

Megan rushed forward. "What on earth?"

"It's Mom," Lil gasped.

Katy went rigid, thinking the worst.

Lil waved a hand in front of her face. "I'm sorry. I didn't know I was going to do that. It's just. . .she won't get out of bed. My dad doesn't know what to do with her. I've never seen him so worried. So stressed."

Relief flooded over Katy that Mrs. Landis wasn't injured or worse. She'd never had to deal with anyone plagued with depression. "Has she been to the doctor?"

"No. She won't go." Lil swiped a hand across her eyes and met Katy's gaze. "I know this is such bad timing, but she needs me. I told Dad I'd come home for a while to help out and try to get Mom out of her slump."

Katy bit her lip, and her stomach knotted. What was she saying? Was Lil moving out? She searched her friend's face, looking for some other explanation, but when she saw the grief etched on Lil's countenance, she knew she hadn't misunderstood. She remembered talking to Lil about her mother's empty-nest syndrome and realized that this was probably the right thing for Lil to do. Wrong for Katy, but right for Lil and her family.

Earlier in church, Katy had thought that she'd already faced dead winter. How wrong she'd been. Within a short twenty-four hours, Katy had lost so much. First Jake. Now her roommate. Megan would soon be going off to her mission trip. It was hard to accept that Lil was actually moving out. She gripped the back of a chair, her mind searching for something to hold on to, something. . .anything stable. For in actuality, Lil was the motivating force of the trio of friends. Without her, Katy might shrivel up and. . . No, she wouldn't. She could be just as strong as Lil. Even if she was afraid of the dark and afraid to be alone in the doddy house at night. She bit her lip. She would show Jake that she was a survivor, that she didn't care if he flew back into Jessie's arms.

Matters with Lil's mom had to be serious for Lil to abandon her dream. Katy didn't blame her. But if she moved out permanently, Katy wouldn't be able to afford the doddy house. As it was, she could only afford a few more months on her present income.

Then a disturbing question shot through her mind. Was God punishing her for pursuing such a selfish dream to begin with? For testing Him? Would she end up moving back home, having failed at everything?

"I'm sorry, Katy. I saw what happened to you at church," Lil said. "The pastor's sermon was so good, and then all this happened. Where is spring in this?"

"I don't know," Katy replied.

Megan stirred uneasily. "He didn't promise us spring today. His sermon was supposed to give us hope. Remember, he said faith is the beauty of winter."

Katy and Lil exchanged glances, reading each other's minds and wanting to tell Megan they weren't in the mood for wishful thinking. Their friend couldn't relate because she didn't have any worries. Her parents allowed her to do whatever she wanted and paid for it, too. They meant well, but Megan hadn't experienced much in the line of hard work or disappointment. Megan could always say the right thing, but was it heart knowledge or head knowledge?

Yet watching her now, just her sunshiny appearance lightened the room. She was always the exquisite butterfly, the epitome of spring manifest, and who could squash her optimism? If they did, then who would be there to brighten their lives? Someday life would challenge Megan. In the meantime, Katy couldn't bring herself to put a tear in Megan's wings.

Evidently, Lil's thinking followed the same path, because she said, "Thanks." Then she looked at Katy. "I hate to leave you like this. I haven't talked to Jake, but I want to wring his neck. What was he thinking?"

Feeling her eyes narrow with a sudden surge of her own hatred, Katy tried to think of a nasty retort to describe Jake, but she got stuck in the dark recesses of her mind until Megan spoke again.

"I'll stay with Katy tonight. It's spring break! I have a meeting tomorrow about the mission trip. And I have some stuff planned with my folks, but I can stay tonight, for sure. We'll pick up your car later or tomorrow. Then maybe I can stay another night, too."

"See. I'll be fine. You need to go," Katy urged Lil with a wave of her hand. "Take lunch over for your dad, too."

Lil turned and lifted the lid off a pot of stew. "I will take some.

There's plenty for all of us. You sure you'll be alright?"

"Yes. Go."

Lil started toward their bedroom. "I need to pack a few things. I'll call you soon as I can."

Katy turned and smiled at Megan, wishing her friend hadn't volunteered to stay over, even though she needed a way to get her car. Always the optimist, Megan would make it her job to help Katy out of her grief, but all she really wanted was to crawl into bed and revisit those dark recesses of her mind. Even if she was afraid of the dark.

~&~

That night, Katy sprawled across the bed from Megan while they looked at color brochures of the Bangladesh mission project.

"Tell me about it. Everything." Anything to get her mind off herself.

"I'll be going through SEND Ministries. An acronym for Service, Evangelism, Nurture, and Discipleship. The trip is June 25 through July 11."

"That's not so long. I thought you were going to be gone all summer?"

Megan raised a blond eyebrow. "Then you haven't been listening."

Katy frowned. Had she tuned Megan out? "I'm sorry. I'm listening now."

"Forgiven. So far there's four of us going. They take up to eight. We'll be involved in English Bible camps doing manuscript studies, worshiping, learning activities, and maybe some prayer walks."

"Wow. So you're not building huts?"

"No." Megan tilted her head, studying her like she was a foreign specimen, and Katy felt ashamed that somehow she'd distanced herself from her friend, hadn't been listening to her dreams.

"If this is an English camp, what language do they speak?"

Megan smiled. "Bangla."

"Of course." Katy smiled back then tried out the word. "Bangla. Where is it?"

"In Asia, between Burma and India."

"You're kidding! I thought you were going to Africa."

Megan ruffled Katy's hair. "You're a mess." They giggled, and then Megan said dreamily, "I wish you could go with me. You could. They still have four more openings. Will you think about it?"

Katy tried to imagine herself in Asia, teaching English Bible. There was no use even considering it; it wasn't anything she felt interested in. "No. It's not for me. Strange as it might sound to you, I've never had the desire to be any kind of missionary."

Megan scrutinized her, and Katy inwardly squirmed. Some people had to carry on with life, working to pay the way for others to go do the mission work or live together in doddy houses. That's what Katy was. A worker, she rationalized. She enjoyed working. She enjoyed seeing the completion of what she'd done with her own hands. "If I ever went on a mission trip, it would have to be some kind of cleanup. Like after a hurricane or tornado or something."

Megan waved a slender finger at her. "I'll remember you said that. With Mennonite Disaster Service, there's lots of opportunities for cleanup. I'd like to do that myself sometime."

They lay back on their pillows, silently studying the ceiling, each thinking their own thoughts. Then Katy said, "I wonder how Lil's doing. I thought maybe she'd call by now."

"Let's call her." Megan closed her brochure and placed it on the nightstand. She pulled out her phone and punched in a speed-dial number. The conversation was short with Megan mostly listening. Katy heard her end with a promise to pray.

"So?" Katy prompted.

"Her mom spent the day in bed, but Lil got her to eat. Lil said tomorrow she's making a doctor's appointment for her." Megan's expression turned contrite. "She was on the other line with Jake when I called."

Katy felt as if she'd taken a blow to the stomach. "And?"

Megan shook her head. "She didn't say anything about him. But she said her old room seems strange, and she misses it here."

"I miss her, too." Katy pushed Jake out of her mind and smiled. "Honestly, at first I thought one of us would murder the other one."

Megan didn't seem surprised. She teased, "But then your nonresistant teaching brought you to your senses."

"Maybe. Mostly, I started to understand her. She has a lot of insecurities."

"I know. If only she could realize how great she is," Megan replied. Then she sighed. "We all have our insecurities."

"You?" Katy gently probed.

Megan twisted a long shank of shiny hair and shot Katy a reproachful glance with her blue eyes. "You're kidding, right?"

Stretching her arm beneath the coolness of her pillow, Katy yawned, but not from boredom. This conversation intrigued her because Megan was the one who always had it together. "But you're so gorgeous and smart."

Megan rolled on her back and stared at the lamp-lit ceiling. "This trip we've been talking about? After that, my folks expect me to find a job. You and Lil expect it, too. I'm part of that pact we made, living together and everything."

"Don't you want to?"

"Move in? Sure." Then Megan yawned. "Wow, why are those so catchy? Anyway, not the job part. I'm not lazy. I'm just scared. August. That's when I'll have to go job hunting. Yuck. I have no clue what kind of job to get."

Katy winced inwardly. If she didn't get more work soon, there wouldn't be any doddy house for Megan to worry about. "Something will turn up. Something that suits you."

"You really think so?"

"Yes."

⁓

Late the following afternoon, Katy stepped into the quiet doddy house and plopped an armful of mail onto the kitchen table. After breakfast, Megan had taken her for her car, and Katy had gone straight to work. In addition to her normal cleaning, she had tackled some dreaded tasks she'd been putting off, like defrosting Mrs. Kline's ancient freezer and going through her storage boxes to locate her spring wreath.

Weary and discouraged, she glanced at the stove. Even though Lil hadn't always been home when Katy was, it felt lonely to know that her friend wouldn't be preparing their dinner. She glanced down the hall, her bed beckoning and tempting. She wanted to answer its call, curl under her covers, and sleep for at least a year. But that wasn't reality. Her growling stomach was demanding nutrition. Anyway, if she went to bed too early, she might not be able to sleep later, when the house was creepier.

She trudged to the refrigerator and found some cold roast beef. She added Swiss cheese from the local Amish cheese house, store-bought tomato, and pickles, then headed to the kitchen table.

She rolled up the dark green shade and peered outside. The trees were budding, but she lived in perpetual winter. She noticed David's shiny black sedan, and her interest perked. His car hadn't been there earlier. He certainly was a contradiction, not the nice boy her mom always raved about, but hot-tempered and still holding a grudge toward her.

She took a bite of her sandwich, wishing things weren't strained between them. She'd enjoyed his company, shared his obsession for cleanliness. That day at Megan's dorm, her friend had pointed out that Katy had a temper. She had that in common with David, too. Feeling melancholy over all that had happened between them, she wondered if she might have grown to love him if Jake hadn't returned.

She shook her head at the turn of her foolish thoughts and noticed her unopened mail. Using her table knife, she sliced through the envelope. Her car's license needed to be renewed. Great. She flipped through a spring clothing catalog, frowning at the worldly styles and wondering how she'd gotten on that store's mailing list. She turned it over to see if it had Lil's name on the address label, and an envelope fell out of its back cover.

She had almost missed it. After setting down her sandwich and wiping mayonnaise from the corner of her mouth with her napkin, she took a closer look. The letter was addressed to her. It was from Florida. She only knew one family from Florida. Sure enough, the return address revealed that the letter was from her old employer, Mrs. Beverly. Her heart sped up with anticipation, wondering if she was returning. Her hands anxious, she opened the envelope and unfolded a rose-patterned stationery that displayed artful, beautiful handwriting:

Dear Katy,

How I've missed your dear face. I don't know if you're still looking for any jobs, but a neighbor from the old neighborhood is looking for a housekeeper. She's looking for someone two days a week, and she'll probably even pay more than I did. She's a sweetheart and will be easy to work with.

The first line of the letter filled Katy with warm nostalgia, envisioning the sweet old woman sitting at her white, rolltop desk, her aged hand taking a pen from a rose-patterned cup. It brought a lump to her throat to realize that Mrs. Beverly was still concerned over her welfare. But when she read about the job opportunity, her heart leapt with excitement. Quickly she read on:

I never thanked you for your handwritten note inside the Christmas card you left us. I was so flustered that day. But I just wanted you to know that I am a Christian. Jesus was my anchor when I lost a daughter to leukemia, giving me peace and hope to continue on.

Katy hadn't even known she'd lost a daughter. Poor Mrs. Beverly. She quickly read on:

I remember how I'd wake in the middle of the night with a song on my lips, the words just what I needed to see me through the next day. The Lord has helped me to make the transition into a retirement facility. I always thought retirement centers were the end of the road, but knowing that I have heaven to look forward to, gives me joy.

With shock, Katy received Mrs. Beverly's testimony into her heart. It rang of truth. As she took it in, she felt a heat in her bosom, like she had the previous Sunday at church. It was a confirmation that her past employer truly knew Jesus. The same Jesus Katy knew, for Mrs. Beverly had the same experience with Him, the reassuring songs that came in a time of despair. Surely, it was God's way of showing her that Mrs. Beverly was a Christian. She stared at the letter with a new understanding of her past employer.

> *We aren't ready to give up yet, however. We're still golfing and enjoying life and good health. If you're ever in Florida, stop in and see us.*
>
> > *Love,*
> > *Sonja Beverly*
>
> *P.S. My friend, Betty Rucker, is a godly woman, too. But watch out for her husband, Herb. He's a hopeless tease. Here's Betty's address and phone number, 777 Springtime. . .*

Springtime? Katy's jaw gaped. God couldn't have made His reassurance any plainer had He penned it across the sky. Either God was exhibiting a sense of humor, or else He thought she needed things spelled out in a clear manner. This was her spring. This job was from Him. Another dream job, according to Mrs. Beverly, and working for a godly couple. An even better job, moneywise, than her other jobs. God had heard her prayers. Gripping the letter with both hands, Katy's vision blurred, and her shoulders shook. She didn't deserve this. She hadn't even been trusting God. If anything, she'd been blaming Him. And here was God smiling down on her.

She felt ashamed for all the times she'd cleaned for Mrs. Beverly and felt sorry for her, assuming she wasn't a Christian just because she was an outsider and did things Katy would never have the conscience to do. She remembered the embarrassing pictures on the paperback novels, and the R-rated movies. The dusty Bible. Perhaps Mrs. Beverly had kept a different Bible in her nightstand drawer? How could she have been so quick to judge? She didn't understand it all, but she couldn't doubt Mrs. Beverly's sincerity. As she looked back, she remembered how the older woman always acted with love and kindness. How could Katy have been so blind?

Bitter remorse sickened her for all the times she'd judged outsiders. How many times had she dismissed people as if they were unredeemable? Suddenly her words came to her, the ones she'd spat out at Jake and their ensuing conversation: *All outsiders are the same.* She remembered his shock. *That's rather harsh. Isn't it?* And then she had lashed out at him. *Or are you so close to them that you can't see the difference?* His description of her was accurate. *Self-righteous. . .mean-spirited. . .good on the outside. . . unforgiving.*

Katy brought her fist to her quivering mouth. *Oh God. Forgive me.* She'd been so wrong. So foolish. Crossing her arms on the table, she hid her face in their cradle and sobbed over her sins.

She saw her own ugliness, and as she prayed and asked for forgiveness and renewal, she felt God's flames of love burning through her, cleansing her. She prayed and pleaded and thanked the One who was in control. She realized that only God deserved to be in control. She'd been wrong to usurp that privilege, trying to move other people like checkers on a game board. Grievous as she felt, when she lifted her head, she felt spring bubbling up inside her.

Never could she have drummed up that much hope for the future on her own. But it now fell over her like a fresh rain. God cared. The Lord was with her. And finally, she wanted to trust Him with her life.

She wasn't sure how to do that, but God would teach her. Rising from the table with a smile, a song bubbled up inside her. She took a fresh tissue and blotted her eyes, then broke into song, not caring if she was hopelessly off-key.

She remembered how Brother Troyer's sermon had seared her heart. Then her hand stilled, and she had another epiphany. This was how Jake felt after his falling away. This was what he'd been trying to explain to her all along about the feeling of a new beginning. With that, she also realized that she didn't hate him any longer. God had removed that burden. It was like she could see him in her mind's eye like God might see him. With compassion. Not all-knowing, but with a patient love.

As she moved around the room, cleaning the table, she spoke out loud to God as if He was a friend present with her in the room. *I give Jake to You, whatever Your will is for us. I might actually be able to be his friend now. With Your help. And forgive me for my poor attitude toward Erin and even Jessie. I know You love them, too.* Then she paused when she caught movement from her side vision. Outside, David was walking to his car. She saw him glance at the doddy house, and she felt a surge of God's love toward him and a powerful urge to make things right between them. Quickly dabbing her eyes again, she ran to the door, acting before she lost her courage.

Swinging it open, she called out. "Hey, David."

He froze. Stared at her.

"Can you come over a minute?"

CHAPTER 35

Katy waited in the open doorway, her heart racing at her impetuousness yet unable to deny the prompting she had felt in her spirit.

David reached the front stoop and halted.

Katy smiled, her eyes pleading for his forgiveness.

His narrowed. His jaw hardened.

She ran her tongue over her dry lips. "I have chocolate mint ice cream. I thought maybe you'd like some."

He glanced back at his car, his expression telling her that he remembered their last conversation as clearly as she did. She knew she was opening herself to another curt rebuff.

He rolled back his shoulders. "Not really."

Lord, help me here. "Please?"

He shifted his stance. "Why?"

She shrugged. "I miss our friendship." When he still seemed skittish, she flashed him another tentative smile that came out a bit more tremulous than she'd intended.

"I heard about Lil. I guess you're real hard up for company."

"That's true," she grinned. "I have some mocha ice cream, too."

"Oh, in that case." He strode past her into the doddy house.

Wondering if she should apologize again, she got the ice cream out of the freezer and placed the containers and some bowls on the table. "Here we are."

In silence, he dipped a scooper into the round container of mocha. His hand paused. "So you miss our friendship. And?"

"Yes." Their gazes met as she tried to convey that reconciliation—not dating—was her intention.

He handed her the ice-cream scoop. "I heard you broke up with Jake."

So that was it. He thought she was on the rebound. She felt her face heat as she scooped ice cream into her bowl. "Yes, we did. I couldn't forgive him. . .until now. . .after it was too late."

"Slow down. You forgave him. After you broke up?"

She took the ice-cream containers back to the freezer and joined him at the table with a sarcastic chuckle. "Right. I need to work on my personal problems. I'm a mess. But with God's help, I plan to change. Anyway, I hate the way it was left between us. You and me."

He displayed his dimple. "Such a pretty mess."

Her face heated again. "So is there any way that you and I could, um"—she took a spoonful of ice cream, feeling self-conscious, and once it had melted in her mouth, she finished—"be friends again?"

He twirled his spoon, making her squirm. "Let me make sure I'm getting this right. You only want to be friends? Or do you want to start up where we left off?"

She couldn't help but smile at his frankness. "No. I just want to be. . .buddies. Play games, chat. I want you to flash your dimple at me like you are now, instead of your nasty scowl. I didn't like that much."

He shrugged. "I overreacted. It's no big deal anymore." Then as if it was settled, he took a spoonful of ice cream.

She settled back, relieved. After a comfortable pause, she asked, "How's Elizabeth doing?"

"Good. Better than this ice cream. How long's it been in the freezer anyway?"

She laughed and made a face. "It's awful, isn't it?" She pushed her bowl away. "We don't have to finish it."

"Too late. I sacrificed myself for friendship." He leaned back in his chair and studied her intently.

She squirmed. "Do I have chocolate on my chin or what?"

"I don't get it. You wanted me to forgive *you*. But you can't forgive Jake."

"I forgave him after it was too late," Katy corrected. She didn't explain that she'd just forgiven him an hour earlier, that she'd just had a renewal experience right before she'd invited him inside. But now that they'd made their peace, she questioned the wisdom of entertaining him inside while she was living alone in the house. She worried her lip. If he lingered, she would call Megan and ask her to join them. They could play Rook.

"So why don't you tell Jake now? That you forgive him?"

She stared at him, having lost track of their conversation. "What?"

He repeated the question.

She reasoned aloud. "Because he hates me. Anyway, he was with Jessie on Sunday."

"Who's that?"

She felt a twinge of pain. "A girl from school. I think they may be getting back together."

"That girl with Erin? Standing in the foyer?"

Katy nodded.

"I didn't get a good look at her. I was too busy looking at Erin. But Jake would never go back to her."

Looking at Erin? She raised an eyebrow. "How do you know that?"

"Because he came back to the church, and unless she changes a lot, that's not going to work out."

"Maybe he'll leave again."

"Not if he's changed."

"Maybe she'll change."

"I doubt it."

She wanted to ask him if he thought Jessie was pretty, but he'd claimed he hadn't looked at her very much. Instead she argued, "But she's friends with Erin."

"That is strange." He wore an unreadable look, one that made her wonder if he had a crush on Erin. Then he shook his head. "Forget about Jessie. You should tell Jake you're sorry."

Katy planted her elbow on the table and cradled her head in her hand. "It's over."

He shrugged. "Maybe you haven't really had a change of heart."

"Don't say that. I have so."

"Prove it."

She narrowed her eyes with suspicion. "Why are you so anxious to see us get back together? You don't even like him." She didn't want to bring up the fistfight.

"I have my reasons."

She stared at him, saw a vulnerability in his expression. Maybe he didn't want Katy to be available because he didn't want to get hurt again. Or maybe David wanted to square things with Jake so he could date Erin. Whatever the reason, he had the right to his opinion. She swallowed.

"Call him," he urged.

⸺ ᔐ

Loud, uplifting refrains filled the cab, and Jake tapped his palms on his steering wheel keeping time to the beat. He willed the inspirational message into his wounded spirit as he mouthed the words. Meanwhile his truck sped across miles, putting distance between him and the object of his heartbreak.

When he stopped for gas, he checked his phone, surprised to see he had messages. His heart wrenched. Three calls from Katy in the past two hours. He could only hope he wouldn't have answered her calls anyway. Two missed calls and one voice mail.

He hesitated, wondering if he should listen to the voice mail. It would be like her to leave some message saying she was sorry. If he listened, he might be tempted to take her back. He wouldn't do that again. He wouldn't weaken. He needed to move on with his life. Clenching his jaw, he erased the message. Grimly, he set the phone to vibrate and jammed it in his pocket.

Climbing back in the cab, he worked the interior lights and checked his road map. After breaking up with Katy, he'd jumped at the opportunity to get away. He needed time to heal, time to forget about her, and mostly time to resolve that he wouldn't go back to her again.

He pulled back onto the highway, sparse with traffic now, intending to go at least a hundred miles before he stopped for the night.

After another thirty miles, his radio started to break up so he turned it off. It was peaceful at that time of night with nothing but twinkling stars overhead and the occasional headlight. Up there somewhere was God. He drove on. Peace stole over him because he knew God answered prayer.

The afternoon he and Katy broke up, he'd driven straight to OSU. Erin had listened to the entire story, helping him work through it. But the most amazing thing was that God had used Jake's pain for His glory. For when Erin saw how his falling away had destroyed his relationship with Katy, the only girl he'd ever loved, and when she saw how this had devastated him, she determined that she wouldn't allow the same thing to happen to her.

They'd talked until late that night, and he had witnessed the miracle of seeing his sister repent of her rebellion. That's why she'd come to church on Sunday. And after the services, the impossible had happened. Jessie had actually stepped inside the meetinghouse, too. She hadn't come for the services, but she had come, nevertheless.

He grinned inwardly. Erin and Jessie made an odd couple, about as odd as he and Jessie had once made. But they'd met through him, and Jessie had helped convert Erin to the world. He wondered if Erin would now be God's instrument to draw Jessie. Would that be the ultimate good that came out of his repentance?

Nah. Jessie would never become Mennonite. He remembered their talks, and Jessie's arguments against the Conservative way. But she might become a Christian. He wouldn't give up praying until it happened.

Erin's repentance had given him a joy that softened the pain of his broken relationship with Katy. For the first time in his life, he didn't center his future around her, and the joy of answered prayer was quietly upholding him. He knew that God was behind the Texas job opportunity he had received. Everything had fallen into place so quickly and perfectly, with Erin moving back home to help his mother. He'd felt compelled to jump in his truck and follow his dream.

CHAPTER 36

Katy paused on the Bylers' front porch. A robin's chirp drew her attention to the large ash tree on the side of the house. The empty swing reminded her of her escapade with Jake's grandma. The robin swooped down to the ground, then flew into the weeping willow, the same tree where she'd gotten her first kiss from Jake.

She felt like an intruder, embarrassed to be chasing a man who'd undeclared himself. She couldn't bring herself to step up to the door. "He's not home. His truck is gone."

"Maybe it's in the barn," David replied, undeterred.

Katy glanced in the direction of the barn. "If he won't answer his phone or return my calls, then he doesn't want to see me," she argued. "He made it clear to me that we were through."

"We've already discussed that. I'm a guy. Trust me. He needs to know you've forgiven him."

"I didn't know guys could be such nags." She scowled at David and stepped up to the doorbell.

When the door opened, Katy's mind reeled from shock, her hand involuntarily covering her pitching stomach as she stared across the threshold at the woman responsible for much of her grief. Jessie was the

286

last person she had expected to see in Ann's kitchen.

On the other hand, Jessie seemed nonplussed with her. She merely tilted her blond head, quietly studying them, until her smoky rimmed eyes widened. "You're Katy." When she sensed Katy's confusion, she added, "I saw you in church."

Jessie didn't seem resentful or jealous. Rather she acted like she was genuinely glad to meet Katy. Her personality came across much softer than Katy had imagined it. There was something beneath all the makeup that was refreshing. But that didn't keep Katy from feeling like she'd walked into a daytime nightmare. Praying for Jessie and actually speaking to her were two entirely different things. She bit her lip and looked up at David.

He quickly introduced himself and asked, "Is Jake here?"

"No. But come in. I'll go get Erin."

Katy's feet seemed nailed to the porch flooring, but Jessie motioned them in as if she were hostess, and when David pushed her elbow, Katy found herself begrudgingly inside Ann's kitchen.

As soon as Jessie left the room, Katy hissed at David. "Let's get out of here. This is a mistake."

"Not so fast. Let's find out what's going on first."

"No. It's obvious. I'm out. She's in. I need to leave before Jake comes back and finds me here."

"You know they're going to tell him anyway. She must be visiting Erin. Otherwise she'd be with Jake."

"Not necessarily. I think—"

Erin burst into the room, ending the argument, her expression bearing delight. Oddly, so did Jessie's. Katy was curious. Maybe David was right. Still. . .

"Have a seat." Erin motioned at the table. "Can I get you guys a soda?"

"No!" Katy quickly replied, her pride pushing aside her curiosity.

"Yes, please." David gave Katy an obstinate look.

She tightened her lips and placed her hands on her lap to keep from yanking his perfect hair from his stubborn head.

"Great." Erin talked while she moved with ease about her mother's kitchen. Her gaze flitted from David to Katy. "What are you guys up to?"

David elbowed Katy. "We were looking for Jake."

"Oh?" A flicker of wariness crossed Erin's expression.

Katy felt both girls studying her with inquisitive gazes but couldn't think of anything to say that would satisfy their curiosity without giving herself away.

"He's not returning her calls, and she needs to tell him something important," David clarified.

Katy's jaw dropped open with disbelief, and her face heated from humiliation. Now she wanted to pull his hair out by its perfect roots.

Erin joined the others at the table, her eyes so like Jake's now filled with concern. "Then I'm very sorry you missed him. He's hurting bad."

It seemed the only one with the brains to skirt the issue was Katy. Her face still burning, she glanced at Jessie, but even she wore a sympathetic expression. David squeezed her arm. The encouragement was her undoing. Her pretense fell away. "Me, too," she admitted, easing gently from his touch.

"I know it wouldn't be the same, but I could relay a message for you," Erin offered hopefully. "It isn't any of my business, but if it would help you guys get back together?" Her gaze held a definite yearning, then it dropped to the table, and she continued more softly, "But if I'm reading this wrong, then I don't want to—"

She looked up again. "I love you, Katy, but I just don't want him to get hurt again."

"I don't blame you." Katy wanted to tell her that she'd changed and how she'd forgiven Jake, but it felt awkward with Jessie present. She studied the petite woman who had her chin propped by a silver-cuffed hand. Katy sucked her lip in then released it. "Are you and Jake back together?"

Jessie pointed at herself and the bracelet jangled. She tossed her short blond mop and laughed. "No. Absolutely not. We're just good friends." Her smoky gaze shifted to Jake's sister. "I'm just hanging with Erin over spring break. Taking a country vacation."

"Lame, I know." Erin shrugged.

Katy could tell that they spoke the truth. Otherwise, Jessie wouldn't have been acting so nice. It appeared that Jessie wasn't as stuck on Jake as Katy had expected her to be. There was no evidence that Jessie was experiencing any kind of pain. This new piece of knowledge lightened Katy's heart and planted new hope.

Nodding, Katy explained, "I've been a fool. God showed me some things about myself, some ugly things. After that, I was finally able to forgive Jake for. . .the past. I know it's too late. But David keeps nagging me, telling me I owe it to Jake to let him know I forgive him."

Erin's eyes filled with respect for David, and she cast him a smile. "He's right. Even if you don't get back together, it'll make Jake happy to know you've found peace. When you guys broke up, he came to see me. He blamed himself for causing you to change. I'm sure that was hard for you to admit. Thanks for sharing it."

Katy sighed. "But he won't answer my calls. He hates me."

"He's hurting," Erin repeated. "He's protecting himself. Now that I know the importance of what you want to tell him, I believe it would be much better hearing it from you. I'll tell him you dropped by and ask him to call you."

"He won't," Katy replied. "I don't blame him."

"I know," David said. "Just give Katy a call when he returns, and she can come back. I think he'll listen if they're face-to-face."

"There's the glitch," Jessie piped up, tapping a red fingernail against a porcelain cheek.

Katy and David both snapped their heads in her direction.

Jessie's hand fell gracefully to the table. "He's run away."

"What?" Katy exclaimed, glancing fretfully at David.

"He got a job offer," Erin explained. "In Texas."

Katy reeled from yet another hard blow then sat in stunned silence. She covered her mouth with her hand, taking in all the implications. How many different ways could she lose him? "I guess we're not to be," she said, glumly.

Jessie leaned forward. "I know you're more important to him than a job. Let me call him. Maybe he'll listen to me."

"No!" Katy blurted, unable to accept Jessie's interference.

For the first time, Jessie's eyes snapped with indignation. "Look. I'm not an idiot."

"I—" Katy started.

But Jessie interrupted, her gaze softening again. "I know I'm partly to blame for all this. I want to help. Make it right somehow."

Katy met her gaze and held it. "That's not necessary."

The foursome sat in quiet contemplation. "There must be something we can do," Erin blurted out as she rose. Katy thought she was getting up to pace, but then she saw she was getting a bowl of chips and dip. She plopped it on the table as if food would provide a solution to their problem.

David dove in, crunching happily.

"I know!" Jessie exclaimed. "You can e-mail him. Pour out your heart. It's perfect because you can say everything you want to say without him interrupting."

A flutter of hope tickled Katy's spine. Jessie was right. He might read an e-mail. Her heart began to race, and she shot Jessie an appreciative look. "You're a genius. It is a perfect idea because our last argument started with a disagreement over using the Internet. It would shock him and at the same time validate my change of heart."

Jessie glanced up at Katy's covering, then back down to her face. Katy blushed, realizing how silly such an argument must sound to an outsider, much like all her many run-ins with Tammy.

But Erin caught her enthusiasm. "This could work."

"Got any more of that dip?" David asked.

All three girls rolled their gazes heavenward. Ignoring him, Katy went on, "Only. . .he might not read it when he realizes it's from me."

"But that's the beauty of it. He'll think it's from me!"

Katy gave Jessie a sideways frown, trying not to let her irritation show.

Jessie went on undeterred, "And once he gets into it, he'll be too hooked to stop reading. Come on. Let's go do it before you chicken out."

Katy worried her lip and glanced at David, wondering how everyone pegged her inner wavering so easily. He motioned as if she were a five-year-old. "Go."

Erin blushed. Katy understood why when she offered, "I'll stay and get David some more dip."

Starting to feel like a third wheel, Katy scooted her chair back and followed the enthusiastic Jessie, who seemed to be as self-willed as David. In the short time she'd known Jessie, she saw that Jake's assessment of the girl was accurate. She was helpful and straightforward. Didn't make a big deal out of social differences. And she looked like she would probably be fun, too. To her own amazement, she could see how Jake had gravitated to her when she extended a helpful hand through the maze of campus life. And she imagined Jessie hadn't intentionally led him astray. Well, possibly she had an ulterior motive at the time, too. Jake was good-looking, even in his conservative clothing. To someone like Jessie, it had probably only made him intriguing.

Still, she couldn't believe that she was taking advice from Jake's old girlfriend. A worldly girl's advice. When they passed through the living room, Jessie drew her finger to her lips. Katy saw that Minnie was resting in an armchair. Her head hung to the side, and her mouth emitted soft snoring noises. They tiptoed past.

"Is Ann gone?" Katy whispered.

"Yes. Grocery shopping. Should be home soon."

And to think they weren't having a bit of trouble with the ornery older woman. The longer she stayed in this home, the more her pride was brought down from its lofty throne. The only thing that would clinch it would be for Ann to come home and find her chasing after her son. Katy hoped she was gone before then. Ann might not want Katy at the house again after all her blunders. Yet if things went as she hoped with Jake, she would have to face Ann sometime.

When Katy realized where Jessie was leading her, she instinctively hesitated.

Jessie placed a hand on her black belted hip. "I'm staying in Jake's room while he's gone. I brought my laptop along."

A pang of hurt shot through Katy. But she quickly closed her mind to it, and when she did, the thought came to her that it was just her pride rearing up again. Pride was a hard foe to quell. Much of the hurt and jealousy she had battled against was caused by the injury to her pride. No wonder God had allowed her to get to this place. Feeling more humbled than ever, she followed Jessie into Jake's room.

Jake's room was different, chaotic from all of Jessie's belongings. Even her perfume overpowered his masculine scents. His computer was missing on his desk, replaced with her backpack and her laptop. Katy couldn't tell if the objectionable photograph was still gone because the nightstand was draped with feminine clothing. So was the bed. Clothing also spilled from an open suitcase. Katy's gaze lingered on the high-heeled shoes cluttering the floor in the middle of the room, the ones Jessie had worn on Sunday. Katy couldn't imagine how anyone could wear them without breaking their neck.

She felt a touch on her arm and looked up.

"I know this is hard for you. It's kind of weird for me, too. First Jake getting all religious, and now Erin. Then Jake running away. You showing up while I'm staying in Jake's room—"

Katy interrupted, "Erin's religious? Was that why she was at church on Sunday? Do you know? Is she returning to the church?"

"Yep." Jessie's face contorted. "Claims she's had some epiphany." She stooped, picked up the heels, and dropped them into the suitcase. "That's why I followed her here for spring break. I'm trying to figure out how this family operates."

Katy gave Jessie her first genuine smile. "It doesn't have to be weird with us. I never thought I'd say it, but I kinda like you. In fact, you're a little like my roommate." Her lip quirked into a smile. "Wouldn't you love to see the look on Jake's face when he realizes I e-mailed him from *your* computer?" It wasn't necessary to add, *Because you were the reason I couldn't forgive him.*

Jessie's dark-rimmed eyes lit with amusement. "He's going to flip!" As they booted up Jessie's computer, they giggled.

Jessie pulled up Jake's e-mail address and a page from which Katy could send her message. "You want me to leave?"

"Do you mind?"

"Not at all."

"Thanks, Jessie."

Jessie waved her appreciation away as if it were a natural thing for the two of them to conspire together. She started to leave then paused. "I'm going to go see what's going on between Erin and David. I didn't see that one coming. Did you?"

"Actually, he hinted to me earlier that he had a thing for her."

"They're cute together. Does he always look so. . .perfect?"

"Yes, he does. But he doesn't always act that way."

"Interesting."

Katy couldn't blame David for his ulterior motives. Once Katy was alone, she glanced at the empty e-mail form. This was it. Her last chance, albeit a slim one. After that, it was up to God.

Breathing in Jessie's perfume in the quiet of Jake's room, Katy paused to collect her thoughts. "It's up to You, God. Whatever Your will, I accept it." She began to type.

CHAPTER 37

Jake stood on the newly laid street, looking over the construction site. In a sense, the streets were laid with gold because the barren dirt lots would someday hold fifty new brick two-story houses. The project could line his pockets and secure his future if this interview went right. But he hadn't driven across the country for the lure of money. He'd never been money hungry. He'd come for peace of mind. Working with his hands and building something for other folks to enjoy brought him satisfaction. And he needed that now to forget about Katy. He needed to make new dreams and to numb the raw pain that kept him on his knees.

Inside the mobile office earlier, he'd noticed that the project's landscape mock-up included grass and trees and winding roads, even a few ponds and playgrounds. The houses would be for middle-class people, but definitely upscale, a worthwhile project.

Yet he held some reservations. Texas wasn't what he'd expected. He wiped the sweat from his forehead with the back of his sleeve. He hadn't known the place could be so hot in April, but the newspaper he'd read in his hotel room the night before had predicted eighty degrees for the afternoon. In April! Would he be able to get used to the heat?

He'd checked Houston out on the Internet, and the temperature could rise past one hundred degrees in the sultry thick of summer. He tried to imagine what that might feel like. And then there was the threat of hurricanes.

With this project, the grid of lots would soon face change, and if he accepted the position so would his own life. He hoped he presented himself as confident, but he felt out of place, an Ohio farm boy gone to the big city. Why, he'd even seen his first palm tree.

"Wasn't easy diverting the bayou," the contractor drawled in his southern manner of speech. "Even had to transport a stubborn alligator."

Jake crossed his arms, mirroring the other man's stance. "Never dealt with alligators, but I had a mad bull chase me around the pasture one summer."

Ben Rawlins, of Rawlins Construction, chuckled. "I think that would be worse." He tilted his face, studying Jake. "I like you. And Tom gave you a high recommendation."

Tom was Jake's college professor. He was a brother-in law to Ben Rawlins and had recommended Jake to the contractor. The job opportunity was a superintendent position for Rawlins Construction's current land-development project.

Rawlins excused himself to take a call, stepping away and turning his back to Jake. They had spent the better part of the day together, going over the project, the job requirements, and just getting to know one another. Jake had been invited to the Texan's home for barbecue. When the contractor got off the phone, he told Jake he had to go take care of a problem. Rawlins dismissed him with directions to his place, hollering over his shoulder, "I'll e-mail you those blueprints, and you can look them over before you come out to the house later."

Back at his hotel, Jake popped open a cola from the little refrigerator in the kitchenette and cranked on the air conditioner. Then he sank in a comfortable chair and pulled out a phone book. He propped his feet on the desk and leafed through, checking to see if there were any Mennonite churches in the area. He found one, but it didn't mention anything about being Conservative Mennonite. Another change he'd have to make. He'd told Katy that he could fit in at a more liberal church, but he had no idea how liberal this one would be. Maybe he just didn't know the names of all the suburbs. Hopefully, there was a Conservative church in the area.

With a sigh, he checked the time on his phone and saw he had a few minutes before he needed to shower. That was just enough time to check the computer for those blueprints the contractor had promised to e-mail.

While he waited for the computer to boot, he considered the pros and cons of the project. He liked the contractor, although he didn't really know him. Yet if Jake's professor was recommending him, in a backward sort of way, he was recommending the contractor, too. The job had dropped in his lap as if it was God's doing. And the offer was better than he'd expected, but since he'd arrived in Texas, he'd had a niggling unease that something wasn't right about it.

Rubbing the back of his neck, he tried to figure it out. Was it the job or the move that bothered him? He wasn't one to run away from his problems, and he'd discovered how long the road was between Texas and Ohio—from his family.

He worked the mouse, considering Erin. She and Jessie were staying at the house over spring break. Then they would return and finish their semester. After that, Erin would move home for good. The timing was right, for Erin would be available to help their mom. Still, he'd learned not to proceed when he didn't feel peace about a situation.

He had e-mail. Only it wasn't from the Texan. His brow rose. From Jessie? That surprised him, although they did e-mail on occasion. Inquisitive, he clicked open the message.

─୧

Katy dipped a long-handled squeegee into a bucket. Starting at the top and stroking downward, she removed winter's grime from the exterior of her kitchen windowpane. Although she was tired from already working at the Brooks', she wanted to get the window cleaned before dark. As she worked, she prayed for Lil and Mrs. Landis. They were seeing a doctor today. She also prayed about the e-mail she'd sent Jake.

Normally under such circumstances, the waiting would have been unbearable, but amazingly, God had provided her with peace. Oh, she had moments when she wondered if she'd been crazy to send that e-mail, but then she remembered that God was in control, come what may.

She heard the crackle of gravel and turned, expecting to see Megan. Surprised to see Ann Byler's car instead, Katy dropped her squeegee in the bucket. Her heart tripped when she saw Jessie crawl out from behind the steering wheel.

"Hey!" the short blond hailed with enthusiasm.

Katy waved back, but her nerves were acutely aware that she probably bore news about Jake.

"Wow. Show me how that works," Jessie said, eyeing the partly cleaned window and the squeegee.

With a chuckle, Katy gave her a demonstration. "Want to give it a try?"

"Sure."

The girl wore a supple leather jacket, jeans, and high-heeled boots— so different from Katy's own calf-length skirt. Jessie gave a little shriek when water dripped over part of what Katy had already cleaned, and then she surrendered the tool.

"Don't worry. I'm going over it again."

"Guess I'd better live in apartments until I can afford a maid." Then Jessie clutched Katy's arm. "I'm sorry. I didn't think."

Katy's face went hot. "I like my job."

"I just wish I *had* a job. My dad always makes me get a summer job. I'd like to keep one all year, but it never works out that way."

Katy bit her lower lip, considering. Earlier that day, she'd discovered that Tammy was still having trouble finding a replacement nanny. "You like kids?"

"I love them. Kids are so fun."

"One of my employers is looking for a nanny for a seven-year-old girl and an eleven-year-old boy. They live in Old Arlington. Think you'd be interested?"

"Are you kidding? That's close to campus!"

"Tammy, the wife, had a bad experience with another college student. But I think she'd like you."

Jessie clutched Katy's shoulders, and she suddenly felt herself pulled into the smaller woman's embrace. At first she flinched, but then she awkwardly patted Jessie's back. When they drew apart, Jessie exclaimed, "Thanks so much!"

"You're welcome. I can finish this later. Want to come inside?"

"I'd love to. Jake told me he did the remodel."

So they'd been in touch since he'd come back to Plain City. Pushing that out of her mind, Katy led the way into the doddy house.

"This is so cute," Jessie exclaimed. After their tour, she admitted, "You must have thought I was a slob when you saw Jake's room."

Katy remembered with a grin. Then she pointed a finger at Jessie. "If you get the Brooks' job, don't let the kids tear up the house."

"Oh man." Jessie sighed. "But I need the job. You've got a deal."

"I'm going on an interview myself. Tomorrow. My dream job." They sat in the living room, and Katy explained about Mrs. Beverly and the loss Katy had experienced when the older couple moved to Florida. She found herself talking about the letter and its effect over her. She watched the vulnerability cross Jessie's face.

Afterward, Jessie sighed. "I could never become like you. I'd have too much to change, too much to give up. I don't want to lose Erin as a friend. But it seems we're doomed. She's not going to be going to parties with me anymore. I'll have to move on."

"Perhaps our lifestyle isn't what God has for you." Katy thought of Mrs. Beverly and said what she'd never thought she'd say, "But you could still be a Christian in another denomination."

"That's what Erin says. We'll see. I really came over to say that I hadn't gotten any e-mails from Jake. Wondered if he'd called."

"No."

"I'm sorry. Maybe he just needs more time. You sure you don't want me to call him, give him a little push?"

"Please don't. It's just the way it should be."

⁓

As hard as it was for him, Jake didn't call Katy. Instead after the barbecue, he told the Texas contractor that he was going home to think over the offer. Ben Rawlins had seemed surprised that Jake hadn't jumped at the opportunity. Even slightly offended, although his southern hospitality kept him from saying so.

Jake had explained that first he had some business to take care of that would determine if he accepted the superintendent position. He explained that although it was a great opportunity, he wanted to be able to give it his all once he accepted. The cross-country move would be life altering, and Jake needed to make sure it was the right move.

That appeased the other man somewhat, and he agreed to wait one week. After that, he'd call his brother-in-law for another name. Jake agreed, and they parted on good terms.

Later along the interstate, Jake mulled over the offer. By the size of the insects that plastered the truck's windshield and splattered the front grill, the saying that everything was big in Texas seemed true. This job offer was a giant-sized decision, too. It was the type of decision that could affect his entire future. As he weighed his choices, a major portion of the return trip was spent praying.

He also listened to Christian radio stations. At times he broke out into audible laughter, trying to imagine Katy and Jessie conspiring together. That was what made Katy's e-mail smack of honesty. She couldn't have faced Jessie without forgiveness. It seemed she had really changed.

Still, he wanted to see her expression when they talked about it. In order to believe her, he needed to see that her guarded expression was gone. It had been shadowing her eyes ever since he'd come back to the Plain City church. He hoped his childhood companion had returned. Because anything less was not enough any longer. He was done chasing a past love. His future companion needed to be a soul mate who would accept him in every way.

He couldn't take Katy back if she was going to slip back into her judgmental attitude or go through life with the emergency brake on. Yet hope kept him buzzing along Interstate 40. If God could change his own heart, filling it with a love that saw beyond the outer facade, then God could have done a miracle in Katy's life, too. Maybe even Jessie's. He breathed another prayer of thankfulness. He wouldn't be headed home if he didn't believe God had already performed such a miracle.

꘡

Katy relaxed on her sofa, her legs flung over the armrest and her phone cradled against her ear. "It's going to be a dream job, just like Mrs. Beverly said. She accepted me on the spot. Mrs. Beverly told her Mennonites are hard workers."

She heard Lil laughing on the other end. "Guess I need to remind my boss about that. I think he senses my lack of interest at the restaurant. I need a better job, too." She sighed. Katy knew Lil had quit searching the newspaper ads. "But not until Mom gets better. Anyway, congrats. We'll celebrate soon. I can't wait to move back to the doddy house. I miss it. Miss you. You're being such a great sport about this."

"So what did the doctor say?"

"He suggested counseling, and we have a follow-up appointment. He'll have the results of the blood work by then. And if that doesn't help, then there's always medication."

"What does your mom think about that?"

"She claims she won't take any drugs. But I think she might agree to see a Christian counselor. I'm going to set up an appointment."

"So is she still in bed all day?"

"She gets up late and takes long naps. But she's up some. I came up with a great idea, but she turned me down flat."

"What was it?"

"I wanted her to take a cake-decorating class with me. Get her back into the kitchen."

"That would have been perfect. Maybe soon she'll—Someone's at the door, Lil. Can I call you back later?"

Katy stuck her phone in her pocket and squinted through the peephole that Jake had installed in the front door when they'd remodeled the doddy house. She nearly fainted to see her handsome remodeler in the flesh, holding a bouquet of daffodils, no less. Her heart racing, she flung open the door.

"Jake?" It was all she could do to keep from flinging her arms around his neck.

When he grinned, she realized how much she'd missed him. "Can I come in?"

"Yes!"

Inside, he tentatively held out the bouquet. "For keeping you waiting. I wanted to talk to you in person."

She clutched the flowers. "I can't believe you came. I mean, I hoped you would. That you'd give me a chance to explain some things. But I didn't think you would."

He leaned one shoulder against the wall. "Your e-mail definitely piqued my interest."

Although his stance was nonchalant, she knew that this was her one moment in the universe when she was being given the chance to restore their relationship. *Just say it*, the quiet voice insisted. "I was wrong."

"Wrong?" He crossed his arms, tilted his face.

"Not to forgive you. Not to believe in you. I was too proud." She gave him a tremulous smile. "But I've changed."

He straightened. Then slowly he reached up to touch her cheek. "Can you tell me what happened?"

She nodded, never allowing her gaze to leave his. "I got a letter from my old employer." Katy poured forth the entire story. She ended it by telling him about her visit to his house and Jessie's idea of sending him an e-mail. When she finished speaking, she was still standing in the same place, clutching his bouquet.

The corners of his eyes crinkled with sympathy. "That must have taken a lot of courage."

"I had my eyes set on the goal."

"What goal?"

"I hoped you could forgive me, too."

He tilted her chin up, looked deeper in her eyes. "Is that all you hoped, Katy?"

Another sliver of her pride slipped away, and she thought surely there must not be a shred remaining. "I hoped you'd give me another chance."

He released his hand, studied her with a serious expression, and she thought it was too late. Her hopes sagged.

And then he quirked the left side of his mouth. "Maybe I could learn to tolerate you a little bit."

She grinned. "If you could, then would you please. . ."

"Yes?"

"Prove it," she whispered.

He lifted a brow. "What do you want, Katy?"

She stared at his lips.

He pulled her close, crushing the flowers. Although his arms held her close, his lips remained gentle and tentative. She threw both arms around his neck and drew him closer, eager to express her love and joy and drawing him into a deeper kiss. When she finally drew back first, she gazed again into the face of the one she thought she'd lost. His return was as glorious as the kiss. He stood there before her, accepting her and giving her another chance. But his gaze didn't hold the awe she felt. It held something else. . .satisfaction, amusement even.

He touched his lip. "That was tolerable, but I think we ruined your flowers."

"That doesn't matter," she said, turning and tossing them on the counter. She turned back and leaned her head against his chest, her arms slipping around his trim waist. "Spring has arrived anyway."

CHAPTER 38

Where are you taking me?" Katy asked.

The black-fringed scarf that Jake had tied over her eyes kept her from seeing where he was driving. Even without the blindfold, she would have known he was up to something because their date was scheduled later than usual. He'd mumbled something over the phone about picking her up after dark to take advantage of a full moon.

His voice broke into her thoughts. "We're almost there, and I don't want to spoil the surprise."

Katy gripped the passenger-seat armrest, deliriously happy ever since Jake had accepted her apology. In the past two weeks, they'd been making up for wasted years. Emotionally, Katy had opened up to him without reservation. The vulnerability of placing her heart in a man's hands left her a tad breathless. Not frightened, exactly. More like exhilarated, climbing a mountain, anxious to see the view from the top, and unsure what was on the other side.

They had both grown so much since their high school dates. They hadn't talked much yet about what was on the other side of the mountain, except that he had turned down the Texas job and planned to stay in Plain City.

303

Getting to know him was surprising in many ways. She had discovered that he preferred dawn over sunset, because it symbolized new beginnings. He wore his pants tight because otherwise his leather tool belt pulled them too low, making it uncomfortable when he worked. She was glad to know that wouldn't change.

Although he couldn't always express himself eloquently, he was a good listener, a tease who knew how to bring a smile to everyone's lips, whether it was Minnie in one of her moods or his hired help after a day of hard manual labor. It took a lot to anger Jake, but she'd discovered that when he was frustrated, he always stuck his hands in his pockets and his eyes saddened around the outer fringes. Best of all, he'd admitted that he prayed for her every night before he fell asleep. How had she ever doubted him?

Through an open window, a gentle breeze brushed her cheeks. With the distinct scent of wet fields and the absence of traffic sounds, she knew that they were still driving on rural roads. The truck slowed and gently bounced onto a rougher surface that crackled like gravel. He killed the engine.

"Are we there?"

"Yes. I'll come around to your side and help you down."

She waited, eager to find out what he had planned. Had he gotten a job and taken her to a construction site? Would it be a prelude to talking about building or buying a house of their own one day? No, a construction site would be too dangerous after dark.

As she waited for him to open her door, her thoughts continued along that vein, sharing a house with Jake. Of late she dreamed more about marrying him than fulfilling the vow of living in the doddy house with all three of her friends.

The door opened, interrupting her musings and quickening her pulse. He reached in and caught her by the waist, then swung her down and set her on her feet. Tottering a bit, she gripped his firm arm until she had her balance. Then he led her across gravel onto softer ground. Something tickled her face, and she swatted it away.

He stopped. "Ready?"

"Yes," she replied.

Gently he untied the scarf. She blinked, looked around. "Our tree?" The weeping willow made a romantic canopy around them beneath the moon's soft glow. In wonder, she added, "Where we first kissed."

"I remember."

He grinned and drew her close. His lips claimed hers. It wasn't a tentative kiss like that first one so long ago, or even like the one a few weeks ago when they had finally gotten back together. It was a confident kiss but urgent. When she opened her eyes, the silvery moonlight shone across his face. His expression held a need that delighted her.

He buried his hand in her long tresses and said in a low rumbling voice, "I love your hair. When I was a kid, it was such a temptation."

"I remember."

"I like it down like this, too."

"You're getting romantic on me, aren't you?"

"Maybe I am."

His work-roughened hand captured hers again. His calluses made her proud of him, of his hardworking attitude. They helped her accept her own work-worn hands. His husky voice turned her thoughts toward him again, "Come with me," he urged.

Her heart swelled with affection. She wondered why he was taking her away from the house until she saw a circle of stones and a pile of firewood topped with tinder. "What's this?"

He answered with a self-satisfied smile. "Do you remember the summer we went to camp?"

"Of course." How could she forget about the vows she and her friends had made around the campfire? It was there that Katy had blurted out, *I know who I'll marry. Jake Byler.* Later she'd found out that Lil had told Jake about it before they'd even left the campgrounds. And even though they'd been mutually attracted to each other for years, Katy had always surmised that his crooked grin had something to do with being privy to that information.

Her gaze next took in two lawn chairs, and she suddenly understood. The kissing tree. The campfire declaration. He was going to propose. She tried to pretend that bubbles of joy were not dancing inside her as she feigned ignorance. "The surprise is a campfire?"

He nodded, then released her hand and motioned. "Sit down. I'll light it."

She eased into the lawn chair and watched him stoop before the fire pit. As he struck the match, his muscles bunched his shirtsleeve. She felt flushed even before the flames leapt from the neatly arranged firewood. While he worked over the fire, a shrill bird cry broke the silence. Some crickets chirped from the direction of the weeping willow. When the sound of crackling wood joined the other night sounds, Jake stood and brushed his hands.

He strode back to her and settled into his chair with a wink that curled around her heart. His hand caressed hers possessively, but he looked into the fire when he spoke. "You had some dreams that year. When I heard about them, they ignited a fire inside me. I didn't know it at the time, but it's been burning there ever since I heard you wanted to marry me."

She stared at the growing blaze, aware of the burning desire he alluded to but wanting to hear more from him than a smug reminder of her own feelings. "That was a long time ago. I was just a little girl."

He turned his gaze on her. The firelight cast golden glints of determination in his eyes. "I want you, Katy. I've always wanted you." He leaned close and kissed her. "Marry me?"

Breathless, she touched his cheek. She wanted him, too. And he knew it. And she didn't care if he was smug. His self-assurance was part of what she loved about him.

"Yes, I'll marry you."

"I love you," he breathed. He slipped his arm around her shoulders, leaned his head against hers, and whispered, "I don't have much to offer you."

Heads bent together, peace and contentment settled over her as they whispered their most intimate thoughts. After assuring him that he was more than enough to meet all her dreams, she asked, "Are you sorry you turned down the job in Texas?"

"Not at all. This is exactly where I want to be."

CHAPTER 39

In Katy's mind, one couldn't have spring without doing some spring-cleaning, and she'd enlisted Lil and Megan to help her prepare the doddy house for her upcoming marriage. The wedding would be just before Megan left on her mission trip in June. Katy and Jake would live in the doddy house. The three friends had set up a tentative plan that by September, Lil and Megan would take over the doddy house. They hoped that was enough time for Katy and Jake to find a place of their own, for Megan to find a job, and for Lil's mom to recuperate.

Now Katy stood on a small ladder she'd borrowed from Jake and handed dishes down out of the cupboards while Lil and Megan stacked them on the counters, the green sink hutch, and the kitchen table.

As Lil restacked plates, she announced, "I have news."

"What?" Katy asked.

"I complained to my mom that I didn't know how I was going to manage your wedding cake, that it was more than I should have agreed to do, and that I was worried about it."

Katy's jaw dropped. "But I didn't know you felt that way. I would never—"

"Ah!" Lil lifted her hand to interrupt Katy. "I don't really feel that way. I just had this hunch, and it worked. Mom's mothering instincts took over, and she told me she'd help me. We'd get through it together. That maybe we should sign up for those cake-decorating classes I had mentioned, after all."

Katy paused from wiping down the cupboard. She turned and perched on the top rung of the ladder. "So you want to do my cake?"

"Yes, silly. And Mom's agreed to help me with it. This is going to be so good for her."

"And she even suggested it? That's great." Katy shook her head, thinking how great Lil was at helping others to move in positive directions. "You're amazing."

"And our first class is next Tuesday."

Megan put a bucket in the sink and ran some water. Once she'd turned the faucet off, she said, "Things are coming together, aren't they? Hey, Katy, you're not still scared at night, are you?"

"Not scared. Just lonely." Katy pointed at the cupboard under the sink. "Can you add a little vinegar to that?"

Megan opened the green cupboard door and found the vinegar.

"I do still use my night-light. But something amazing happened. When I trusted God for Jake and my job, my terror of the dark fled." She tilted her head, thoughtfully. "I don't think I'd ever choose to live alone. Nights aren't exactly pleasant. But I can make it a few more weeks."

Megan lifted the bucket up to Katy and filled a second one to wash the baseboard and windowsills.

"This place really isn't that dirty," Lil stated. "It hasn't been that long since we moved in."

Considering that remark came from someone who didn't make her bed or pick up after herself, Katy couldn't help but protest, "I think some of that construction dust settled after we moved in."

Lil shrugged and started on the baseboards. "Jake told me you guys had decided on your honeymoon, but he wouldn't tell me where you're going."

Megan turned from where she was working at the sill to listen.

"Sarasota, Florida. I want to thank Mrs. Beverly in person."

"That's awesome," Megan replied. "You'll love it."

Katy knew that Megan's family often drove down over the Christmas break during her school years. They had extended family in Sarasota, and there was a Mennonite community there.

"Jake's going to do some research on the Internet to find us a place to stay."

"The Internet?" Lil asked, drawing out and exaggerating the word *Internet.*

Needing to move her ladder, Katy came down. She got herself a cold drink and couldn't resist placing the cold glass against the back of Lil's neck.

"Ah! Stop!"

"Actually, Jake was willing to get rid of the computer, knowing my reservations. But I suggested we keep it for business only, and that any other use should be discussed between the two of us first. That way, it won't be so easy to use it for frivolity and get pulled into the world."

Lil had turned away from the baseboard and now sat cross-legged on the floor. Her expression turned dreamy. "That sounds like a great plan."

Megan poured two more glasses of water, handed Lil one, and joined them. "While we're on the subject of computers. . ." Her voice became tentative. "There's something I wanted to give you for a wedding gift if you don't think it's too worldly."

Katy tilted her head. "It sounds like you're up to something. Let me guess. A computer cam so that we can talk to you in Bangladesh?"

Megan scowled, looking beautiful as ever. "How did you know about those?"

"Jessie explained them to me."

"Oh. I knew you wouldn't agree to that. Anyway, you'll be on your honeymoon. But one of my friends at school is great at photography. He does his photos on the computer. I'd like to arrange for him to shoot your wedding."

Katy smiled with pleasure. "I'd love it. As long as we keep it simple."

"Great. You won't even know what he's up to, I promise. I think my parents will chip in. We'll definitely keep it simple."

"I'm so blessed," Katy whispered. "I wish your photographer was here today. This is a day I always want to remember. . .with the three of us together."

"Don't worry," Lil said. "We won't let you forget anything." She reached out to give Katy a hug and knocked her covering askew.

With her heart swelling with fondness for her friends, Katy reached up to straighten it, suddenly realizing that neither of her friends wore theirs, and it didn't hurt her any longer. She said with choking emotion, "Once Jake and I find another place and you guys live here, if Jake ever has to take an out-of-town job, I'm joining you for a sleepover."

Lil scowled. "Duh? That's just a given."

EPILOGUE

Katy and Jake faced each other for the first time as husband and wife. She drank in the masculine planes of his clean-shaven face, his fresh haircut, the softening of his dark eyes, and three things struck her at once: the intensity of his love for her, its sincerity, and that it was hers for the taking. She stood on tiptoe. His head lowered to give her the traditional wedding kiss. When she heard clapping, she drew away blushing.

"I love you," he whispered.

"Love you, too," she replied.

A white rose petal drifted down and landed on the grass at their feet.

Their kissing tree had become their wedding tree. Katy's idea of placing satin bows of purest white and sprinkling white primroses throughout the weeping willow branches made it a lovely altar for their vows. Since they'd had their first kiss beneath it, and since Jake had proposed there, the Byler farm had been deemed the perfect place for their June wedding.

They turned and looked out over their guests. Jake had made benches for the ceremony, and together they had painted them white. The picturesque white sparkled clean against the lush summer lawn and the more distant green cornfields. Their friends and family brightened the benches with color and laughter.

Holding hands, they moved down the center aisle, greeting guests as they moved along. Her gown swished over the freshly mowed grass, but for once, Katy wasn't worried about stains.

Her gown was everything she'd ever dreamed it could be. Her mother had sewn the satin dress in a simple, yet elegant style with a high neck and quarter-length sleeves. She had embroidered the neck and the hem. Now it glistened in the late afternoon sunlight.

The mothers of the bride and groom had conspired to find a stringed head covering that Minnie had once made—when she designed and sewed bonnets for extra income. Mrs. Yoder had removed the strings and added longer, wider satin ribbons that now streamed down Katy's back, serving as her wedding veil.

Katy's hair was twisted and pinned up beneath the covering. Before the wedding, when she'd fixed her hair, she daydreamed of her new groom removing the pins. For once, she wouldn't slap his hands away, like she had so many times before when he was just a mischievous little boy who took pleasure in yanking her ponytail.

Now as they edged forward, Katy's left arm held her bouquet so that the white roses nestled in the hollow of her skirt, adding the perfect adornment to her plain gown. From her tiny cinched waist, the fabric draped elegantly over the slim curve of her hips to the ground. Having taken a good look at herself in the full-length mirror Lil had purchased for the doddy house closet, she'd felt more of a Cinderella than she had the night of the ballet.

She blushed now to remember the silk white negligee that was packed in her suitcase. It had not been cut with such modesty. Thankfully, it was not being captured on film. It had been a gift from Lil. And Katy had wondered if Jake had put his cousin up to it.

Beside her, Jake looked handsome in his new black suit. He wore a white shirt and a vest made from the same material as Katy's wedding dress. But it was the possessive look in his eyes that made Katy's heart turn somersaults. She hoped the photographer would catch that look as well as the lopsided grin sometime before the day was over.

Their attendants trailed behind them. Lil was paired with Cal, and

Megan with Chad Penner. Karen walked with their oldest brother, and Erin with David. The bridesmaids wore simple lavender dresses, hand-sewn from a Butterick pattern Katy had found at the discount fabric store.

When they reached the last row, Jessie stood beside the Brooks, holding Addison's hand. When Jessie gave Jake a hug. Katy didn't resent it one bit. In fact she took pleasure in seeing the rare occasion of Jake's blush.

"I didn't initiate that," he whispered, his voice thick with his Dutch accent, as they moved toward the table that had been set up for the wedding party.

"We'll discuss it later," Katy replied, feigning displeasure.

He glanced at her to see how much trouble he was in, and she affectionately squeezed his hand.

When it came time to cut the wedding cake, Katy and Jake took their places to do the traditional first bites. Their arms interlocked, Katy stared at the piece of cake that hovered in front of her face. He pushed it closer, and she closed her lips, teasing him. He had already licked his bite greedily clean. His mouth quirked in a grin, then his lips grew serious, and he gave her a most sincere gaze, one she'd come to love of late.

"I'll never force you to do anything, Katy. I'm not that kind of guy." Forgetting about their enraptured audience for a few seconds, she touched his cheek, inadvertently getting frosting in his black hair. She opened her mouth and accepted the creamy confection. Maybe the S word woouldn't be so bad after all. "You're getting more tolerable all the time."

"And you haven't seen anything yet."

When they stepped away from the table, Katy pointed toward his sparkling truck. "Did you see what David did?" When she had enlisted David to wash it, she forgot how easy that would make it for him to tie a string of cans from its hitch.

Jake gave her a sideways frown. "I saw. He's after Erin, you know. I mean to have a frank talk with him when we get back from our honeymoon."

"But he's such a nice guy," Katy couldn't resist saying, thinking of her mother. Just before the wedding, her mom had predicted again, *I know marriage will make you happy.* And although she hadn't added that Jake was *such a nice boy*, Katy knew that Jake had won her mother over the day he took her little brothers fishing so that Mrs. Yoder could run some wedding errands.

With fondness, she also remembered how her dad had called her *dumpling* when he walked her down the aisle. Although he'd given his blessing on the marriage weeks earlier, he'd also given Jake a private talk, a rather stern one if evidenced by the pale expression Jake had worn afterward.

She blinked out of her reverie. "I need to talk to Mrs. Landis before the cake table is inaccessible."

"All right. I'm going to go see what damage David did to my truck."

Katy praised Mrs. Landis for her work on the triple-layer cake. "I'm so glad you took care of finding servers for me."

"Oh, it's nothing. I enjoy doing this," Mrs. Landis replied. The woman seemed happier than Katy had seen her in months.

A few minutes later, Jake returned and drew her off to the side.

"Everything all right?" she asked.

"Elizabeth went into labor. David went with their family to the hospital."

"How exciting!"

Jake glanced around the milling crowd. "How much longer do we need to stay here?"

Everyone was having fun, but now that the cake had been served, the party would soon wind down, and they wished to make their exit before that happened. "Why—" She cut her comment short when Minnie marched up to them.

The older woman stopped, toe to toe with Katy, her eyes squinting at Katy's covering, staring far longer than normal or polite. Katy began to feel uneasy. She'd seen that look in Minnie's eyes before. And when Minnie stretched forth her arm, Katy squeezed Jake's hand, hoping he saw what was happening, too. Minnie was going to make a move for her covering again!

But the old woman was too quick for Katy or Jake, and her hand flashed out and up, nabbing one of the satin ribbons. She wound it around her age-worn fingers, cracked from hours of quilting. Katy froze, waiting for her to yank it off her head. This time, she determined, she wasn't going to make a fuss. Yet she had envisioned allowing Jake to remove it. It was her wedding veil, and it symbolized so much for her. She sucked in her breath, afraid to move.

"Now Gram," Jake began, "that's Katy's wedding veil."

"I made this, didn't I?" Minnie asked, ignoring her grandson and narrowing her eyes with unmistakable mischief.

"Yes, Minnie," Katy softly gasped. "And I'll always cherish it."

Emotion flashed in Minnie's eyes, and she dropped the ribbon. Her mouth moved almost fishlike. Then she suddenly shook her head in protest, emphatically thrusting her finger against Jake's suit jacket. "This! This!" she insisted loudly.

Aghast, Katy looked at her groom. Then slowly, understanding dawned. "You want me to cherish your grandson instead? Oh Minnie, I do cherish him."

Minnie didn't reply, but she dropped her hand and got a big grin on her face as she dismissed them by marching off toward the cake table.

Katy let out a sigh of relief then grinned up at Jake. "That was a close one. She's right, you know."

Jake demonstrated *his* agreement by sweeping Katy into his arms right next to the willow tree, for all the world to see. He kissed her until there was no doubt left in her mind that he cherished her, too, and that it was time to make a dash for that shiny, black pickup truck.

Cleaning Tips

Cold or hot coffee cleans drainpipes.
Vinegar in front-loader washers kills mildew on seals.
Keep home cleaner by sweeping driveways and entryways.
Use paintbrushes to dust cracks and hard-to-reach places in
telephones, stereos, etc.
Shine a stainless steel sink with vinegar or a touch of oil on a cloth
to make the sink sparkle
Cleaning my feather duster: Keep dipping and swirling in soapy
water and rinsing in clear water until the water stays clear.
Then dry with feathers up.

Miscellaneous Tips

Ice cubes sharpen garbage disposal blades.
Chopping onions takes rust off knives.
Outsiders: peel like an onion to see what's really inside before
discarding. Stop judging their actions without understanding
their motives. "Every way of a man is right in his own eyes:
but the LORD pondereth the hearts" (Proverbs 21:2).
Do not underestimate the elderly. Though their feet move slower,
their hands remain lightning fast and their thoughts are as
mysterious as the universe.
Kissing trees make wonderful wedding altars.

Stains

Burned food in dishes: fill with water and 2 tablespoons baking
soda. Soak. Scrub.
Ring around the collar: shampoo cleans the body oils away.

Gum: first cool and harden, then scrape most off with hard edge, then rub remainder with egg whites.

Tomato stains: run cool water until clear, then blot with white vinegar. Note: Removes the stain but does not remove memory of the incident. I remain in search of that particular cleansing agent, that can renew my mind.

Later entry: It is forgiveness.

Removing Jake's scent: sprinkled a pinch of baking soda on my white blouse where our shoulders touched. Do not give in to temptation to sleep with untreated blouse under my pillow.

Hand Cream Home Remedies

Recipe One
2 ounces beeswax
1 cup sweet almond oil
1 cup water
Heat, heating water separately, then blend. Cool and store in jar or tin.
Use as hand lotion.

Recipe Two
½ cup olive oil
A few drops of scented lavender drops from dollar store
Wear gloves until it soaks into skin

Recipe Three
1 banana
1 teaspoon honey
Juice of one lime
1 tablespoon butter
Mash banana and add to honey, lime juice, and butter. Blend and put in container. Leave on at least two hours with gloves.

Spring-Cleaning Tips

Use a natural sponge. Wash down kitchen backsplashes with
vinegar water.

Use dishwasher to clean odds and ends.

Check expiration dates of medicine-cabinet and refrigerator items
and make a shopping list for employer.

Check smoke alarms before they go off in the middle of the night
and frighten little Addison.

Window blinds: use a white glove and dip in vinegar water (equal
parts vinegar and water).

Toss shower curtains in washer.

Personal note 1: to survive winter until spring arrives, stir up my
faith, wrap myself in God's hope, and watch for Dutchman's
breeches. God is able.

Personal note 2: new beginnings are not only possible but
wonderful!

Cleaning Recipes

Wood-Paneling Recipe:

1 pint warm water

4 tablespoons white or apple vinegar

2 tablespoons olive oil

Apply with a clean cloth. Let soak a few minutes, and wipe off
with a dry cloth.

Windows Recipe:

2 cups water

3 tablespoons vinegar

½ teaspoon liquid dishwashing detergent

Squeegee

Tip: Clean one side horizontally and the other vertically so you
can determine which side has streaks

Cleaning the Microwave:
1 cup coffee
1 slice lemon
Microwave a few minutes, let it set, and it softens the spills. Wipe
down with warm, soapy water.

The Head Covering

"But I would have you know that the head of every man is Christ,
and the head of the woman is the man; and the head of Christ is
God. Every man praying or prophesying, having his head covered,
dishonoureth his head. But every woman that prayeth or prophesieth
with her head uncovered dishonoureth her head: for that is even all
one as if she were shaven. For if the woman be not covered, let her
also be shorn: but if it be a shame for a woman to be shorn or shaven,
let her be covered. For a man indeed ought not to cover his head
forasmuch as he is the image and glory of God: but the woman is the
glory of the man. For the man is not of the woman: but the woman of
the man. Neither was the man created for the woman; but the woman
for the man. For this cause ought the woman to have power on her
head because of the angels. Nevertheless, neither is the man without
the woman, neither the woman without the man, in the Lord. For as
the woman is of the man, even so is the man also by the woman; but
all things of God.

"Judge in yourselves, is it comely that a woman pray unto God
uncovered? Doth not even nature itself teach you, that, if a man have
long hair, it is a shame unto him? But if a woman have long hair, it is
a glory to her: for her hair is given her for a covering. But if any man
seem to be contentious, we have no such custom, neither the churches
of God."

1 CORINTHIANS 11:3–16

Journal disclaimer: Cleaning tips and recipes try at your own risk.
Same with applying Katy's personal tips.

About the Author

Dianne Christner enjoys the beauty of her desert surroundings in Phoenix, Arizona, where life sizzles when temperatures soar above 100 degrees. She and husband Jim have two married children and five grandchildren. Before writing, Dianne worked in office management, in admissions and as a teacher's ̶ ̶ ̶ ̶ ̶ ̶ ̶ ̶ stian school, and owned an exercise salon in Scott̶ ̶ ̶ ̶ ̶ ̶ ̶ ̶ ̶ ̶

Her first book was published in 1994, and she now writes full-time. She has published several historical fiction titles and writes contemporary fiction based on her experience in the Mennonite church. Her husband was raised on a farm in Plain City, Ohio, in a Conservative Mennonite church. Dianne was raised in an urban Mennonite setting. They both have Amish ancestors and friends and family in various sects of the Mennonite church. Now Dianne and Jim attend a nondenominational church.

You may find information about her other books at www. diannechristner.net where she keeps a blog about the Mennonite lifestyle.